Misery Cove

by

Jan Rydzon

Cover Art by *Teddi Black*

The Wild Rose Press, Inc.
PO Box 708
Adams Basin, NY 14410-0708
Visit us at www.thewildrosepress.com

Publishing History
First Edition, 2026
Trade Paperback Print ISBN 978-1-5092-6404-9
Digital ISBN 978-1-5092-6405-6

Published in the United States of America

Dedication

This book is dedicated to my incredible husband, Tom Rydzon, who encouraged me through all the twists and turns of my writing life, and my sister, Margie Spitzer, who reads everything I write and gives fantastic feedback.

I'd also like to acknowledge my critique partners: Cindy Harrison, Theresa Falzone, Mary Michayluk, and Christian Belz for their unfailing support spanning many years, as well as my fabulous non-writer beta readers: Marianne Gaulin, Barb Washburn, Judy Hayes, and Maureen Iman. Thank you!

The Wild Rose Press, and especially my editor, Claudia Fallon, have been wonderful! I appreciate everything you've done as I make my debut entry into the publishing world.

Chapter One

The old billboard on the outskirts of town was gone. The one where "Misery Loves Company" spanned the blue sky and a grinning sunglasses-wearing sun hovered over a beach filled with cartoon people. In its place, a tasteful black and gold sign read, "Welcome to Historic Misery Cove." Was it there the last time she came into town on one of her guilt trips? Erin Brady didn't remember, and it didn't matter. Her mother was dead, and she was late for the funeral.

She left her car in St. Jude Church's parking lot, steeling herself before entering the cemetery. Past rows of headstones, and stands of maple and pine, a priest recited prayers for the dead.

"Eternal rest grant unto her, O Lord. And let perpetual light shine upon her…"

Her mother had planned her funeral months ago, saying only her children should attend. She said she didn't want her friends to see her "getting planted." Mick sat in one of two chairs facing the open grave. The other was empty.

The priest placed a hand on the coffin. "Rest in peace, dear friend."

Mick shook his hand, handed him an envelope, then approached Erin. "So, you managed to show up. Good for you."

After an eight-hour flight, she wasn't ready to deal

with this. "My flight was—"

"Yeah, sure. It's always something."

She didn't respond. Nothing she said would make any difference.

"You are coming to the wake, right?" her brother asked.

"Yes. In a few minutes."

He shook his head and walked away.

Erin sat in the chair she should have occupied, dropped her head into her hands, and sobbed.

She left the cemetery a few minutes later and drove to downtown Misery Cove instead of going straight to The Sand Bar, where the wake was probably going strong. As much as she wanted to see her daughter, she wasn't looking forward to more of Mick's sarcasm.

Misery Cove hadn't changed much since the last time she visited two months before. Still a rundown beach town. During the past year, it had upscaled a bit, thanks to the promise of a new lakefront development project. The old mercantile was now Zinc Bar and Grille. A restaurant, antiques store, and bakery had replaced the old burger joint, souvenir shop, and cheap bathing suit store. But to Erin, it seemed like the same grungy place.

She couldn't avoid the wake any longer, so made a U-turn, drove a mile back, and turned onto a cracked asphalt lane winding through a bare-branched forest. It ended at a wide clearing where her family's Paradise Beach Motel squatted on five hundred feet of the eastern Lake Michigan shoreline.

Erin parked her rental behind three rows of cars and started toward The Sand Bar, but slowed when she spotted Rhonda's rusty ten-year-old compact car. She'd been so proud of it. Took care of it like she'd taken care of nothing else. Erin inhaled deeply, then walked into the bar.

A banner reading, "We'll miss you, Rhonda," drooped from ceiling brackets. From overhead speakers, Jimmy Buffett loudly assured everyone it was five o'clock somewhere. Erin almost gagged at the odor of stale beer and pine-scented disinfectant, but at least her brother had put some effort into cleaning the place.

Mick left his spot behind the bar. "Glad you could make it."

"Where's April?"

"In the house with Shirley."

"How is she doing?"

Mick half-smiled. "Pretty broken up, but she puts on a brave face."

Yes, that was her incredible daughter. How did she get so lucky? "We have to talk, Mick, but I need to see April first."

She found April in the living room and overwhelming love filled her soul. She swept her daughter into a hug. "I missed you so much, honey."

"I'm so glad you're here." April's voice trembled. "Granny died." She buried her head in Erin's shoulder.

"I know, honey. Are you okay?" Damn the flight connections. She should have been here two days ago.

"I'm really sad." April sniffed. "I knew Granny was going to die soon, but not this soon."

Erin kissed the crown of April's head and released her. "Where's Shirley?"

"In the bathroom, I think."

"Is it okay if I go talk to Uncle Mick for a while?"

April nodded. "You're not leaving here again, are

you?"

"No, honey." They'd both be leaving soon. As Erin headed for the front door, she stopped at the hallway entrance. "Hey Shirley, I'm home," she called. "And I'm going back to The Sand Bar to talk with Mick."

Back in the bar, she found Mick talking to a group of guys. "Sorry to interrupt. Mick, can we talk outside for a minute?"

He scowled, then nodded. The cool afternoon breeze carried the scents of seaweed and fresh-cut cedar, along with painful waves of nostalgia.

"You didn't tell me much on the phone. How did Rhonda...What happened?"

"Don't pretend you give a shit."

"Hey—"

"Now Mom's dead and her only daughter couldn't show up on time for her damn funeral."

She stiffened. It was going to be a long couple of days.

"I told you about the flight delays. Why couldn't you postpone the funeral for one lousy day?"

"I didn't think you cared all that much."

"That's not fair. Just please tell me what happened."

He looked down and kicked some loose stones. "Mom came into the bar that night and took a bottle of her favorite merlot back to the house. We didn't talk. If I'd known it was the last time..." He swiped a sleeve across his eyes.

The fast-food burger Erin picked up on the drive from the airport roiled in her stomach. Rhonda was dead. It wasn't possible. She'd seemed immortal.

"Mom wasn't in the house when I locked up the

bar, so I went to the beach to find her. She usually walked out there when she couldn't sleep." He drew a shaky breath. "There was a full moon that night and I found her right away. She was by the old dock, partly in the water. I pulled her onto the beach and shook her, but she didn't move and wasn't breathing. I took off for Shirley's."

"Why didn't you call 9-1-1?"

"I wasn't thinking straight, all right?"

"Where was April?"

"Spending the night with one of her friends." A screen door squeaked. He looked toward the bar, smiled and waved. "There she is."

April rushed to her. She was twelve and growing up way too fast. Her red, swollen eyes pivoted between Erin and Mick. "Is everything okay?"

"Everything's fine, honey." Erin swallowed against the ache in her throat and wrapped her arms around her daughter. They video-called each other several times a week, but it didn't compare with holding her daughter close. "Everything's fine. Your uncle and I just have a few things to discuss."

"I'll see you inside, okay, Mom?"

"Sure. I'll be right there."

Erin watched her daughter drift away. It just about killed her every time she had to leave for a job.

The Sand Bar's door opened again, and Shirley Cochran wandered over. Her tropical caftan billowed around her like a parachute. She gave Erin a fierce hug. "You made it to the cemetery?"

"Yes, but a little late."

"Your mom wouldn't have minded." Shirley gave Erin another hug. "You still look like the wind could blow you away."

She needed those warm and safe hugs. Shirley was Rhonda's best friend and had been her rock growing up. A person to confide in when her mother was on the beach meditating, thrift store shopping, or otherwise unavailable.

"I'm so happy to see you, Shirley."

"I'm happy to see you too, love. So, are you two coming back in or what?"

"We're just about finished," Erin said. "See you inside in a minute."

When Shirley was gone, Erin turned back to Mick. "The motel looks deserted. Are any units booked?"

"Long story short, no. Six weeks ago, the county shut us down. Something about it not being up to code."

Their grandfather had built the motel sixty years before and she doubted anyone had monitored building codes since then. "Rhonda didn't want to sell, right?"

"She got offers, but wouldn't take any. A couple months ago, she said she wanted the motel fixed up and reopened. Planning it gave her something to think about besides the cancer."

Strange. Rhonda hadn't cared about the motel for years. "Did she say when it would happen and how she was going to pay for it?"

He shrugged. "No. She wanted it to be a surprise. Did you know she was seeing a psychologist?"

"No. Why?"

"She got depressed about dying sometimes. Are you coming back in or what?"

"For a while, but then I'm going to my room. I'm exhausted."

"Yeah, fine, whatever." Mick headed back to the

bar.

She hadn't even been in town for an hour and already the weight of millions of past battles and another brewing exhausted her.

The motel's paint-blistered exterior needed a lot of work. Six units formed a semicircle to the left of the office and the adjacent Sand Bar. Another six curved to the right. Her family's two-story beach-facing home shared a wall with the back of the office. The office's rear door led to the home's foyer. The deterioration started after her father died. Before then, the Paradise Beach Motel was a modest, well-maintained twelve-unit resort where vacationers had to reserve summer rooms two months in advance. Now the place looked like it could be a theme park attraction named The Haunted Motel.

Erin made her way into the bar and through a cacophony of condolences. She'd disconnected herself from the town a long time ago, but Rhonda thrived in it, making new friends every time she went to the grocery store. And it looked like they were all there.

Shirley waved her over to the bar where a man behind it mixed drinks. "Hey Bill, bring Erin and me a couple of margaritas," she yelled.

Erin glanced around. "Where's April?"

"She went back in the house for a while."

Erin didn't blame her. It was a big noisy party with no other kids to talk with.

"I'm sorry for your loss, Erin," Bill Farrell said. "It's not gonna be the same around here without Rhonda." He pulled out a tequila bottle and started on their drinks.

"I didn't know Bill worked in the bar," Erin said.

"He does whenever Mick needed help, which isn't often these days."

"Here you go, ladies." Bill slid the drinks toward them.

Erin took a tentative sip. Pretty good. "Is Bill still doing maintenance work on the motel?"

"Yeah. Rhonda felt sorry for him. He needs the money." Shirley leaned over her glass and licked salt from the rim.

"I hope she didn't pay him much. The motel is a wreck."

"She didn't, and it is. You get what you pay for."

At a light touch on her shoulder, Erin turned. "There you are, honey."

"You okay, Mom?" April asked.

"I am. How are you?"

April's smile wobbled. "Okay, but I miss Granny so much. Mom, I don't want to stay in here with everyone laughing and drinking. Is it okay if I go back to the house?"

Erin pulled her daughter close. "Yes, of course. I'll be in later and we can talk."

"Okay, see you later."

"I love you, honey."

"Love you too, Mom."

"She's a wonderful kid," Shirley said when April disappeared into the crowd.

Erin sipped again. "She inherited the best parts of Sam and me." She glanced around the room. "Who's the woman talking to Dean?"

"The one in the slinky black dress and five-inch stilettos? It's your brother's newest girlfriend, Melanie Addington."

"Interesting funeral attire. Should we take a bet on how long this one will last?"

"It's been over three months now. A record."

"Hmm." Erin scanned the crowd. "I don't recognize many people."

"Sure you do. We're all just looking a bit older. And let's face it, when you come home, it's only for a few days at a time and you don't hang around us much. Steve from the pharmacy is over there with Zachary, the shrink."

"I know Steve, but not Zachary. Who's that ov—"

"To Rhonda, ex-hippie chick, lover of nature, kind soul," someone in the center of the room shouted and raised a glass.

Everyone followed. "To Rhonda."

From behind the bar, Mick raised his glass. "To Mom."

Erin met his gaze, raised her glass and downed the margarita. Rhonda would have loved the toasts, laughter, and dancing that continued throughout the evening. She glanced at her watch. April.

The house was quiet when she walked in and took the stairs to April's bedroom. The door was partway open. April was curled into a fetal position, sound asleep. They could talk tomorrow. She crept down the stairs and went back to the bar.

After drinking margarita number three, Erin bent over the bar. "Mick, make sure that everyone either has a safe ride home or let them sleep it off in one of the motel rooms."

"Do you think I'm a goddamn idiot? I've been managing this bar ever since I was eighteen while you were off traveling around the world and not doing shit to help us out."

"Starting right up, aren't you?" She moved off the stool. "I'm getting my suitcase and going to my room."

Chapter Two

Erin woke the next morning, disoriented, and glanced around. She was in her childhood bedroom. And Rhonda was dead. She stumbled into the shower, depressed and dizzy, then dressed and headed downstairs to the empty kitchen. Mick and April must still be asleep. She made a pot of coffee, poured a cup, and went down the hall to her mother's bedroom.

The room was clean but cluttered. Brightly colored leis, Mardi Gras beads, and flamingo light strings hung from mirrors. A collection of small plaster mermaids, mother, and child figurines, and vases of plastic flowers fought for space on the dressers. She itched to sweep everything into a garbage bag.

Inside the closet, jeans and exotic print tunics consumed most of the space. Dressier pants and shirts hung in the back. Erin slid Rhonda's favorite batik shirt off a hanger and buried her face in it. Her mother's scent still clung to its folds. So familiar. So alienating. *Damn it, Rhonda.*

She was mentally exhausted but the need to organize and clear out Rhonda's junk took over. Her mother's messiness had always driven her crazy. Starting with the dresser, she pulled the top-drawer handle. It didn't budge. She yanked harder and stumbled backward when it flew open. Tangled layers of gaudy bracelets, necklaces, and earrings lay inside.

She picked up a handful.

Fast, heavy footsteps, then Mick burst in. Sleep had matted his hair on one side and it stuck out on the other. She almost laughed, but his angry face stifled it.

"What the hell are you doing? Put that stuff back."

She dropped the jewelry into the drawer. "Since I'm leaving in a day or two, I thought we should go through Rhonda's things and—"

"Do not touch Mom's stuff." He scanned the room, his gaze lingering on the bed pillow, still bearing a faint imprint of Rhoda's head.

April walked in, eyes puffy with sleep. "Mom, what's going on?"

"Nothing, we're fine."

"Are you and Uncle Mick arguing again? Don't say no because I heard you."

Mick ruffled her hair. "Everything's okay, squirt. Your mom and I are just looking around Granny's room."

"Well, okay…"

Erin wanted to get away from Mick and be alone with her daughter for a few minutes. "I bought you something in London," she said. "Let's go to my room."

Once in her bedroom, Erin removed a small jewelry box from her tote bag and handed it to April. It was getting tougher picking out gifts for her daughter, something April wouldn't think was babyish. She'd settled on a slender gold bracelet with a small diamond charm.

April opened the box and squealed. "Oh Mom, I love it. And it has my birthstone." She threw herself into Erin's arms. "Thank you! Thank you!"

Erin hugged her back. "You're welcome, honey. I love you."

"I love you too, Mom. Can I go over to Olivia's and show her my bracelet? Remember, I told you about Olivia? She's my best friend."

"Of course you can go. Do you want a ride?"

"No thanks, I'll take my bike."

"Stay in the bike lane and watch for cars coming up behind you, okay?"

"I will, thanks." She bolted out of the bedroom.

Erin watched her daughter pedal down the driveway, then returned to Rhonda's room. "Mick, I'm sorry. I just wanted to help. You shouldn't have to deal with all this by yourself."

"Showing up for late Mom's funeral shows exactly how much you give a shit about anything around here."

"Here we go…"

"Yeah, here we go. You're always off doing something or going somewhere. While I was stuck in this dump for years, you were having a good time away at college, then traipsing around the world with your job. You made it clear you didn't care about me and Mom."

"That's not true. I love you both."

It was like this every time she came home. Within a few minutes of arriving, old painful arguments resurfaced, brightly polished and ready to be tossed around like daggers.

"You didn't see how Mom jumped every time the phone rang, hoping it was you."

"My relationship with Rhonda was between her and me and has nothing to do with you, little brother."

"You don't know shit. You—"

"Whoa, whoa, take it easy." A voice as calming as a warm summer breeze came from the doorway. "Have a minute, Erin?"

She turned, and the fight drained out of her in a rush of embarrassment. Justin Rourke. "Sure."

"Sorry you had to hear that." Erin headed for the living room, but stopped at the entrance to the kitchen. "Want a cup of coffee?"

"Sounds good." A concerned expression crossed his face. "Are you and Mick okay?"

"We are. Everything's fine. We're just a little emotional right now."

Everything was not okay. She should have realized how much Rhonda's death would have affected Mick. And now he was alone in her room, surrounded by remnants of her life and years of memories. There was an awkward silence as she poured Justin's coffee and refreshed her own. Should she go to Rhonda's room to comfort Mick? No. He'd probably resent her intrusion.

They sat on Rhonda's lumpy couch, facing the sliding glass doors. Beyond them, a covered porch led to sandy patches of grass, then to a beach that stretched to the shoreline. Overhead, seagulls circled a pile of debris, then dive-bombed it, squawking.

She stole a glance at Justin. After all these years, he still made her heart kick. They were together in high school but grew apart when she went to the University of Denver and he attended the University of Michigan. After college, he became entrenched in Misery Cove and never wanted to live anywhere else. She'd wanted to live anywhere else.

"Hope you don't mind that I let myself into your house." Justin set his cup on the coffee table. "I rang the doorbell, but no one answered. The door was unlocked, so I…"

"You know it's okay."

She and Justin went back a long way. His mother would drop him off on summer mornings on her way to work, to play with Mick and her. He'd stay until she picked him up in the late afternoon. Sometimes, when her dad finished working for the day, the two families would roast hot dogs over a beach bonfire. Justin had been like a brother until they started dating. So long ago.

"Rhonda said you're seeing someone."

His eyes brightened. "I met Catherine six months ago. She's an attorney in Great Rapids."

"Is it serious?" Oh God, why did she ask that? It was none of her business.

"I'm not sure. Maybe."

She smiled, but her heart ached a little.

"I've wanted to tell you how sorry I am about Rhonda. Is there anything I can do?"

"Not really…I didn't see you at the wake."

"I went to the church service but had to leave when my editor called. There was a fire at the Fordham Winery."

"Do you still enjoy working for the *Great Rapids Times*? You've been there awhile."

His lips twitched into a grimace-like smile. "The *Times* never runs out of emergencies to throw at me. But how about you? How are you feeling? Really?"

"I don't know. Rhonda's accident is so unbelievable. I was prepared for her dying from cancer, but not this way. Mick didn't tell me much about what happened. Did your law enforcement friends say how she died?"

"Apparently, she went for a walk on the beach and climbed onto the old dock. Then slipped, hit her head, and tumbled into the water."

"I don't get it. She'd been on that dock a million times and never slipped."

"She'd had a couple glasses of wine. It was late, between eleven-thirty at night and one in the morning, and she was probably tired."

"Did they say anything else?"

"Well, uh...I'm not sure—"

"Tell me."

He took a breath. "Okay, they found blood and hair on one of the dock's iron pilings. There was a concave contusion on the side of her head and water in her lungs. Hitting the piling must have knocked her out. She drowned."

Erin swallowed hard. "Anything else?"

"Just that the medical examiner ruled it an accidental death at the scene."

Rhonda was dead. She still couldn't process it.

"I saw her a few weeks ago and she said you and April still live in Denver, but April is—"

His phone buzzed, and he glanced at the screen. "I have to go. Any chance we can catch up sometime this week?"

"I might not be here that long."

Erin walked him to the foyer and opened the front door. "Thanks for stopping by."

"If you decide to stay a little longer, let me know so we can get together for dinner." Justin hugged her.

"I will." She probably won't.

He turned around and waved as he walked to his

car.

Mick's voice drifted through the second door in the foyer, which led to the motel office. "No, Melanie, I need more time...More than that...Please...Okay. See you soon." Then silence.

She knocked once and opened the door. "Okay if I come in?"

"Why the hell not?"

Mick sat behind a large oak desk. Messy stacks of paper, unopened envelopes, and crumpled snack bags covered its entire surface.

Erin resisted commenting on the clutter and sat in the chair across from him. "I'm sorry about this morning."

He blinked a few times, then gathered some papers into a pile. "I'm sorry too. So much shit's going on, I don't know what to do next. Seriously, Erin, I am glad you're here."

"Me too...What was Rhonda like the last few weeks before she died?"

"Up and down. She was glad you let April stay with her for the school year. It took her mind off the cancer."

"April was glad to be here. She wanted to get away from that trouble at school."

"Yeah, she told me. By the way, yesterday she asked if she could stay here until school's out for the summer."

"What did you tell her?"

"I said she could, but it's up to you."

"It's going to be hard telling her she's going back to Denver with me."

"Come on, let her stay. I can handle it. She's a

good kid. And Melanie can help me with the girly stuff."

"I'm not sure a thirty-seven-year-old guy is mentally equipped to handle a twelve-year-old girl, but thanks anyway. We'll work it out. Like you said, she's a good kid. I'm going to the cemetery in a little while. Want to come along?"

"Yeah, sure."

"See you outside in a few."

Ten minutes later, Erin spotted Mick leaning against the hood of a sleek silver convertible. In front of him, Melanie thrust her index finger at his face.

"What do you mean you haven't talked to Shirley yet, you useless clown?"

Erin's body tensed. Big sister outrage? It was one thing when Mick made her mad, but it was another when his girlfriend humiliated him. And what did she see in Mick, anyway? She looked like a CEO fashion doll and probably rated her boyfriends based on status and income. Mick had neither. And what did Mick see in her? He usually went for the hunting and fishing types. He must be in big trouble, though, because Melanie's finger punctuated each word with a poke to his chest.

"Why. Haven't. You. Talked. To. Shirley. Yet?"

His head drooped "Well, uh, Mom and the funeral and—"

"Don't give me that shit. The contract has been ready for days and Shirley already said she'd sign it."

Erin crossed the parking lot. "Mick, what's going on?"

His gaze swiveled from Melanie to Erin. "Uh, Erin, this is my...this is Melanie Addington. Melanie, this is my sister Erin."

Melanie shot Mick a dismissive look and held out a hand. "Erin, I'm so glad to finally meet you. Mick told me about your exciting job. Travel writer, right?"

"Nice meeting you, too. Mick, what's this about Shirley and a contract?" As far as she knew, Shirley had nothing valuable enough to write a contract on.

"Well, we need—"

"It's not a big deal, Erin. Let's go to lunch sometime while you're in town, okay? Mick, we'll talk later." She blew him a breezy kiss, slipped into her convertible, and roared out of the parking lot.

Chapter Three

Dread knotted Erin's stomach at the idea of seeing Rhonda's grave again. *This time, the coffin will be under six feet of dirt and Rhonda's death will feel very final.* She tapped her fingernails on the car's steering wheel to redirect some of her nervousness. She had to think about something else. "What's the deal with you and Melanie?"

"Would you quit doing that?"

"Doing what?"

"Making that clicking noise. It's driving me crazy."

"Sorry." She moved her hands to the nine-and-three o'clock positions.

Mick opened the window a crack. "I've been seeing her for a couple of months."

Months? How on earth did he keep up with Melanie's obviously expensive lifestyle? "How did you meet her?"

She caught his wide smile out of the corner of her eye.

"I was at Charlie's Tavern one Saturday night with the guys and this hot blonde tapped me on the shoulder and asked me to buy her a drink."

"Lucky you. So, what are you supposed to talk to Shirley about?"

"She's thinking about selling her place, and Westside Development wants it for their new lakefront resort. Paradise Beach is more valuable to them because it's next to land they already own, the piece that runs along the lake and into town. They want Shirley's land because it's on the other side of ours. Melanie's handling the whole thing."

"But Rhonda wasn't planning to sell, right?"

"Well…uh." Mick cleared his throat. "You know, a couple weeks ago, the doctors told Mom she only had a few months to live and—"

Erin swerved onto the shoulder and braked. "And you'll inherit the motel and sell it to the developers. Were you and Melanie sitting around waiting for her to die?"

"Oh my God, no. Absolutely not. But, well, Mom was going to die soon. The doctors said so."

"How else is Melanie involved in this?" Erin eased back onto the road.

"She's a big-time real estate agent and will sell the condos south of the new marina once they're approved for construction."

"Is this why Melanie was poking your chest?"

"Yeah, I'm supposed to talk Shirley into signing the sales agreement. It'll be good for her. She'll get a bundle for her place, but they'll pay a lot more for ours. They said there's nowhere else on the coast that'll work for a development this big. Melanie's helping me with the details."

Of course she is. "So, Melanie has a pretty big interest in this deal, doesn't she?" She glanced at Mick. His eyes had narrowed. "Rhonda told me she was against the new resort. She said property values will skyrocket along with property taxes and everything else, pricing residents out of their homes."

Mick shrugged. "She knew I wanted to sell. Wasn't happy about it, but…"

"Rhonda made it pretty clear she was leaving everything to you, so do whatever you want. But do not pressure Shirley about selling her place."

****

Erin slid out of her car in St. Jude Church's parking lot and waited for Mick to catch up with her. The once beautiful church had grown shabby over the years. The aging parishioners relied on Social Security checks for daily expenses, with not much left for the Sunday collection basket. But today, scaffolding climbed the front of the building. Workers were installing new stained-glass windows and nailing shingles to the roof.

"When did the restoration start?"

"About three months ago. Mom said most of the new homeowners wanted the church restored and they're willing to pay for it."

They wandered into the old churchyard, where the air was heavy with the scents of damp earth, spruce, and decaying flower arrangements. Tall obelisks, weathered tombstones, and simpering-faced statues marked graves in the older section of the cemetery.

"Do you remember playing hide-and-seek in here when we were kids?" Mick asked.

"Of course I do. You always found me."

She usually let her little brother win and laughed when he'd run in circles, yelling, "Found ya, found ya," when he did. A treasured summer memory before life turned upside-down.

Erin didn't know many people buried in St. Jude's. Their father wasn't. Rhonda had him cremated, then sealed his ashes in a plastic storage container so her kids would remember him and he'd be near his beloved lake. It still sat on the back porch railing. When Erin was older and learned the whole story, she'd believed it was Rhonda's way of punishing him for running off.

They walked by a gray-haired woman crouched in front of an established grave. She placed a single red rose on it.

"Who's that?" Erin whispered.

"Mrs. Masters."

"I didn't recognize her. She must be close to eighty."

Truthfully, Erin was a bit afraid of the old widow. She'd yell at kids who accidentally trampled her grass or talked too loud on their way home from school. Erin and her friends called her the old witch. She picked up her pace.

A mound of raw earth heaped with bouquets marked her mother's grave. Erin shoved icy hands into her pockets and imagined Rhonda lying inside the coffin, eyes closed, hands folded, and dressed in whatever Mick decided she should wear. The weight of six feet of dirt trapped her underground. The image was so vivid Erin stumbled backward.

Mick didn't notice. He'd bent down, brushed the bouquets aside, then rested a hand on the dark soil. "Oh, Mom," came out with a sob. "Why did you have to go out on that stupid dock in the middle of the night?" Tears dribbled down his cheeks. He swiped them with his hand then got to his feet and faced Erin. "Why didn't you visit her more after she found out about the cancer?"

His question jarred her into defensiveness.

"She knew I was on a two-month assignment in

Amalfi when she found out. I came back as often as I could and called every week to talk with her and April. I honestly couldn't bring myself to believe she was dying."

That was only part of it. She'd been a coward, afraid to face Rhonda's mortality. Afraid to witness the fear of death in her mother's eyes. She'd worried about her own feelings instead of thinking about Rhonda's.

"And then you didn't even make it home in time for the funeral."

"How many times do I have to tell you I tried, but had a hard time getting a flight? Then when I finally did, it was delayed by a storm."

"I don't believe you."

"What?"

"You've used that excuse for years. You could have found a way to get here."

She tensed. "Where in the hell do you get off being so righteous? You could have postponed the funeral."

After giving Rhonda's grave one more look, Mick hurried away.

"Wait, Mick."

He exited the cemetery, sprinted through the parking lot, and started toward Paradise Beach before Erin got to the car. She drove up alongside him. "Get in."

"I'd rather walk."

She'd found herself sucked into another fight. "Fine. But don't forget about our appointment with the lawyer at two."

Chapter Four

Erin arrived at Dean Scott's law office a few minutes before two. He half-rose when she entered, then sat when she settled in a chair across from him. He'd been a longtime friend of Rhonda's and looked like who he was—a sixtyish, finicky, old-fashioned bachelor.

"Good to see you, Erin."

"You too, Dean."

She didn't know him well but could tell from the precise arrangement of the papers and pens on his desk that he'd rather die than color outside the lines. Not a bad quality for an estate planning attorney. Next to her, Mick tapped his knees. Melanie, on his other side, stared at Dean as if he were Misery Cove's equivalent of God speaking from the burning bush.

Dean cleared his throat. "Thank you all for being here."

Erin jiggled her foot. This was a waste of time.

"As you know, I am the executor of Rhonda's will, which I will read presently, and I—"

The office door opened and a woman in a tailored suit poked her head in. "Please excuse the interruption." She waved to Mick and Melanie, approached Dean, and spoke softly to him.

Dean pushed back his chair and crossed to the doorway. "This is Laura Nowak, an attorney who's consulting with me on a case. I know this is irregular, but would you mind if I left for a moment?"

"Not at all," Erin said. When they were gone, she turned toward Mick. "Do you know her?"

Mick nodded. "She's one of Westside Development's lawyers."

Dean returned to his desk minutes later and picked up several papers. "Sorry for the interruption. I assume everyone is ready to begin." He slipped his glasses on. "I, Rhonda Brady—"

"Can't we just cut to the main part?" Mick leaned forward, looking like he was about to launch himself out of his chair.

Melanie whispered in his ear, then slipped her arm through his.

Why was he so wound up? It would be blah, blah, blah. Everything goes to Mick and everyone can go home.

Dean set the documents on the desk and looked over the top of his glasses. "Fine with me. Is a summary agreeable to you, Erin and Mick? I could read the whole thing out loud, but its meaning is fairly straightforward. Either way, you both will receive notarized copies."

In a rare moment of sibling synchronicity, Erin and Mick looked at each other, rolled their eyes at Dean's formality, and nodded in unison.

"Very well. Your mother was concerned that the two of you didn't communicate often enough or well, and it would worsen when she was gone. She believed family was most important and that you can't trust anyone else the same way. She wanted you two to have each other to rely on."

The room was so quiet, Erin could hear everyone breathing. She sat up straight. Why had Rhonda been concerned with her and Mick's relationship? Something bad was coming.

"Fine, then." Dean removed his glasses and fiddled with the stems. "Erin and Mick, you will jointly inherit the Paradise Beach Motel and property, but only if together the two of you bring the motel up to code within four months and run it for eight. The will further stipulates you cannot accept help from Westside Development or any other development-related corporation."

Mick jumped up. "What the hell, Dean? Mom said she was leaving the motel and property to me."

Dean's face was expressionless. "She changed her mind for the reasons I stated. She wants you and Erin to earn the property by working together before you inherit. Now please sit."

Melanie pulled on Mick's arm and he lowered himself to the edge of the chair.

Dean's words finally penetrated Erin's shock and sunk in. "I am absolutely not staying here for a year to restore the motel."

"Erin, if you'll allow me to proceed..." Dean's tone had an edge to it.

"Sorry, go ahead." She had the feeling she wouldn't like whatever else Dean had to say.

His piercing gaze slid from Erin to Mick, then down to the will. "If the terms of the will are not met, ownership of the Paradise Beach Motel and property will revert to Compassionate Care for Canines and Cats, a local charity also known as C-4, for the purpose of replacing Paradise Beach Motel with a cat and dog senior center and adoption facility. C-4 will not be permitted to sell the property for five years from the date its ownership begins."

Erin couldn't move. Rhonda was trying to manipulate her from the grave.

"As Rhonda's executor," Dean continued, "it is my responsibility to ensure her wishes, precisely as stated in the will, are satisfied before ownership is granted to the two of you. Again, any failure to abide by the will's terms will result in C-4 becoming the owner of record. The twelve-month countdown begins a week from today. Questions?"

"But there's no money to fix the place up." Mick sounded close to tears.

Dean lifted another document from the desk. "Actually, there is."

Mick's head snapped up. "There is?"

"How much?" Melanie asked.

Dean frowned at her and focused on Erin and Mick. "You have seventy thousand dollars to work with. It should be enough to bring the motel up to code if you manage the money wisely."

"Christ," Mick whispered. He turned to Erin. "Where did Mom get that kind of money?"

"No idea," she said through clenched teeth.

"Your mother purchased a seventy-thousand-dollar life insurance policy after your father died and paid it off several years ago. You two are the named beneficiaries. I notified the insurance company of her death and will deposit the money into the account of your choice as soon as it arrives."

Erin had to hand it to Rhonda. She'd come up with a scheme to prevent Mick from selling Paradise Beach to the developers without his big sister's cooperation. *Well, it wouldn't work. The charity can have the damn property.*

Melanie pulled Mick close. "This is a frigging catastrophe," she hissed. "You know what this means for the project? Delay, delay, delay. Do something!"

"Chill, Melanie. This isn't about you." Erin was near her breaking point.

Melanie glared and wrapped her arms around her midsection.

So that's why she'd latched onto Mick. He must have told her about the original will when they'd first met. He'd wanted to impress her.

"All those years, I took care of the motel for Mom and you didn't do shit, Erin," Mick choked out. "How could Mom do this to me?"

"Pulling the permits takes months," Melanie said. "The timeline is impossible."

"Rhonda was a clever woman," Dean said. "She had the permits drawn up and signed several months ago."

"She could have at least warned us this was coming," Erin said.

"Maybe she would have, but because of the accident, she didn't have time." Dean rose. "I know this has been a lot to absorb. You need to talk between yourselves. Let me know what you decide by a week from today."

Erin stormed out of the office and into her car. Why couldn't Rhonda leave the old will in place? But no, she had to have control over the next year of Mick's and her lives. Interesting. She'd always been hands-off with her kids, which makes the will situation all the more strange and frustrating. Didn't she realize it would have the opposite effect from what she wanted?

For years, they'd had a distant relationship. It didn't help that Rhonda dressed like a hippie well into her fifties. But she had an almost magical allure that drew people in. Even Erin was completely mesmerized once.

She closed her eyes and leaned back into the seat, remembering a warm summer evening when she was six. Her father had built a bonfire on the beach and they roasted marshmallows while his radio played. When Rhonda's favorite song about not stopping believing came on, she rose to her feet and spun under the stars, her waist-length hair, peasant skirt, and layers of beads twirled with her. She'd adored her mother and believed she was the luckiest girl in the world. Not long after that day, the adoration turned into resentment.

Somewhere a horn blared, snapping Erin into the present. Without a doubt, Mick would try to convince her to stay in Misery Cove, to work with him to restore the motel, and to eventually sell it to Westside. He'll think half the money was better than none. So, she was in for the mother of all fights when she told him she wouldn't stay. She just couldn't.

She started the car. If she didn't vent to someone, she'd explode.

****

Shirley emerged from the woods behind her little house carrying a wicker basket as Erin pulled into the gravel drive and left the car.

"Do you have a few minutes?"

"Sure. How about we talk while I plant these ferns? Don't want the roots to dry out." She set the basket on the bare patch next to the porch and knelt beside it.

Erin sat on the lowest porch step. Her anger had morphed into incredulity. "Mick and I were just at Dean's office for the reading of Rhonda's will. She changed it a couple of months ago. Did she tell you?"

Shirley sat back on her heels. "No. That's strange. Rhonda always told me everything. Or I thought she did." She got back on her knees, dug six holes, and placed a tuft of ferns into each. "What'd it say?"

"She left Paradise Beach to Mick and me equally, but only if we brought the motel up to code, and then ran it together. The whole thing will take a year. If we don't, the property goes to an animal charity."

Shirley laughed so hard tears spilled down her face and she almost toppled sideways. "That is so Rhonda." She brushed dirt from her hands, got to her feet, and sat next to Erin.

Erin frowned. "It is so Rhonda, and it's not funny."

"Maybe it'll turn out okay, love."

"I doubt it."

There was no way in hell she'd spend a year in Paradise Beach, but she wouldn't tell Shirley yet. She'd work out the details first. Like what would happen to Mick when Dean handed the motel over to C-4.

"So, what are you going to do?"

"I don't know."

"The way I see it, your choices are to stay and help your brother or leave and deal with the mess when Paradise goes to the charity. Either way, it wouldn't hurt if you stuck around for a while, right?"

"Okay, I'll think about it." Maybe for two seconds.

Shirley turned on the hose and watered the ferns. "Did Mick tell you he doesn't think Rhonda's death was an accident?"

"What? No, that's crazy. Why would he think that? If it wasn't an accident, it had to be suicide and there's no way Rhonda would kill herself."

"Well, there's also murder, but it's hard to believe anyone would intentionally kill Rhonda. But if by any chance it was murder, the killer had to be some kind of psycho weirdo who had the urge to kill because there was a full moon or his dog told him to do it or something. If that's the case, we all better keep a baseball bat around."

"You got that from one of your cop shows, right? Anyway, Mick always jumps to the worst-case scenario. It had to be an accident."

Erin's phone rang. Mick.

"Erin, come home right now. It's important."

Damn. "Why?"

"Just get here." He ended the call.

****

"That was fast." Mick was sprawled on the living room couch, holding a beer can.

What the hell? "What's the big emergency, Mick? Did you need another beer or something?"

He sprung upright, spilling beer down the front of his shirt. "Shit." He dashed to the kitchen and returned, pressing a paper towel to the wet spot and holding another beer can. "Why did you disappear after we left Dean's? Didn't you think we needed to talk before you went running off?"

"Not really. There's nothing to talk about."

"Wrong. There's a lot to talk about, but first I need to tell you something about Mom."

"It couldn't wait until I came home from

32

Shirley's?"

Typical Mick. When he wants to tell you something, he has to do it right now.

He returned to the couch. "This is really important, Erin...I don't think Mom's dying was an accident."

Her brain hurt. How much information could she possibly process in two days? She let out a breath and sat next to him. "Shirley believes the medical examiner. Why don't you?"

"Mom would never go out to the dock that late at night, let alone climb on it. It's broken. Part of it tilts into the water because last winter's ice flows rammed it. She always warned me and April off of it."

"We both know Rhonda never followed her own advice."

"Right, but there's other stuff like the way she was dressed. When she came in the bar to get the wine, she had on her good clothes, her hair was all fixed up, and she wore lipstick and that eyeliner stuff. Some of the guys even whistled. If she was just going to the beach, she'd wear jeans and a sweater or something."

That stopped her. "Exactly what was she wearing?"

"Her best black pants, a fancy white blouse, and her new black leather jacket."

He had a valid point about the clothes, but there could be a million reasons she dressed that way. She couldn't think of any, though. "So, you think someone else was here?"

"Yeah, I do. That's probably why she got the wine. Maybe they had a few glasses and went to the beach. Then he killed her." His voice shook. "And there's another thing. Stuff's missing. I couldn't find the wine bottle. What if the killer hit her with it, then kept it? It wasn't in the garbage or anywhere else in the house."

"What about dirty wine glasses? Did you find any?"

"No, which is weird. Mom always drank wine out of a wine glass."

"Are any missing?"

"Do you seriously think I know how many wine glasses we have?"

"Not really, but I do." She went to the kitchen and opened the cupboard.

Mick followed her. "Well…?"

"Ever since I broke a glass last year, there have been five. Five are here now. So there goes your theory."

"The killer could have washed the glasses they used and put them away. And another thing. Her phone is missing."

"Did you look for it?"

"Sorta. I called her number, but didn't hear it ring."

"That's it? That's all you did?"

"Hey, a lot was going on in the days after Mom died."

"Did you tell the police about the bottle and phone?"

"Yeah, of course. They said she could've tossed the bottle anywhere. And her phone could still be in the house."

She might be pressing too hard. He was having a rough enough time.

"Okay, sorry. I get it. You haven't told April any of this, have you?"

"No way." He leaned over and grabbed her hand. "Please don't go back to Denver until we figure out what happened to Mom. And we need to figure out the stuff about the will. What do you think we should do?"

"I can't deal with this right now."

****

She woke at two-thirty in the morning and couldn't get back to sleep while questions about Rhonda swirled through her mind. Was her death really an accident? Why did she wear dressy clothes to the beach? Maybe she had a visitor, but that didn't necessarily mean the visitor killed her. The missing wine bottle and phone were odd, though. Justin described the injury to Rhonda's head as concave. Could a wine bottle have caused it? Was Mick right about Rhonda being murdered?

Everything she knew about Rhonda's death was secondhand information. In the morning, she'd go to the police station.

Chapter Five

"Ms. Brady, I'm Detective Caroline Mackey. Sorry for your loss."

"Thank you."

Mackey's stiff navy blazer, tight bun at the back of her head, and stern expression reminded Erin of every authoritarian boss she'd ever had the displeasure of working with.

"Please sit. What can I do for you?"

Erin settled into one of the wooden visitor's chairs. "I understand you investigated my mother's death."

Mackey nodded and glanced at the open folder on her desk. "Yes, I have her file right here."

"Then you know about her missing phone. And that the wine bottle she took from The Sand Bar is also missing. Have they turned up?"

"Since the medical examiner ruled Mrs. Brady's death accidental, no further investigation was or is necessary."

"My brother and I think it's possible our mother's death wasn't an accident and would like the investigation to continue."

"Ms. Brady, I understand how you must feel, but that's not possible. Her case is closed. There could be reasonable explanations for the missing items. For example, Mrs. Brady could have misplaced her phone and tossed the wine bottle into the lake."

Mackey explanations were reasonable. The same thing crossed her mind the day before.

"There's another thing. Rhonda wouldn't have dressed up to go to the beach. We think she had a visitor."

"Are you suggesting Mrs. Brady is the victim of a homicide?"

"I don't know. But she must have dressed up for someone. If she was alone, she would have worn something more casual, like jeans and a pullover."

"Do you know of anyone who would want to harm your mother?"

That was the problem. Everyone loved Rhonda.

"Not really."

"Ms. Brady, I'm very sorry, but without evidence to the contrary, there's nothing we can do."

Of course, detectives needed evidence. "I have one more question. Does the medical examiner think it's possible a wine bottle could have made the depression in my mother's head?" She pictured someone standing behind Rhonda, raising the bottle above her head, and… She closed her eyes a moment, trying to wipe that image out of her mind. "If it *is* possible, my mother could have gone to the beach with someone who hit her head with the bottle, then drowned her."

"If the M.E. believed any other means of death were possible, she wouldn't have ruled it accidental."

"Please, could you just ask her if it is possible? Maybe she didn't know about the missing bottle."

The detective hesitated for a moment, then said, "Sure, I'll call her later and let you know."

Erin guessed she had no intention of contacting the doctor. "Can you call her now? Please?"

Mackey sat back in her chair and sighed. "Sure. Okay." She picked up the phone, asked a few questions, nodded, and hung up. "The doctor said Mrs. Brady died from drowning, resulting from her head injury and fall. She stands by her original finding of accidental death." Mackey's face softened. "I'm sorry. When an accidental death happens, we want to find a reason for it. We want something or someone to blame. But often, it's just an accident."

****

Early the next morning, Erin booked two seats on a flight to Denver for the following day, after seeing April on the school bus. She glanced at her watch. Seven-thirty. Mick won't be up for a while, but as soon as he comes downstairs, she'll tell him she won't be helping with the motel renovation and she and April are flying home tomorrow. It'll be a hard conversation and she blamed Rhonda. If only she hadn't written a new will.

She'll wait until Mick has a cup of coffee before telling him the bad news. Once things settle down, she'll call Dean and tell him to begin the transference of Paradise Beach to C-4. When the final papers have been signed, she'll return to Misery Cove to help Mick pack up the house.

Of course, he'll be devastated and she wouldn't be surprised if he lost Melanie along with the property. Not a bad thing, in her opinion. From what she'd seen, Melanie didn't deserve Mick. She didn't treat him well, not that Mick seemed to mind. Probably not a coincidence they'd become a couple right after Rhonda found out she didn't have long to live.

A pang of guilt unsettled her. Mick will lose his

home, but again, it's Rhonda's fault. She'll ask him to move to Denver with her and April. He could live in her condo and take classes at the university if he wanted.

She'd just poured a second cup of coffee when Mick burst into the kitchen. "We need to talk."

"Sure. Come upstairs and keep me company while I pack. April and I are leaving tomorrow."

"What about the will? Mom wanted us to work together on the motel. If you leave, Paradise will go to that fucking animal charity. Do you really want that to happen?"

"Let's talk upstairs."

Once in her room, she dragged a suitcase out of the closet and opened it on the bed.

"Listen, I have an idea about the will," Mick said.

"You have an idea or your girlfriend has an idea?"

"Doesn't matter. If the current will is disqualified, the old one rules, right? Then I will inherit Paradise Beach and we'll all live happily ever after."

She pulled a stack of tops out of a drawer and set them in the suitcase. "I think that's right. And it's invalidated, not disqualified."

"Whatever. Will you stop and sit down for a minute?"

"Fine." She sat on the edge of the bed.

"All we have to do is convince the judge to invalidate the new will because Mom wasn't in her right mind when she wrote it. We have to work on it together since the new will benefits both of us."

No way Mick came up with this on his own. "Rhonda's mind was fine, and you know it. Anyway, I have to get home and back to work."

"Don't you care that someone might have killed

Mom? And if you leave now, this place will go to that dumb ass dog and cat thing. And what about April? Mom wanted Paradise Beach, or rather the money we'd get from selling it, to go to her eventually. If you don't care about my future, at least think about your daughter's." He breathed deeply, then exhaled. "Please, stay at least long enough to get the new will thrown out. We can talk to Dean tomorrow."

He was right. April should benefit from the sale of the property.

"How does Melanie think we can prove Rhonda wasn't in her right mind when she wrote the will?"

"The idea wasn't just Melanie's." Redness crept up his neck and colored his cheeks. "We could say Mom had horrible headaches, took too many pain pills for the cancer, and continued drinking. That she didn't know what she was doing half the time."

Definitely Melanie's idea. Mick was so dazzled by her, he probably figured she was a gift from God. But maybe it would work and couldn't take more than a week. "Okay. We'll talk to Dean. I'll stay if he thinks there's a chance a judge will agree to invalidate the new will."

Mick planted a noisy kiss on her cheek. "Thank you!"

"Listen, if this works and you inherit, promise me you'll get a good financial adviser and set up a trust for April with half of the money you get from selling the motel."

"I promise." He walked out of the room grinning and returned as Erin was replacing her clothes in the drawers. "We have an appointment with Dean tomorrow at ten."

****

Later that afternoon, after canceling their flight reservations, Erin found April gliding on a swing in Paradise Beach's play area. She sat on the only other unbroken one and pushed herself off to the screech of rusty chains. After swinging a few minutes, she skidded to a stop. "Uncle Mick and I are meeting with Granny's attorney tomorrow to see if we can get her will invalidated."

April dragged her feet in the sand to slow down, then jumped to the ground. "What's that mean, invalidate the will?"

"It means we want the judge to decide the current will isn't correct and we should use the old one instead."

"Why? The new will is what Granny wanted."

"Did she tell you that?"

"Not exactly, but if she wrote it, it's what she wanted."

April was right and amazing and astute.

"It's a little complicated, but your uncle and I agree he should own the motel property."

"You don't want to stay here and help him fix it up, do you?"

"It's not that."

Oh, Lord, now she was lying to her daughter. When had April become so insightful? She'd have to be more careful about what she said and how she acted. Life was so much simpler when April believed everything she told her.

"We have to go home, but I want your uncle to keep the motel. We'll be staying for a week or two until everything's settled."

"I hope the judge doesn't invalidate it. I love it here, Mom. Can't we live here?"

"What do you love about this place?" Erin tried to keep the disbelief out of her voice.

"The beach."

"Denver has beaches."

"Yeah, but we don't live on one. And I have a lot of friends here. They're nice, Mom. Can we please wait until I finish out the school year?"

Erin's heart hurt. She'd allowed April to stay with Rhonda for the current school year, because the previous year, a pack of mean girls bullied her. They called her a baby and worse because a nanny lived with her while Erin traveled. Also, Rhonda deeply loved April and wanted her at Paradise as diversion while she dealt with her diagnosis.

"I'll think about it."

Another lie and more guilt. April would leave when she did. She'd deal with the bullying problem when they got home. No one would ever bully her daughter again.

"Thanks, Mom… Did you love Granny?"

"Of course I did." True, but it was complicated.

"Did you love Daddy?"

Where did that come from? April hadn't asked about her father in years.

"Yes. When I met him, he was a good man."

"Were you sad when he died?"

"Of course, sweetie. Like the way you feel about Granny dying."

Another lie. She'd lied more in the last ten minutes than she had in a long time. She hated lying.

April's phone sounded, and she answered it.

"Yeah…okay, I'll ask. Mom, can I go to Olivia's? She has a new kitten."

"Sure."

She ached for her daughter. She'd have to find a different school in Denver for the next school year. Or maybe they'd move to a different city. Anyway, there was absolutely no way she could stay in Misery Cove. She'd feel trapped. After her father died, every day was like sinking into quicksand, sucking her deeper into the life Rhonda had.

She couldn't go through that again.

Chapter Six

"Contesting a will is a serious business," Dean said the next day.

"Mick and I believe our mother's judgment was impaired when she wrote it. Take a look at this." Erin set a plastic grocery bag on the desk. Inside was a jumble of prescription drug containers. "These are her pain-killers, cancer meds, anti-depressants and sleep aids." Actually, not all the pills were Rhonda's. Erin increased the bottle count by including some of hers and Mick's, thinking Dean wouldn't examine them too closely. "Worrying about the cancer and dealing with her pain affected her judgment."

"Right," Mick said. "She was always forgetting things and getting lost and—"

Erin nudged Mick. "Mick means she hadn't been herself. Under a lot of stress. As you know, she was seeing a psychologist."

After taking a cursory look inside the bag, Dean handed it back to Erin. "The day she told me about changing her will, she didn't seem mentally impaired to me."

"If she was right in the head, she would never have written a will like that," Mick said.

Dean pressed his lips together and looked from Erin to Mick. "I suppose it wouldn't hurt to have the judge take a look. And maybe...well, who knows?"

Dean jotted a few notes, then slipped the first and second wills into a manila envelope and set it aside. "I have a meeting with the judge tomorrow on another matter, and I'll bring this with me. I'm not sure how long it'll take him to reach a decision. Maybe a week. Maybe more. As executor, I have the authority to suspend the so-called ticking clock. I'll restart it when I contact you with the judge's decision."

"Could you ask him to speed it up? I've got to get moving on this thing with Melanie," Mick said.

Dean interlaced his fingers. "What thing?"

"Doesn't matter. Let's go, Erin."

As Erin joined Mick, she turned back. "Dean, would the charity be allowed to build an animal facility on the property?"

Dean grinned. "Oh yes, Rhonda cleared it with the zoning board a few months ago."

"Can I sell Paradise Beach if I inherit it?" Mick asked.

"Yes," Dean said slowly. "There's no restriction on what you can do with the property after you inherit it."

****

Erin dropped Mick off at Melanie's condo, then continued to Paradise, praying the judge would invalidate Rhonda's current will. If so, she'd talk to Dean about representing Mick on the negotiations with Westside, reviewing the final contract, and setting up April's trust.

Drafting the purchase agreement could take a while, so she and April would head to Denver as soon as she got word that the old will was in play. She'd return to Misery Cove for the closing and to help Mick clear out the house. She was almost giddy imagining being free of Paradise Beach and having money secured for April's future.

April met her at the front door, her face scrunched with anxiety. "What happened, Mom? Are we going home?"

This was going to be tricky because whatever the judge ruled, they were returning to Colorado. "Let's grab a soda."

They took drinks from the refrigerator and sat at the kitchen table.

"Well, are we going home?" April locked gazes with Erin.

"Not for another week, at least. Mr. Scott has to talk to the judge before we know what happens with the will."

"What happens then?" Tears quivered on the edge of April's lower eyelids.

This was so hard. She wanted to leave as much as April wanted to stay, and hated it. She held her daughter close. "We'll see."

Later that evening, Erin's phone blared a weather emergency signal. A severe thunderstorm watch was in effect until eleven that night. She'd let April sleep unless the storm grew worse and they had to take cover.

From the back porch, she watched angry clouds tumbling in from the west. Feeling a chill as the wind shifted, she moved inside and started a fire in the living room hearth. When the blaze was strong enough, she set a log on top.

"I could have helped with that."

She jumped. Justin was right behind her.

"You almost gave me a heart attack. Please knock or something when you come in."

"Sorry…I brought you something." He gave a sheepish smile and handed her a bottle of wine.

"Thank you." She glanced past him through the glass doors where the plastic bowl holding her father's ashes teetered on the rail. "Oh my God." She flew to the back porch and set the bowl on the floor behind the loveseat.

Justin slid the door behind her when she came back in.

"Thanks. You're staying for a glass of wine, aren't you?" Was he just being nice or…?

He grinned. "I hoped you'd ask." He opened the bottle, poured wine into two glasses, and handed her one. Then they sat on the floor in front of the fireplace.

"What will you do with your dear old dad now that Rhonda is gone?"

"Well, there's a complication." She told him about the terms of the will and that she and Mick were trying to get the will invalidated. "Whichever way the judge rules, we'll have to find a place for him."

"Have you considered burying him in Rhonda's grave?"

"She'd hate that. Keeping your husband's ashes in a plastic bowl isn't exactly a sign of a happily-ever-after marriage."

"What will you do if the judge rules the current will stands?"

"Mick wants me to stay and help him bring the motel up to code and April wants to live here forever, but I just can't. I know it sounds selfish, but I hate everything about this place."

She watched his face for a reaction. There wasn't one. Not even a flicker.

"Even when we were kids, you said that if you left, you'd never come back."

"I still feel that way. Anyway, Mick doesn't think Rhonda's death was an accident."

"He doesn't believe the medical examiner?"

"No. What do you think?"

Lightning flared, illuminating the dark sky with white light. A crash of thunder shook the windows. Erin jumped.

"I want to check on April."

She rushed up the stairs and peered into her daughter's dimly lit bedroom. April lay sound asleep. What an amazing kid. Love drove everything else out of her mind.

She returned to her seat next to Justin and sipped her wine. "She's sleeping through it. Where were we?"

"You asked what I thought about Rhonda's death. I believe the experts."

"I spoke with Detective Mackey. She said the police did some preliminary investigation but didn't need to continue once the medical examiner ruled Rhonda's death accidental. Mick said the police questioned him, but do you know if they talked to anyone else?"

"One of my detective buddies said they interviewed everyone who'd been in The Sand Bar that night. No one admitted seeing Rhonda after she left with the wine, and no one remembered anyone leaving the bar before Mick closed the place at one."

"So, a bunch of guys, probably drunk out of their minds, remember exactly who was in the room every minute that night."

"Think about it. It would have taken a lot of time to

go to the house and beach and…well, everything else."

Thunder rumbled in the distance.

"Did they say if there were any unfamiliar cars in the parking lot?"

"They recognized all the cars."

"Someone could have walked here, though. It's only a mile from town. I know everyone loved her, but maybe someone had a secret grudge."

"It sounds like you think her being murdered is a fact. It's not."

"I'm not sure I believe someone killed her, but I think getting wine from the bar that late in the evening and being dressed up means she was expecting someone."

****

Erin walked through the woods to Shirley's property after April left for school the next morning, crossing the gravelly driveway to the cabin's front porch. The beach was invisible from there, although only forty yards away. Shirley wanted it that way. She said the forest was more peaceful than the lake.

Before Erin had a chance to knock, Shirley threw open the front door. Her eyes were teary. "I was hoping you'd stop by."

Erin hugged her, then stepped inside. "How are you holding up?"

"You know…"

"Yes, I know."

She handed Shirley a small package, then sat in one of the ancient leather recliners, the one she'd sat in a thousand times while Shirley listened to her childhood problems. Across the room, a small fire sputtered in a stone fireplace. She let out a long, comforting sigh.

Shirley shook the package. "What's this?" She opened it. "Oh my God, thank you! My favorite French cologne." She sprayed some on her wrists and set the bottle on the table. "So, what's going on, kiddo?" She lowered herself onto the other recliner and studied Erin's face. "You look serious."

"Mick has a crazy idea to invalidate the will, and I agreed to stay and find out if it's possible."

"Invalidate the will so he'd inherit? That's clever. It was Melanie's idea, right?"

Erin laughed. "Of course it was."

"I know you're not happy about the whole thing, but I am. I like having you around. Anyway, it's difficult to invalidate a will, so you'll be on your way soon enough."

Erin wiggled more deeply into the chair and looked around. She loved Shirley's cabin. Humble but comfortable and cheerful. Small living room, dining room, kitchen, two tiny bedrooms and a bathroom, all neatly squeezed into nine hundred square feet. Shirley had lived there her entire life. First with her parents, then with her husband, now alone. More alone now, without Rhonda next door.

Shirley gazed into the fire. "To tell you the truth, I miss your mother a ton. We were friends almost sixty years and every time I saw her, she brightened my day. I can't believe she's gone." She took a crumpled tissue from her pocket and wiped her nose.

"Someone told me you were with her the day she died."

"We went to the mall in Great Rapids that afternoon to exchange the sweater she bought April for her birthday. Then we window-shopped a little and stayed for a late lunch in the food court. On the way home, I dropped her off at her shrink's office. You know she was seeing Zachary Smith, right?"

"Mick told me."

"While she was there, I went grocery shopping at the Stay and Shop. After that, I drove her home. Bill was there, working on the motel roof. Oh, I forgot, we stopped by the pharmacy after Zachary's. She had to pick up a prescription. That was about it."

"I would never have guessed Rhonda would go to a psychologist."

"It wasn't a regular thing. Sometimes she'd get bummed out thinking about dying, so she saw Zachary to talk about it."

Sorrow swelled inside Erin, unraveling all the excuses she ever had for avoiding Misery Cove and Rhonda. How much depression and anxiety had her mother gone through, knowing she'd probably be dead before Thanksgiving? Her thoughts tumbled into a deep, dark pit. *Pull up. Now.* She couldn't afford to lose it.

"Then you took her home?"

"Right. That was the last time I saw her. Excuse me a minute."

Shirley left the room and returned with two small glasses of what looked like cream. She handed one to Erin. The scents of chocolate, vanilla, and whiskey tickled her nose. "Is this what I think it is?"

"Yes. Don't judge me, I need it." Shirley downed hers in one swallow.

Listening to Shirley talk about the last day of Rhonda's life was painful, but she had to know the rest.

"Did you see her after you dropped her off at the

house?"

"No. I got into my sweatsuit, turned on the TV, and dozed off." Shirley paused, her eyes distant. "Oh, wait. She called me that night and I—"

When she didn't continue, Erin said, "And…?"

"Darn." Shirley massaged her temples. "I can't remember what she said. Ever since she died, my brain's been foggy. If I remember what she said, I'll let you know."

Chapter Seven

Two days later, Erin drove to downtown Port Elizabeth with Shirley, thinking about her conversation with Justin the other night. He'd blown off the idea Rhonda might have been murdered. Maybe he was right. It had been a friendly visit. They were friends. She used to like that word. Would his girlfriend Catherine mind if she knew he'd visited his friendly ex? Erin researched her after Justin left. In pictures that she hoped were digitally altered, Catherine looked beautiful. They probably looked great together. *Damn*.

"Erin, did you even hear what I said?" Shirley asked.

"What? Oh, I'm sorry, I was daydreaming."

"I said I gave myself a headache last night, trying to bring up that phone call from Rhonda, but no dice."

"Don't worry about it." Erin continued slowly along Front Street, passing several pubs and restaurants, upscale apparel shops, local artisan jewelry stores, and art galleries. Maybe she and Shirley could do a little shopping when they finished lunch.

"Every time I'm here," Shirley said, "I wonder why I don't come more often."

"I know what you mean."

Unlike Misery Cove, ten miles to the south, Port Elizabeth was a vibrant east-coast-like beach town. When she was a teenager, she longed to live there. All the cool kids did. They considered Misery Cove low class, and she was embarrassed to admit she lived there.

She found a parking place down the street from Georgia's Lakeside Grille. Georgia Owens, the grille's owner, greeted them at the door and gave Erin a smothering hug.

"I'm so sorry for your loss, honey. We all loved Rhonda."

Erin nodded. "Thanks." She didn't know what else to say.

Georgia squeezed Shirley's shoulder. "Sorry for your loss, too." She led them to a table next to a wall of sliding glass doors overlooking a deck that overlooked the lake.

After seating and handing them menus, Georgia asked, "What can I bring you ladies?

"I'm not sure yet," Erin said. "Will you give us a couple of minutes?"

"Sure, water in the meantime?"

"Yes, please."

When Georgia left, Shirley said, "Thanks for coming to lunch with me. There's something I need to talk to you about."

"What's up?"

"Westside Development. You know how they've been bugging Rhonda and me to sell them our land?"

"Bugging you?"

Shirley leaned forward. "They visited both of us a few times, but no one had been around since Rhonda died. Then Mick and Melanie showed up at my place last night."

Erin tensed. "What did they want?"

Shirley lifted an envelope from her purse and

handed it to Erin. "They wanted me to sign this. It's a sales agreement for my property."

Erin set the envelope on the table. "Mick mentioned you were thinking about selling. Did you change your mind?"

Georgia discreetly placed glasses of water on the table and left.

"I don't know yet. But with Rhonda gone and the town going to hell with the enormous Westside Development project coming up, Misery Cove doesn't feel like home anymore."

"I'm guessing this is where Mick and Melanie come in."

"Melanie works for Lou Guthrie, Westside's chief financial officer. She's top dog on Westside's sales team. She and Mick strongly encouraged me to sign the sales agreement right away. They said if I sign now, I'll get above the market price. If I wait until Paradise Beach is sold, I'll get a lot less. Melanie showed me a sketch of the entire development and what I'd be living next to if I didn't sell. Did you know that most of the trees between my land and yours belong to Paradise Beach?"

"No."

"Me either. If I don't sell and Paradise does, the trees will be cut down and they'll build a ten-story condo complex with a kiddie pool right up against my property line. She said they'll put up a wall, but you know and I know a wall won't keep out the noise."

Georgia appeared at their table. "Ready to order lunch?"

Erin fought to control her anger. How could Mick and Melanie pressure Shirley to sell only a week after

Rhonda died? "I want a vodka martini."

"Sounds good," Shirley said. "Make mine a double, Georgia."

Georgia raised her eyebrows. "All righty then. Comin' right up."

When their drinks arrived, Erin drained half her glass. "You know, I'm not helping Mick fix up the motel."

"I figured."

"If we're successful in getting the current will thrown out, Mick will sell right away and you'll have a decision to make. Stay and get ready for mega-resort neighbors or hurry and sign your sales agreement before Mick signs away Paradise."

"But if the current will stands," Shirley said, "the pet charity gets Paradise Beach and I'm up the creek. Who'd want to buy property next to a cat and dog place? The thing is, I really love my little shack, and just this minute I decided I don't want to sell. So, I'm pretty much screwed." She slumped over her martini.

Erin hadn't realized that refusing to help Mick renovate the motel would also affect Shirley. That it impacts the three most important people in her life. She clasped Shirley's hand.

"Don't worry, we'll figure something out."

****

Dean Scott phoned two weeks later. "Erin, the judge reached a decision on the validity of Rhonda's will late yesterday. They consulted her physician, oncologist, psychologist, and a few of her friends, including me. Everyone said Rhonda was of sound mind. Laura Nowak, Westside Development's attorney, produced a list of witnesses willing to testify that

Rhonda had become increasingly confused in the months prior to her death and took it to the judge. As you know, Westside has an interest in ensuring the old will remains valid. The judge saw through that maneuver and ruled that the current will stays in effect."

Erin sagged into a chair. "Thanks for the update."

Rhonda was probably jumping for joy in whichever sphere she occupied. Well, she won't be happy for long. Erin braced herself before going to look for Mick.

He was in the office, talking on the phone. "I said I'm sorry, Mel." He looked up and saw Erin. "Listen, I have to go…Okay, see you later." He ended the call. "You look pissed. Is something wrong?"

"The judge won't invalidate the will."

Mick's face went white. "Holy shit. What are we going to do?"

This was an agonizing dilemma. If she refused to work on the motel, she'd hurt both Mick and April. If she stayed, her worst nightmare would come true. She knew it was selfish, but she could not live in Misery Cove. She'd make it up to them somehow.

"There's nothing we can do. Dean will prepare the paperwork to transfer Paradise Beach to C-4, and April and I will head home in a few days. Come with us. We'll return to clear out the house once the papers have been signed, then go back to Denver. You'll love it there. Think about it, okay?" She started for the door.

"Wait. This can't happen. We have to do something."

"I'm so sorry, Mick."

She walked out disgusted with herself. Rhonda had forced her into this mess, but it had been her own stubborn selfishness that would hurt everyone. *Rhonda, did you think this through? I can't believe you wanted this to happen. If you're up there somewhere, please help me think of a way out.*

Erin found April on the back porch reading her phone, and sat next to her. "I have something to tell you. Remember when we talked about Granny's will? The judge said it's valid."

"What does that mean?"

"It means the animal charity will take over the motel." Not take over, they'll knock it down and build an industrial-looking shelter. What a waste. The property is beautiful and valuable. Maybe Rhonda really was losing it before she died.

"If you and Uncle Mick fixed it up, you'd both own it. We could live here, Mom."

"I'm sorry, but we're flying home at the end of the week."

"But why? I can help clean up the motel. It'll be fun."

How could she explain to her twelve-year-old the deep dislike she had for the house, motel, and town? The shabbiness that touched something deep inside her? Repulsed her? She couldn't. "No, honey. We have to go home."

"Please, Mom. School ends in six weeks and I want to be with my friends. Uncle Mick said I could stay."

"You can't stay with Mick. Who will cook and clean? Who'll take care of you when he goes out with his friends?"

"Then you stay with me. It's only six weeks."

"No, I'm so sorry."

Saying no was hard. But every day she stayed in

Misery Cove, she was losing herself, the smart, focused, logical person she'd been in Denver.

April jumped up, and her book tumbled to the floor. "I hate you! You can't make me go to Denver!" Her words ended in a sob and she raced into the house.

****

Erin tossed her suitcase onto her bed and jerked open the lid. Later, she'd call April's Denver school principal and tell her April will join her old class the following week, and ask about ways they could prevent the bullying. Or maybe she'd find a way to work from home and homeschool April for the rest of the school year.

Footsteps clomped in the hallway, then Mick swaggered into her bedroom, grinning. "I have a great idea."

"I don't want to hear any more of your great ideas." Erin carried three pairs of shoes from the closet and laid them in the bottom of the suitcase.

"Just stop and listen for two minutes, okay? It's a compromise." Another grin. "And before you ask, I came up with the idea by myself. Haven't even mentioned it to Melanie. Please, Erin."

She sighed, "Okay, let's hear it." She settled onto the vanity chair and forced herself to be patient.

"Regardless of what you said before, I know you think our family should own Paradise Beach, not that animal charity, right? Especially if the charity is a fraud?"

"What? Who told you it's a fraud? Rhonda wouldn't leave the motel property to a fraudulent charity. Dean probably checked it out when he wrote the will."

"I don't know about that, but I looked it up on the internet."

Erin grabbed her phone and searched. "Looks like the IRS has a list of registered charities." She scrolled down. "Hmm, C-4 isn't on it." She continued searching. "And there are several legal cases pending against it. I guess you're right."

"See, I told you."

There was no doubt in her mind Rhonda expected her to research C-4, and had deliberately selected it because it was shady. She'd known Erin would think twice before leaving millions to criminals.

"So, what's your great idea?" She'd try to be objective.

"Get this. We tell Dean we agree to the terms of the will, but here's the good part. You won't have to stay here the whole time. If you check in with Dean by phone every week or so, and visit him once or twice a month, he'll think you're on the job. In a year, you can sign Paradise over to me and go on your merry way. And I'll sell Paradise for a shit load of money."

It actually might work. *Rhonda, is this your answer?* Now she was losing it, talking to a dead person.

"And another thing. I know April wants to finish her school year here. Let her stay and I'll take care of her."

"You have no idea how to take care of a twelve-year-old girl. And what happens when you decide to go out with your friends or spend the night with Melanie?"

"We'll figure it out. She can stay some nights at Olivia's. Olivia's mom Kelly won't mind. And Shirley will help. It's only a few weeks, Erin."

"Give me a minute." This might be the only way that Mick and April benefit from the inheritance. "Okay, I admit it's a good idea. We'll visit the township office tomorrow morning to find out exactly what's needed to bring the motel up to code."

Mick pulled her out of the chair and gave her a quick hug. "Thanks, Erin. I promise you won't be sorry. I'll call Dean and tell him we're on." He kissed her cheek. "You're the best. See you later. I'll be at Charlie's, celebrating."

I'm still mad at you, Rhonda, but thank you.

Chapter Eight

Erin drove straight to Shirley's house after meeting with the township the next day and found Shirley on her porch swing, reading the latest mystery about a thoughtful inspector in a quiet village

"I haven't read that one yet," Erin said. "How is it?"

"Great as always. Looks like you have something on your mind."

"A nightmare. We—"

"Stop." Shirley got to her feet and pointed to the swing. "Sit." Then she headed inside. A few minutes later, she returned with two glasses of iced tea, handed one to Erin, and sat beside her. "Now, tell me what happened."

Erin took a sip. "What's in this beside iced tea? Vodka?"

"Never you mind. Have another sip and tell me what's going on."

She did and with a long sigh, set the glass down. "Mick came up with an idea about how we can work together on the motel without me actually being here full time. We just got back from visiting the township to find out what needs to be done to bring the motel up to code. They said smoke detectors and room sprinkler systems have to be installed. The black mold has to be eradicated. We need new toilets, sinks, and showers.

Holes in the walls have to be repaired, and the mildewed furniture replaced. The rooms have to be wheelchair accessible, and the roof has to be re-shingled. There's a lot more."

"I'm not surprised."

"Why did Rhonda neglect the motel for so long?"

"Your mother was a wonderful woman, but she only saw the shiny side of life. She never wanted to manage the motel in the first place. She must have told you how she inherited it from her parents, right?"

Erin nodded. "Yes."

"Well, after your grandparents died, she and your father ran the place, and it did well enough. When he took off, she held on, hoping he'd come back. But once he died, Rhonda pretty much gave up."

That was an understatement. But then she remembered what she'd gone through when Sam died. Marrying him had been the most impulsive thing she'd ever done and, in a few years, she regretted it. But by then they'd had April and she decided to stick it out for her daughter's sake. Although she hadn't been in love with him for a long time, his death shook her. He'd been alive one minute and dead the next. April was only two when he passed. Passed. That word sounds so peaceful. His drunken single-motorcycle accident was anything but.

Shirley rearranged herself on the swing. "Mick tried taking care of the place after you left for college, but his heart wasn't in it."

"It still isn't, and we need someone to manage the work if we have any shot at all at getting everything done. Do you know anyone reliable?"

"George at Great Lakes Construction is the best

person around. He'll give you a good deal—tell him I sent you."

"There's one more thing. I'll be flying between here and Denver for a while. Just enough so Dean thinks I'm around. April wants to stay in Misery until the end of the school year. Mick said he would take care of her, but you know…"

"Don't you worry about a thing. I'll move over to Paradise until you're ready to take her home."

****

Erin had only been home a few minutes when someone knocked impatiently on the front door. She opened it a crack. Melanie, the last person she wanted to see. "Mick's not home."

"Good. I wanted a chance to talk with you alone."

"Not now, okay?" She couldn't handle any more aggravation.

She started closing the door, but Melanie shouldered her way in.

"Just give me five minutes."

"What do you want?"

"Can we please sit?"

Erin went to the dining room and sat on the nearest chair. Melanie settled across from her and put her briefcase on the floor. "Mick told me about the compromise."

"That was fast."

"Listen, I want to make it easy for you while you're in Colorado. I'll keep a close eye on the motel renovation, so all you'll have to do when you're here is check the units, visit Dean, and be on your way. I'll also check in with April. Maybe we can go to the movies or something."

"Shirley will take care of April. And I can handle the motel oversight." When Melanie frowned, Erin said, "I'm surprised you'd want to spend your time on a construction site and babysitting. Why are you really here? Does it have something to do with what's in that briefcase?"

Melanie blushed, but her smile stayed bright. "Well, as a matter of fact…" She opened the briefcase and removed a sheet of paper. "Mick told me you agreed to sign your half of the inheritance over to him when the will's conditions have been met." She paused.

"And?"

"And we want you to understand this is a business transaction. Westside has a lot on the line here."

"*Westside* has a lot on the line?"

"Well, yes. Mick said he would inherit with no strings attached, but because of the new will, construction will be delayed for a year."

"What's the problem? Work can continue on other sections of the resort."

"The problem is that you might change your mind about transferring your half of the property to Mick and won't sell it to Westside."

"I won't change my mind. Mick can have it as long as he puts my half in a trust for April when it's sold."

"Then you won't mind signing this." Melanie held out the paper.

Erin didn't reach for it. "What is it?"

"Not a big deal, Erin. We had our attorneys draw up an agreement that states that when you and Mick inherit Paradise Beach, you will transfer the ownership of your portion to Mick."

"I'm not signing anything."

Melanie was a manipulator. Something else was going on here.

Melanie's expression darkened, but she quickly recovered with a polished smile. "Lou Guthrie, Westside's CFO, just wants a guarantee to protect all parties concerned."

"Sorry."

"What *is* the issue here?"

This was getting tedious. "I don't have to explain anything to you."

"So, what should I tell him?"

"I really don't care."

Chapter Nine

Erin was in the kitchen reading the morning news, two mornings later, when a text from Mick popped up. He was on his way back from picking up building supplies. She was shocked. This was early for him. Interesting how the motivation of a few million dollars got him moving.

The roar of engines and the slamming of heavy truck doors sent Erin outside where Mick and three other guys unloaded lumber from the back of a semi.

She looked around. "Mick, where's George?"

"I fired him. Bill, Gary, and Roy are going to help me get this place back into shape." A goofy smile appeared on his face, like he was proud of himself but worried about what she'd say.

His words flipped the anger switch in her head. "Come with me." She headed to the office and slammed the door behind him. "What the hell were you thinking? We agreed—"

"I couldn't pass it up, Erin. Roy used to work for Great Lakes and is way cheaper than George. Gary knows a lot about plumbing and electricity. And, of course, Bill knows this place backwards and forwards. We'll save tons of money and get the work done faster."

"You should have talked to me first."

"Maybe, but I bumped into Roy when I was getting

coffee this morning and the idea hit me like a ton of bricks. I told him about what we needed and he said he'd like to work with us. Besides, it's my ass on the line now. If I mess up, we won't inherit Paradise Beach and Melanie will kill me."

She turned her back to him, tears burning her eyes. Every time she had everything under control, Mick cannonballed it, destroying her plans to return to normality, far away from Misery. "I swear, Mick, you pull one more thing like this and I'll call Dean and tell him I'm not working on the motel. You know what happens then, right?"

"You wouldn't."

"If you think that, you don't know me at all."

****

Erin spent Saturday morning grocery shopping and bought enough so Shirley wouldn't have to go to the store for a week. She'd already booked airline tickets, texted her boss the date she'll return to work, and did the laundry.

Mick and April were in the living room watching cartoons when she walked in. "Why aren't you two outside? It's beautiful."

"Not in the mood," Mick said. His eyes were bloodshot, and an aspirin bottle sat on the coffee table in front of him. "Hey, are we okay? Sorry I didn't let you know about firing George the other day."

She was still mad about that, but will see if it works out. "Okay, but from now on, let's make decisions about the motel together."

"I swear, I will."

"By the way, you guys got a lot done yesterday. Keep up the good work."

They'd worked two ten-hour days in a row, and cleared out bathroom fixtures from all twelve units, removed bedroom furniture, tore out carpeting and probably a lot she couldn't see.

"What was that big delivery last night?"

"Mostly building materials and plumbing stuff. So, are we okay?"

"We are. Hey, I'm going to Shirley's to say goodbye. Is anyone interested in coming with me? April?"

April jumped to her feet. "Sure. When's Shirley moving in?"

"The day I fly out. She'll stay in my room." Erin hadn't been sure how Mick would feel if Shirley stayed in Rhonda's bedroom. Anyway, Rhonda's room was still crammed with her things. "How about coming with us, Mick? Might clear your head."

"Forget it," Mick grumbled.

"Come on, it's a beautiful day."

"No, thanks. Tell me all about it when you come back."

"I can't be gone long, Mom. Remember, I'm going to Olivia's and spending the night."

"Right."

****

A few minutes later, they were walking on hard-packed sand near the shoreline. Erin slowed near the rickety dock where Mick found Rhonda. Her heart thudded.

April sorted through a pile of seaweed the waves had washed up during the night. She plucked a pink seashell from the tangle, turned it over in her hand, then placed it on the dock. "Granny loved this color... Mom, do you miss her?"

"Yes. A lot."

"Do you miss Denver when you're here?"

"In a way." That was a colossal understatement.

"Do you wish you were there now?"

"I do." She'd give almost anything to be home in her condo right then. Her new, clean, organized condo. "Are you looking forward to going home when school's over?"

"No. I love Paradise Beach. I feel like Granny is here, and I'll miss her more when I'm home. Can't we live here with Uncle Mick forever?"

"No, honey, we can't."

"Why not? What about school?" April's lower lip trembled. "I can't go back to my old one and get bullied again."

"We'll figure something out, I promise. In the meantime, you'll be here with Shirley."

"Well, that's okay. I love her. She reminds me of Granny."

They entered the path through the woods linking Paradise Beach to Shirley's land, ending at Shirley's driveway. A few feet in, Erin stopped near an overturned trash barrel. Grimy soda cans, beer cans, and wine bottles had spilled out, along with soggy fast-food wrappers and bags.

"Why can't people carry their trash with them?"

Disgusted, Erin kicked the pile. A wine bottle much cleaner than the rest rolled out. She flipped it over with the toe of her shoe to read the label. Her breath caught as she fumbled for the phone in her pocket.

"Mick, are you still home?"

"Yeah, what's up?"

"Stay there." She ended the call and snapped a photo of the label. "We're going back to the house."

"Do you think this is the bottle Granny got from Uncle Mick?"

"How did you know about that?"

"Uncle Mick and I looked for it in the house before you came. So, do you think it's the same bottle?"

"I don't know, honey." If it was, how did it get there?

Mick was on the phone when they entered the house. "Okay, Mel, be right there." Mick ended the call. "What's going on?"

"Guess what?" April grinned. "We found a wine bottle."

Erin opened the photo app on her phone and handed it to Mick. "Is this the wine Rhonda took from the bar that night?"

He expanded the photo and squinted. "Looks like it. Where'd you find it?"

"By the trash barrel in the woods," April said. "I bet it's Granny's." Her eyes were brighter than they had been in days.

"Let's go pick it up," Mick said.

"I'll come with you," April grabbed his hand.

Erin took her phone back. "We shouldn't move it. There might be fingerprints."

"Someone might take it," Mick said.

"I doubt it."

"We should at least call the cops."

"We will, but not just yet."

"Why not?"

"They ruled Rhonda's death an accident, and

they'll need something more than a bottle from a trash heap to even consider opening her case."

****

An hour later, the sliding glass doors scraped open, then closed.

"Erin, are you home?"

"In the kitchen, Shirley."

Shirley came in, panting. "I need to tell you something." She put her hand to her chest and inhaled deeply a few times.

"Sit down and catch your breath. Would you like a glass of water? A coffee?"

"Will you please stop hostessing me and listen?"

Erin leaned back against the sink. "All right, go ahead."

"You know, a couple weeks ago when I started telling you about Rhonda calling me the night she died?"

"That's right. I think her will drove it out of my mind."

"Well, I didn't remember either until the mail guy rang my doorbell a little while ago with a package." She sat at the kitchen table. "When Rhonda called me that night, she said something had been bothering her for a while. I asked her what. She didn't say a word for a long time. I kept saying 'Rhonda, what is it?' Then she said to never mind, that she took care of it, but wasn't sure she'd done the right thing."

"Took care of what?"

"I asked her what the hell she was talking about. She started to say something when I heard her doorbell ring. She said she had to go and hung up."

"What time was it?"

72

"About ten-fifteen."

Rhonda never had guests that late, at least not when she'd visited.

"Did you tell the police?"

"No, like I said, I forgot about it. Anyway, after the call ended, I couldn't fall asleep, so I started reading one of my cozy mysteries and dozed off. Didn't wake until Mick pounded on my door like a crazy man. I'll never forget how he looked. His eyes were huge, and he flung his arms around and screamed, 'It's Mom.' He literally dragged me onto the porch. When I finally got him calmed down a little, he said Rhonda was on the beach, dead and we took off running. It was the most horrible sight I ever saw." Shirley covered her face.

Erin had no trouble visualizing Shirley's story and a clammy, sick feeling coursed through her.

"At first, I didn't believe Rhonda was dead, and I shook her." Shirley pulled a tissue from her pocket and wiped her eyes. "I called 9-1-1. EMS people came. Then the medical examiner checked her over and examined the dock. The police looked at it too, then talked to Mick and me. Mick took them into the house, where he said they looked around. I couldn't look when they put her in the body bag."

Erin leaned down and hugged Shirley as she sobbed. She fought against breaking down herself. When Shirley's crying slowed, Erin said, "That's enough for now."

"No. I want to finish. I blocked out the call Rhonda made to me that night under everything that happened afterwards and didn't think of it until the day I mentioned it to you. Then my stupid brain forgot about it again until today."

Someone had been in the house that night. Someone Rhonda expected. "April and I found a wine bottle in the woods on our way to see you earlier today. Mick says it had the same label as the wine Rhonda took from the bar."

"I should've realized something strange was happening when that doorbell rang. I should've checked up on her. It's my fault she's dead."

"Don't. It's no one's fault except the person who killed her...I didn't mean that. It slipped out."

"So now you think someone killed her, too?"

"I'm not sure. It still could have been an accident." Erin paced the kitchen. Who would want to kill Rhonda? Who did she know well enough to invite into the house that late? So much didn't add up. Especially the doorbell. The police had to reopen the case. She picked up her phone.

"Who are you calling?"

"Detective Mackey. I need to tell her I have more information about Rhonda."

Chapter Ten

At four o'clock that afternoon, a young officer escorted Erin to Detective Mackey's office.

Mackey looked up from her desk. "Take a seat, Ms. Brady. What can I do for you?"

Erin sat in a visitor chair opposite the detective. "Thank you for seeing me so quickly. I have some additional information about my mother's death." Erin located the wine bottle photo on her phone and passed it to Mackey. "Please look at this."

Mackey squinted as she scrutinized the picture. "What am I supposed to be seeing here, Ms. Brady?"

"The wine bottle in the trash pile."

Mackey fingered the image, making it larger. "I see…You're thinking this is the missing wine bottle, am I right?"

"I think it's a possibility."

"Where'd you find it?"

"In the woods past the dock where Mick found Rhonda…my mother."

"And you think it's the exact bottle she took from The Sand Bar?" She set the phone on her desk and pushed it forward. "Unlikely."

"Detective, the woods where I found the bottle is on Paradise Beach property, not far from the spot where my mother's body was. Sometimes tourists walking the beach toss their garbage in that trash barrel, but not at this time of year. All the other cans and bottles looked weathered like they'd been in there since last summer. This bottle hasn't been there that long."

Mackey reached for the phone and stared at the screen. "Even if it's the same bottle, Mrs. Brady could have thrown it in there herself. Where's the bottle now?"

"I left it where it was, thinking it might be evidence."

"When did you find it?"

"Earlier today."

"Did you touch it?"

"Not with my hands. I nudged it with my shoe so I could see the label."

"Ms. Brady—"

"There's something else, Detective. Shirley Cochran told me Rhonda called her at ten-fifteen the night she died. She said a doorbell rang while they were talking."

"And you think it was the killer."

"Possibly. The missing wine bottle shows up close to where Rhonda was found. Her head has a concave injury on it. Someone rang her doorbell late at night, an hour or two before she died. I think it warrants an investigation."

"Okay, fine, I'll have a couple officers stop by your place to pick up the bottle."

"What about the doorbell?"

"It could have been anyone. Someone who was lost or wanted a room in the motel."

"After ten at night? And with the motel sign off? And why was Rhonda dressed up if she didn't know someone was coming?"

"Ms. Brady, there could be a million reasons. Like I said, I'll send some officers over to take a look. If the wine bottle was used as a weapon, there could be traces of DNA on it. And if forensics finds anything, there's a good chance we can reopen the case."

Erin's heart lightened. "Thank you. Can the officers come today? I'm leaving for home in a couple of days and want this settled."

"I can send them tomorrow. Getting results from forensics usually takes longer than a few days, but I'll see what I can do."

Finally, some cooperation. Shirley and Mick should be around when the police came. She'll ask Justin to come by too. Good excuse to see him again.

****

"The cops were polite enough," Shirley said the next afternoon. "But you must be so embarrassed."

"I can't believe the bottle wasn't where we left it."

The police had looked at her as if she were crazy or lying. Erin slumped in a kitchen chair after walking the officers to the door. She wasn't only embarrassed but mad at herself. Why had she carelessly left the bottle out in the open? She should have at least covered it up.

"I told you not to leave it in the woods." Mick said.

"I know. I know. Are you trying to make me feel worse?"

"You had the right idea," Justin said. "Unfortunately, whoever took the bottle must have realized leaving it behind was a bad idea."

"It's been there since Rhonda died, and disappeared the day after I found it. Don't you think that's strange?"

"Maybe whoever took the bottle just remembered

and didn't want anyone finding it," Shirley said.

"But we'll never know, will we, Erin?" Mick said.

"Stop rubbing it in, okay? Besides, only you, me, and April knew about the bottle. Did you tell anyone, Mick?"

"Uh, no. No, why would I?"

"You went to Charlie's Tavern last night. Maybe you told your buddies about the bottle because it made a good story."

Mick's face reddened. "If I did, so what? Anyone could have moved it."

"Damn it, Mick—"

"Erin, did you tell Mick and Justin about the doorbell?" Shirley broke in.

"I did."

"Are you sure it was a doorbell, Shirley?" Justin asked. "My mother sets reminders on her phone to remind her to take her meds."

Shirley glared at him. "I know what a doorbell sounds like."

"I've had enough fun for one day," Mick said. "I'm going to Charlie's."

****

Erin, Justin, and Shirley were on the back porch enjoying a spectacular Lake Michigan sunset when Erin's phone buzzed.

"Erin, this is Detective Mackey. I talked with the chief about the doorbell Ms. Cochran heard the night Mrs. Brady died, and showed him the photo you sent of the wine bottle. He said since the bottle, along with its possible DNA, is missing, there's not enough cause to open Mrs. Brady's case."

"Thanks for getting back with me, Detective." Erin

ended the call. She wanted to throw something, hit something. Yell. She wished Rhonda hadn't died. She wanted to go home.

"Not good news?" Sympathy filled Justin's eyes and touched his voice.

"Without the bottle, they can't do anything. It's my fault. I should have reported it right away."

"Don't be so hard on yourself. Something else is bound to show up. Always does on the cop shows." Shirley gave a half-smile.

"Would it bother you if you never found out what happened to Rhonda?" Justin asked.

Erin couldn't answer. Mackey's call had crushed her.

"I'll be back in a minute."

She stumbled to Rhonda's room and buried her face in the bed pillow. Just the faintest whisper of her mother's scent lingered, and it tugged at her heart. She couldn't let it go. Her anger and frustration with the police had hardened something inside her. She flipped onto her back and stared at the ceiling. The police were convinced Rhonda's death was accidental and weren't interested in investigating further. She had to do it herself.

"Are you okay?" Justin asked when she returned.

"Fine. But to answer your earlier question, it would bother the hell out of me if I didn't know what happened to Rhonda." She picked up her phone, discouraged, resentful, and committed.

"What are you doing?" Shirley asked.

"Changing my flight. Tomorrow I'm going to Denver for a few days to pack up some of my and April's things. Then I'll talk to my boss about a leave of absence. When I get back, I'll turn in my rental and use Rhonda's car. Looks like I'll be sticking around here for a while."

Chapter Eleven

A week later, Erin spotted Justin in a corner booth at Georgia's. She'd driven there straight from the airport, because he said he had something important to tell her. Her heart pounded crazily. What if he was getting married?

When she reached his table, he kissed her cheek. "Get everything done?"

She slipped into the seat opposite him. "Pretty much. There wasn't a lot to pack, just clothes and some other things April and I will need for the year." She'd said a sad goodbye to her lovely condo, dreading the twelve months ahead.

A server appeared at their table and handed them menus. "Can I get you anything to drink while you decide on lunch?"

"A glass of the house cabernet, please," Erin said.

"Make it two."

When the server left, Erin glanced at Justin. He didn't look much different from when they'd been together. Being in a restaurant with him, looking at each other across the table, seemed like a first date. Awkward.

"So, what did you want to tell to me?"

"Let's wait until we have some wine."

"Why?" *Oh God.* What if it's worse—he's going to be a father?

"Just humor me, okay?"

His smile sent a shiver curling up her spine. She needed to stop this. He wasn't available.

"What's Catherine up to today?" She really didn't care, but couldn't think of anything else to say.

"Shopping, I think. How's April? I mean, is she adjusting to Rhonda not being around?"

Their back-and-forth questions seemed like strangers making small talk. It broke her heart that they sort of were.

"She's getting there. Kids are resilient."

The server arrived with the wine and poured it.

"Cheers," Justin said.

"Yes, Cheers. Now, what were you going to tell me?"

"Can we wait until after we eat?"

"Justin, come on."

"Okay… Some of my friends at the lumberyard told me Mick is buying the cheapest boards he can find for the motel. Also, the cheapest drywall, bathroom fixtures, paint, carpeting, electrical equipment. Basically, everything."

"Are they just inexpensive or…?"

"No, it's also the quality. I know Westside will tear down the motel once they buy it, but you'll be lucky if the place doesn't fall apart before then."

She gulped down the rest of her wine. "Let's go."

****

Erin's car skidded into the motel parking lot, her mind so full of ways to torture Mick she didn't remember driving. The lot was empty. No vehicles, no people. It was two in the afternoon, for God's sake. She called Mick and angrily counted the number of rings before his voicemail came on.

"You got Mick. Leave me a message."

"Where in the hell are you? Call me immediately." She got out of her car and slammed the door.

Justin left his car next to hers. "I want to show you something." He walked to a stack of lumber. "See those dark patches? It's wet rot. The wood was probably stored outside during the winter. Maybe more than one winter." He stooped next to a stack of paint cans. "This is one of the worst brands on the market for beachfront property. Not mildew or mold resistant."

She knew how her brother operated. Why hadn't she paid more attention to what he was buying? "I need to see the rooms." She retrieved the master key from the office and unlocked the door to Unit 101.

What a disaster. Cracked drywall and splintered boards lay in haphazard piles. Tools were scattered among empty food containers and beer cans. A sawhorse lay on its side under crumpled sheets of brown paper. Pipes jutted out of a wall.

Justin flipped on the bathroom light. "You better see this."

A new plastic surround covered half of the wall above a new plastic bathtub. Black splotches marred the other half of the wall.

. "Oh God! Is that…?"

"Yep, black mold."

"I want to see what's behind that plastic thing."

Justin left the bathroom and returned with a chisel and hammer. "I'll probably damage it."

"I don't care."

A few minutes later, the surround was off. Black mold thrived underneath.

"I've seen enough," she said. She started for the house.

"What about your suitcases?"

"I'll get them later."

Inside, she tossed her purse on the kitchen counter. "How could he be so stupid?"

She grabbed her phone and dialed. After several rings, Mick's voicemail kicked in.

"He's still not answering. He and his idiot friends are probably at the bar, thinking they put in a good day's work." She grabbed her purse and hurried out the front door.

"Where are you going?"

"I'm going to kill Mick. He's probably at Charlie's Tavern."

"I'm coming with you. Can't have you going around murdering people."

"Fine, but I'm driving."

****

Justin followed Erin as she burst through Charlie's front door. It was a scruffy place that survived the downtown gentrification project by being popular with the town's rougher crowd.

Mick leaned against the crowded bar, his arm slung over Melanie's shoulders. She slid onto a bar stool, pulled Mick between her thighs, and brought his face down to hers. They kissed an uncomfortably long time. The motel renovation guys whooped congratulations and raised their beer bottles.

Erin tugged on the back of her brother's shirt until he turned around.

His eyes widened. "What are you doing here?"

"What are you celebrating, Mick?"

Melanie gave a smug smile and held out her left hand. "We just got engaged."

Even in the dim light, the diamond gave a two-caret wink.

"We need to talk. Outside," Erin said.

"Don't let her boss you around," Melanie slipped her arm around Mick.

His gaze flicked between Erin and Melanie. "I'll be back in a minute, Mel."

Justin hung back while Erin faced Mick on the sidewalk in front of Charlie's.

"You paid for that ring with the money Rhonda left us to renovate the motel, didn't you?"

"I was going to repay—"

"Repay it? With what? Your only job was working on the motel and you screwed that up."

"No, I—"

"You financed that ring by buying cheap supplies and taking risky short-cuts. Did you really think the building inspector wouldn't find the black mold under the tub surround? And did you really think I wouldn't find out the renovation account was missing several thousand dollars?"

"You didn't seem to care all that much about what was going on."

"Maybe I stayed away because I hoped you could handle it. I was wrong." Erin stepped closer to Mick. "Here's what's going to happen. You are going into the bar, take that ring from Melanie, and bring it out to me."

"No, I can't—"

"If you don't, I'll tell Dean the motel will never pass the inspection. He'll turn the property over to the animal charity." She locked gazes with him. "I want that ring now."

"Shit, Erin, I can't do that. You don't know—"

She pressed a number on her phone . "Hi, this is Erin Brady. I'd like to speak with Dean—"

"Wait. Hang up. I'll do it." When she ended the call, Mick said, "Just give me a minute. I have to think of something to tell her."

"Tell her I want to see the ring in daylight."

"She'd never believe that."

"I don't care what you tell her. Get in there and get that ring."

Mick lowered his head and slouched back to the bar.

A few minutes later, Melanie appeared in the doorway. "You bitch!"

She threw the ring at Erin. It missed and fell to the ground.

"Good throw." Erin retrieved the ring and smiled.

Melanie stormed back into the bar.

"That was interesting," Justin said. "Want to go back to Georgia's?"

"No thanks. I don't think I could eat right now."

****

Erin was still seething when April bounced into the living room an hour later, and it took her a few seconds to pull up a smile. "Come over here and give me a big hug. I missed you, honey."

The hug was a good one and brought tears to Erin's eyes. She loved her daughter so much it almost scared her. She'd be thirteen next year, then only a few years until she graduated from high school, then she'd go away to college. Oh God, she couldn't think about that now. She gave April an extra squeeze and kissed her cheek.

"I missed you too, Mom." April untangled herself from Erin's arms. "Did you find my purple sweater and bring it with you?"

"Of course. I put everything in your room. How was school this week?"

"It was fine. But Mom, there's this boy in history class that I sort of like, and guess what?" Her eyes sparkled. "He sat next to me on the bus on the way home from school today."

"That's great, honey." To have your life turn shiny and bright because someone you like sits next to you was one of the Universe's gifts to the young.

"I'm going to call Olivia and tell her. Then I'll come down and help you with dinner."

"I can manage. It's frozen pizza night."

While April charged up the stairs, Erin called George at Great Lakes Construction. "Are you still available to work on the Paradise Beach Motel?"

"Mick said you didn't need me."

"That was a mistake."

"I'm sorry. I picked up another job."

"Please? I really need your help."

"To tell you the truth, I'm not sure I can work with Mick. Especially if he's going to be my contact on the job."

She didn't blame him for feeling that way. "You will only deal with me on the renovation."

"Will Mick be working on the motel with my crew?"

"Yes. Also, Bill. He maintained the motel for my mother for a long time. If they don't work out, let me know and I'll take care of it. Give them cleanup work if you don't trust them to do anything else."

"Well…okay. How about I start the day after tomorrow? There are a few things I have to attend to."

"Not a problem. Thank you so much. See you then."

Erin ended the call and leaned back on the couch, head whirling and exhausted. *Thank God George agreed to take the job.* Now she could concentrate on convincing the police to reopen Rhonda's case.

Mick sauntered into the living room, wearing a sullen face. "I'm sorry. I tried to save us some money."

"You didn't think it through. The work would never have passed—"

"I get it. I get it. I'll take care of everything."

"Yes, you will and you'll be working with George."

His face twisted. "That's bullshit and, by the way, thanks a lot for that bit with Melanie. You'll be happy to know she broke up with me."

"What makes you think I'm happy?"

Chapter Twelve

Three days later, Erin woke to the sound of idling trucks and the odor of diesel fumes. She'd spent the day before with George, purchasing replacements for the materials Mick bought and they were being delivered now.

After throwing on jeans and a shirt, she knocked on Mick's bedroom door, then pushed it open. Mick and Melanie were asleep in a face-to-face tangle of sheets and blankets. Two empty wine bottles lay on the floor next to the bed.

"Mick, get up! George is here."

He rolled toward her and opened one eye. "What the hell time is it?"

"It's time she got out of here." Melanie frowned and sat up, not bothering to cover her bare torso with the sheet that was bunched up at her waist.

"Didn't you break up with Mick?"

Melanie pinched Mick's cheek. "I can't stay away from this guy for long."

"Whatever. Mick, get out of bed."

Melanie stretched her arms and yawned. "You sound a little grouchy this morning, Erin. No warm body in your bed last night? Maybe you need a good—"

"Thanks for your concern, Melanie." Unfortunately, it was partially true. Sex seemed like a distant memory. "I hope April doesn't know Melanie spends the night, Mick."

"When did you get to be such a prude? Mom had her guys here all the time, and it didn't damage our fragile morals. Anyway, April spent the night at Olivia's."

"I know. Meet me in the office in five minutes."

Erin wiped down the desk chair and sat, inwardly groaning at the mess facing her. Then swept everything covering the desk into a box to be organized later.

Mick stormed into the office, wearing cutoff shorts and flip-flops. Negative waves poured out of him like sweat. He plopped into a chair. "Well, I'm here. What do you want to talk to me about?"

Negative waves poured out of her too, and she fought to keep her voice neutral. "First, this is my office. From now on, don't touch anything on or inside the desk. Second, George is managing the motel renovation and you'll take direction from him."

"Take orders from George? Seriously? I'll look like a dumb ass in front of the guys."

"You made yourself look like a dumb ass."

"Like I said, just trying to save us a little money. And talking about money, I know Dean closed Mom's bank accounts and put the money into the same account as the renovation funds. I need debit and credit cards for that account."

"I'm holding onto those. You'll get paid a salary, exactly the same amount George pays his crew. Until you screw up. Then the whole deal is off."

****

On Saturday, Erin drove to the pharmacy in downtown Misery Cove to meet Shirley for lunch. Steve Herrera, the owner/pharmacist, had also resisted

Westside's gentrification push. The yellowing sign in the pharmacy's window, "IN MISERY? WE CAN HELP," had been there as long as Erin could remember. She walked inside to the jingle of an old-fashioned overhead bell.

Five aisles of bare wood shelving displayed all the emergency supplies a vacationer or resident might need. She found Shirley behind the cash register in the pharmaceutical section and handed her the toothbrush she'd picked up in aisle three.

"I need a new one, since I'll be hanging around here for a while."

Shirley rang it up and glanced over her shoulder at Steve, who was attaching a label to a pill container. "Okay if I take my lunch break now?"

"Sure, go ahead. Hey Erin, good to see you."

"Good to see you, too."

"Have a pleasant lunch, ladies."

Outside, Erin started toward The Cove Restaurant, which she'd discovered had the best whitefish tacos around. Shirley grabbed her arm.

"How about we sit by the water for a few minutes first?"

As they ambled toward the beach, Shirley said, "I miss Rhonda so much. There's a great big hole in my life ever since she died. You've been filling it, though, Erin. You're a kind, warm-hearted person and I love you."

Erin's cheeks warmed. She didn't deserve Shirley's compliments. It was easy being kind to kind people.

The beach was empty except for scavenging gulls and dog walkers. Spring was in the air, warming the outer edge of the cool breeze coming off the lake.

Shirley shook her head as she surveyed the coastline. "I just can't picture it. A new marina, eight-story hotel, condos. Strangers will take over our town. We won't even recognize it in five years."

Erin didn't care what happened to Misery, but saw Shirley's point. The multi-story buildings would hide the beautiful Lake Michigan view from everyone except hotel guests, condo owners, and boaters.

"Don't worry. Sometimes things don't turn out the way we're afraid they will."

"There's always that." Shirley sighed. "I've been thinking. Once Mick sells Paradise Beach, I should probably get rid of my place and get a condo somewhere in a fifties-plus community. There's a nice one in Great Rapids."

"Last time we talked, you said you didn't want to move. You've been back and forth on selling. Are you sure?"

Shirley didn't answer for a moment. "No. But with Rhonda gone..." She pulled a tissue from her pocket and blew her nose. "Well, it's just not the same around here."

Erin wished for magic words to comfort Shirley, but all she could do was take her hand. That kind of sorrow can't be quieted with words.

"Let's sit on that bench by the water."

They sat together, snuggling for warmth. In the distance, a freighter heading toward Chicago drifted along the horizon, but no boats moved into or out of the small public marina. It was always quiet here and downtown before Memorial Day when tourists arrived. Eerily quiet, like everyone was holding their breaths waiting for something to happen.

"Why wait until Mick sells to decide? You'd get a better price for your property now."

"I'm just not ready to make up my mind yet." She kicked at the sand with the toe of her shoe. "So, what's going on with you?"

"Everyone's working hard on the motel. You should stop by. Also, Mick's getting along with George, thank God, and April is looking forward to summer vacation."

"I asked about you."

"I'm going to find out why Rhonda died." She watched a seagull dive into the lake. It came up empty, and the targeted fish got to live another day. She mentally applauded it. "I've been thinking about the doorbell you heard."

"You're starting to believe she was murdered, aren't you?"

"I don't know. But since it seems likely someone visited her, they might have seen something."

"Or they could be the killer."

"Like I said, we don't know anything yet. So, who would she dress up for?"

"Let's see. There are the lawyers Dean and Laura, also Zachary and Steve. Probably Father Joseph from St. Jude's." She squeezed her eyes shut, then opened them. "That's about all I can think of right now."

"Did she dress up to see any of them before?"

"I think if she asked any of them over for a drink, she would. She dresses up a little when she, Dean, Steve, Zachary and me get together at Georgia's for dinner a couple times a month. We're all spouse-less, you know. About Father Joseph, I just assume that since she dresses up for church, she'd dress up if he came over."

"Did Father Joseph ever visit her at home?"

"Not that I know of."

"You said the Tuesday before she died, you were all at poker. Anything unusual happen? How did Rhonda act?"

Shirley's face crumbled briefly, then she took a breath. "She was a little edgy at first. The game was at Dean's and she and Dean were off in the corner talking when me, Steve, and Zachary got there. She said something like, 'It's none of your damn business what I do.' And he said, 'You don't have any idea what the repercussions would be. I'm making it my business.'"

"What were they talking about?"

"They wouldn't say."

"Do you know of any reason anyone would want to kill Rhonda? As far as I know, she didn't have any enemies."

"It doesn't have to be an enemy, you know. It could be anyone who'd benefit from her being out of the way. Unless it was some wacko. But she wouldn't get dressed up to have a wacko over for drinks, right?"

Erin smiled. "True. Let me know if you think of anyone else."

"I will. By the way, did you get an answer from your boss about the leave of absence?"

"She said there's no guarantee my job will be available when I return. I'm fine with that."

Shirley raised an eyebrow.

"No, really, Shirley. It's okay."

They sat, not speaking for a few minutes, then a loudspeaker voice blasted toward them from downtown, followed by a concert-audience-like roar.

Shirley jumped up. "What the hell?"

Erin grabbed her purse. "Let's see what's going on."

A woman's electronically amplified voice blasted from a podium at the top of the town hall stairs. "They'll turn our beloved hometown into a grid-locked tourist trap. Those devils will drive up our property taxes, home prices, apartment rentals, the cost of our groceries and gasoline. Double our permanent population and redouble it during tourist season. They've already destroyed many of our historic buildings."

A crowd of sign-wielding protesters bellowed their agreement.

Erin had never witnessed a demonstration in Misery. It was kind of exciting.

"This is crazy," she said into Shirley's ear.

"I sort of agree with them," Shirley said.

"Me too."

Another burst from the podium. "And what about the opera house? It could have been used for lectures, cultural events, art exhibits. But nooooo. Now it's a salesroom for personal watercraft." She sniffed disgustedly, then glanced to the right as the town hall's side door opened and a woman in a gray business suit scurried toward the street. "There she is, Ms. Laura Nowak, attorney at law!" the voice screeched. "The person who had the old schoolhouse and playground knocked down to put up her fancy mansion."

The crowd booed and waved signs in Laura's face as she fast-walked toward a car.

Erin tapped Shirley's arm. "I met her the day Dean read Rhonda's will."

"You know she works with Westside, right?" Shirley asked.

"Yeah, Mick told me."

The speaker continued. "The schoolhouse could have been re-purposed as Misery Cove's Historical Society, which is presently located in the basement of Calvary Methodist Church. The basement! That schoolhouse was built in 1888, just after our town was founded. It has historical significance. But do the developers care?"

"Nooooo," the crowd shouted, moving in Laura's direction as she jumped into the car.

"Our town is being invaded, polluted by outsiders. They're like a cancer, growing by destroying everything in their way."

Shirley leaned close to Erin's ear. "Laura's not an outsider. She was born in Misery."

"I don't think they care."

Screaming people surrounded Laura's car, slamming fists on the trunk, hood, and windows, as she edged the car slowly down the street.

Erin pulled out her phone. "I'm calling 9-1-1."

Chapter Thirteen

After lunch at The Cove, Erin walked Shirley back to the pharmacy and returned to Paradise Beach. She found Mick lounging on the couch in the living room, drinking beer and watching baseball. She pushed his legs onto the floor and sat next to him. "There was a big anti-development demonstration downtown. The crowd reacted like a bunch of zombies."

"George says they'll probably bring a protest to the motel one of these days. They know if it's not finished on time, I won't get the inheritance and Westside won't get Paradise Beach."

"How do they know you're going to sell to Westside?"

"You've been living in Denver too long. Remember how the grapevine works around here? Everybody knows everything."

"Anyway, Shirley told me the names of people who Rhonda might have invited over the night she died, but I also want to talk to people she knew around town. Any ideas?"

"The check-out lady, Holly, at Stay and Shop, knows everything that goes down around here." He drummed his fingers on the side of the beer can. "Also, she stopped by to see Mrs. Masters once in a while. Other than that, it was mostly Mom and Shirley, plus her poker group. She knows lots more people, but wouldn't invite them over for a late drink."

"Thanks, I'll talk to Holly. Can I have a sip of your beer?"

"Really? Didn't you used to say every alcoholic drink except wine, bourbon, and vodka was low class?"

"I never said that."

He smirked and handed her the beer. "Sure. Here you go." She took a quick sip and gave it back.

"Talking about selling, you've done a lot of work on the motel in the last two weeks. Do you want to see it torn down in a year? If you kept it, you'd always have a roof over your head. And I think keeping it is what Rhonda wanted."

"No way in hell. I've spent too much of my life here. And I'll always have a roof over my head with the millions I'll get when it's sold. Besides, Melanie would kill me if I didn't sell. And I love her. I really do." He took a swig of beer.

"So, what will you do with the money?"

"I don't know. Buy a hot sports car. Buy a boat and take it to Mackinac Island. Melanie will help me figure it out."

Of course she will.

"What about work? What will you do all day?"

"You know, I was having a decent day sitting here with my beer and watching the game, then you showed up and ruined it."

"Sorry." She was so used to thinking baby brother Mick needed help working things out, she'd overlooked the fact he was in his thirties.

"Anyway, while we're at it, have you found out anything more about Mom's murder?"

Murder. A frightening word. Not one she'd ever

have associated with Rhonda. Last night, when she couldn't sleep, she went over everything she'd learned since she'd arrived in Misery. The case for accidental death was less substantial than the case for murder, at least to her, Shirley, and Mick. She'd proceed with that view and collect all the information she could.

"Erin, did you hear me? Have you found out anything about Mom's death?"

"Some, but not much yet. How many guys would you say were with you in the bar that night?"

He sat up straight and turned down the volume on the TV. "Eight or nine."

"Eight or nine? Can you be more precise?"

"Okay. Eight guys were there. Nine including me."

"And you didn't lose sight of them the entire night."

"We all had to take a piss at some point, and some guys went out front for a smoke, but I swear, no one was gone more than ten minutes, tops."

"They went out front? You mean the parking lot, not the beach?"

"Yeah. The bar's back door has an alarm, so no one could leave without paying. This was when the bar used to be open to the public."

Rhonda wouldn't have dressed up for any of his friends, anyway, and ten minutes wasn't enough time to kill her. Kill her. It surprised Erin how she could separate the intellectual challenge of finding out if someone killed Rhonda from the horrible reality. "Do you think the guys saw anything?"

"No. I already asked."

"Did you see Rhonda the day she died, other than when she took wine from the bar?"

He rubbed his eyes. "I saw her in the kitchen that morning. She said she was leaving to meet Laura for coffee and going shopping with Shirley later."

"Why did she meet with Laura?" She was starting to sound like a rapid-fire TV detective. Not necessarily a good thing.

"I don't know."

"What time were they meeting?"

"She left around nine, so I guess it would be a few minutes after that."

"Did you see her any other time?"

"She was still gone when I left the house for a few hours. When I came back, she was yelling at Bill because she said he'd been drinking on the job and the roof repair was supposed to be done the week before. He said he ran out of shingles. She was mad and said he could have bought some. Then she fired him."

"What time was this?"

"Not exactly sure. Maybe around five-thirty or six."

"Was Bill upset?"

"Nah. It didn't mean anything. She was always firing him."

This was going nowhere.

"Okay, just one more thing. You said Rhonda was dressed up when she came into the bar to get the wine. She didn't dress up very often, right?"

"She never did except when she and her friends went out for dinner in Port Elizabeth. Oh, and when she went to church."

"You didn't think to ask her why she was dressed up?"

"I was busy behind the bar. She came in and took a

bottle and left."

Erin remembered Shirley mentioning that one of the people Rhonda would dress up for was the priest. "Did Father Joseph ever visit her here?"

"Yeah. A few times."

She was surprised. "Why?"

"I don't know. They'd just talk and drink wine."

"Rhonda drank with a priest? When did that start?"

Mick raised the beer bottle to his lips, then set it down without drinking. "I'm not sure. Maybe a couple of months ago. It was weird, but Mom said she and Father Joseph helped each other."

"With what?"

"She never said."

"Okay, thanks." When Erin pushed herself to her feet, her hand slid between the couch cushions and felt something hard and smooth. She pulled it out. *What the…?*

Mick stared at her hand. "That's Mom's phone."

Oh my God! She pressed the power button. Nothing happened. "It's dead." She plugged it in and a few minutes later, still charging, she checked for voicemails. None. Next were the texts and emails. *Jackpot.* She picked up her tablet and began typing.

"What are you doing?" Mick leaned closer.

"I'm copying the names, dates and times of Rhonda's texts and emails from her last week." As soon as Rhonda's phone had enough charge, Erin unplugged it.

She had to talk with Shirley.

****

"You look frazzled," Shirley said. "What's happened?"

Erin sat in her usual chair. "I found Rhonda's cell phone between the couch cushions."

Shirley sat in her own usual chair. "I'm surprised the police didn't find it."

"I don't think they looked since the medical examiner said her death was an accident."

"Anything good on it?"

"Not sure yet. The incoming calls Rhonda received the day she died were from Laura, you, and one from an unknown caller. The only outgoing calls were to you and Father Joseph."

"Did you search for the unknown number or call it?"

"Both. No results. When I called it, I got an out of service message. Whoever it was, they only spoke a few minutes."

"It's probably a burner phone. Murderers use them all the time on cop shows. What time was the call?"

Erin checked Rhonda's phone. "Six thirty-six p.m."

"Maybe you should tell the police."

"Not yet. I need something more substantial."

Shirley's face lit up. "Okay, let's find it. What else? What about emails?"

"The incoming were mostly doctor appointment reminders and spam. The only outgoing ones were to me, Mick and April."

"Texts?"

"None. We both know Rhonda hated texting."

"Right, dumb question. I don't suppose you had any trouble getting past her phone security password."

"Very funny. It's still one-one-one-one."

Shirley shook her head. "She's lucky no one ever stole it. Anything else?"

"The previous week, Mick, April, and you called her. She called you, her oncologist, Bill, April, and Laura."

"No unknown numbers?"

"No. Either Rhonda and her killer arranged the meeting in person or they set it up during the call from the unknown number."

"Unless one of us killed her... Don't look at me like that. I'm joking."

"I know. Anyway, I checked out her oncologist. He was on a Caribbean cruise that week." Her breath caught thinking about Rhonda's struggle with cancer. Just when her emotions were under control, grief blindsided her. She paused a moment. "And that's about it. Using the email and call history, I filled in some gaps in the timeline I created."

"Timeline?"

"Yes, of what Rhonda did that day." Erin opened the Notes app on her phone. "Let me know if I have the times right, based on what you know. First, Laura called her at eight-thirty that morning. Mick said Rhonda met her for coffee about nine."

"The time seems right. I wasn't there, but Rhonda told me about it. She said Laura wanted to talk to her about selling Paradise Beach. She told Laura she wasn't interested. Then they talked about old times."

"Rhonda knew Laura?"

"Remember, I told you Laura was born in Misery? We all went to high school together. She moved away when she went to college and didn't come back. Now she's here working for Westside."

Erin glanced at the timeline. "I don't know what time she came home from seeing Laura, but you picked her up at eleven-thirty."

"I think it was closer to twelve."

Erin corrected the entry on her tablet. "You and Rhonda went shopping at the mall, had lunch around two-thirty, and left the mall at three-thirty. That's only about two hours of shopping since the mall is half an hour away."

"Rhonda wanted to exchange a sweater she bought April, and we just wandered around after that, mostly window shopping."

"You dropped her off at the psychologist's office at four."

"That's about right. I was glad she went because she'd been more bummed out than usual lately."

"Why?"

"Wouldn't you be bummed out if you knew you only had a few months to live?"

Erin's heart clenched. "Right. How long was her appointment at the psychologist's office?"

"Less than an hour."

"Next you drove her to the pharmacy a little after five, then took her home."

"Yep."

"Then about five-thirty, Mick says she fired Bill."

"Poor Bill. She was always firing him."

Going through the details of Rhonda's last day broke Erin's heart and she fell silent for a moment. "She called Father Joseph at six and talked to him for fifteen minutes."

"I'm surprised. We spoke to him after Mass some Sundays, but I didn't know she'd talked with him any other time except in confession."

Erin remembered Mick saying Father Joseph

visited Rhonda, and they'd talk and drink wine. Why wouldn't she mention it to Shirley? "She received the call from an unknown number at six thirty-six."

Shirley headed for the kitchen. "I'm making us some tea." She returned a few minutes later and handed Erin a crockery mug. "Okay, what's next?" The excitement on her face had faded. She looked weary.

Erin wrapped her hands around the mug, absorbing the comforting heat. "Mick said Rhonda came to The Sand Bar a little before ten to get a bottle of wine."

"I just don't get that. As far as I know, she never had anyone over that late."

"She called you at ten-fifteen and you heard a doorbell."

Shirley nodded. "That unknown phone call is bugging me."

"Me too, but there's no way to trace it at this point. It could be something or nothing."

Chapter Fourteen

Erin dreaded Mother's Day. Always had. And today, most store windows in downtown Misery still displayed cheery signs filled with hearts and flowers, although Mother's Day was over a week ago. Mother's Day meant sorting through stacks of sickeningly sweet cards that didn't come anywhere close to expressing her feelings about Rhonda. The cards she sent were always generic. "Happy Mother's Day" on the front and some form of "Thinking of you" on the inside. She'd signed them "Love, Erin" because she knew Rhonda expected it. If her mother was alive now, she'd buy a mushy card and sign it "I love you, Mom."

The corners of her eyes prickled, and she dropped onto a park bench in the town square. April had given her a beautiful card again this year. Another card she'd always treasure. She wondered what happened to all the bland, unemotional cards she'd sent to Rhonda.

"Erin, mind if I sit?"

She startled, looked up and attempted a smile. She recognized him. "Not at all."

He lowered himself onto the bench. "I'm Zachary Smith, your mother's psychologist. I'm so very sorry for your loss."

"I saw you at her wake. Thank you for coming."

He studied her face. "You look upset. Can help?"

She took a tissue out of her pocket and blotted her

eyes. "No, I'm okay. There's just a lot going on."

"I don't doubt it. I was on my way for a coffee at Full of Beans. Join me?"

"Sure. I'd like that, Doctor Smith."

"Please call me Zachary."

He ordered their coffees while Erin found a table. Women at the counter sneaked glances at him. Zachary carried himself with confidence, clearly no stranger to the gym. Good-looking, although probably old enough to be her father. He balanced the cups on a small cardboard tray as he crossed the room to their table and sat, placing a cup in front of her.

"How long will you be in town?"

He must be the only person in Misery who didn't know the inheritance story.

"About a year."

"You don't sound happy about it."

"I'm not." She wanted to ask him about Rhonda, but it would be awkward. Another time.

"Mother's Day was last week, so it's no wonder you're upset. I hope you can take some comfort knowing Rhonda loved you very much and was proud of the travel articles you wrote."

The words caught her off guard and warmth rose in her cheeks. Rhonda never once said she was proud of her. Why not? Now she'd never know. But since Zachary mentioned Rhonda, she had the opening she needed. "I'd like to ask you about—"

Zachary's phone rang. He picked it up and glanced at the screen. "Sorry, be right back."

He went outside where Erin could see him through the coffee shop's picture window. He smiled as he talked.

He was still smiling when he retook his seat. "Sorry about that. It was my daughter, Sara. She's coming to spend a few weeks with me this summer."

"Wonderful. Does she live near here?"

"No, Arizona."

"Are you from Arizona?"

He smiled. "No. I've always lived in Michigan. Now, where were we?"

"I have a few questions about Rhonda."

He smiled sadly. "Your mother was a vibrant and interesting woman. We all miss her."

"I've been wondering about the way she died. Do you think it was an accident?"

He leaned back and sipped his coffee. "Do you think it wasn't?"

"I don't know."

"The medical examiner called her death an accident, and from what I know of Rhonda, there's no reason to believe it was anything else."

"The whole thing feels odd to me. Walking on the beach late at night and falling off the dock—it's not like her."

"How much do people actually know about each other? How much did Rhonda know about your life, for example? Not just superficial things like where you travel or what your hobbies are. What about your personal life—how much money you earn, political and religious beliefs, relationships with co-workers, friends, lovers?"

He was right. How much did she know about Rhonda's life? How much did anyone know about their parents?

Her phone vibrated, and she checked the screen.

"Sorry, now it's my daughter." She stepped outside. "What's up, April?"

"Melanie's here, and you gotta come home."

April almost never called her, so it must be important. "Be right there."

She went back to Zachary. "I have to go home. Thanks for the coffee and conversation."

"You're welcome. And Erin, if you ever need anyone to talk to, professionally or otherwise, just call." He handed her a business card.

****

The drive home took less than five minutes. As Erin pulled into the parking lot, the construction crew was packing up. She glanced at her watch. Right. After five.

April dashed out the front door, grinning and still wearing school clothes. "Come with me and be very quiet."

Erin followed her through the front door, into the foyer, and to the hallway staircase. April sat on a step and pulled Erin down next to her.

"You're being very mysterious. What's going on?"

"Shh. Just listen. She's on the phone."

Melanie's voice came from the kitchen. "No, she won't... I already told you we tried... I'm caught in the middle here... Yeah, and what are we going to do about it?" She paused, but the sound of her fingernails tapping the laminate counter top didn't.

April nudged Erin and mouthed, "See?"

"See what? Who's she talking to?" Erin whispered.

"I don't know, but you should have heard her before."

Melanie's voice grew louder. "Lou, you're right, it

109

would be nice if we could get to her sooner, like... Right... Don't worry, I'll take care of it. Yes, of course I want to be Vice President of Marketing... All right fine... What?... No."

Enough spying. Erin headed for the kitchen, but stopped when Melanie's voice turned sultry.

"Tonight is perfect. Seven at your place...Can't wait to see you, babe."

"Stay here, April."

Erin strode into the kitchen, seething. Melanie was cheating on Mick.

Melanie's body went rigid. Then a lopsided smile appeared. "I didn't hear you come in."

"Where's Mick?"

"In the shower."

"Oh, weren't you talking to him?" She was curious to see what Melanie would say.

Melanie dropped the phone into her pocket and laughed. "No, I was talking to one of my college classmates who's staying in Great Rapids for a few days." She picked up her purse. "Nice seeing you, Erin. I have to rush off for a house showing. Tell Mick I'll call him later." She headed for the door.

April came into the kitchen and sat at the table. "You know she's lying, right? I hate her and wish they'd break up."

"Didn't they just get back together a few days ago?"

"They did, then broke up the next day. Now they're together again. You gotta pay attention, Mom."

"As long as I have you keeping track, I'm good." Erin opened the refrigerator. "Want a snack and soda?"

"Sure. But what do you think about what she said?

Obviously, she was talking to some guy."

Erin set a can of fizzy fruit-flavored water, a glass, and a plate of cookies on the table. "Why did you call me?"

"She was saying how much money they'd make off the condos and other stuff, and that they needed to get papers signed on Paradise Beach and Shirley's place right away."

Erin tamped down her anger. "Don't worry, Uncle Mick will take care of it."

"I love Paradise Beach. I hope he won't sell it. Do you think he'll do it?"

"A year is a long time. Anything could happen between now and then."

April seemed to think about that. "What about Melanie seeing that guy tonight? Should we tell Uncle Mick?"

"I don't think so. First, we could have misinterpreted what she said." Unlikely. "And second, your uncle wouldn't appreciate us interfering. Especially if we're wrong. Let's forget it for now."

"Okay. I'm going to my room to change." April picked up her drink and cookies and headed for the stairs.

Erin was still in the kitchen when Mick came in.

"Where's Melanie?"

"I don't know. She was talking on the phone, then left."

"Probably a work call." He pulled a phone from his pocket and started walking out, then turned. "What do you think of her? Pretty special, isn't she?"

"She's something, all right."

****

Erin poured a third cup of coffee and carried it to the back porch. During the night, the bowl with her father's ashes had toppled off the railing and onto the sand. She picked it up and considered tossing it into the lake but then set it back in place.

She was angry he died. Her life would have been very different if he hadn't. She remembered being happy in the years before. Summer days filled with sunshine, swimming, and barbecues. Fall evenings with the four of them sitting around beach bonfires, singing and telling ghost stories. Winter gatherings by the living room's stone fireplace, toasting marshmallows and playing board games.

The screen door behind her slid open. She turned around, expecting Mick.

"Good morning," Justin handed her a carryout coffee cup. "Black, no sugar, right?"

She smiled. "You remembered."

He lifted the plastic bowl from the rail and shook it. "I see your dear old dad is still here. I don't think I ever got the entire story about what happened with him and Rhonda."

"Not much to tell, and I didn't want to talk about it back then. He crept out in the middle of the night when I was seven. A few months later, Rhonda told me he was dead. She went to Texas to identify his body and left Mick and me with Shirley. A week later, she came back with his ashes in that food storage bowl. A unique revenge."

He set the bowl back on the rail, then settled on the rattan loveseat next to her, slinging his arm over the back. His hand brushed her shoulder. She moved slightly, and hoped unobtrusively, away.

"I remember you had a tough time when she came back from Texas."

"She was a wreck. She'd forget to buy groceries and pay the utility bills. Just gave up. I learned to do the laundry and clean the motel rooms. She didn't take care of us. Do you remember when we'd find her on the beach smoking a joint and knotting macramé wall hangings to sell at the craft shop?"

"That's when you stopped calling her mom."

"She wasn't a mother to me anymore. I idolized her before my father died. But in the years after, a thousand small things shredded my feelings for her. Thank God for Shirley."

"She snapped out of it, eventually."

"Sort of, but by that time I was in my late teens and it was too late."

A year after she graduated from college, the annual guilt trips started. On those visits, her uncomfortable relationship with Rhonda occasionally eased when they'd had a few drinks and let their guards down. But any closeness they'd shared in the night burned off with the next morning's sun.

"I'm so sorry you went through that." Justin got to his feet. "And I'm sorry I have to leave now. There's a meeting at the office in twenty minutes."

"Wait a minute. Why are you here?"

He smiled. "I'm not really sure."

Chapter Fifteen

Later, Erin staggered to Shirley's front door clutching two oversized Stay and Shop bags packed with groceries and cleaning products. The bags began a slow slide out of her arms.

The door flew open and Shirley snatched one. "Wow, this weighs a ton."

Erin steadied the other bag with her now free hand. "You got here just in time. Your groceries almost ended up all over your porch."

"You're a doll." Shirley led the way to the kitchen, where they left the bags. "Working ten hours a day this week, I didn't have time to go to the store."

"No problem. I was going anyway."

"Hey, do you have time to sit on the front porch and talk for a while?" Shirley grinned wickedly. "I made us a pitcher of Cosmos."

"Bring it on."

Shirley pulled a pitcher from the fridge, poured vibrant light pink liquid into two martini glasses, and they settled on the porch swing.

Erin sipped her drink. "Delicious." She sipped again and set the glass on a table. "I met Holly at the checkout counter. How long has she worked at Stay and Shop? I haven't been in there for a long time."

"Must be about eight years now. Why?"

"She knew I had coffee with Zachary yesterday."

114

Shirley laughed. "She's the town gossip. Knows everything about everyone. So, what about Zachary? What did you two talk about?"

"Not much. A little about his daughter. What's the deal with her living in Arizona?"

Shirley downed half of her Cosmo, coughed, then quickly got to her feet. "Be right back." She returned a few minutes later. "Went down the wrong pipe. Anyway, Zachary's wife died when Sara was just a kid. About ten, I think. Zachary went through a bad patch and knew he wasn't in any shape to take care of her. He sent her to her aunt in Phoenix and she's lived there ever since."

"She never came back to live with him?"

"No. She's in college out there now. Wants to be a psychologist like her daddy. Anything else?"

"I asked him if he thought Rhonda's death was accidental. He said what everyone does, that the medical examiner ruled it accidental, so it must be true. I've been wondering why people commit murder and looked it up. Most articles have a version of love, vengeance, and power. I can't imagine anyone killing Rhonda for love, can you?"

"No way. We're way past that passionate stage."

"Then there's vengeance. I can't see Rhonda's death as a revenge killing."

Shirley shrugged. "No idea. People are strange these days."

Erin didn't speak for a moment. "Money is power. Before Rhonda changed her will, Mick planned to sell Paradise Beach to Westside Development. Rhonda had already turned them down, so the company would have benefited from her death."

"I hate to say this, but so would Mick. The money he'd get selling Paradise Beach."

"There's no way he'd ever hurt Rhonda."

"I know. I'm just saying that everyone knew she was leaving Paradise to him and he was planning to sell to the developers. By the way, Melanie would also benefit. She'd make a huge commission on the sale of the condos."

"True. And when she married Mick, she'd make sure the money he'd get from selling Paradise Beach was community property. But I really don't think Melanie would kill Rhonda. She only had to wait a few months until Rhonda died from cancer."

"That woman is a nightmare. Know what I learned yesterday? That she's sleeping with Lou Guthrie, her boss, you know. Poor Mick. Do you think I should tell him?"

"I don't think so. I accidentally overheard a phone conversation she had with someone. Lou, I think. Sounded like they were seeing each other that night."

"Talking about man friends, what's happening with you and Justin?"

"Nothing, and that's okay with me. As far as I know, he's still happily engaged to Catherine."

"I'm old, but I'm not stupid. I see that look in your eye whenever I mention his name."

She never could hide anything from Shirley. "You're imagining things. I got over him a long time ago. But we *are* meeting for dinner tomorrow."

Shirley grinned. "I knew it. You've had that look on your face."

"Can we drop it? And honestly, I don't want to talk about him. It's ancient history."

Shirley raised an eyebrow. "Fine. Okay. What's going on with your investigation?"

"Tomorrow I'm visiting Laura Nowak, since she had coffee with Rhonda the day she died."

****

Laura's contemporary home rose two stories, all flat rooflines and wide glass windows. It straddled the spot where Misery Cove's historic one-room schoolhouse once stood. Erin remembered how she and her friends spent summers playing in the abandoned building, happily ignoring the posted condemned signs and getting away with it. Over the years, it deteriorated further, eventually becoming an eyesore. To many of the townspeople, but not the preservationists, the house was a major improvement.

The front door swung open on Erin's third knock. "Laura, hi. I'm Erin Brady. Sorry, I should have called first. Do you have a few minutes?"

"Of course. Come in. It's wonderful to finally meet you."

Erin followed her through the foyer and into the living room, shocked that it resembled the old schoolroom. The wood panels she remembered lined three walls, but were now a soft white. The distressed floor planks glowed with golden-brown warmth. She imagined rows of desks leading to a chalkboard at the far end of the room, as Rhonda had described when she was a kid.

Why hadn't she mentioned having a friend named Laura? But then she didn't talk to April about her high school friends either. "Your home is gorgeous."

"Thanks. When Melanie told me the schoolhouse and its property were for sale, I couldn't resist buying them to build my dream house. It's partially nostalgia. I attended school there until sixth grade. So did Rhonda. I'm so sorry she's gone."

"Thank you...I remember playing in the old schoolroom. It looks like you built your house around it."

"It was falling apart, and the builders had to tear it down. But I had the living room constructed with the same dimensions, using the original wood from the walls and floor. Despite working for Westside, I'm a preservationist. Would you like coffee or something else?"

"Coffee sounds great."

Laura led Erin through a wide hallway to a kitchen gleaming with white oak cabinets, white granite counters, white granite island, and a gray granite floor.

Six black leather bar stools hugged the island. Erin pulled one out and sat while Laura poured coffee.

"This kitchen is absolutely incredible." She nodded toward a frosted glass door with a shiny black wine cellar plaque. "I've always wanted a wine cellar, but there's not much room in a condo."

"I'd show it to you, but I haven't gone down there in a few weeks."

"Oh?"

"Somehow rodents found their way in, probably while the house was being built." She shivered. "I hate mice. The exterminator isn't available until next week and I can't put the house on the market until all the creatures are gone."

"You're selling? Why?"

"I left Westside Development and moving back to the east side of the state."

"What a shame."

She smiled. "It's for the best. I don't suppose you're here to talk about me, though. Is there something I can help you with?"

"There is. You had coffee with Rhonda the day she died. Would you mind telling me what you two talked about?"

"It wasn't much, considering we hadn't spent time alone together since I moved back here. My fault. I worked long days setting up Westside's contracts, clearances, and all the other paperwork required for a development of this size. Rhonda wasn't happy I worked for Westside, said they were destroying the town. She was right."

"Did she seem worried about anything else?"

"She talked about her cancer and said that she was afraid you and Mick would never see each other after she was gone. She was pretty sure she fixed that, though."

"She sure did. Anything else she was concerned about?"

Laura's gaze darted around the room, then to her watch. "No. Sorry, but I have an appointment in half an hour."

She was hiding something.

"Can we get together again? Maybe for lunch? I'd love to see you before you leave. You knew my mother as a young woman and I'd like to know what she was like back then."

"How about next Tuesday? After that, I'll be spending most of my time in Oakland County."

Erin checked her phone. "That works. Georgia's at noon?"

"Fine." Laura entered the date into the calendar app on her tablet. "I'm so happy I finally met you. Rhonda and I didn't correspond a lot, but when we did, she always said how proud of you she was."

Rhonda told everyone except her. What a difference it would have made in their relationship if she had.

****

When Erin returned to Paradise, the work crew was finishing up for the day, putting away tools and stacking lumber. George, and Mick were at the far end of the parking lot, facing each other. George's frizzy, gray-streaked ponytail swished back and forth as his arms gestured wildly. Mick's shoulders sagged, and he'd stuffed his hands in his pockets. Trouble.

When Mick stalked away, she approached George. "Is everything okay?"

"Don't you worry about me and Mick. We'll be fine." His voice was a rough drawl. Like he'd grown up somewhere way south of Michigan and had been smoking for a long time.

"Thanks, George. For everything." She started for the house.

"Hey Erin, wait up." Bill left the crew and hurried to her. "I tried to talk to you at the wake, but you seemed pretty busy. I'm real sorry about Rhonda. She and me was good friends."

She doubted that.

"Yeah, Rhonda was one of the good ones," he continued. "Always was." He grinned. "We used to tease her with that Rhonda song whenever she passed by us guys at school. We knew she didn't like it, but she was a good sport. I was really glad she offered me a job when no one else would."

"You knew her from school?"

"Yep, grammar and high school."

Another thing she didn't know. "Then Shirley was in your class too, right? And Laura?"

"Everyone knew everyone. Only fifty-five of us in our class, from Port Elizabeth and Misery Cove combined. Small towns, small school. Out of those fifty-five, only forty-seven of us are left standing. Can't help but wondering if old Satan will come for me next."

"Don't worry, you'll outlive everyone. Someone said you talked with Rhonda the day she died."

His eyes narrowed. "Yeah…I was working on the roof. Why?"

She shrugged. "No reason. Someone mentioned they saw you."

"It was Shirley, right?"

Erin shrugged. "What time did you talk to Rhonda?"

"About five, five-thirty, I guess."

"Anything unusual happen?"

"Nope, just said hello and goodbye. She went into the house and I quit for the day soon after."

"What about the argument?"

He stepped back. "Ah, shit, Erin. It wasn't really an argument. The roof wasn't finished yet, and she fired me. Didn't mean nothing. It was the third time she fired me that month. Didn't seem like herself when she did it, though."

"What do you mean?"

"Well, usually when she'd get pissed at me, she'd get loud, wave her arms around. That day, she just said, 'That roof should have been finished three weeks ago.

You're fired,' then went into the house."

"Did you see anyone or anything that didn't seem right?"

"Not really. I knew I wasn't really fired, so I worked on the roof another half hour then went to The Sand Bar. Mick had it open for a few friends."

"How long were you there?"

"Until closing. Ask anyone. Ask your brother."

Chapter Sixteen

Erin barely made it into the house before April grabbed her hand and dragged her to the living room couch. "Mom, I have to ask you something."

"Weren't you going to the mall with Olivia and staying at her place tonight?"

"I changed my mind." April bounced excitedly on the balls of her feet. "This is more important. You know that actress, Marilyn Mitchell?"

"I saw her on Broadway a while ago. What about her?"

"She's in Misery for the summer to give the seventh and eighth-grade kids acting lessons. And at the end of the summer, we get to be in a school play if we're good enough. She did the same thing last year too, but I wasn't here when the classes started. And when we came to Misery in July, Granny was getting sicker, remember?"

"I remember."

How could she forget? Rhonda started chemo that month and wanted April to stay with her for the summer and coming school year. She said April would be her reason to get up in the morning. Erin had several overseas assignments that year too, and April would rather stay with Rhonda than her nanny. That was the only thing bad about her job: being away from her daughter. As soon as she and Mick satisfied the terms of the will, she'd find a job in Colorado that kept her close to home.

"Classes start in two weeks on Saturday and are three times a week during the summer. Can I do it? Please? Granny talked to Ms. Mitchell when she came here back in February. She said it would be okay with you if kept my grades up."

"Your grades are great, so yes. You'll have fun."

"Thanks, Mom. I love you." She skipped upstairs and returned a few minutes later, waving a sheet of paper. "Here's the summer schedule. You have to sign at the bottom." She pressed some numbers on her phone. "I have to tell Olivia I can take the class." She headed back upstairs.

Mick came into the living room and plopped into a chair. "I'm pissed off."

"About what? I thought you were going out with Melanie tonight."

"She called off our date. Said she had a couple of house showings. You know, she's been doing that a lot lately, breaking our dates. I wonder if she's actually working or seeing another guy."

"Ask her."

Erin worried about Mick's future with Melanie. Soon enough, he'd find out that he wasn't her first love—money was.

"If you don't have any other plans, do you mind staying home with April? She was supposed to spend the night at Olivia's, but now she isn't."

"No prob." He smiled. "It'll be fun. Maybe I'll take her out somewhere…Where are you going?"

Erin couldn't help grinning. "Justin and I are going to dinner." He'd called earlier and said he'd pick her up.

He smirked. "That's interesting."

"It's nothing. Just old friends getting together."

"Yeah, sure." Mick headed for the kitchen. A few minutes later, he called, "Erin, Justin's just pulled up."

She started for the stairs. "Tell him I'll be down in a minute."

****

Erin told herself she wasn't especially excited about seeing Justin. They were just getting together to catch up. That was all. They found two open bar seats in Zinc, the town's newest restaurant, cozy with dim lights, slate fireplace and not overly contemporary, like some of the other makeovers. Erin ordered a glass of wine. Justin, a craft beer.

"Where's Catherine tonight?" She didn't know why she always asked. Maybe hoping to learn they'd broken up.

"Girls' night out in Great Rapids."

"I'd like to meet her sometime." Erin forced a smile.

"Actually, we're not on good terms right now."

"Oh, I'm so sorry." *Not really.*

Justin sipped his beer. "So, you're looking into Rhonda's death."

"Who told you? Shirley?"

He smiled. "I'll never tell." The smile disappeared. "Erin, Rhonda died because of a freak accident."

"I don't think so."

"You're guessing. But if you're right and whoever caused her death learns what you're doing, you could get hurt."

"I've just asked some people a few questions...Is

that why you asked me to dinner? To warn me off?"

"Partly, but—"

"Sorry for interrupting," the woman next to Erin said. "But this is the first time my husband and I have been in this area. Do you live around here?" She held a glass of what looked like a chocolate martini.

Erin smiled. "Justin does." She nodded toward him. "I'm only here for a short time." She must really hate Misery. She didn't even want a stranger to know she has a connection to it.

The man leaned over his wife. "We're from Ohio and on a road trip along Michigan's coastline. We're spending the night at the motel outside town. But on the way here, we saw a protest and wonder if it's safe."

"Some residents of Misery Cove don't like the changes being made to the town, but no one is really dangerous. I'm Erin, by the way. And this is Justin."

"Ray and Sharon," the man said. "Pleased to meet you."

Sharon elbowed Ray out of the way. "Why is this place called Misery Cove? Such a sad name for such a nice town."

"Justin, you tell them the story."

He set his glass of beer on the bar. "Misery Cove used to be a lumber town called Oak Cove, but in the early 1920s, the woods were lumbered out and most residents moved north. The families who stayed were on their own through some miserable winters. Then a former lumberjack built a bar he named 'Moon Over Our Misery,' for the full moon over the cove the night the bar opened for business. Not long afterward, the town was officially named Misery Cove."

"Interesting," Sharon said.

They went back to their drinks.

"Did you make that up?" Erin whispered.

Justin gave a non-committal smile.

The door opened and three business-suited men stumbled in and sat at a nearby table. After a few minutes, one of them yelled, "Hey, where's a waitress?"

"I think those guys work at Westside Development," Justin said. "I'm almost positive the one facing this way is Lou Guthrie."

"I bet this isn't the first place they've been drinking tonight."

A petite red-haired woman in blue jeans and a Zinc logoed black t-shirt sashayed to their table. "What can I get you gentlemen?"

"Are you on the menu?" Lou leered.

"Come on Lou, you got that little honey waiting for you back at your place tonight. Give the rest of us a chance."

The red-haired woman frowned. "I need your orders now, or you can get your own drinks."

"She's a feisty, one. Good looking too," one of the guys said.

"That she is," Lou said. "But she's got nothing on Melanie."

Erin startled.

"Do you think he's talking about Mick's Melanie?" Justin said.

Erin slid from the stool. "Let's go somewhere else."

****

Erin was afraid to open her eyes. It must be morning, because daylight filtered through her closed eyelids. Nausea churned in her stomach. A movie-like scene played in her head of Justin helping her into bed. Was she still dressed? She slipped her hands under the covers. Shit. Only underwear. Had she slept with him? She couldn't remember. Maybe she had a way-too-much-wine induced dream.

She blindly stretched her arm to the other side of the bed. It was warm. Had she drunkenly seduced him? Or was it the other way around? What the hell had she been thinking, ordering that last drink? She sat up, defiant. Why should she feel anything but bad-ass? Anyway, he was gone, and she'd avoid him for the next few weeks.

After dressing, she opened her bedroom door and stepped into the hallway, where the comforting aroma of coffee wafted up the stairs. She froze. Mick had no idea of how to make coffee. *Oh God.* Back in her room, she pulled off her jeans shorts and tank top, and pulled on her ripped University of Denver sweatshirt and baggy sweatpants. She didn't want to give him any morning-after ideas.

Justin sat at the kitchen table, reading his phone, looking fresh out of the shower. His wet hair was just beginning to curl as it dried, and his face was shiny— almost radiant. Over his jeans, he wore a blindingly white sleeveless undershirt. Her heart kicked. He looked good.

He smiled up at her. "Good morning. Mick drove April to Olivia's and said he had to pick up some supplies. Do you want me to make you some toast?"

"No thanks."

Why was it that men always looked so cheerful and pleased with themselves after a night of sex? Like they'd accomplished something amazing. She was glad he didn't try to kiss her. Her feelings about the whole thing were still unsettled.

"Coffee?" He poured her a cup and set it on the table.

She tried for a breezy pose. "So, what's going on in the news?"

"Listen, about last night…"

She perched on a chair and reached for her cup. "I don't want to talk about it."

He grinned. "Don't worry, nothing happened."

"Oh…really?" *God, how embarrassing. He knows I think… Damn.*

"It was late when we got here. April was asleep, and Mick asked if I would take care of you if he left for a while. I said I would. I didn't want to leave you in your condition."

"What do you mean?"

"You were tired and maybe had a little too much to drink. I was worried you'd get sick and choke on…something, so I stayed with you."

"I'm so sorry. I—" Her phone rang. She picked it up, listened, and slowly set it on the table.

"What?"

She could barely get it out. "Laura Nowak is dead. The housekeeper found her this morning at the bottom of the basement stairs."

Chapter Seventeen

Laura's funeral was held four days later. Fewer than twenty people clustered near the grave, listening to Father Joseph's droning eulogy. Erin knew some of them—Shirley, Bill, Melanie, Mick, Lou Guthrie, Dean, Mrs. Masters and Zachary.

"I just can't believe it," Shirley said. The hollows under her eyes were wet. "I hadn't seen her for years until she moved back to town a year ago to work for Westside. She, Rhonda, and I talked about going out to dinner. Now boom, they're both gone."

"I'm so sorry." Erin handed her a tissue. And she was sorry, not only for Shirley but because she'd only spoken with Laura that once and liked her. Both she and Rhonda were too young to die. "Do you know if anyone from Laura's family is here?"

Shirley sniffed and touched the tissue to her nose. "She was a widow with no children, no parents, and no sisters or brothers. No one except friends to be sorry she's gone. I feel so bad. She died alone." Sobs shook her body.

Erin held Shirley in her arms and patted her back. "It's okay. Everything's going to be okay."

She knew her words were nonsensical, but they seemed to work. Shirley hiccupped twice, and the tears slowed.

"...that concludes Ms. Nowak's service," Father

Joseph said. "Mr. Lou Guthrie asked me to invite everyone to a memorial lunch at Zinc Bar and Grill at two o'clock."

"Do you want to go, Shirley?" Erin asked.

"Not really. I want to go home."

As they started for the car, Shirley stopped. "Look, over there. Mrs. Masters is standing by her daughter's grave. Zachary is with her." She approached them. "How are you doing, Mrs. Masters?"

"As well as can be expected on this terrible day," Mrs. Masters said. "First the Lord took Rhonda, then He took Laura. It's hard for an old woman like me to go to funerals, especially funerals for younger people."

"It is hard when someone you know dies," Shirley said. She pulled Erin forward. "This is Rhonda's daughter."

"Of course, I know Erin. Since she was a little girl. I also know she never comes home to Misery much." She sniffed. "Leaves her daughter here for months on end while she goes running around all over the place."

Erin stiffened.

"That's unkind, Mother," Zachary said.

Mrs. Masters bent down and stroked the grass covering her daughter's grave as if it were a blanket. "My girl was everything to me. Seems like only yesterday that she passed." She straightened up and glowered at Erin. "You're lucky to have a living daughter. It's a shame you're throwing away precious time you could be spending with her."

Erin tried to stop herself from responding, but failed. "You know nothing about my relationship with my daughter and it's none of—"

Shirley pulled Erin's arm. "We have to be going.

Goodbye, folks." As they walked away, she said, "That old biddy thinks she knows everything about everyone. Forget her. She's always been a mean-spirited witch, but she's getting worse."

Erin swallowed her anger before she spoke. "Is Zachary her son?"

"No, son-in-law."

"I didn't know they were related."

"Well, you weren't around much once you moved out west. There's a lot about our little town you don't know."

Justin broke away from a group of mourners strolling to their cars.

"I didn't realize you were here," Erin said. "Did you know Laura?"

"I met her in the coffee shop when she was there with Rhonda, so I wanted to stop by to pay my respects."

"Did your police friends tell you how she died?"

"She fell down the basement stairs. The medical examiner estimated she died between six and nine at night and ruled it an accident."

Erin hesitated. "Something's off. Laura told me she wasn't going into the basement until the exterminators cleared out the mice."

"Maybe they'd been there."

"I don't think so. I was at her place the day before she died, and she said they weren't coming for a week."

****

After dropping Shirley off at her place, Erin returned home to Melanie yelling in the living room.

"What do you mean, take it easy? I hated that bitch. She wanted to destroy everything."

132

Silence for a moment, then Mick said, "Then why did you go to her funeral?"

"I wanted to make sure they covered her with at least six feet of dirt. Let's go to Zinc for the memorial lunch. I need a martini."

"I get it, but why—"

"Shut up and let's go."

As Erin walked toward the living room, Melanie rushed past her without speaking.

Mick looked at Erin, shrugged and followed Melanie out the door. He came back a few minutes later.

"Weren't you and Melanie going to Zinc?"

"Nah, she's no fun in that mood."

"Why does she hate Laura?"

"Laura was going to report Westside to the EPA for environmental issues or something, and they fired her."

"She told me she didn't work for Westside anymore and she was moving back to the east side. She didn't say she was fired."

"Well, she was, but Melanie's still pissed."

"Why?"

"Because Laura was going to file the report, anyway."

****

The next morning, Erin woke at seven. By the time she showered, made breakfast and walked April to the bus, George had arrived and motel work was underway.

Mick hadn't left his room yet, and Erin didn't call him. He was an adult, for God's sake. Even April, who slept until ten on weekends, didn't need anyone to remind her to get up for school. Erin loaded breakfast dishes into the dishwasher and headed outside for a motel progress report.

"We're doing pretty good so far," George said. "Mold has been eradicated in all twelve units. We've almost finished repairing the roof and replacing siding in units one to six. The exterior of units seven through twelve are next. You'll be happy to hear the project is on schedule and will stay that way, as long as nothing out of the ordinary happens."

Even in its unfinished state, the motel looked better than it ever had. Erin wondered how she'd feel when, in a little under a year, bulldozers knocked it down and hauled it away, with nothing left but sand.

"It looks great, George. Thanks."

He dug into the gravel with the toe of his work boot. "Do you have a few minutes to have a private talk?"

Oh God, what now? "Sure, let's go to the office." Erin had spent several hours in the office cleaning, sorting paperwork, and paying bills, and now she could enter it without cringing.

She perched on the edge of the desk. "What's up?"

"I, uh…well, I hate to tell you this. It's about Mick."

Of course it was. "What has he done?"

"It's more like what he hasn't done. He's not here half the time. Acts like he's the boss, walking around talking to the guys and not lifting a hand to do the work. Takes long lunches and leaves before quitting time. He's a bad example for the rest of the crew."

"Have you talked to him about it?"

"Sure I have. He just grins and reminds me that he owns the place."

"I'm so sorry. I'll talk to him." She kept her voice steady despite her growing anger.

"Don't. Not yet. I've been thinking this over and have an idea that just might work. But I want your thoughts first."

"I'm listening."

"Mick doesn't like to ask for help and gives up too easy when he's not sure how to do something. Then he gets frustrated and walks away from the job. He seems to like the work, though. Maybe I could take an hour or two a day and teach him the right way to do things."

"That's a great idea."

"It means that, for that hour or two a day, I wouldn't be working at top speed. I'm afraid it might push us over in cost or time or both."

"Just do it. Hire another person if you have to, someone Mick could replace when he gets up to speed."

George grinned. "Are you sure you two are related? It's like you come from different planets."

"Thanks, George." Erin about-faced and marched into the house.

"You couldn't wait until after breakfast to ambush me?" Mick sat up in bed, holding a pillow to his bare chest.

"This isn't an ambush. It's a wake-up call. George has been at work for an hour already. Get dressed and come downstairs."

In the kitchen, Mick retrieved a box of sugary children's cereal and a jug of milk from the refrigerator. "Well, go ahead. What did I do now?"

She considered what George said, the possibility Mick might not be careless and lazy. At least not about the motel renovation. "Is something bothering you?"

He shrugged. "Like what?"

"Maybe something about working on the motel. George said he expected you to be more interested in it since it'll be yours a year from now."

Mick poured cereal and milk into a bowl, scooped up a spoonful, then slammed it back into the bowl. "So, you two have been talking behind my back? Christ, what do I have to do to get some respect around here?"

"It's just that you don't seem too excited about how well the work is coming along, and I wondered if something was wrong."

Mick stared at his cereal.

"Come on. What is it?"

He swirled the cereal around the bowl. "I'm just not cutting it. The guys George brought along are experts at this renovation stuff, and I don't know shit. They're probably laughing at me behind my back."

She hadn't expected that. "Do you like the work?"

"Well enough, yeah. I like working with my hands, but I can't even drive a fucking nail straight."

"George could teach you."

"I don't think he likes me too much."

"He said he's willing to work with you if you put in the effort."

"You two figured out what to do about dumb ass Mick? That's bullshit, Erin."

"It wasn't like that. He says you have a good feel for the work and wants to help."

Mick ate a spoonful of cereal. Then another. "Okay. Maybe we could work together before starting time and after work, if he's interested."

"Are you interested? Can you stick to it?"

"I'll do my best."

Chapter Eighteen

Erin gazed at the lake as the sun's lower edge met the horizon, wishing she could capture the tranquil beauty of the evening. But a burning sensation roiled in her chest. Mick's work issues were a problem. And the short gap between Rhonda's and Laura's deaths bothered her—a coincidence, or could there be a connection?

Back in the house, she found Mick slouching on the living room couch, drinking beer. Melanie leaned against his shoulder with a glass of white wine. It was one thing knowing Mick loved Melanie, the gold digger. But her irritation reached an entirely new level to see Melanie relaxing in Rhonda's living room as if it were her own.

Mick straightened. "Where have you been?"

"Staring at the lake. How did work go today?"

"George and I talked. I think everything's going to be okay."

"That's great news." As Erin started out of the room, Melanie elbowed Mick.

"Wait," Mick said. "Mel and I want to talk to you about something."

"Not now, Mick." This was going to be something Mick and Melanie dreamed up, and she didn't want to hear it.

"Please?" Mick wore his endearing, lopsided smile.

She sighed and sat on the edge of a chair. "Go ahead."

Melanie slid several sheets of paper from a folder on the table and held them out to Erin. "We want you to—"

Mick pulled Melanie's arm back. "Wait. Let me." He leaned forward. "Remember the last time Melanie asked if you'd sign the agreement to turn your inheritance over to me and you wouldn't?"

Erin grew dangerously still.

He took the papers from Melanie and laid them on the table. "We, I mean I, wonder if you'll just think about it. These papers say what you and I talked about before, that when we complete the terms of the will, you'll give your half of the property to me and I'll sell the whole thing to Westside."

Irritation tightened the muscles in her neck. "How many times do I have to tell you I'm not signing? If you don't trust me—"

"No, it's not that—" Melanie started.

"Melanie, stop. I got this," Mick said.

She shot him a deadly look. Erin stifled a smile. Her baby brother had finally shown Melanie some backbone.

"Fine. Take care of it yourself." Melanie stormed out of the room, then returned seconds later. "No. I'm not leaving. I have an interest in this too. Erin, Westside Development needs assurance that when the motel is up and running, you'll sign your half of the inheritance over to Mick."

"And they want to make sure I'll sell Paradise to them," Mick said. "They're not happy about waiting a year with nothing more than my say-so, and said they'll move the project farther north if you don't sign."

"You believed them?" Erin said. "They're not going anywhere. They already have a lot of money invested here."

"Just sign the papers," Mick said. "Please. If you do it now, they'll sign a purchase agreement to buy our property."

"Contingent, of course, on the terms of the will being satisfied," Melanie said.

"Right," Mick said. "If you don't, we'll lose out." His voice had a desperate edge.

He was so gullible.

"I'm not signing. Period."

"You're a selfish bitch, Erin." Melanie's gaze bored into hers. "After all your brother has done for you."

Erin laughed. This was bordering on the ridiculous.

Mick grabbed Melanie's wrist. "Stop it. You're not helping."

Melanie glared at Mick. "Is this how it's going to be when we're married? Taking your sister's side against your wife?"

Erin pointed to the door. "Get out, Melanie."

Melanie stalked out of the room.

"For God's sake, Erin!" Mick hurried after her.

****

"Mom!" April rushed to the back porch, where Erin sat with her morning coffee. Her red-gold hair hung to her shoulders in messy curls. She was beautiful. And smart. And her eyes looked troubled. "I had a really bad dream last night." Her lower lip trembled. "And when I woke up, it felt real."

"What did you dream, honey?"

"That it was my fault Granny died."

Erin pulled April onto the loveseat next to her and kissed the top of her head. "No, honey. It was not your fault."

"But if I hadn't been spending the night at Olivia's, she wouldn't have walked alone on the beach that late. We would have walked together after dinner." She buried her face in Erin's chest.

Erin hugged her tight. "Shh. It's not your fault."

"Are you sure?"

"I am. Don't think about it anymore, okay?"

"I'll try." April swiped her tears with the sleeve of her sleep shirt. "Mom, do you think it was an accident when Granny died?"

"Why? Do you?"

"I don't know."

Erin had avoided answering similar questions. "To be honest, I don't know either."

Laura's death made her question every strange aspect of Rhonda's. Especially the late-night doorbell. Something wasn't right.

"Are you telling me the truth?"

"It's as close as I can get to it right now."

****

After Erin walked April to the school bus stop, she returned to the back porch with her tablet to brainstorm. Of the five people Shirley said Rhonda would dress up for, she'd spoken with two, Zachary Smith and Laura Nowak. Laura died soon afterward. Erin went cold every time she thought about it. She'll talk with Dean Scott next. He'd been Rhonda's attorney and friend.

At three that afternoon, Dean opened his office door and waved her into a chair. "I'm glad you called," he said. "I stopped by Paradise Beach the other day. The renovation seems to be progressing well, and it's on budget. Looks like there won't be a problem finishing the work on time. Soon you and Mick will begin running the motel and well on the road to completing the terms of the will."

"I have a question about getting the motel up to code in four months and running it for eight. That's twelve months altogether. What if the township agrees it's up to code sooner?"

Dean laughed. "Oh, I see. You want to know if the motel work is completed in, say, three months and you run it with Mick for eight, can you return to Denver in eleven months? The answer is no. Rhonda wanted you two together for a full twelve months."

Damn it. "I knew you'd say that. But that's not the reason I'm here."

"I didn't think so. What else can I help you with?"

"Westside was trying to buy Rhonda's and Shirley's properties. After they refused to sell, did the company ever try invoking eminent domain?"

"Where did that come from?"

"One of my friends was forced out of her home because her neighborhood's property was needed for a public park. Could that happen with Paradise Beach?"

"How much do you know about eminent domain?"

"That the government can take over private property without the owner's consent, and sometimes at the request of a third party, if it's for the common good—public use."

"That's correct. And yes, Westside requested the government enact eminent domain on some properties in Misery Cove. Apparently, Lou Guthrie has friends in influential government positions and assumed he could get it through. It was one of Laura's assignments. In any case, Westside wasn't able to prove its project was solely for public purposes."

Good. Westside couldn't make a land grab. "I also have a question about Rhonda. Do you think her death was accidental?"

He frowned. "Yes, of course. What else would it be?"

She knew everyone would say that, but wanted to introduce the idea that Rhonda's death could be something other than accidental. Might yield more information later. "I'm not sure. When was the last time you saw her?"

"The Tuesday before she died. Shirley, Steve, Rhonda, and Zachary came to my place for our weekly poker night." He fiddled with the cuff of his suit jacket.

"Anything unusual happen?"

"No. Everything was fine."

"Did she seem upset about anything? Argue with anyone?"

He shrugged. "I don't think so. She drank more wine than she normally did. Steve asked her if she had something on her mind. She said no, but looked worried."

"Do you have any idea why?"

"No."

A few minutes later, Erin was in her car, trying to understand why Dean didn't admit he and Rhonda argued.

Chapter Nineteen

The early morning crowd had thinned out in Brioni's Cafe by the time Erin and April walked in. Erin breathed in the warm earthy aroma of freshly ground coffee and cinnamon rolls, bringing memories of her father and her coming here every Sunday morning to buy donuts for Rhonda. She sighed, ordered a latte for herself, and a hot chocolate for April, then found a table in front of a window.

"Summer vacation is coming up in a few weeks. Anything special you want to do?"

"Not really. Just—" April grabbed Erin's wrist. "Mom, that's my acting teacher. She's coming in here." April waved. "Hey, Ms. Mitchell."

A tall, angular woman with straight black hair came to their table.

"April, how wonderful to see you. And this is…?" She nodded at Erin.

"I'm Erin, April's mother. Can you join us?"

"I'd love to. Let me grab a coffee."

"This is so cool, Mom." April stared at Marilyn as she strode to the counter. "Please don't embarrass me."

Erin nodded solemnly while inwardly grinning. She wished she had a dollar for every time she'd said that to Rhonda.

Marilyn returned to the table and slid into a chair. "About Rhonda, Erin. I'm so sorry for your loss. I wanted to fly in from New York for the funeral, but was told it was a small affair."

"You knew her?"

"Yes, we go way back."

That was a shock. Rhonda didn't tell her she knew a Broadway actor. What else didn't she know about her mother?

"April is very excited about your class."

April frowned and kicked her under the table.

Erin struggled to hold back a smile. "I understand you're returning to New York in the fall."

"Early September, actually. It's good to be back in Misery for a while, though."

"Were you responsible for establishing the theater group in town a few years back?"

"Not only me. The town council and I planned it together. My passion, though, is teaching young people to act. This is my second summer at April's school. I'm glad she could join us this year. We're running a play with the students in mid-August."

"Which play?"

Marilyn winked at April. "We're not telling, right, April?"

"Right." April's eyes glittered as she winked back.

Erin loved seeing her daughter excited instead of depressed, as she'd been in Denver last year.

"Erin, I understand you live in Colorado. How long will you be in Michigan??"

"About a year. April and I will return to Denver after that."

"That's too bad. I was hoping she could join me next year, too."

April's mouth trembled. "I don't want to leave

here. But maybe Mom will let me come back next summer. Mom, can I?"

"We'll see."

"That would be wonderful." Marilyn got to her feet and held out a hand. "I'm glad to finally meet you, Erin. And April, I'll see you soon."

April watched Marilyn cross the room and leave. "Mom, isn't she amazing?"

"Yes, she is. When you're finished with your hot chocolate, I'll drive you to school. I have a meeting with Father Joseph in twenty minutes."

****

The stained glass windows inside St. Jude's Church threw jagged patterns of sapphire, ruby, and emerald across the pews and floor. In the semi-darkness, saintly statues gazed solemnly toward heaven and a sad Jesus looked down from the cross. She hadn't been inside a church for decades, but the almost otherworldly sense of being in a holy place hadn't disappeared.

Father Joseph knelt in the front row of pews. His forehead rested on his folded hands. She sat behind him until he raised his head.

"Father?"

He turned and smiled. "You must be Erin. Please excuse me. Just getting a little meditation in. You wanted to talk about something, right? Is here okay, or would you rather go to the rectory?"

"The rectory."

It would be awkward to question him as a potential suspect in Rhonda's death here, especially now that her respect for the church had apparently resurfaced. Misery Cove was having a more of an emotional impact than she'd expected.

She followed the priest across a stone courtyard to the rectory. Its brick facade mirrored the Gothic architecture of the church. He opened the door and led her down a paneled corridor to a comfortable sitting room. They sat in cozy club chairs in front of a dark fireplace.

"Mary Margaret," he called.

A plump, middle-aged woman entered the room, wiping her hands on a towel. "Yes, Father?"

"I'll have a cup of green tea and please bring Ms. Brady whatever she wants."

"Just water, please."

Father Joseph nestled back in his chair. "Sorry I couldn't meet with you this morning as you requested. Every Monday morning, I say Mass at Good Shepherd's Senior Center."

"It worked out for me too."

"Rhonda told me so much about you, Erin. I feel as if I know you."

Erin's cheeks warmed as she wondered which of her many offenses her mother shared. "You knew her well?"

"As well as a person can know anyone, I suppose."

Mary Margaret returned and placed a tea service on the table next to the priest and handed Erin a bottle of water.

Father Joseph slowly sipped his tea. "What was it you wanted to talk with me about?"

Erin set the bottle down. "I've been told Rhonda was upset before her death, and I'm wondering if you thought the same."

"This is very difficult. Although she received the

sacrament of confession often, there were other many times when we spoke, and it's difficult to separate them. So, I must consider whatever Rhonda told me in confidence is bound by the seal of confession or the seal of friendship."

Damn. "I'm not asking what she said. I'm asking about her mood. She called you the night she died. Can you tell me why?"

The priest steepled his hands. "Something troubled her."

"What?"

"I'm sorry, but I can't reveal that."

This was so frustrating. "You visited Paradise Beach several times and shared wine with her."

"We spoke of many things. The weather, you, your brother, her granddaughter." A slow smile crossed his lips. "This is going to sound odd, but we were becoming wonderful friends. As you might imagine, in my profession, good friends are hard to come by."

"Anything else?"

"Well, she had a grudge against Westside Development, like half the town. Said they were going to ruin Misery Cove."

"Were your meetings a secret? Shirley didn't know about them."

He laughed. "Rhonda didn't want anyone to know we met at Paradise Beach. She said she wanted to protect my reputation." He laughed again.

Erin could see why Rhonda liked him. He was kind and easy to talk to.

"You said she was troubled the day she died and that sometimes you spoke about the past. Was there anything in particular you could tell me about her past?"

He didn't speak for a moment. "Just that impetus for violent actions occurring in the present can often be traced to the past."

"Are you saying she died because of something that happened in the past?"

"I said no such thing, Erin." He rose to his feet. "Now, if you'll excuse me, I must prepare this week's sermon."

Driving home, Erin wondered why Father Joseph abruptly ended their conversation. He knew more than he was letting on. Something about the past. But how far in the past? Last month? Last year? Last decade?

Rhonda would have talked to her psychologist about the past. But would he be willing to tell her anything? Probably not, but it was worth a shot.

****

Two days later, Erin followed a winding stone path from Zachary Smith's driveway to the office at the back of his house. A plaque affixed to the office door read Zachary Smith, PsyD. She entered to the faint buzz of an alarm.

Three chairs and a small table lined a wall in the small reception area. The opposite wall held several professional-quality photographs of sailboats and yachts, and a second door, which she assumed led to an inner office. She sat, feeling jumpy and didn't know why. She'd interviewed hundreds of people for her travel reviews.

A few minutes later, Zachary opened the door with a dazzling a smile. "Erin, I'm so glad to see you again. Come in." He led her down a short hallway to a sunroom where, beyond floor-to-ceiling windows, a perfectly manicured lawn sloped toward the beach. He sat behind a large glass top desk and gestured to one of the two leather armchairs facing it. "Please sit. On the phone, you said you wanted to talk to me about your mother. Are you seeing another psychologist currently?"

"I'm sorry if I gave you the impression I wanted therapy. I just have some questions about Rhonda."

"And I'm sorry I misunderstood. I'll answer whatever I can."

"She had an appointment with you on the day she died. What was her state of mind?"

His brow furrowed. "I'm not sure I—"

"Some of her friends said she'd been nervous and distracted that week. And when I spoke with her on the phone, she sounded worried but wouldn't tell me what was wrong. Did she tell you?"

"Sorry, our sessions were confidential. I'm curious about why you're asking."

"I want to know what was bothering her. When I discussed Rhonda's death with one of her friends, they said that often violent actions have roots in the past. Did she ever mention anything about that?"

"Again, I'm sorry, but I can't comment on that."

His reluctance to talk about a patient didn't surprise her. "I get it, but assume her conversations during the poker games aren't off limits."

"No, of course not." He laughed.

"Can you tell me what she talked about during the last few poker nights? Anything bothering her?"

"Nothing out of the ordinary. The last time we all met would have been a few days before she died. She seemed a little anxious but wouldn't talk about it in front of her friends."

"You said in 'front of her friends.' Did she talk about it during her session with you that week?"

"As I said, I can't disclose anything Rhonda said during our sessions." He reached for a pad of paper and a pen. "Did the two of you have the kind of relationship where you and she felt safe exchanging confidences?"

Erin squirmed. She couldn't remember the last time she and Rhonda had a heart-to-heart conversation. Maybe never. "Didn't you and she talk about this?"

"Of course, but I'm curious about your perspective."

"Can we move on? Did you see her other than during a psychological session or poker games?"

He grinned. "Are you asking if Rhonda and I dated?"

"Did you?"

That would be interesting. She'd never seen Rhonda show the slightest interest in dating. But of course, she might not know because her visits to Paradise had been infrequent until April stayed for the school year.

"We didn't date, and I didn't see her except in the office, at poker, and when the poker group went out to dinner." He glanced at his watch. "Sorry. We're out of time. I have a patient coming soon and for their privacy…"

"Of course." She got to her feet. Even if Rhonda told him anything the week she died, he wouldn't tell her. She'll try again, but use a different tactic next time. "Thanks for seeing me."

"Erin, Rhonda was perfectly fine. As her friend, I can tell you she faced death with more strength than most people."

Chapter Twenty

Erin took the long way home. Her car was the one place she could count on being undisturbed. Zachary saying Rhonda faced her prognosis with strength brought overwhelming guilt. She'd been a coward about her mother's cancer. She should have visited her more, called her more, been there for her.

The day Rhonda told her she had terminal cancer, her brain had auto piloted into defensive mode and she'd ended the phone call quickly. Her mother had probably been scared and depressed, but instead of comforting her, she'd forced herself to write an article about London pubs. Days afterward, she hadn't allowed herself to feel the sadness living just below the surface. As long as Rhonda was alive, there was hope, and she'd refused to envision a world without her mother in it.

She parked in the motel driveway, avoiding the restoration chaos, and went into the house. As she reached the kitchen, a powerful boom sounded, shaking walls and rattling windows. Fear shot through her and she rushed outside. George, Mick, and the rest of the crew stared toward Shirley's property, where a wall of orange flames spiked from the clearing where Shirley's house stood.

"Let's get over there," Mick yelled, jumping into his truck.

Erin swung into the passenger seat beside him.

Shirley was supposed to be working, but what if she wasn't? *Please, please, Shirley can't be home.*

Mick headed down the driveway with neck-jarring acceleration while Erin called 9-1-1. George and the crew were in a van behind them. Mick jammed on the brakes as a school bus stopped at the end of the driveway, blocking access to the road. April hopped out, spotted the flames, and sprinted to the truck

"Mom, what's on fire?"

"Honey, go to the house and stay there. I'll call you when I find out."

When the school bus pulled away, Erin braced her feet against the back of the footwell as Mick made a sharp right turn onto the road. After a few minutes, the truck swerved into Shirley's rutted driveway and stopped at the far edge of the parking area where they had a clear view of the house. Flames surged through the roof, two front windows and the open front door. Small fires sputtered in the forest where the explosion had propelled sections of the roof and siding.

George braked the van behind the truck. Mick leaned out his window and motioned for George to back up.

"We gotta get out of the way so the fire trucks can pull in. Park on the shoulder."

"At least Shirley's car isn't here." Erin's pulse slowed a little. "I have to call her."

Shirley picked up on the third ring. "What's up?"

"Are you at work?"

"Yeah. You sound weird. What's going on?"

"You have to come home right now. Wait, Mick's talking…"

"Tell her to park on the side of the road near the

motel," Mick said. "The fire department will need room to get through."

"Shirley, park on the shoulder between your place and Paradise."

"Is everything all right?"

"No." Erin's voice trembled. "Your house is on fire."

Once Mick parked, Erin jumped out of the truck. Sirens blasted in the distance and within minutes, two fire trucks sped into Shirley's driveway. Shirley was right behind them and tried to follow. A firefighter stopped her.

After gesturing and arguing, she backed up, parked near Mick's truck, then sped toward Erin. "Is my house gone?"

"I'm so sorry." Erin pulled Shirley into a hug. She fought to control her tears.

The smell of burning wood spiraled toward them on a hot wind, along with the crackling, popping, and sizzling sounds of boiling tree sap. Tall sheets of water glowed rusty-gold over spiky flames.

"It's almost beautiful," Erin whispered.

Shirley pulled away and stared at her glowing house, then covered her eyes. Tears leaked under her hands and coursed down her cheeks.

Feeling helpless, Erin stayed close, her heart breaking.

Justin walked over to them. "Shirley?"

Shirley lowered her hands.

"There's not much they can do about your house, but they'll prevent the fire from spreading into the woods. The fire chief said there'll be an investigation into the cause. I'm so sorry."

"How'd you know about this?" Erin asked.

"One of my cop friends called me."

Shirley attempted a smile. "Thanks for being here."

Justin gave her a hug. "Do you have somewhere to stay tonight?"

"She does," said Erin. "Shirley, you're staying with us."

****

Night had fallen by the time the firefighters left and Erin, Shirley, and Mick plodded back to Paradise Beach and into the house. April looked up from the living room couch and turned off the television when they came in. Silently, they lowered themselves into their seats. A cold wind blew into the room through the open glass doors. The late May evenings had been chilly the past week.

"This is going to sound dumb ass, but do you want me to build a fire?" Mick asked.

"Go ahead." Shirley said. "It'll be cozy." She blotted her eyes with a tissue. "I'll be right back." Her head drooped as she headed of the room. When she returned to the couch, her smile was heart-tugging. "I can't believe my home is gone. My father built it. I grew up there and lived in it when I got married. You kids would run over to see me there from the time you could walk. Now everything is gone and what am I going to do? I don't have insurance."

Erin wrapped both of Shirley's cold hands with hers. "You know you're welcome to stay with us as long as you want." She took the afghan from the back of the couch and draped it over Shirley's shoulders.

"Will someone please tell me what happened?" April asked.

"Shirley's house burned down," Mick half-whispered.

"Why did it burn down?"

"Might be an accident," Erin said. "Justin said there'll be an investigation."

Mick disappeared for a few minutes, then returned with a tray of glasses. He handed a glass of amber-colored liquid to Shirley. "It's the good stuff," he said. "And here's your pinot grigio, Erin." He handed April a glass of orange juice. "Here you go, squirt." He sat with a can of beer.

"Turn on the TV, please April," Shirley said. "But not the news."

The three people she loved most in the world stared mindlessly at a show about Egypt. Everyone was trying to distance themselves from what happened next door.

Shirley swallowed the last of her bourbon. "I think I need some time alone."

"I'll get a bed ready for you." Erin left the room, frustrated because there was nothing she could do to ease Shirley's pain. She returned ten minutes later. "I put clean sheets on Rhonda's bed. Use any of her clothes you want."

"Thank you all for everything." Shirley trudged into the hallway.

"Mick, are you okay with Shirley staying in Rhonda's room?" Erin asked when Shirley was out of earshot

Mick tipped the beer can into his mouth, getting the last few drops. "Of course. It's what Mom would have wanted." He gave a half-smile. "Now, aren't you glad I didn't let you throw out Mom's stuff?"

"Oh, shut up."

****

After a surprisingly dreamless night, Erin wandered into the kitchen and found a note from Shirley next to the half-full coffee carafe.

I'm meeting the fire chief at my house, what's left of it, anyway.

Be back soon.

Erin could only imagine what Shirley was going through. Yesterday was bad enough, but confronting the wreckage of her home in the daylight must be unbearable. She poured a cup of coffee and a glass of orange juice, then sat at the kitchen table. What was going on? First Rhonda's death, then Laura's so-called accident, now the burning of Shirley's house. She opened her tablet, reading through her notes and adding details. Rhonda, Laura, and Shirley—three friends, three tragedies.

"Any coffee left?" Shirley dropped into a chair. Her eyes were bleary and her eye bags more pronounced.

Erin poured coffee into a mug and handed it to her. "How are you doing?"

Shirley gave a wry smile. "What do ya think?"

"Sorry, stupid question. What did the chief say?"

"That it was probably arson, but they have more investigating to do before they know for sure." She stared at her hands. "Rhonda, Laura and me. It's like we've all been targeted. Now, do you finally believe someone murdered Rhonda?"

Murder. It wasn't a word you'd normally associate with the death of your mother or someone you knew. And Shirley's fire was a third violent action against women who were friends. Couldn't be a coincidence.

"You and Rhonda refused to sell your property to Westside, and Laura was planning to report Westside's environmental issues to the EPA. I believe their deaths weren't accidental, based on the circumstantial evidence we've found and the connections to Westside. And whoever killed them might have set fire to your house."

"So what are you gonna do about it?"

"I think I'll have another chat with the police."

Chapter Twenty-One

Detective Mackey sighed. "So, Ms. Brady, you think there's a crazy perp running around town murdering women and burning down houses?"

Erin fought for patience. "I believe the same person murdered my mother and Laura Nowak, and probably set fire to Shirley Cochran's house. And that person is associated with Westside Development."

"May I remind you the medical examiner ruled your mother's and Ms. Nowak's deaths accidental?"

"Detective, I'm asking you to reopen Rhonda's case because there's a connection to another death and a fire. The Westside project touches all three and there's only a short time period between them. Please, at least discuss it with your boss."

"Okay, even if it's just to get you out of my hair for a few hours."

"Thanks. When will you let me know?"

"Soon."

As she drove back to the motel, flashing lights appeared in her rearview mirror. *Damn.* She glanced at her speedometer and saw she'd been driving fifteen miles an hour over the speed limit. Undoubtedly a byproduct of her frustrating conversation with Mackey.

She pulled over and watched the rearview mirror as the officer studied his tablet and left his car, then leaned into her window.

"Driver's license and registration, please."

She handed them over and he walked away. It seemed a long time before he returned.

"You have a Denver driver's license and the car is registered to a Rhonda Brady. Do you have her permission to operate this vehicle?"

"Rhonda Brady is…was my mother. She died two months ago. I'm here to manage her business with my brother, who lives here."

"What kind of business?"

What difference does it make? She took a breath and managed an even tone. "She owned a motel. Paradise Beach."

He nodded. "If you plan to keep her car, I suggest you have it registered in your name."

"Good idea, officer. Is that all?"

He straightened. "Yes, ma'am. In the future, keep an eye on your speed. Have a good day."

Without warning, Erin found herself in tears. She would not have a good day. She hadn't had one in days…months.

"Something wrong ma'am?"

"No." But something was. Her entire life. As she pulled onto the road, her phone rang. "Ms. Brady, Detective Mackey here. I know you were anxious for an answer from the chief, so I got to him right after you left. He said there's no reason to believe the deaths of your mother and Ms. Nowak are related to each other or to the fire at Mrs. Cochran's home, which has been ruled an arson."

"But—"

"I know you're not happy about this, but we have limited resources and are in the best position to determine how to use them." The detective paused. "If you have any other questions, my door is always open."

Erin pulled onto the shoulder and slammed her fist on the dashboard. It had been so obvious to her that Westside was the common thread connecting the three women's catastrophes. Westside and its desire to turn Misery Cove into another Saugatuck. But she reluctantly understood the detective's point. No evidence, no crime.

Back to square one. If Westside was behind the deaths and arson, it's possible that similar incidents occurred at their other construction projects. She'll look into it.

Erin found Shirley making April's favorite chocolate chip cookies when she returned home. "How did it go with Mackey?" Shirley asked, pouring the last spoonful of cookie batter onto a baking tray.

"Same old story. There's no evidence of murder, so they can't do anything."

"So, what are you going to do now?"

"Research Westside's other projects. Could you supervise things around here while I bury myself in the Great Rapids Library for a few days?"

"No problem."

****

For the next three days, Erin scoured public records, property records, and media reports for any sign of suspicious activity related to Westside Development. By the last day, she reluctantly accepted that if there were other incidents, Westside had done an excellent job of covering their tracks. She left the library, got into her car, and slammed the door. Back to square one. She went to bed that night discouraged, but determined to keep at it.

At nine the next morning, her phone buzzed.

"Ms. Brady, this is Detective Mackey. I've been thinking about what you said when you were here a few days ago and have something to discuss with you. Can you meet me in the Woodbridge Mall's food court at three this afternoon?"

"The food court?"

"I know it's unusual, but believe me, it's necessary. Can you meet me or not?"

"Sure, okay."

Mackey hung up before Erin could ask what the meeting was about.

****

She almost didn't recognize Mackey. Her dark hair fell in loose waves to her shoulders. She wore eyeliner and mascara, and a white t-shirt over jeans. "Detective Mackey?"

Mackey smiled. "Yep."

"Are you off duty or undercover?"

"Off duty, so today you can call me Caroline. Take a seat."

"Okay, and call me Erin. So, Caroline, why are we meeting here instead of your office?"

"Because I have something to tell you that I probably shouldn't." Mackey's gaze darted around nervously. "If you tell anyone what I'm about to say, I could get fired. Or worse. That's a lot I'm asking, so it's up to you. Do you want to hear what I have to say or not? If yes, do you promise not to tell anyone?"

Erin was stunned. Mackey was doing her a favor? "I absolutely want to hear what you have to say and I promise not to tell anyone where the information came from."

"Okay, your case interested me, Erin, especially after Mrs. Cochran's fire, and I poked around. Seems that a government agency has been investigating Westside Development for years and monitoring upper management's phone calls, internet, and Wi-Fi traffic, emails, travel, and more. Several state-wide departments are assisting with the investigation."

"What government agency? What's being investigated?"

"I can't discuss that. I asked the officer in charge if there was any possibility Westside Development was involved in your mother's or Ms. Nowak's deaths. They were willing to take a look because I told them a federal crime may have been committed. Murder for hire." She smiled slyly. "That wasn't actually true, of course. They got back to me fairly quickly. Although several major crimes are being attributed to Westside Development, no homicides are among them."

"Why aren't they being prosecuted for the crimes they are committing?"

"Because the investigation encompasses more organizations than Westside, and that's all I can say."

"What about Shirley's fire?"

"Arson doesn't rise to the level of importance for an investigation of this type. I shouldn't tell you this, but locally, we uncovered some suspicious activity involving Melanie Addington. We're keeping her in our sights."

"What suspicious activity?" Shirley's fire? Melanie tried to get Shirley to sell her property and maybe it occurred to her that burning Shirley's house would expedite the process.

Mackey shook her head. "I've told you too much already."

"Is it anything that could endanger my family?"

"No."

"Getting back to Shirley Cochran, the arsonist may have been trying to kill her."

"According to the fire department's report, her car wasn't at her residence at the time of the fire, so the arsonist would have known she wasn't home, right? We continue to work with the fire department to find the perpetrator."

"I guess that's all I can ask. Are you positive no one associated with Westside could have killed my mother?"

"If someone murdered her, and that's a big if, it's highly unlikely Westside Development is responsible."

She'd been dead wrong about Westside. Now what?

Chapter Twenty-Two

Erin looked up from her tablet when Shirley plodded into the living room, dropped into a chair and gave a long exhale.

"Nonstop customers in the pharmacy all day and my feet are killing me. I should've driven to work today.

"You should have called me. I'll pour you a glass of wine, then I have something to tell you."

"Your face is telling me it's not good news. While you're pouring, I'll change my clothes and be right back."

Five minutes later, Shirley settled into a chair with a cold pinot grigio. "Okay, what's up?"

"I don't think Westside is responsible for Rhonda's and Laura's murders."

"What? I thought you were pretty convinced Westside was the culprit."

"I changed my mind."

Shirley narrowed her eyes. "Someone must have told you something. Spit it out."

"Can we drop it for now so I can ask you a few questions?"

"Okay, but I'm gonna want the whole story at some point."

Erin paged back to the beginning of a document on her tablet. "I've been racking my brain, trying to come up with other suspects. Remember when I said jealousy is one of the reasons people commit murder? You, Rhonda, and Laura went to high school together, right?"

"We did. Marilyn too. What are you getting at?"

"Were the four of you popular?"

Shirley paused for a moment. "Laura and Marilyn were more popular than me and Rhonda. We were more second-tier popular, if you know what I mean."

"Was anyone jealous of you or anyone in your group?"

"No, I don't think so."

"Did your group ever do or say anything that would make one of your schoolmates angry or hurt?"

"Hell no. What's the deal?"

"Someone told me that violent acts often have roots in the past. You four went to school together."

"Oh, I get it and we didn't do any of that. You know, you're pretty good at this research stuff. I feel like I'm being questioned by a cop. Have you ever considered changing careers?"

"You're hilarious." Erin paused. "Just to confirm, you're saying none of you ever bullied, teased, or harmed anyone at school to the point that they'd want revenge now?"

"At school? No."

****

At two-thirty the next day, Erin pulled into the driveway of a gray and white New England style cottage facing Lake Michigan. A row of modest bungalows across the road enjoyed obstructed views of the lake, if they had any view at all.

Marilyn greeted her at the door. "So happy to see

you again, Erin. Come in."

The small living room had a beachy vibe with pale blue walls, sand-colored throw rugs, and a blue and white striped couch. Open play scripts covered the coffee table and the desk under the window. A sweater hung from the back of the desk chair.

"Your cottage is lovely." Erin wished the Paradise Beach house looked like Marilyn's place, minus the clutter.

"Thanks. I'm considering buying it. Melanie came by the other day and told me it was going on the market."

Melanie certainly gets around. "You want to live here permanently?"

"No. I'm retiring from the stage at the end of the year, and this is a perfect place to get away from the city. And, of course, I'm sentimental about Misery. Next year, I'd like to play a larger role in managing the community theater."

Marilyn's phone rang. She looked at the screen. "I'll be just a minute, Erin." She went to her desk and opened a book with a blue reptile cover. "Yes, next Wednesday looks good... Great, I'll see you then." She jotted a few notes in the book. "Sorry about that. I've been waiting for that call since yesterday."

"That's your appointment calendar? It's gorgeous. Crocodile?"

"Yes. A gift from my very extravagant mother last Christmas. She even had the cover embossed with my initials. She knows I'm not fond of calendar apps."

"Why?"

"I'm always afraid I'll screw something up. I have a lot of meetings when I'm in New York. and paper and pen are easier for me." She laughed. "Even here where I'm not so busy, I schedule everything, even calls to my mother." She glanced out the back window. "It's a beautiful day. Let's chat on the deck." She led the way to a pair of white Adirondack rocking chairs facing the lake. "Can I get you something to drink? Coffee? Iced tea? Something stronger?"

"No, thanks…You're probably wondering why I'm here."

"Something to do with April and the acting class?"

"It's about Rhonda. April said you talked to her last March."

"We had lunch at Georgia's. I came in for a week to set things up for the summer class." She shook her head. "I can't believe she died just a few weeks later."

"Do you mind telling me what you two talked about?"

A shot rang out, and they both jumped.

"What was that?" Erin cried.

Marilyn grimaced. "It's Mrs. Masters from across the street. She shoots at the squirrels getting into her bird feeder."

"Does she kill them?"

"I don't think so. Last week, I talked to her about firing weapons in a residential area and she chased me off her property with a shotgun. Now she gives me the evil eye whenever I run into her."

"She doesn't exactly consider me her best friend, either. Anyway, what did you and Rhonda talk about, if you don't mind telling me?"

"It wasn't much. Old times, high school friends, what we'd been doing lately, and of course, how Misery Cove is changing."

"How did she seem to you?"

Marilyn hesitated. "Knowing she wouldn't live to see April grow up devastated her. And she'd wanted to see you and Mick settled before she left the planet. Her words."

Erin's heart lurched. *Oh God, Rhonda.* "You knew about the cancer?"

"She told me about it last year. We didn't communicate much when I was in New York, but we visited whenever I was here. We'd planned to get together when I returned to Misery to teach the class. But then her accident happened."

"Do you think it was an accident?"

Marilyn raised her eyebrows. "Don't you?"

"There are reasons Shirley, Mick and I believe it wasn't. I talked with the police a few times, but they aren't interested in reopening her case."

"So, you think what? Someone murdered her?"

Erin didn't speak for a moment. "I do."

"Laura died not long after Rhonda. Do you think someone murdered her, too?"

"Yes."

"Then someone set Shirley's house on fire."

"We think the three incidents might be connected…You, Rhonda, Laura, and Shirley went to school together and were friends."

Marilyn smiled. "So many great memories. We were a fun group and adored The Fab Four. We knew every song by heart. Even called ourselves the Fab Five. Crazy, right?"

"Five? Who was the fifth?"

Marilyn excitedly pointed toward the lake. "Look! It's one of the tall ships, so majestic and beautiful."

"It is. We were talking about your fifth friend. Who was she?"

"Oh, just someone who moved on a long time ago."

"What was her name?"

"It's been over forty years. I don't remember. What does this have to do with Rhonda?"

Nice job of evading the question. Either Marilyn didn't remember the name or didn't want to talk about her.

"Nothing, just curious." She'd circle back to that later. "Okay, another question. Did anyone at school envy your group? Or did anyone in your group bully anyone?"

Marilyn frowned. "Absolutely not."

"Do you think it's possible that someone took revenge on Rhonda, Laura, and Shirley?"

Marilyn didn't respond for a moment, then her face paled. "Oh, my God!"

Her voice sent chills up Erin's back. "What?"

"Am I next?"

"Why would you be next?"

She rose unsteadily. "Erin, I'm sorry. I need to cut this short."

Chapter Twenty-Three

The line of red taillights Erin followed through downtown Misery came to a dead stop about an eighth of a mile from the motel. Inching closer, she saw a crowd of protesters blocking the motel driveway and surging toward the house. She glanced at the time. Four o'clock. April would be home from school and terrified. Erin's call to her went to voicemail.

She drove the car onto the shoulder, slid out, and called Mick. "Where are you?"

"In Great Rapids. We all are. George gave us the rest of the day off. What's up?"

"Protesters are blocking the driveway." She dodged cars and gawkers, clutching the phone to her ear. "April's not answering her phone and I can't get to the house. Hear that?"

Protesters yelled, "IF YOU SELL, YOU'LL GO TO HELL!"

"I'm leaving now, but it'll take me about forty-five minutes to get there."

"Just get here as fast as you can. I'm calling the police." Her phone buzzed. "Gotta go, it's April."

"Mom, where are you?"

"Near our driveway. Where are you? Are you okay?"

"I'm in the house and I'm scared. People are running around our parking lot, yelling and tipping over

Uncle Mick's construction stuff."

"Stay where you are. I'm coming."

"Hurry!"

Erin called 9-1-1 as she dashed to a group of huddling protesters. "Please move out of the way. This is my house and my daughter's in there."

"Hey, everyone," one of the women sneered. "This here is Erin Brady, the famous travel writer." She leaned in close to Erin's face. "Misery Cove is our home and we don't want a hotel and condos on our beautiful beach. If you and your brother sell to the damn developers, you'll be very, very sorry."

"The police are on the way. You should leave."

"Hey, everyone, get this. Erin called the police." She laughed.

Several people closed in, circling Erin. Someone yelled, "Grab her. We can use her as a hostage."

The sneering woman and a man gripped her wrists and shoved them behind her back.

"Let go of me!" Erin kicked and twisted but couldn't get away.

Another man joined them and they forced her to her knees. Twigs and gravel pierced her skin and her breath came in shallow gasps. She wasn't getting enough air. This couldn't be happening.

"What should we do with her?" someone asked.

"Take her to the truck."

Two protesters grabbed her upper arms and hauled her to her feet. She struggled against them and their hands tightened.

"Let me go!" She shoved her elbow into the belly of one of the people behind her.

Hard rock music blasted from a motorcycle racing

along the shoulder, aiming straight for the crowd. People scattered and the hands holding Erin dropped away. She fell to the ground. The motorcycle roared up next to her. The driver reached down and pulled her up.

"Jump on."

Erin leapt behind him, almost tumbling off when he accelerated toward the motel. Protesters scrambled out of his way. Sirens wailed in the distance.

The driver jumped off the bike in front of The Sand Bar and pulled out a pistol. "LEAVE. NOW!"

Protesters gaped and scurried into the woods.

He watched them, grinning, then pulled off his helmet and ruffled his hair. "You okay?"

Erin stared. Tall, slender, dark hair, white shirt under a black leather jacket, jeans. He looked like a magazine cover model.

"Yes…Thank you." Her hammering heart slowed down, but not all the way down.

"I'm Patrick Roth. Happy to help." He held out a hand.

She shook it. His grip was firm but not bone-breaking. "Erin Brady."

Rotating lights flashed on the trees as a magnified voice blared. "Break it up. Go home unless you're looking for some jail time."

A police car pulled into the parking lot. Two officers exited.

"We understand you were restrained, ma'am. Are you hurt? Do you need medical assistance?"

"I'm fine, just a little shaken." She glanced at the house. April leaned out of Erin's bedroom window. "Honey, stay in the house. I'll be inside soon."

"I'd like to get your statement. Is now okay?" the

officer asked.

"No. I need to get to my daughter. Doesn't look like there's any damage, so no statement is necessary." She didn't blame the protesters. She sympathized, but was still angry they showed up at the motel and scared April.

"If you change your mind, come to the station."

"Thanks, officer."

Patrick moved toward his bike. "I'll be on my way. Nice meeting you."

"Would you like to come in? For a coffee or something?" With the shortage of available male company in Misery Cove, she hated to see him go.

"No, thanks." He put the helmet on and buckled it under his chin.

"Are you just passing through?" *Say you're not.*

"No, I'll be here awhile. Maybe I'll run into you in town."

****

April burst out of the front door, heading straight for Erin. "I was so scared, Mom."

Erin folded her daughter into her arms and kissed the top of her head. "Everything's okay, honey."

They looked up as a car pulled into the parking lot and Mick jumped out. "Are you guys okay?" He scanned the motel, construction supplies, and equipment. "It's a mess, but it looks those assholes didn't hurt anything."

"Thank God," Erin said. "Let's go inside."

Mick's face was ashen. "I was worried about you two."

He put one arm around Erin and the other around April as they entered the house and stepped into the kitchen. "I love you guys," he said, squeezing them.

"We love you too," Erin said, shocked.

He'd never said that before. At least not to her.

His eyes brightened. "Hey, I have an idea. Why don't I make dinner? I'll pull out the barbecue and grill us some burgers."

"Really?" said Erin.

April grinned. "Sounds great, Uncle Mick."

Erin and April exchanged stunned glances.

"Thanks, Mick." Erin said.

They walked through the living room and onto the porch.

"I got really scared when all the yelling started," April said. "You and Uncle Mick and Shirley weren't here. I really miss Granny. She was always here when I got home from school."

"I'm sorry I wasn't here. I'll make sure someone is always around when I need to be away."

"Where were you, anyway? You're always going somewhere."

Mick came out of the house, pulled the barbecue grill from under the porch, and lit it. "Burgers in half an hour."

"He's different," April said when he disappeared around the side of the house.

"I think so too."

She realized she and Mick hadn't argued in a long time. Maybe Rhonda had been right about forcing them to stay together for a year.

"To answer your question, I miss Granny and I've been asking her friends about how she was before…you know."

"Before she died, right? You never asked me."

"I was afraid it might make you sad."

"It probably would, but you should've asked me, anyway."

April was right.

"Okay, did you notice anything different about Granny the week she died or before that?"

"Hmm. She forgot stuff sometimes and didn't smile as much. Once when I passed by her bedroom, I heard her talking to herself."

"What did she say?"

"Something like, 'Should I? Shouldn't I?' And then, 'It'll help me, but will it hurt anyone?' I thought she was talking about killing herself and ran into her room. I asked what she was talking about and she said not to worry and to forget what she said."

"When was this?"

April scrunched her face. "I think about two weeks before she died."

It never occurred to Erin that Rhonda might have considered suicide.

"Mom, she didn't kill herself, right?"

"No way. For one thing, the medical examiner ruled out suicide. And for another, she loved us too much to do it. She must have been talking about something else."

****

"I hoped I'd find you out here, Erin," Shirley said. "The pharmacy wasn't too busy, so Steve said I could leave a little early."

Erin slid over to make room for her on the rattan loveseat.

"I just saw April riding her bike down the driveway. Is she okay? Someone told me about the protesters. And what about you? Was it scary?"

"We're both fine. Just a bunch of agitators blocking the driveway. But get this. A hot guy on a huge motorcycle saved me from them, then drove me to the house."

Shirley leaned back into the cushions and sighed. "Hot guy on a monster bike? Why doesn't anything like that happen to me?"

"It's a first time for me, so maybe your day is coming... April told me she heard Rhonda talking to herself two weeks before she died, and it sounded like she was considering suicide. Was she?"

"No way in hell."

"I agree. April misunderstood."

"She absolutely did. You met with Marilyn today, right? Find out anything?"

Erin picked at a loose strand of rattan. "Not sure this is something or not. I asked her if your group bullied anyone and—"

"Hey! I told you we didn't."

"Marilyn said the same thing. She also told me about your old group, the Fab Five. What was that all about?"

Shirley hesitated. "We were crazy kids."

"Who was the fifth in your group?"

"It was a long time ago. I really don't remember. Marilyn have anything else to say?"

"Just that she wondered if she'd be next."

"Next what?"

"Next one to be killed. Why would she think that?"

Shirley paused. "I don't know, but you're on the wrong path with this bullying thing, though."

"Maybe, but I'm checking everything. Steve is next

on my list for a chat."

"He didn't go to school with us."

"I know, but he saw Rhonda the day she died and I want to know if she said anything." Erin got to her feet. "Since the pharmacy isn't busy now, I'll go talk to him."

Chapter Twenty-Four

When Erin reached the pharmacy, Steve was flipping the cardboard "Open" sign in the window to "Closed." He'd been the trusted town pharmacist for as long as she could remember. And he probably knew the medical history of almost everyone in Misery Cove. She remembered her embarrassment the first time she picked up birth control pills. Thankfully, he didn't blink an eye.

He unlocked the door. "What can I do for you, Erin?"

"Sorry to bother you, but can we talk for a few minutes?"

"Sure, come on in." He locked the door behind them and led her to his office, where they sat on opposite sides of his desk. "How can I help?"

"Shirley said Rhonda came here to pick up a prescription on the day she died."

"She did."

"What was the prescription for?"

"It was a refill of her anti-anxiety meds."

"How did she look? Did she say anything?"

"She appeared a bit out of sorts. Shaky. The prescription was for a ninety-day supply and she said she wondered if she'd be alive when it was time for a refill."

Remorse knotted Erin's stomach as she

remembered the times she'd distanced herself when Rhonda made remarks like that. Sometimes she even got annoyed. Once, when Rhonda opened a package of 100 coffee filters, she'd said, "I probably won't be around to use the last one." Erin told her she was being morbid. Now she wished she'd shown more empathy. But back then, she wouldn't allow herself to believe Rhonda was dying.

"Did she say anything else? Buy anything?"

He half-smiled. "Yes, she bought a bag of potato chips, a couple boxes of chocolate-covered peanuts, and some pretzels. I asked if she was having a party and if so, why wasn't I invited? Teasing her, you know. She said it wasn't anything like that."

"Did you think she was seeing someone that night?"

"I don't know. Why are you doing this, Erin? Let it go."

"I can't. Do you think Rhonda's death was an accident?"

He lifted a pen from his desk, twirled it through his fingers and dropped it into the coffee mug he used as a penholder. "I honestly don't have a clue."

"Did she ever mention anyone threatening her?"

"Not really threatening, but once she told me Westside Development was pressuring her to sell Paradise Beach to them. Offered her a pretty sizable amount plus one of the new condos, but she said no."

"When you, Shirley, Dean, Zachary, and Rhonda played poker that last time, how did she seem?"

"What do you mean?"

"Different? Quiet?"

"No. Actually, the opposite. We played at Dean's

that night. Zachary, Shirley, and I arrived at about the same time. Rhonda was already there. She was madder than a hornet at him. I asked what was wrong, but neither one would talk about it."

Later, Erin wondered why Dean didn't mention his argument with Rhonda.

****

Erin checked her reflection in the bathroom mirror the next morning and gave her hair a final mist of hairspray.

April peeked in the open doorway. "Where are you going?"

"I'm meeting Ms. Mitchell for breakfast."

April frowned. "To talk about me?"

"It's not about you. I want to ask her about Granny again. Find out what she was like a long time ago." And why she expected to be the next victim."

"Can I come?"

"Sorry, no. You have school."

"But she's my friend, not yours. Can't I come for just a few minutes?"

"She can be friends with both of us. Just like we're both friends with Shirley. How about if I arrange for the three of us to go to lunch next weekend?"

"I guess so. But if you do talk about me today, promise you won't say anything embarrassing."

"Cross my heart. Now go get your breakfast." While April rushed down the stairs, Erin went to her bedroom to dress.

A scream froze her in place. She raced down the stairs and into the living room. April knelt in front of the television, eyes inches away from the screen.

"What is it? You scared me half to—"

April moved to the side, revealing a reporter gesturing toward a house behind her. "The police were called to the scene at six forty-five this morning by a neighbor, who reported she was taking a package to Marilyn Mitchell. When no one answered the door, she went to the back of the Mitchell residence, where the sliding glass doors were open. In the primary bedroom, she found Ms. Mitchell's fully clothed body on the bed. The neighbor said she tried to wake her, then called 9-1-1. Ms. Mitchell is currently at St. Jude Memorial Hospital, where she's in critical condition."

The reporter glanced over her shoulder, then back at the camera. "Here comes a police officer... Excuse me, what is Ms. Mitchell's condition?"

"Nothing has changed since I spoke with you fifteen minutes ago, ma'am. We're waiting for word from the hospital." The officer pressed her earpiece. "What? Okay. I'm on my way." She left to join a group of officers gathered at the side of the cottage.

Shirley entered the living room, gripping a cup of coffee. "I've been glued to the TV ever since the news about Marilyn came on." She shakily set the cup on a side table and collapsed into a chair. "I can't believe this."

April's voice quivered. "It could be a mistake, right, Mom?"

"I hope so, honey." It didn't look good, though. She pulled April into a hug. How was this going to affect her daughter?

"I can't go to school today."

"It's okay. We'll watch the news together."

The reporter's voice broke through. "We just received word from the hospital. Ms. Marilyn Mitchell was pronounced dead thirty minutes ago."

Oh God. Another death.

Shirley sprung out of her chair, heading for the hallway.

"No! She can't be dead!" April hurled herself into Erin's arms, almost knocking her over.

"I'm so sorry, sweetie." Everything went silent for Erin. She was only aware of her daughter's body snuggled into hers.

April's phone buzzed. She wiggled out of Erin's embrace and answered it as tears trickled down her cheeks. "Mom, Olivia's mom said she could stay home from school, too. Can she come over?"

"Of course she can."

****

April and Olivia sat cross-legged on the floor, staring at the TV. Erin settled beside them.

"You two have been here for hours. I don't think we'll learn anything else today. Why don't you go outside for a while and I'll let you know if they find out anything new?"

"Where did Shirley go?" April's eyes were unfocused, like she'd just woken from a dream.

"She's in her room."

Erin's initial shock had faded a little, replaced by annoyance with the media mixing facts and suppositions, interviewing shocked neighbors, and asking inane questions of everyone who had the slightest connection with Marilyn.

She went to the back porch. The girls wandered along the shore. The day was one of the perfect ones—sunny, faint breeze, temps in the mid-seventies, the water an especially brilliant blue. A day where it seemed impossible that anything bad could happen. Her phone sounded. Justin.

"I knew you'd want to hear the latest right away," he said. "A friend in the medical examiner's office said preliminary findings show that Marilyn Mitchell most likely died from a drug overdose between eight and ten last night. A probable suicide."

****

Later that day, Erin and Justin sat side by side on a weathered bench facing the lake. He didn't look as put together as he usually did. His clothes looked like he'd slept in them, his eyes were weary, and he hadn't shaved.

"Are you okay?"

Justin stared at the water where sailboats swanned past Hope Island. "We can talk about it later. First, I want to know what you want to talk to me about."

She kicked off her shoes, and dug her toes into the sand, still cool despite the especially warm mid-June weather. "Okay, how much do you know about Marilyn's suicide?"

"She didn't leave a note, and no one seems to have had any idea she was depressed enough to kill herself."

"Apparently, she took antidepressants. Did she overdose?"

"There was a nearly empty vodka bottle next to her bed and just a few pills left of the antidepressants. The medical examiner said it was most likely the combination of alcohol and drugs that killed her. He won't know for certain until the toxicology results come in. Might be several weeks or even longer."

"She said she was happy to be in Misery Cove when I saw her. Loved teaching acting to the kids and getting away from New York."

"You talked with her? When?"

"Two days ago."

"What did you talk about?"

"Rhonda and Laura. She said she was afraid she'd be next to die. Three women, all dead within a couple of months. Add Shirley's arson to the mix and what are the chances?"

She was so frustrated and angry she wanted to scream. How could the cops be so blind?

"Now I'm back to where I started because Westside wasn't involved."

"I know they're not. How do you know?"

"Can't say. How did you find out?"

"I can't say either." He looked into her eyes. "You've been thinking about this a lot."

"They all grew up in Misery Cove and all went to the same school. I wonder if there were resentments, jealousies, hurts from their high school days. Someone wanting revenge."

"But—"

"I know what you're going to say. It's been over forty years since they graduated. But what if something happened recently that touched off the jealousy or whatever?"

Justin stared into the distance. "I see what you mean, but it would have to be something fairly devastating for someone to murder three women."

"Right? Any ideas?"

"Well, Holly at the grocery store said someone from the cat and dog charity is taking bets that you and Mick won't finish the motel. They said they're looking forward to moving in."

Erin chuckled. "Now I've heard everything. Really, any thoughts about the deaths?"

"You know what the police believe, right?"

"Accident, accident, suicide. I have to keep digging."

"If you're right and the supposed killer knows you're investigating, you'll be in danger."

"I don't want to talk about that now. So, what's going on with you? You look terrible."

He met her gaze. "It's Catherine. She wants us to pick a wedding date."

Erin's heart dropped. "Why?"

He smiled ruefully. "She thinks I'm spending too much time with you."

"We've only seen each other a few times since I've been back."

"I made the mistake of telling her about our previous relationship." He smiled, a genuine smile this time. "And she thinks you're trying to seduce me away from her."

Not a bad idea. She brushed sand from her feet and pulled her shoes on. "Well, did you do it? Set a wedding date?" *Please say no.*

"Not yet."

Chapter Twenty-Five

Four days later, Shirley maneuvered her way into the house, carrying two huge grocery sacks. "Boy, do I have something to tell you."

"Let me help." Erin eased the sacks from Shirley's arms and took them into the kitchen. She pulled out a bag of caramel and milk chocolate mini-bars and held it up, smirking.

Shirley snatched the bag and set it aside. "Don't judge me." She nudged Erin out of the way to shove the candy, dried spaghetti, cereal, and jars of marinara sauce onto a shelf. "I found out some stuff about Marilyn."

"When is the funeral? April and I want to attend."

"No funeral or memorial service in Michigan. Apparently, her husband and parents flew in from New York yesterday to take her home." Shirley leaned against the sink. "Holly at the Stay and Shop told me that Karen, who cleans offices at the police station, said Marilyn definitely committed suicide. She swallowed antidepressants with vodka."

"No way she killed herself. She loved teaching the kids and wanted to buy the pretty cottage she was renting. I've got to find out who's doing this."

"Stay out of it or you might win a place on the killer's hit list." Shirley started a pot of coffee, then turned it off. "Screw this." She pulled a bottle of pinot grigio from the fridge, poured two glasses, and handed one to Erin.

"Thanks. Even though I'm sure Westside had nothing to do with the murders, I had Mick ask Melanie if Marilyn had any connection to Westside."

"What'd she say?"

"That Marilyn wasn't even an investor. There's still the school connection, though. Are you sure there wasn't anything someone blamed Rhonda, Laura, Marilyn, and you for?" She included Shirley, even though it was possible that the murderer hadn't started the fire.

Shirley stared into her glass. "I keep telling you, we were good kids. Must be something else."

"I keep thinking about the Fab Five. Who was the fifth?"

Shirley frowned. "I can't remember the names of everyone I went to school with. That was what, over forty years ago?"

"Please, try to remember."

"Why is this so important to you?"

"Because she might have something to do with the murders. Did the four of you kick her out of the group or something?"

Shirley scowled. "You're way off track here, but I'll think about it and let you know. Satisfied?"

"Yes. But be careful. Promise me."

"No problem. I'm getting a little weirded out, anyway." Shirley got up. "I'm watching TV in my room."

Erin stayed in the kitchen, staring into her wineglass. Her head was stuffy, like she coming down with a cold. And a headache threatened. Another glass of wine and she wouldn't care. Why is everything so complicated?

An unfamiliar text appeared on her phone.

—This is Patrick Roth, the guy who gallantly saved you from the protesters the other day. Are you available for dinner tomorrow?—

How did he get her number, but who cares? Maybe he'll clear the murders and Justin out of her head for a few hours.

—Sure, just text me the time and place.—

****

The next evening, Erin parked in front of the pharmacy and walked to the foot of Fish Landing, an old fishing pier that jutted out into the lake, where Patrick suggested meeting. The sun, low in the sky, cast shadows on the street, and lights around the cove created shimmering lines in the water.

She found him studying a sign displaying Westside's proposed glass-enclosed galleria, replacing Fish Landing's quaint historic stores and restaurants with a cold industrial monstrosity. Her thoughts darkened a moment, but then Patrick turned. A current of air from the lake lifted the hair grazing his forehead. His smile was teasingly wicked.

"I was just thinking it was incredible how we met in the middle of a protest."

"With you rescuing me." She glanced at the picnic basket dangling from his hand. "What's that?"

"It's such a beautiful night. I didn't want to waste it inside a stuffy restaurant. I found us a spot on the beach."

After stepping onto the sand, Erin slipped out of her sandals and dangled them from her fingers as they walked along. She should be nervous, alone with a stranger on a beach in the dark with a murderer hanging around. But she wasn't and not sure why.

Patrick stopped at a bench halfway to the water, set the basket down, and removed a plaid blanket and bottle of French champagne. Then popped the cork and poured the bubbly, pale gold liquid into two flutes. They touched glasses and sipped, glancing at each other over the rims.

Wow, she hadn't expected this wildly romantic night. She wanted to reach out and touch him. Next, he wrestled a puffy silver bag from the basket and unzipped it. Erin's mouth watered as the tangy, sweet, and cheesy aroma of pizza drifted out.

She laughed. "Champagne and pizza. I love it."

So far, he was checking all the boxes.

They sat and balanced pizza slices in one hand and flutes in the other. Patrick made a sudden move to keep his pizza from falling onto his khakis and spilled champagne on Erin's white pants. She laughed so hard her pizza landed in the sand.

Patrick grinned. "How do you like my impromptu icebreaker?"

"Cleverly executed."

"When we're finished eating, let's take the blanket, sit by the water, and drink the rest of the champagne."

"Sounds perfect."

They strolled to a spot near the water's edge. Patrick spread the blanket on the sand and they sat side by side, watching a brilliantly lit freighter slowly drifting south. Her pulse kicked up a few beats. This was straight out of a romance movie.

"Someone in town mentioned you lost your mother

recently."

"Yes." The night Rhonda died must have been a lot like this one, only colder. She took a long swallow of her drink. "She died suddenly."

"Heart attack?"

"No. I don't want to talk about it, okay?"

"Of course." Patrick refilled their flutes, and they talked nonstop about movies, music, and friends.

Erin finished her third glass of champagne, feeling a little buzzed. "I should get back."

He rose and helped her to her feet. "I had a great time and hope you did, too."

She smiled. "I did."

Back at the bench, they repacked the basket. She picked up her sandals, Patrick walked her to her car, then softly kissed her cheek. The warmth of his lips lingered when he pulled away.

"Want to do this again?" he asked.

"Sure."

Justin who?

****

Shirley looked up from a rerun of her favorite crime drama when Erin came into the living room. "So, how was your date?"

"Really nice. Great, in fact."

Shirley raised an eyebrow. "Did you...you know?"

Erin's cheeks grew warm. "You're not really asking if I went to bed with him?"

"Why not? You haven't had a man around since you've been here and it's not natural. I remember what it was like being young."

Erin sank into the couch. "I love you, but I won't discuss on my sex life with you. Now or ever. But just to answer you this one time, I did not have sex with him."

Unfazed, Shirley said. "Too bad. Sometimes I worry about you."

"Seriously, don't. Please." All she needed was Shirley monitoring her dating life.

"Okay, moving on."

"Thank you."

"Loosen up, girl. Anyway, I called the cops to see if there's any new info on who burned my house. After a lot of cop-talk, they said they're still investigating."

"At least they're working on it."

"Right, but get this. A couple of hours ago, Melanie came by with another purchase agreement for my property."

"What did you tell her?"

"That I don't want to think about it right now. It stresses me out."

"Good."

"She wasn't happy when she left, but tried to hide it. Smart move."

Erin picked up the TV remote. "Okay if I turn this off?"

"Sure, I've seen it before, but I just can't get enough of that cute special agent."

"What's with you and your TV men? Get a real one, for God's sake."

"Have you actually checked out the men my age around here? Anyway, anything new on finding Rhonda's murderer?"

"I'm running into a brick wall and wonder if I've been wrong assuming the same person killed her, Laura, and Marilyn. There could be two or even three killers."

Shirley frowned. "Seems way out there." She started for the kitchen. "I gotta get some wine. Want a glass?"

"No thanks, I've had enough for tonight."

"I haven't. Another month of this crap and I'm signing up for rehab." A few minutes later she came back with a half glass of wine. "See? I'm cutting down." She returned to her seat. "Zeroing in on our original question. Who would want Rhonda dead? Everyone loved her."

"Maybe not everyone. You know, she called Father Joseph that evening. Maybe she invited him over."

"And what, he killed her?"

Erin shrugged.

"No way," Shirley said.

"She didn't tell you she had him here several times, right? Maybe there was a dark secret she told him or he told her."

"So what? Why would he kill her? Because he thought she'd tell someone?"

"Maybe. Try to keep an open mind, okay? How about Dean? She had a fight with him earlier that week and no one knows what it was about. He lied and said there hadn't been a fight. He could have visited Rhonda that night and intentionally or accidentally killed her."

"You've got a seriously disturbed mind. Maybe you should write murder mysteries."

"Ha ha. Now moving on to Laura. There was no love lost between Laura and Melanie, and it could have been about more than just the Westside business. Also, the pro-development protesters hated Laura because of the EPA thing. One of their fringe members could have killed her. They probably didn't know Westside had already fired her. Last but not—"

"I should be taking this all down," Shirley said. "Maybe I should write the murder mystery."

"Are you finished with the sarcasm?"

"Yes." Shirley smiled innocently.

"Okay, last but not least, Marilyn. What if she had an abusive husband, and that's why she's been coming here the last two summers? She wanted to buy the cottage she was renting. Maybe to get away from him. No one knows what he looks like. He could have killed her. She also told me she's had some run-ins with Mrs. Masters."

"Oh, come on now. Mrs. Masters is about eighty."

"Wasn't there some talk about how her daughter died?"

"Who told you that? Mrs. Masters worshiped the ground that girl walked on." Shirley leaned back into the cushions. "This is getting way too complicated."

"I know."

The glow from Erin's date with Patrick was gone. Buried under too much speculation.

Chapter Twenty-Six

The next morning, while Erin updated the research notes on her tablet, a loud crash jolted her out of her chair and an earthquake-like shudder shook the house. She dashed to the parking lot. The back end of a semi-truck protruded from the left side of the motel. Mick, George, and the rest of the crew fixedly stared at it.

"How did this happen?"

Mick shrugged. "The truck came up the drive pretty fast and couldn't stop, I guess."

"Is anyone hurt?" She moved closer to the truck and a groan came from inside. "Mick, call 9-1-1."

She angled her way through the space between the breached motel wall and the truck, and startled when the passenger door flew open and a man slid out. He landed on his feet and doubled over.

"Are you okay?"

He drew a few deep breaths, then straightened his back and flexed his arms and legs. "I think so." Blood poured from his nose. He didn't seem to notice.

"What's your name?"

"Joe. Don, that's the driver, is in worse shape than me."

"I'm Erin. Stay where you are for a minute."

The man nodded.

Erin hoisted herself onto the passenger seat. The driver's head rested on his bloody hands, gripping the steering wheel.

"Don?"

He slowly turned toward her. Blood streamed down his face from a gash on his forehead. Erin searched for something to staunch it and spotted a crumpled fast food bag on the floor. She found unused napkins inside and pressed one to the driver's forehead.

"Can you hold this?"

He nodded and lifted his right hand. His left arm dangled at his side. She held out a napkin to Joe.

"Tilt your head back and hold this to your nose."

The driver groaned and closed his eyes.

"Don?"

He didn't respond. The napkin on his forehead had slipped. Erin reached out and held it in place.

"Erin, the EMS, and the fire department are on the way," Mick called. "Is everyone all right?"

"The driver's unconscious. He's bleeding. He might have a broken arm, and it looks like he's wedged in. Come in and help Joe. He's standing by the wall."

Mick shoved his way inside, slung Joe's arm over his shoulder and slowly worked his way to the hole in the wall. "Hey, guys, I need some help here."

George came running and helped Mick move Joe out of the narrow space.

Erin stayed with the driver, speaking to him soothingly, although he probably couldn't hear her. She glanced toward the break in the wall as the sound of sirens grew nearer. *Thank God.* A few minutes later, vehicle doors slammed and people shouted to each other. A firefighter ducked into the motel room and worked his way to the passenger side of the truck.

"You can go back out, ma'am. We have this."

Erin crawled out of the truck. The firefighter let her pass, then boosted himself into the passenger seat. She stumbled to the parking lot, but stayed near the truck.

Two more firefighters reached the back of the truck. One stuck her head inside the motel room.

"What's the status in there?"

"We need to tear down the front wall on the left to get the driver out."

"On it." The firefighter turned to Erin, Mick, George and the crew. "We need all of you to stand back out of the way."

The ambulance arrived a few minutes later and two paramedics entered the truck and the firefighters exited.

"Status?" a firefighter called to the paramedics.

"We need to get him to the hospital as soon as possible."

Erin's phone buzzed. "Justin, you heard what happened?"

"Yes. I was on my way there, but was called to a two car collision on the expressway with multiple injuries."

"Is everyone okay?"

"Unknown. I'll be here for a while. How's it going at your place?"

"The driver and passenger were injured in the crash, and the motel is a mess."

"I'm sorry. I'll stop by when I'm finished here."

****

When the last emergency vehicles left an hour later, Erin, Mick, and George surveyed the damage.

"Doesn't look good," George said. "The front of units three and four are totally destroyed, and I suspect structural damage to all six units. Looks like the roof buckled. I'll know more once we can take a good look at the building. First, we'll have a safety inspector out to tell us what we need to do to make the motel safe to work on."

Erin prayed the injuries weren't serious. The animal charity will probably jump for joy when they hear about this.

Mick stared at the motel and shook his head. "We were nearly finished with half the units, now they're basically gone. What the hell are we going to do now?"

****

Erin sat on the back porch, distractedly watching a ferry pull into a dock on Hope Island, and thinking about the last few hours. What a disaster.

Shirley came out and handed her a glass of wine. "Don't look so upset. Could have been a lot worse."

"I called the motel's insurance company. They'll be by tomorrow for an assessment. George called Great Lakes' insurance company and the trucking company called theirs. Those assessors are coming out tomorrow too. George says he thinks insurance will cover most, maybe all, the damage."

"That's good news, right?"

"Right, but we still have the problem of getting the motel finished on time. I called Dean to see if there are any provisions in the will for accidents. He said no, so Rhonda's time frame stands."

"Could you get more crew?"

"This is prime building season. George is going to check, but it'll be a couple of days before he knows if anyone's available."

"Where is that damn truck driver? I'd like to punch his lights out."

"Take it easy, Shirley. It was an accident."

"I know, but still… Did Justin come over?"

"He was tied up earlier, but stopped by an hour ago for a few minutes."

"Just a few minutes?"

"Catherine's making dinner." Erin gave a fake smile, then rose to her feet when someone knocked on the front door.

"No, you stay here. I'll go." Shirley left the porch and walked around the outside of the house. She was back in a few seconds. "You got company."

Patrick pulled Erin out of her chair and hugged her. "I came as soon as I heard. Can I help?"

Tears gathered in her eyes. Everything seemed so hopeless. "Thanks, but I need some time alone to figure it out."

"No worries." He kissed her cheek and left.

****

The next morning, after a towing company removed the damaged truck, Erin lingered outside the gaping hole in the motel's facade and wanted to cry. So much destruction. Thank God the truck driver wasn't badly hurt. It was unusually quiet. George and the crew were absent, waiting for the insurance companies' inspectors to assess the damage.

She turned when a car drove into the parking lot. Patrick got out, glanced at the motel, and pulled her into his arms.

"I'm so sorry, but it's not too bad."

"Yes, it is." She stepped back. "George thinks it'll be hard to find the additional crew he needs to finish the restoration."

"I know you're under a lot of pressure because of

your mother's will."

Anger flashed through her. "Who told you about the will?"

He chuckled. "It's all over Misery, small towns, you know. Anyway, I think I can help."

That stopped her. "Help with what?"

"My uncle has a small home building business. Maybe he can spare a few workers for a couple of weeks."

"That would be amazing. Thank you!" She kissed him lightly on the lips and he drew her into a lingering kiss. "Wow," she said, when they finally broke apart. He was a great kisser. "I...uh...I was about to get myself another cup of coffee. Want some?" She hoped she looked more composed than she felt.

He smiled, all confident and gorgeous. "I could use a cup."

After pouring two coffees in the kitchen, she led him to the porch, where they sat together on the loveseat.

The cloudless sky was so blue it almost hurt Erin's eyes. Sailboats skimmed the water while jet skis buzzed them like persistent mosquitoes. A ferry carried day trippers to Hope Island. So peaceful.

"You must love living here," Patrick said.

"Paradise Beach and I have a love-hate relationship. My brother Mick loves it, though."

"I saw him and Melanie in Georgia's yesterday," Patrick said. "Overheard them talking about Westside Development and you."

She frowned. "What did they say?"

"That Westside wants you to sign something and you won't."

Great! They know better than to discuss business in public. "How do you know them?"

"Saw them at Charlie's Tavern a few times. They—"

"I thought I heard voices back here." Justin appeared from around the side of the house. "Oh, I hoped to catch you alone."

Awkward. Erin forced a smile, and it probably looked it. "Justin, this is Patrick. He's visiting the area for a while. Patrick, Justin is an old friend."

Her heart skittered. Why was Justin here? Was he surprised by Patrick's presence? Did he feel even a tiny twinge of jealousy?

"Nice to meet you, Justin." Patrick pushed himself out of the loveseat and held out a hand.

Justin shook it. "That's your red convertible out there, right? Didn't I see you driving it out of Westside's parking lot yesterday?"

"You probably did. My company does business with Westside. What business are you in?"

"How do you know Erin?" Justin's smile was thin.

"I helped her get rid of some protesters at the motel a while back." He leaned down and kissed Erin's cheek. "Lucky day for me."

Did Patrick kiss her to get a rise out of Justin? She didn't like it. She shot a sideways glance at Justin. What was going through his head?

"Oh, that was you." Justin's expression hardened.

Erin sensed an ego battle coming. She got to her feet. "Justin, can I talk with you a minute? Alone?"

They went into the house.

"What in the hell was that all about?" she asked.

"What?" He gave an innocently puzzled look.

"You know damn well what I'm talking about."

"I care about you, and there's something about that guy I don't trust. You shouldn't either."

He had a lot of nerve warning her away from Patrick.

"You just met him, for God's sake. How do you know what he's like?"

"Okay, fine, Erin. I'll leave." He turned toward the door.

"Wait. Why did you stop by?"

"Never mind."

"Suit yourself." Why did she feel like crying? She didn't need this shit.

Erin returned to the porch. "Sorry about that, Patrick."

"An old boyfriend?" He smiled.

"Something like that. We haven't dated for years."

"Well, I better act fast before he's back in your life again. How about dinner at the restaurant in my hotel tonight? It's supposed to have the best cuisine around."

She wondered if having dinner at his hotel had a secondary purpose. It'll be interesting to find out. And Justin could go to hell.

"Sounds great."

"Okay, I'll pick you up at seven."

"Not necessary. I'll meet you there."

What would happen tonight? Whatever it was, she was ready to purge the Justin what-ifs out of her brain.

Patrick's kiss was warm and urgent. "See you tonight."

Chapter Twenty-Seven

Erin left her car with the hotel valet, then crossed the lobby to Restaurant Margaux. Within the softly lit interior, sophisticated jazz played in the background while servers moved among the tables. She spotted Patrick sitting at the far end of the bar, chatting with the bartender.

He was so good-looking. And kind, thoughtful and intelligent. She could get used to having him around. He caught her staring at him and a smile lit his face. The power of that smile shot through every nerve in her body. When she slid onto the stool next to him, he kissed her cheek.

"You look beautiful."

"Thank you."

Her short black dress crept up her thigh and she tugged it down. He placed his hand over hers and stopped her.

The bartender lifted a golden bottle of Champagne from a silver wine bucket and held it out to her as if it were a very special gift. Surprisingly, the bottle itself was clear. It was the champagne that was golden.

"Beautiful," she whispered, sliding a glance at Patrick.

After the bartender poured, they touched glasses and Erin sipped, loving the feeling of Champagne bubbles bursting on her tongue.

Patrick set his glass down and met Erin's gaze. "Tell me about your day."

In this romantic room, with this gorgeous man, she was lost for words and said the first thing that popped into her mind. "Nothing very interesting, just keeping an eye on the insurance investigators." *Oh God.* What was wrong with her?

"I'll get you some construction help soon. What needs to be done besides repairing the truck damage?"

The bartender refreshed their glasses as she explained the work needed before the township issued occupancy permits. After the second glass of Champagne, a pleasant little buzz set in. "What time is our dinner reservation?"

"How about dinner in my suite, if that's okay with you?"

"It is." Her pulse spiked. Was she ready for this?

Patrick signaled for the check, signed it, and grabbed the unfinished bottle of Champagne. His hand was warm on the small of her back as they crossed the lobby to the elevator.

When the doors closed, he said, "I've been waiting to do this all day." He pulled her close, and they passionately kissed, breaking apart only when the door opened on his floor.

Inside his suite, more sips of Champagne and a round of feverish kissing left her weak. His phone buzzed, and he reluctantly disengaged himself to glance at the screen.

"Sorry. I have to take this."

He walked toward a corner of the room talking and returned a few minutes later, his hand covering the phone's mouthpiece. "I'm going to be a while. Dinner will be arriving soon." He kissed her forehead. "I'll be with you as quickly as I can." He flashed a regretful frown over his shoulder as he entered the bedroom and closed the door.

Erin briefly wondered what was so important, but the Champagne had pretty much dulled any questions she had except one. When? If this was his idea of foreplay, it was working.

She wandered to the balcony doors, where reflections of city lights wavered in the dark water below. Almost as beautiful as the starlit sky. She finished her Champagne. What was taking so long?

The doorbell rang. She passed the bedroom door on her way to answer it. Inside, Patrick was speaking.

"Yes... I think so... Don't worry, I've got this."

Erin unlocked the door and opened it. A server with a wheeled tray of covered dishes waited in the hallway.

"Dinner for Mr. Patrick Guthrie," he said.

Patrick Guthrie? "Come in." She stepped aside.

The server set the dining table with a white linen cloth, China plates, crystal glassware, and shiny silverware. Then placed a low bouquet of dark red roses in the center. Next, he set a wine bucket on one end of the table and nestled an unopened bottle of Champagne among the ice cubes. "Would you like me to stay and serve?"

"No. Thank you." Patrick Guthrie. Her desire melted away.

The server nodded and left.

Patrick emerged smiling from the bedroom and walked to the table. "This looks terrific. What do you think?"

"You said your last name was Roth."

Suspicion and anger fought for control.

His smile dimmed. "It is."

"Then why did the server call you Patrick Guthrie?"

Patrick studied her face for a moment. "My surname is Roth-Guthrie."

"Are you related to Lou Guthrie, CFO of Westside Development?"

He reached for the Champagne bottle, slowly uncorked it, and poured two glasses. "Let's not talk about this right now." He handed her a flute and picked up his own, then walked to the glass doors and slid them open. "It's beautiful out here. Let's enjoy our Champagne on the balcony."

She didn't move. "I want to know if you're related to Lou Guthrie."

He hesitated, then slowly turned toward her. "He's my uncle."

"And he asked you to what…to get to know me, so you could convince me to sign an agreement to hand over my inheritance to my brother?"

A shadow crossed his face. "It might have started out that way, and I'm glad it did. I wouldn't have met you otherwise. But I really care about you, Erin. With or without you signing anything."

Erin set the Champagne glass on the table. "I can't believe I've been played like this." She grabbed her purse and started for the door.

"Don't go. It's a good deal for you and your brother. The Paradise Beach property is a key piece of the development plan. You can practically name your price. All they want is a guarantee you'll sign your inheritance over to Mick."

She marched to the door and pulled it open.

"Erin, please don't go. I promise I won't mention the property again."

"Go to hell."

****

Erin's Champagne headache the following morning helped her focus on the two thoughts fitting between the rhythmic thuds at her temples. What to do about Patrick's betrayal and how to cope with the damaged motel without exceeding the will's timeline? The Patrick issue was trivial, but the motel problem had to be figured out. After dressing, she went outside to where George studied a clipboard and glanced at motel units one to six.

He looked up. "So, do you want the bad news or the bad news?"

Her headache pounded. "Just tell me, please."

"In order to make the restoration deadline, I need more crew. I called every construction company within fifty miles. No dice. There might be workers available from farther out, but when you factor in the cost of gas, housing, and food, it wasn't worth bringing 'em in."

When she'd agreed to Mick's compromise, she wouldn't have minded missing the construction deadline because she wouldn't have to stick around for another eight months to run the motel. But by the time the truck plowed into it, she'd mentally and emotionally committed to seeing the restoration completed for Mick and April.

George's face was grim. "That's not all. The repair cost is a big problem. I know the insurance money will come through. But between the time it takes to get the money, and finding additional workers, I'm afraid finishing the job on time is looking impossible."

"There must be something we can do. Please. I can get a bank loan."

He let out a long breath. . "As I said before, the main problem is finding help. I'll go back to the office and try to work something out, but I don't know, Erin." His eyes looked uneasy. "Don't get your hopes up."

As he started toward his truck, an ancient motorhome pulled into the parking lot and stopped in front of the undamaged section of the motel. A ruddy-faced, white-haired man leaped out of the driver's side door. His black and red plaid shirt flapped over faded jeans. Tanned forearms protruded from his rolled-up shirtsleeves. He whistled and scanned the wrecked building.

"Looks like a bomb went off. The newspaper picture didn't do it justice."

George sauntered over to him. A wide grin creased his weathered face. "Your RV is a classic. Looks in pretty good shape, considering its age. Is it an '85?"

"An '80. Picked her up cheap about six, seven years ago." He stuck out his hand. "I'm Eddie, by the way."

George grasped the hand. "Glad to meet you. I'm George."

Erin warily joined them. "Can I help you?"

"Erin?" Eddie held out his arms and tears teetered on his lower eyelids. "Are you Erin? You're grown up and so beautiful."

She stepped back. "Who are you?"

He dropped his arms. "I'm your dad."

"My father is dead."

"So that's what she told you." He swiped his eyes and chuckled. "That's my Rhonda. For years, I begged her to let me visit. But she said she'd cut off my balls if I came within ten miles of this place." He lowered his head. "I wanted to come to her funeral, but didn't think it was a good idea, seein' as you probably wouldn't recognize me."

"I don't believe you." She was on the verge of flying apart. Already on aggravation overload, this strange person shows up. "I want you to leave. Now."

George moved between Eddie and Erin. "Sorry, buddy, you better go."

Mick came out of the house. "What's going on?"

"Is that my little Micky? Christ Almighty. It's me. Your dad."

Mick stopped short and stared at Erin. "What the hell is he talking about?"

George rubbed the back of his neck. "I think I'm going to take off unless you need me. This looks like a family matter."

Erin nodded. "Okay, we can handle this."

Eddie slipped a wallet from his pants pocket and pulled out a driver's license. "See?" He handed it to Mick.

"It says his name is Edward Brady," Mick said, "and the birth date is right."

"How can I make you believe me? Rhonda and I were married on September 4th and—"

"I'm getting Shirley," Mick said. "She'll know if it's him."

A few minutes later, Shirley strode up, hands on hips, glowering at Eddie. "I don't believe it, you sack of shit. You were supposed to be dead. How dare you come back after all this time!"

"He *is* our father, then?" Erin asked, disbelief morphing into shock and anger.

Shirley grimaced. "Unfortunately, yes."

Damn it Rhonda. Your non-accidental death, your manipulative will, and now your dead husband? Are you watching me from wherever you are and laughing your butt off?

"Can we just sit down and talk?" Eddie asked.

Erin scowled. "He knows Rhonda's dead and wants the motel."

"You're our dad." Mick's voice was full of wonder, like a child seeing stacks of presents under the Christmas tree.

Tears trickled down Eddie's face. He nodded.

Shirley shot him a disgusted look. "As much as I'd like to stay and hear what this a-hole has to say for himself, I'm going to be late for work if I don't leave now. Do you need me for anything?"

"Not right now. Thanks, Shirley," Erin said.

"Let's go sit on the back porch and hear what he has to say, okay Erin?" Mick asked.

"I don't believe this," she said, but stomped toward the back of the house.

Chapter Twenty-Eight

Erin settled on a porch chair, not wanting to chance Eddie sitting next to her on the loveseat. Of all the crap that happened in the past months, this was close to the worst. Good thing school vacation had started and April was at Olivia's. Erin didn't want her daughter to see her this angry.

"Why did you leave, Dad?" Mick's voice broke.

"I'm sorry, son. First off, I was only twenty-seven-years-old with a wife, two kids and a motel to maintain and run. The world was breaking my back. I'm not proud of this, but I did a runner even though I loved all of you."

Erin sprung out of her chair. "That's enough."

"Just hold on a minute, okay Erin? Let him tell us what happened. Please?"

With a heavy sigh, Erin resumed her seat.

"Go ahead, Dad," Mick said.

"Thanks, Micky. I hoped to get a job on an oil rig in Texas and make some real money. But every young guy in the world hoped the same thing. Texas was where the real growth was, not Michigan. After six months, I missed you all so much I told Rhonda to pack you all up and come live with me. She promised to think about it. Eventually, she came out alone. We couldn't work it out, though. She said the motel was a legacy from her parents. It was home, and she didn't want to leave. Then she found out I'd been seeing someone. It wasn't a big deal. This gal and I just had a few drinks and laughs together. It didn't mean nothin' but she told me to drop dead and left. I guess that's why she told you kids the story she did."

No one spoke for a few minutes, then Mick said, "We missed you too, Dad."

"Speak for yourself." Her headache was getting worse. "You can't miss what you never had."

Eddie pulled out a crumpled handkerchief and blew his nose.

Mick pulled Eddie into a hug. "I'm glad you're here."

"What the hell are you doing, Mick?" Erin shouted. "Rhonda's probably turning over in her grave. It's his fault she was a wreck all those years and that this place is a disaster." She picked up the plastic bowl and opened it. "Rhonda told us this was you." She dumped the ashes over the porch rail.

Eddie's belly laugh was loud and long, and tears spilled down his face. "That Rhonda. What a woman." He gave one more laugh before a shadow crossed his face. "I should have come back anyway, even though she threatened to kill me if I did."

"You're here now." Mick sniffled. "You're staying for a while, right?"

Eddie glanced at Erin. "Well, uh—"

"No!" Erin's simmering anger was about to explode.

"Come on. He's our father."

"I don't give a shit."

"How about for the night? Please, Erin?"

Mick looked so hopeful she couldn't refuse.

"Okay, but I want him gone in the morning and he's not staying in the house."

"Not to worry. That's what the motorhome is for," Eddie said. "You were a pretty little girl and you've become a beautiful woman. I can't tell you the number of times I—"

"Just stop it."

As she entered the house, Eddie said, "She hates me, doesn't she?"

Shirley came back to the porch. "I forgot. I don't need to be at work for another hour." She turned to Eddie. "What the hell do you expect? You left Rhonda with two small kids and a motel, you mother-f... I can't even say it, although that's what you are. Erin's been through a lot and you just make it a hell of a lot worse, asshole."

****

Erin rolled out of bed the next morning and went to the window. *Shit.* Eddie's RV was still in the parking lot. She went to the bathroom and swallowed an antacid. If he stayed out of sight, she just might make it through the day without exploding. A lot going on besides his unwelcome presence, and she needed to be clear-headed. She threw on jeans and a shirt and started down the stairs. Midway, she smelled bacon and coffee. Then Eddie's voice reached her.

She steeled herself and continued to the kitchen where Eddie was at the stove, pushing bacon strips around in a cast-iron skillet, while Mick watched and April sat at the table. "How did you get in here?" Her throat was so tight it was hard to get the words out. "I locked the doors last night."

Eddie looked over his shoulder. "Erin, honey, sit

down. Breakfast is almost ready."

"Don't call me honey. I said, how did you get in here?"

"The door was open, and I wanted to fix my kids some breakfast."

Erin glanced at Mick, who smiled and shrugged.

"Why didn't you tell me I had a grandpa?" April asked. "He told us about working on a ranch in Texas and riding a bull in a rodeo."

Erin's jaw tightened. He's trying to impress her daughter.

"I didn't know myself. Anyway, what are you doing home? Weren't you spending the night at Olivia's?"

"We got into a fight last night and I called Uncle Mick to pick me up. Are you mad at me?"

"No." She pulled a cup out of the cupboard, banged it on the countertop, and poured coffee.

"What time do you have to be at school?" Eddie asked. "I don't want you to be late."

What the hell? He's been here less than a day and already acting like a member of the family.

"It's summer vacation." April grinned.

"Right. Grab some plates for me, will you Mick?" Eddie looked toward the hallway. "Where's Shirley?"

"Still sleeping."

Mick grabbed plates from the cupboard and went to the stove, where Eddie placed a piece of French toast and a few bacon strips on each one. Mick sent the plates on the table.

How could Mick and April betray her like this? Act as if Eddie's showing up was a good thing?

"It's a little too late to play daddy, Eddie. And you

were supposed to stay in your fleabag motel on wheels."

"Come on, Erin. Lighten up," Mick said. "Dad's just trying to help."

"Stay out of this, Mick. Eddie, come out to the back porch with me. Please."

"Okay, okay." Once Eddie turned off the flame and slid the frying pan off the hot burner, he followed Erin outside.

"This is what I see. You didn't want a family anymore, so you took off, leaving Rhonda to take care of everything. And now that Paradise Beach is worth a lot of money and Rhonda is dead, you decide to come back? Well, there's no way. Get into that piece of junk of yours and go back to wherever the hell you came from."

"Will you let me explain?"

"No. Just leave."

Mick ambled onto the porch. "I put our breakfasts in the oven to keep them warm."

"Thanks. Now let's get Eddie off the property."

"No. I want him to stay."

"After everything he did to Rhonda and us, you want to forgive him?"

Eddie half-sat on the porch rail. "I'd like to tell you two what happened."

"I don't care. Just—"

"It's not going to kill you to hear him out, Erin." Mick handed her a mug. "Here's some coffee. Let's just sit down and listen."

Mick might be right, and listening was the least she could do. She sighed.

"Okay, fine. Let's hear it."

"Me and your mom, we were pretty young when we got married. Too young. Then you came along pretty quick, Erin, then your grandparents passed and Rhonda inherited Paradise Beach. A few years later, Mick was born. I..." He took out his handkerchief and wiped it under his eyes. "I was a coward. Couldn't hack all the responsibility, so I took off. A few months later, I wanted the three of you to come out to Texas and stay with me. But like I said yesterday, Rhonda refused. And after her trip to Texas, said I was dead to her and apparently that's what she'd told you. That I was dead. Breaks my heart."

"Why wouldn't you come home, anyway?" Mick asked.

"Running a motel wasn't my thing. And after living in Texas for a while, I couldn't face folks here in Misery, knowing I'd left Rhonda and you kids."

"What kind of father does that?" Erin said. "Runs off and leaves his wife and two little kids?"

"Why don't you ease up a little, Erin? Can't you see he's trying?"

"No, all I see is a father who abandoned his life here, then returns when he wants something. So, Eddie, I suppose you know you own Paradise Beach because it's joint marital property."

"I suppose that would be right, but that's not why I'm here."

"Bull." Erin walked toward the door.

"Listen, I worked on construction for a while in Texas and when I read an article in the newspaper about that truck plowing into the motel, I thought I could help. Before you ask, I keep up with what's going on in the *Misery Cove Times*. I read it online."

"Erin, George said we need help if we're going to make Mom's deadline," Mick said.

"Don't you get it? That whole thing about the will is out the window. Eddie and Rhonda jointly owned the property, so now only Eddie owns it. There's no inheritance and no deadlines anymore. Apparently, Rhonda didn't consider Eddie when she wrote the will."

"Hang on there. Here's what you don't know." Eddie squared his shoulders. "I stopped by Dean's office on the way into town yesterday." He chuckled. "He looked like he'd seen a ghost. Anyway, I told him I don't want Paradise Beach and want to gift it to you two with the exact provisions in Rhonda's will. I figured she knew what she was doing. It'll be ready for my signature in a day or two. So again, I can help with the construction work. Just point me in the right direction."

"Erin, this could be a good thing."

Erin's brain churned. "I can't think right now. Put him to work. But listen, Eddie. Stay out of my way and stay out of the house, do you hear me?"

He winked and saluted.

She went into the house and heard Shirley moving around in her bedroom. Erin knocked on the door. Shirley opened it. Her face was puffy with sleep.

"What?"

"What time do you start work today?"

"Nine."

"Want to go out for breakfast?"

"Sure, give me a couple of hours."

"What?"

Shirley laughed. "Just kidding. I'll be ready in five."

****

Brioni's in Port Elizabeth opened at seven, and it was packed when Erin and Shirley arrived at eight-fifteen. Erin steered Shirley to the counter at the front of the restaurant where they ordered. When their orders were ready, they sat at the only available spot, a counter-width window ledge with three stools. The window faced Main Street, where runners, bikers, and walkers competed for the narrow sidewalk.

Shirley unrolled her napkin and set the silverware on her plate next to the cinnamon rolls. "What's up? We never go out for breakfast. You have bad news?"

"No. The insurance people said the checks won't take long since it's clear the damage to the motel was an accident. A brake failure or something. In the meantime, there's still enough of Rhonda's money left to cover additional labor in the short run. If we can find anyone."

"That's great news." Shirley brushed cinnamon dust from her lips.

"There's something else. I was going to talk with you about it yesterday, but Eddie's arrival distracted me."

"Hurricane Eddie, in my opinion."

"You're totally right. Anyway, yesterday I called Detective Mackey to see if they've uncovered anything new about Rhonda's case. She said I should give it a rest since the case is closed."

The conversation still upset her. She looked down at the runny, brownish, breakfast burrito she'd ordered, covered it with a napkin, and pushed it aside.

"Figures. Some of the cops around here have no imaginations. They should take a look at some of the

218

great crime dramas on TV. Reading a few mysteries wouldn't hurt either."

Erin sipped her coffee. "Anyway, I'm not giving it a rest. I've been waking up in the middle of the night trying to work out what Rhonda's, Laura's and Marilyn's deaths have in common, besides what we already talked about."

"Well, there's no common M.O. unless you consider staging a murder to look like an accident or suicide, an M.O. M.O. is short for *modus operandi*."

"Thanks for educating me." Erin smiled, then let it fade. "What if after a year, I have to return to Denver, never knowing how or why Rhonda died?"

"Take it from me, you won't." Shirley glanced at her watch. "Time to get to work."

Chapter Twenty-Nine

The next day, Erin found Eddie in the kitchen putting away groceries, as if Paradise Beach was his home. "What are you doing?"

"Shirley asked me to pick up a few things at the store."

Why was Shirley treating Eddie like he lived here? This was too much.

"When are you leaving? Today, I hope."

He set a carton of milk in the refrigerator. "Afraid not. I have an appointment with Dean in a few days to sign the papers giving Paradise over to you and Mick. I also told George I know a few guys in the area, some old friends. They're retired plumbers, carpenters, and electricians. We're ready to help with the motel."

"How do you still know people around here?"

"Me and the guys kept in touch all these years. In fact, they visited me in Texas and I got some of them jobs. Most came back to Michigan over the years. Anyways, George said he was grateful and that with the extra labor, we just might make the deadline. Me and the guys are starting first thing tomorrow morning."

"George should have asked me first." She was losing control of everything—who comes into the house, who gets hired to work on the motel. Everything. "You went behind my back."

"Sit down a minute, honey. I have something to

say." Eddie plopped down on a kitchen chair.

She remained standing. "Eddie, what exactly do you want?"

"For starters, I wonder if you could call me Dad."

"Absolutely not."

He wasn't getting it.

"Erin, I'm sorry if I stepped on your toes. I promise to talk with you first if anything like this comes up again. I know you don't want me here, but please give me until the end of the day Tuesday to see if you want me to stay or not. Whichever way it works out, the guys will stay and help."

Silence.

"Okay, let me tell you a story." Eddie got out of the chair and faced Erin. "I really didn't want to spill everything in front of Mick."

"Spill what?"

"I really loved Rhonda, but wasn't good enough for her."

"Wow."

Oldest excuse in the book. She started walking away.

"Can't you please listen for two minutes?"

She sighed, but stopped.

"I had a heart attack last year and was in the hospital for a few days. It scared the hell out of me. A guy about the same age as me was in the next bed. He had a heart attack too but had family coming to see him all the time, a daughter, son and three grandkids. They put big smiles on his face, fussed over him, brought him things. I got to thinking about what I missed—you and Mick growing up, April being born. I swear, if I could do it over, I would never leave."

He looked away for a moment, then back at Erin. His eyes were red. "Honestly, honey, I don't want anything from you. Please, just let me help."

Damn. He was getting to her, but she had the feeling he'd be more trouble than he was worth.

"If George thinks you and your friends can get the motel up and running on time, you can stay, but don't come into the house unless you're invited. By me. And don't call me honey."

****

Later that day, Erin held the front door open, waiting for Shirley as she left her car. "We have to talk."

"You couldn't let me get into the house before you pounced?" Shirley squeezed past Erin and dropped her purse on the entry table. "What's up?"

"You know what."

She was still steaming about Shirley sending Eddie on errands, making him feel part of the family. Little by little, he was easing himself into their lives and he's gone far enough.

Shirley glanced toward the living room, where April lounged in front of the TV. "Let's talk in my room."

"Fine."

Shirley closed the door once they were in her bedroom. "Sorry. I'd been talking to Eddie and decided he is telling the truth about wanting to get to know his kids and grandchild. But now I'm mad. He promised he wouldn't tell you."

"Tell me what?"

"That you, me, and Mick think Rhonda, Laura, and Marilyn were murdered."

"You told him about the murders?" Erin erupted.

Shirley's eyes widened. "Isn't that what you wanted to talk to me about?"

"No. That was about sending him to the store. Why on earth did you tell him about the murders?"

"I figured sooner or later he'd hear it somewhere and it would be better coming from me. He has a right to know."

"You could have talked to me about it first."

Shirley sat on her bed. "Sure, and what would you have said? You've been determined to send him away ever since he got here. But he wants to get to know his kids and granddaughter. Is that a bad thing? Mick and April want him to stay."

"I guess how I feel doesn't count for anything." Erin's eyes stung.

Shirley grabbed Erin's hand and pulled her down next to her. "I'm sorry you feel your feelings don't count. They do. I wasn't happy when Eddie turned up, but then I got to thinking. Eddie has feelings too. Mostly, he's really upset you hate him. I admit it was impulsive and maybe not wise of me to tell him about the murders, but what's done is done."

"He left Rhonda with—"

"I know what he did. He regrets it. Is it so hard to let him stick around for a while? After all, he got guys to help with the motel. They'll be here tomorrow. And he wants to help us find Rhonda's killer. It can't hurt."

Erin remembered Eddie saying Rhonda was the one who kept him away. He said he'd wanted his family with him. She glanced out the window. Eddie was talking with Mick in front of the RV. They looked like a normal father and son, enjoying each other's company.

"Okay, he can stay for a while, but I reserve the right to kick him out if he screws up."

****

"Morning, Erin," Eddie said, starting up the porch stairs as if he were approaching a wild animal. "Nice day to be sitting out here."

Erin looked up from her tablet, feeling slightly guilty about the way she'd acted the day before. "It is. Can I help you with something?"

"Shirley told me you're looking into who could have killed Rhonda. Would you mind telling me what you found out?"

He had a right to know. She figured that out at three in the morning.

"Okay. Only Shirley, Mick and I are in on this, so please don't mention it to anyone."

He smiled and mimed pulling a zipper across his lips.

"Sit down, if you want to."

Eddie lowered himself into the chair next to hers. "I'm sorry I—"

He looked so humble she felt sorry for him. "Let's forget about it, okay? I suppose Shirley told you why we think someone murdered Rhonda."

He nodded.

"That's all we know. Truthfully, I'm stuck. I've been asking her friends if they know anyone who would want to hurt her, but no one has a clue."

"What about if our family and Shirley get together and brainstorms?" Eddie asked. "Not just Rhonda's death, but the others, too. Seems there must be a link in there somewhere."

"You knew them, didn't you? Laura and Marilyn?"

"Not much. A little at school. But once me and Rhonda got together after high school, they were already away at college. So, what do you say? The four of us have a planning meeting?"

Why hadn't she thought of brainstorming? "Sure. Sounds good."

"Hey, I have to ask, when did you start calling your mother by her first name?"

"Don't go there."

Chapter Thirty

It was Eddie's idea to hold the meeting in his motorhome. Erin had been fine with that. The less time he spent in the house, the fewer reminders of him would be around when he left. She'd expected a shabby old man cave. But everything gleamed and smelled of pine-scented cleaning products. The couch and chairs wore gray and black plaid upholstery, and gray vinyl wood-like planks covered the floor.

Framed photos of her, Rhonda, Eddie, and Mick covered walls and counters. Her first Christmas, Mick's and her birthdays, family fishing, and building snowmen. Her mom and dad were happy, and she'd felt safe and loved back then. But Eddie's leaving in the middle of the night and Rhonda's reaction to it had changed it all. For a long time, she'd blamed Eddie for dying and Rhonda for falling apart afterwards. Now she wasn't sure who to blame.

Eddie smiled as he set a plate of chocolate chip cookies on the dining table. A pot of coffee brewed in the galley. He'd respected her request not to enter the house unless she invited him. And she hadn't. Thinking about it now, she sort of regretted it. Paradise Beach had been his home, but she wasn't ready to open that door yet.

Shirley came into the RV and whispered something to Eddie that started him laughing. She turned to Erin.

"Place looks pretty good, don't you think?"

"I'm actually stunned."

"Son," Eddie called out as Mick opened the door. "Please brush that sawdust off your clothes before you come in."

Mick nodded and retreated. Back inside, he headed for the galley, picked up the coffee mugs Eddie filled, and set them on the table.

"When did Mick get so domestic?" Shirley murmured.

Erin shook her head. "No idea."

"Okay, now that everyone's here," Eddie said, "let's sit down and get this thing done. Go for it, Erin."

Another surprise. She hadn't expected this take-charge side of Eddie. But, of course, she barely knew him. "Okay, everyone," she said. "I want to make sure we're all on the same page, so I have a question. Do you believe Rhonda's, Laura's, and Marilyn's deaths, and maybe Shirley's fire are connected?"

Mick nodded. "Totally."

"Yep," Eddie said.

"Of course. Everything happened within the last three months and we were old friends..." Her eyes widened. "Oh my God."

Erin stared. "What's wrong?"

"Nothing." Shirley gasped, then cleared her throat. "Nothing's wrong. Just keep going."

"If you're sure..."

"I am."

"Okay." Erin opened her tablet and paged through some notes. "I learned that senior Westside officers, like the CEO or CFO, weren't implicated in the murders, so who else could it be?"

"Where'd you hear that?" Mick asked.

"I can't tell you, but I believe it. Any ideas on who else could be the killer?"

No one spoke.

"Okay," Erin said, "Here's an idea. We've been treating Westside as a single entity, as in 'Westside probably killed Rhonda.' But what about lower-level individuals who might want to ensure the project goes forward for personal reasons?" She glanced at Mick. "For example, Melanie. She hooked up with Mick a few months before Rhonda—"

Mick slammed his fist on the table, shaking the coffee mugs. "Wait a damn minute. You're saying my future wife could be a murderer?"

Eddie put a hand on Mick's arm. "I know it's hard to swallow, but we need to check out everyone. Even Melanie. From what I hear, she'll be rolling in dough when the condos sell, so she has a huge reason to make sure they get built."

"You want to know who killed your mother, don't you, Mick?" Shirley said.

"Yes, I do, but we're wasting our time with Melanie."

Erin scrolled through her tablet. "There is one more thing. Melanie talked to both Rhonda and Shirley about selling their land. Also, Laura recently asked her about selling her house and Marilyn talked to her about buying the cottage she was renting. She's been in all their homes in the last two months."

Mick's face was red. "Okay! I get it. But Melanie never murdered anyone."

"I don't think you'll like what I'm going to say next, Mick," Erin said.

His face tightened. "Go ahead."

"You and Melanie got together a few months before Rhonda died and before anyone knew Rhonda changed her will. I'm guessing that at some point, you told her that when Rhonda passed away, you'd inherit Paradise Beach. Or maybe she already knew. Many people did. It's possible she seduced you to into a relationship and eventually suggested marriage to make sure you'd sell the property to Westside, since Westside couldn't get anywhere with Rhonda and Shirley. Melanie could have taken things into her own hands and murdered Rhonda."

"Erin!" The red blotches on Mick's face grew darker.

"I think she only planned to kill Rhonda at first," Erin said, "but then Laura planned to call the EPA and report the environmental problems, and Shirley wouldn't sign the sales agreement. Marilyn fits in somewhere, but I don't know how yet."

Mick scooted back from the table. "You finished crucifying Melanie? If not, I'm leaving."

She might have gone a little overboard. "Sorry, Mick. Help us prove she didn't do it."

He moved back to the table. "Okay, but this sucks."

"If the project goes through, Guthrie will make a bundle too," Eddie said.

"Guthrie's the chief financial officer," Erin said, "but it wouldn't hurt to check him out. He might have a personal interest like Melanie. Anyone else?"

"Why him and not the rest of the Westside top brass?" Shirley asked. "They might all have personal interests and they'll all make a lot of money."

Except for herself, no one knew about Guthrie's relationship with Melanie. What if he planned to marry Melanie when she divorced Mick after getting control of the money from the sale of Paradise? She laughed to herself. She was seeing conspiracies everywhere.

"How about we just focus on Guthrie for now? So, who else?"

Shirley lifted her chin. "What about Zachary?"

"Motive?" Erin asked.

"He was one of the people Rhonda would dress up for. And someone she knew."

"Right. We can't eliminate anyone until we check out their alibis," Erin said.

"You said Mom called Father Joseph the day she died," Mick said. "What about him?"

"I've considered that too," Erin said. "She could have invited him to Paradise Beach and confessed something she did that involves Laura and Marilyn."

"Like what?" Mick asked.

"Like they did something terrible in school and someone got hurt or died. What if he gave her absolution, then killed her while she was in a state of grace, thinking he was saving her soul? Then decided to save the other women's souls the same way."

Shirley frowned. "That doesn't make any sense. Why would Father Joseph commit murder and damn himself to hell?"

"A bargain with the devil. Three souls going to heaven in exchange for his," Erin said. "Let's keep him in for now. So far, we have Father Joseph, Mrs. Masters, Zachary, Melanie, and Lou Guthrie as suspects."

"What about the protesters?" Eddie asked.

"We'd have to track down all the fringe elements who were so desperate to see the project fail they'd kill anyone in their way. For now, let's stick with the names we have, plus add Dean and Steve. So, seven suspects."

"Steve and Dean wouldn't hurt a fly," Shirley said.

"But they're on the list of people Rhonda would dress up for if they were coming over for drinks, so let's leave them on for the time being. If we come up empty on the names we have so far, we can circle back to the protesters. Rhonda probably knew some of them well enough to have them over for drinks. Anyone else?"

Silence.

"Okay then," Erin said. "Please let me know by the end of the day if you want to help. Don't forget we're looking for a murderer and it could get dangerous."

Shirley waved her hand. "Danger smanger. We don't have to come out with guns blazing, you know. Remember the fluffy amateur detective from a British book series who seems harmless but isn't? She went around asking grandmotherly gossipy questions to bag the killers."

Eddie got to his feet. "Of course I'm in. No way I'll sit around here doing nothing when I could be out there looking for Rhonda's killer."

"Sorry I was a little touchy, Erin," Mick said. "Thanks for trying to find Mom's killer. Just tell me what you want me to do."

"Thanks, Mick. And I appreciate all of you. Let's meet here tomorrow morning at eight. I'll have a plan ready."

As Mick and Shirley started out the door, Erin turned back. "Do you have plans for dinner, Eddie?"

"Uh…no."

"How about joining Mick, April, Shirley and me, about five? It's pizza night if that's okay with you."

Eddie grinned. "I'll bring the wine."

****

Erin entered Eddie's place at eight-ten the following morning. Three pairs of eyes looked up at her from the dining table.

"Sorry I'm late. I got halfway here and realized I forgot something." She handed Eddie a shopping bag.

He peeked inside. "What's this?"

"Personal safety alarms and pepper spray containers. Pass it around and everyone, please take one of each."

"Seriously?" Shirley asked. "Do you really think we'll need that stuff?"

"Maybe not, but we have to be prepared. Last night, I came up with a plan to catch the murderer. First step is to find out where the suspects were on the date and time a murder was committed."

"You know, everybody's going to say they were home alone when we ask them, especially the murderer," Shirley said.

"Or that they were out for dinner or a movie or something," Erin said. "That's where smart questioning comes in. There's a technique called Cunningham's Law that says the best way to get a right answer on the internet is to post a wrong assumption. In other words, to get accurate information, write something you know is wrong and someone will want to correct it. We could use this to question people."

"I'm confused," Mick said. "How about an example?"

"Say you want to question Mrs. Masters. She's known Laura, Rhonda, Marilyn, and Shirley since they were kids. Get her to talk about them. Then say you were driving on Laura's street the night she died and saw her on Laura's porch. Mrs. Masters will deny it and want to tell you exactly where she was. We'll follow up on what the subjects say. Of course, the killer will be lying."

Mick snorted. "Mrs. Masters hates that Laura built a contemporary home on school property and would never visit her."

"That's the point. According to an article I read about Cunningham's Law, people can't help themselves from correcting false things you say about them."

Eddie grinned. "Pretty smart." His grin faded. "And it could be dangerous. Our suspects are people that have probably never had to comment on their whereabouts to anyone. At best, they'll tell us the truth about where they were. At worst, the killer will know we're on to him or her."

"That's why we need to be clever. Ask questions anyone would ask during a normal conversation. By the way, none of us will question our subjects alone. Each of us will have a partner."

"Who's mine?" Shirley asked.

"Mick. You two will question Dean, Steve, and Lou Guthrie."

"I'm cool with that," Mick said.

Shirley nudged Mick, grinning. "Me too."

They looked too excited, like it was a game. It scared her.

"Eddie and I will question Mrs. Masters, Father Joseph, Melanie, and Zachary."

"Sounds good to me," Eddie said. "Except for one thing."

"What?" Erin asked.

"Mrs. Masters hates my guts."

"We'll figure something out."

"Pairing us up might not be such a good idea," Shirley said. "I get why you want to do it, but it's not natural if you want the meetings to look casual. Mick and I don't hang out together."

Erin paused for a moment. "I understand. What about if we decide with our partner what's best for each interview? The important thing is safety. For example, one of us makes the contact and the other one stays close by. And try to approach your subject in a public place."

"That works," Shirley said.

"If you learn something that eliminates one of your subjects, call a meeting that day. We can all benefit from hearing how it was done and who's off the suspects list. And make sure your phone is always fully charged. I'll stop by the rectory this afternoon and have a chat with Mary Margaret."

"How about if we use our phones to track each other?" Mick said. "That way, we'll know where everyone is. I could set it up. Give me your phones. I'll bring them back when they're ready and show you how to use the tracking app."

"That's a great idea, Mick," Erin said.

She'd never seen this side of her brother. The intelligent and thoughtful side. Maybe it had been there all along and she hadn't noticed.

"It's wonderful that you're trying to find Rhonda's killer, Erin," Eddie said. "And thanks for dinner yesterday. Made me feel like part of the family."

She hated to admit it, but he was starting to grow on her.

"A couple of days ago, Shirley asked me to join the poker group," Eddie said. "There's a game tonight, and it'll be a good time to find out if Steve and Dean have alibis for any of the murders. Zachary too, if it doesn't look too obvious."

Shirley smiled. "Good thinking."

"Anything else?" Erin asked.

"I'm glad we're finally doing something." Mick started for the door. "Shirley, meet me in the living room in ten minutes. I'd like to tackle that asshole Guthrie."

Chapter Thirty-One

Erin marched outside as soon as Shirley's car pulled into the driveway that night. "Wasn't poker only supposed to last four hours? It's been six. You didn't let me know you'd be late."

"Okay, Mom," Shirley said. "Next time we will."

"Sorry Erin. It was my fault," Eddie said.

"I got worried. Where were you? I called, but you didn't pick up."

More than worried. Frantic. They could have been in an accident or something, and a murderer was lurking around.

"Let's go in the house," Shirley said.

They followed her inside and sat at the kitchen table.

"First, sorry about not answering our phones. We always have them on silent during poker and forgot to turn them back on." She gave Eddie a sideways glance. "After poker, we had a nightcap at Zinc."

Oh my God. Was a relationship in the works? She didn't want to think about it. "So, how did you two do?"

Eddie grinned. "I won a hundred bucks."

"I mean about questioning Steve, Dean, and Zachary."

"Just teasing. I knew what you meant, honey," Eddie said. "Tell her the good news, Shirl."

Shirl?

"Steve almost got a Royal Flush tonight," Shirley said. "He told us he got one at The Downtown Casino a couple of months ago. He was there with Dean and a group of guys from church. Dean said it was the night Rhonda died. They forgot all about it when they got home. The shock and all. They remembered later, but didn't think it was a good idea to bring it up. Anyway, they spent the night at the casino hotel and all the guys they went with could vouch for them."

"Excellent." Erin crossed Dean and Steve off the suspects list.

"We didn't work on Zachary," Eddie said. "It would have been awkward to get anything from him after the Royal Flush story. But we'll try again another time."

"Okay, but wait a few days. In the meantime, Eddie and I'll focus on Mrs. Masters."

Shirley yawned. "It's been a long day. Anyway, Mick and I are visiting Lou Guthrie's office tomorrow, supposedly to set up an appointment with him."

****

"Want a cappuccino? Eddie asked when Erin walked into the motorhome the next evening. "Got me a coffee machine this afternoon that has those little coffee pod thingies and a milk frother."

That was a surprise. Eddie seemed too old school to know what cappuccino was. "Sounds good, Mr. Barista."

Eddie chuckled. "Comin' right up."

"Where's April?" Shirley asked.

"Spending the night at Olivia's. Where else?" Erin said.

"She was really close to Olivia and her mother Kelly during the school year." Shirley said. "She doesn't want to go back to her old school."

"I know, and she won't." Erin accepted the coffee mug Eddie handed her. "I'm going to research schools in Denver before we leave for home next year."

Mick and Shirley glanced at each other.

"What?"

"She wants to stay here," Mick said. "Don't give me that look, Erin. You know she does."

Mick wanted April to stay in Misery Cove, and she didn't understand why. Or was it he wanted both April and her here? She couldn't deal with another discussion about it right now.

"Let's change the subject."

"But you know she—"

"Mick, please give your report."

"Okay, fine. We found out that Guthrie was at a three-day meeting in Houston when Mom died. And at a golf tournament in Miami when Marilyn was killed."

"How did you find that out?" Erin asked.

"Are we good or what?" Mick said. "You go ahead, Shirley."

"First, I asked Lou's executive assistant if I could have an appointment with him next week to discuss my land," Shirley said. "I wanted Lou's calendar up on her computer screen. Then I pretended to faint. When I supposedly came to, I asked her to take me to the ladies' room where I said I still felt dizzy. Drew that out as long as I could."

"In the meantime," Mick said, "I paged back on the calendar app to look for what he was doing on the murder dates and he wasn't even in Michigan."

"Outstanding," Erin said.

He'd been a bright kid when he was little. Good grades, good friends. But as he grew older, he'd changed. Maybe it was her fault. She'd left him home with Rhonda while she went to college and he'd hated running the motel. And why not? Rhonda didn't care about the motel either. But now, working on solving Rhonda's murder, he was a different person. Or the same person, but with a job he cared about.

"He could have lied to his assistant about where he was," Eddie said.

"He didn't." Mick stirred the froth on his cappuccino into the dark coffee underneath. "I phoned the Houston hotel later. Said I was Lou Guthrie's assistant, gave the date Mom died, and asked if anyone turned in his black leather portfolio. The clerk asked me his room number, and I said Mr. Guthrie didn't remember. Apparently, the front desk person looked it up and said, 'Yes, we have him in room 412 for three days. But no, I'm sorry. No one turned in his portfolio. We would have called him right away if we'd found it.'"

"We did the same thing for Guthrie in Miami," Shirley said. "I pretended to be his assistant and said he'd left his lucky shirt it the closet. The hotel verified Guthrie was in Miami when Marilyn died."

"So," Mick said, "he's out."

Eddie sat forward. "What if he hired someone to kill them? He had a perfect alibi for both."

"It's possible," said Erin, "but I don't think Rhonda would invite a hit man or hit woman over for a drink."

"But what about—" Eddie started.

"I know what you're going to say," Erin said.

"That Rhonda wouldn't know it was a hit person. But do you think Guthrie hired a murderer who is a good enough friend of Rhonda's that she'd grab a bottle of wine from the bar and dress up for them that night?"

Shirley rested her face in her hands. "I'm starting to get a headache with all these complications."

Mick downed his cappuccino, pulled a beer out of the refrigerator, and held it up. "Anyone else?" When no one answered, he unscrewed the top and sat back down. "I agree with Erin."

"Me too," said Shirley. "And I'm sure we can say Lou Guthrie is not the killer."

"So, three down, four to go and two of them are mine," Erin said. "I'll use the tactic Mick and Shirley used with Guthrie on Father Joseph. Also, I'm calling Zachary for an appointment tomorrow or the next day. I'll go in alone. Zachary might think something's off if both Eddie and I question him."

"Right," Eddie said. "But I'll be close."

"How about Melanie, Erin? When are you and Dad talking to her?"

Mick looked defensive and anxious.

"Isn't she at a real estate conference this week?" Erin asked.

"Yeah."

"Then I'll see if she can meet me next week and I can handle it alone, Eddie. I'll tell her we should talk about the wedding. Mick, have you set a date yet?"

"She won't do it and believe me, I've tried to pin her down."

"Do you think she'll go to lunch with me?" Erin asked. "The last time I saw her, she called me a bitch."

"She was just having a tantrum. She'll go."

****

When Erin returned to the house, she found April sitting cross-legged on the living room floor, watching TV. Erin sat down next to her, satisfied with the progress they were making, eliminating suspects. But the more they eliminated, the closer they were getting to the killer. Above everything else, she had to keep April safe.

April glanced out the window toward the RV. "You've been meeting with Grandpa again." Her eyes sparkled. "Are you actually beginning to like him?"

"Your grandfather and I have a mutual problem to solve."

"It must be about Granny since Uncle Mick and Shirley are in on it too, right?"

Her awesome kid was getting way too observant.

"Yes, they are, and we have a lot of work to do. How would you like to stay at Olivia's for the next week or two?"

"You want me out of the way, right?" She pulled a string dangling from her shirt. "Like I'm a baby or something?"

"I don't think you're a baby and yes, I want you in a safe place."

"That means this house isn't a safe place, so what about all of you? Please don't do this."

"I know it's hard to understand, but we need to help the police with their investigation. So, how do you feel about staying with Olivia for a while?"

"Great, Mom. She asked me to go up north with her and her parents, anyway."

"When?"

"The day after tomorrow. She wants me to stay two

weeks."

"Perfect. I'll call Kelly to get the details. Thanks for being such a cool kid."

April threw her arms around Erin. "I am, aren't I?"

Chapter Thirty-Two

"Hey, you two," Erin said, "how about helping me out when you finish breakfast?"

April and Mick looked up from their phones, wearing identically bewildered expressions at being jarred out of their cyber worlds. April absentmindedly bit into her breakfast sandwich.

"Did you say something, Mom?"

Kids had the amazing ability to filter out everything outside the images on their screens.

"Yes, I wondered if you and Mick could help me after breakfast."

"Help you with what?" Mick looked wary. "It's Saturday, and I was planning to relax all day."

"We haven't cleared out Rhonda's room yet, and Shirley needs more space for her clothes, since she'll be with us for a while. Before she left for work, she asked me save her a few of Rhonda's shirts."

Poor Shirley. On top of her house burning down, she'd lost her best friend, slept in her bed every night, and had to see Rhonda's clothes and personal items every day.

Mick slammed the last of his sandwich onto his plate. "You want to get rid of all her stuff, don't you?"

"No. Honest. You can decide what we keep and what we donate, okay? Also, we can look for clues to why she died. Maybe she kept a threatening note or letter. Maybe a diary."

"She never had a diary, I know that for sure," Mick said. "Okay, let's do it, but I'll be watching you."

April jumped up. "This is so cool. Let's go."

"Mick, can you find us some boxes?"

"To store her stuff and maybe donate, right? Not to trash or sell?"

He was still understandably territorial about Rhonda's possessions.

"Let's not decide anything today and just make room for Shirley. We'll pack all Rhonda's clothes and other things into boxes and store them in the attic for now, okay?"

"I guess."

****

Mick set four cardboard boxes and several large garbage bags in front of the open door to Rhonda's room. "Can you do this without me? I'd rather not see Mom's, you know, underwear and stuff. Feel free to toss that kind of crap away."

"I'll call you if you we find anything interesting."

Erin knew that aside from feeling queasy about his mother's underclothes, his grief was still near the surface. Even being in her room must be painful.

"Thanks." He tousled April's hair. "Keep an eye on your mother for me, squirt."

"Okay," April said, as he left.

"Hey, how about starting with the cedar chest?" Erin said. "Look for a diary, notes, old letters. I'm not really sure what we're looking for, but we'll know it when we see it. I'll start with the bookcase."

April's cheeks were pink with excitement. "Maybe there's a treasure inside." Several minutes had passed when she sat back on her heels, surrounded by old wool scarves, worn winter gloves and torn sweaters. "Look at this." She handed a large bag to Erin filled with unopened, postmarked envelopes.

Erin reached in and pulled out a handful. Each envelope had Eddie's name and Texas address in the top left corner. He'd addressed all of them to either Mick or her. She opened one. A smiling snowman Christmas card was inside. Eddie had written,

I'm sorry I can't be with you guys today, but I love you and think about you every day.

Love,

Your Dad.

She opened a few more envelopes. The holiday and birthday cards held similar messages. All the memories she had of Eddie while he lived at Paradise Beach were of having fun with him and feeling safe snuggling in his arms. How had he felt being kept from his children for years? She wouldn't tell Mick about the cards for a while, unsure about how he would react.

"Anything else?"

"Just some cards from you and Uncle Mick."

"Let me see." They were the Mother's Day cards she and Mick had given Rhonda over the years. She assumed Rhonda had thrown them away. Obviously, the cards from her meant more to Rhonda than they had to her, and she couldn't think about that right now.

"Just put these back in the chest. I'll decide what to do with them later. Want to check the dresser?"

April opened the top drawer and fingered the costume jewelry, lifting out a fake coral necklace and bracelet. "Can I have these?"

"Sure, take anything you want."

"Mom, I don't think we're going to find anything interesting. It looks like the other drawers have Granny's clothes and the last one has Shirley's. Can I please go to Olivia's? I need to know what clothes she's taking on vacation."

"Sure."

"Call me if you need me." April headed for the door.

At least they couldn't say she didn't ask them to help. Erin returned to the bookcase filled with books on astrology, mysticism, and romance novels. She opened each one, looked for notes in the margins, and fanned the pages, hoping something would drop out, but nothing did. She loaded them into a box.

The junk jewelry went into empty shoe boxes for storage in the attic and underwear, pajamas, socks, and fraying t-shirts were tossed into garbage bags for disposal. The shirts Shirley wanted stayed in the closet and the rest folded and placed in boxes.

Nothing was in any of the pockets except crumpled tissues and store receipts. A folded step stool leaned against a closet wall. She opened and climbed it. On the shelf above the clothes pole, a lidless cardboard box occupied a corner. She carried it down and upended it on the bed. Hundreds of loose photographs and a photo album tumbled out.

The first picture she picked up was from her college graduation. That day she'd posed woodenly next to a beaming Rhonda. She remembered being embarrassed by her mother's bohemian outfit: a floral peasant blouse over a purple, ankle-length gauze skirt, and flat brown sandals. Other mothers wore summer dresses with high heels or stylish flats. Her college friends said her mother was "adorable" and "so cute." At the time, Erin wished Rhonda wasn't so stuck in the sixties. Now, she admired her mother's courage to be herself.

She opened the album. On the first page, Rhonda, Shirley, and three other girls played volleyball on Paradise Beach. They looked about April's age. Other pages showed Rhonda and her friends at bonfires, parties, and high school football games. A picture of Rhonda and her four friends wearing caps and gowns came next. The Fab Five. Erin squinted and recognized Shirley, but not the other three. At the back of the album was a loose photo of five women in their mid-forties standing on a dock next to a cabin cruiser, raising Champagne glasses.

She recognized Shirley and Rhonda right away, of course. Bringing the photo closer, she also recognized Laura and Marilyn. But who was the fifth?

****

Shirley staggered through the doorway and dropped into a chair on the back porch next to Erin. "God, I'm exhausted. Steve had me cleaning and organizing the stock room all day. If I'd known he was going to have me do that, I wouldn't have walked to work this morning. Remind me to get a desk job the next time around."

"You should have called me to pick you up, and didn't we talk about you walking to work alone?"

"I'm careful, so no nagging."

"Fine."

Shirley wasn't taking the danger seriously enough. Erin went into the house and returned with a glass of wine.

"Maybe this'll help. Your dinner is in the oven when you're ready." She settled back into her chair. "We packed up Rhonda's things today."

"Thanks, you're a doll. It'll be nice to spread out." Shirley yawned and sipped her wine. "Where's April and Mick?"

"In the RV with dear old Dad."

"Are you letting him stay?"

"Since he offered to bring in his friends to help with the motel work, I don't think I have a choice."

"You always have a choice, Erin, and that was the right one."

"I'm not sure. Anyway, when I was going through Rhonda's cedar chest, I found a box of Christmas and birthday cards from Eddie going back to the year he left. You really didn't know he was alive?"

"I swear to God I didn't. How could she keep something like that from me? How do you feel about it?"

"At first, I was mad at Rhonda for lying and at Eddie for staying away. But now I think I shouldn't judge. Who knows what was going through their minds back then?"

"That's something I never imagined I'd hear."

"What?"

"You giving Rhonda a pass for something you didn't agree with."

"Am I that close-minded?"

Shirley took Erin's hand. "No love, just human."

"Thanks for that." Erin was grateful for Shirley's ever-present love and understanding. "Anyway, about your room. I cleared out the closet and dresser, except for the things you said you wanted. We stored all her other clothes, books, and incidentals in the attic."

"Thanks." Shirley stretched her arms above her head. "I assume that while you were clearing things out, you looked for clues to the person who had it in for Rhonda."

"I did, but nothing turned up. It wasn't like I expected a note that said, 'Hand over your property or else,' but I hoped I'd find something."

"That's too bad. Hey, pour me a little more of that wine."

Erin collected their glasses and refilled them in the kitchen, then picked up the photo album before returning to her seat on the porch. "I found this in the closet."

Shirley moved next to Erin. "Let me see that. I had a bunch of pictures too, but they're all ashes now." She opened the album and slowly turned the pages. "These are all from high school. Oh my God, look at the five of us. We're babies. Here's Rhonda's fifteenth birthday party. And here's the gang at the county fair. Look at Rhonda holding that giant teddy bear. That girl always won something." She turned a few more pages and grinned at a photo of five girls in white caps and gowns holding roles of paper secured with red ribbons. "Our high school graduation."

"Why no more photos after this one?"

"After graduation, most of our friends left Misery for Ann Arbor or Lansing and we didn't see them much after that. Your mother and I weren't great students, but we tried the local community college to see if we could handle it. We couldn't. We were sick of hitting the books and didn't feel like doing it anymore. It wasn't too long after that we both got married. Probably should've stuck with the community college."

Erin leaned over and turned to the back of the album and the loose photo. "This is the only one with all of you as adults. What was the occasion?"

Shirley glanced at the picture, then closed the album. "You know, I feel a little grimy from work. I'm going to wash my face and hands."

When Shirley returned, Erin was studying the cabin cruiser photo. "You all look so happy. Was it a birthday party or something?"

"Wasn't really an occasion. Even though Rhonda and I were the closest, we kept in touch with the other girls now and then, and learned that Laura and Marilyn would be in town at the same time. So, we planned a weekend on the lake."

"When was this?"

"About fifteen years ago." Shirley got to her feet. "I'm tired. I'm going to bed."

"Wait. I have a question. Who's the fifth woman in the picture?"

"Mrs. Masters's daughter."

"The one buried in the cemetery? One of the Fab Five?"

Shirley heaved herself up. "Yes. Can I go to bed now?"

"When did she die?"

"A long time ago." Shirley started for the door. "Good night!"

"Wait. How did she die?"

"She drowned."

****

Shirley wouldn't talk about the fifth woman last night or this morning before she left for work, but promised she'd tell all when she got home.

Erin had something else to think about right now, anyway. She shouted up the stairs, "Are you ready, April? Kelly and Olivia will be here any minute."

"Coming." April bumped her pink and white suitcase down the steps. "They just drove in." She dragged the suitcase behind her through the front door.

Erin followed her to the idling car and leaned into the driver side window, handing Kelly an envelope. "This is a little something to cover the cost of having another mouth to feed for two weeks. Thank you."

"It's no problem and the money isn't necessary."

"Please take it, just in case." Erin stepped back as Kelly slid out of the car.

"Olivia loves April and so do I. I'll take it for now, but return it if we don't need it." She leaned close and whispered. "Having April here keeps me from having to invent ways to entertain Olivia when she gets cranky and bored." She popped the trunk and stored April's suitcase inside.

"Have a great time." Erin hugged April and kissed the top of her head. "Don't forget to help with the chores."

"Oh, Mom, you know I will." April slid into the backseat next to Olivia.

Erin waved until the car was out of sight, then headed for the kitchen. She'd just poured a cup of coffee when her phone buzzed.

"Erin, this is Steve at the pharmacy. Is Shirley sick?"

"No. Isn't she at work?"

"No, and she should have been here an hour ago. I'm concerned because she's never late. Did she have anything going on before working today?"

"No. I'll check around."

A call to Shirley went straight to voicemail. The tracker app reported "No Location Found" for Shirley's phone. Something was very wrong. She grabbed her purse and rushed across the parking lot toward her car.

Eddie stepped into her path. "What's the hurry? I want to show you—" He studied her face. "What's going on?"

"Shirley's not at work. Her calls go directly to voicemail and the tracker can't find her." Erin spotted Shirley's truck in the parking lot. "She walked to work again?"

"Yeah. I tried to stop her, but she said the day was too nice to drive. Said she'd call if she needed a ride home later."

Erin hurried into her car.

Eddie's eyes widened. "Where are you going?"

"To look for her."

"I'm coming with you."

Erin drove the route Shirley took to work while Eddie scanned the side streets. She stopped at Full of Beans, where Shirley usually picked up her morning coffee and donut. The cashier said she hadn't seen her.

In the meantime, Eddie darted into the grocery store, then back to the car. "Holly says Shirley hasn't been in, but she'll ask around and let us know."

When Erin parked in front of the pharmacy, Steve rushed out. "Did you find her?"

Erin shook her head. "It's been over two hours since she left home and we've been everywhere we can think of."

"Can I do anything?" Steve asked.

"Stay by the phone," Eddie said, "and try calling her every ten minutes. Let us know if you hear anything."

Erin sat in the car, paralyzed. "I don't know what else to do."

"Something's happened to her. I know it." Eddie pounded his knee.

"I think so too." Panic tightened her chest. "We need to call the police."

"They can't do anything for twenty-four hours, but at least they can get the paperwork started."

Erin's phone buzzed. She shot a glance at Eddie. "It's Justin."

"I just got a text from my editor," he said. "Shirley's been in an accident and she's in the hospital."

"Is she okay?" Erin's breath came out in uneven gasps. *Please God, let her be okay.*

"They're examining her now."

Eddie tugged on her sleeve. "Is it about Shirley? What's going on?"

"I'll be right there, Justin." She ended the call and made a U-turn. "Shirley's been in an accident."

"Tell me she's okay."

"I don't know if she is."

Chapter Thirty-Three

At a light tap on her shoulder, Erin opened her eyes. She was sitting on a chair, her upper body draped over a hospital bed. She jerked upright.

"About time you woke up, sleeping beauty," Shirley said. "You've been out for over six hours."

Erin reached for Shirley's hand, the IV-free one, as memories of the previous day flashed through her mind. Bandages covered Shirley's forehead. Bruises and scrapes darkened her cheeks and arms. She had two black eyes.

"How are you feeling?"

"Not so hot."

Erin's eyes stung as she struggled to control her emotions. It had been such a close call.

"Do you remember what happened?"

"Yeah, I was hit by a car. Do the cops know who it was?"

"No. Whoever it was left you in a ditch." If she ever found out who hurt Shirley, she'd...

"In a ditch? How'd anyone find me?"

"Thank God, a guy driving on Main near downtown spotted you and called 9-1-1. I don't get it. Eddie and I drove up and down that road. How could we have missed you?"

"Maybe I was already here."

Why hadn't she insisted Shirley drive to work until

after the killer was caught? Guilt threatened to drag her down, but she pulled herself out. She had to stay strong. "Can I get you anything?"

"Another body. Everything burns and throbs, and my ribs hurt like hell."

"You're lucky nothing's broken. Want me to ask a nurse for some pain meds?"

"No, I'm groggy enough." Shirley looked as if she was trying to smile, but it came out as a grimace. "Damn, it hurts to move my face. By the way, you look awful. Go home and get some rest. You must have been here all night."

"I'm not leaving you. What time are the police coming?"

"Who knows? What time is it?"

Erin glanced at her watch. "Six-thirty in the morning."

A metallic rattle came from the hallway, and a nurse appeared with a cart. "I'm here to check your vitals." He strapped a blood pressure cuff around Shirley's right arm and placed a thermometer in her mouth. "Breakfast is coming soon, Shirley, and I ordered coffee for you, ma'am. I figured you could use it."

She peeked at his name tag. "Thanks, Tony. I'm Erin."

After a few minutes, he removed the cuff and thermometer, and checked the results. "Vitals are normal, Shirley. How are you doing?"

"Not exactly ready to run a marathon, but good enough to go home."

"The doctor will be in soon. In the meantime, let me know if I can get you anything."

After he left, Shirley pressed a button on a remote control and the head of her bed moved into a sitting position. "Ouch! Son of a b—" She wrapped her arms around her ribcage and looked over at Erin. "Stop staring at me like that. I said I'm okay."

"Fine. What do you remember about the accident?"

Shirley didn't answer for a moment. "I was walking to work. Then this white car comes out of nowhere and aims right at me. Then a yellow car comes from the opposite direction. Must have scared off the white car because it swerved away, but it got me anyway. That's all I remember."

"It must have grazed you and tossed you into the ditch. Did you recognize the car?"

"No. And I didn't recognize the driver either. All I saw was a long-haired blond."

A food service worker brought Shirley's breakfast tray and left.

Shirley slid the scrambled egg plate away, sipped her coffee, then set the cup on the tray. "There's something I have to tell you."

"You don't need to talk now." Erin pulled the blanket up to Shirley's chin. "Try to get some rest."

"Will you please quit fussing and let me talk?"

Her spunk was intact, but her gaze wouldn't meet Erin's.

"It's something about the deaths, isn't it?"

Shirley picked up a piece of toast, bit into it, and put it back. "Yeah. I think it's about Gloria. I don't know if she's the only connection between Rhonda, Laura, Marilyn and me, but that's the one I know about."

"Who's Gloria?"

"Mrs. Masters's daughter. The fifth girl in Rhonda's photos."

"What about her?"

"I wanted to tell you before, but I really didn't think it had anything to do with the murders. Don't be mad at me when you hear it."

Erin grinned. "I'm not making any promises."

Shirley inhaled slowly. "Damn, that hurts. Anyway, the five of us hung around together growing up, but as I told you before, when we graduated from high school, everyone went their separate ways."

"Did you stay in touch?"

"We tried, but you know what happens over the years. Later, Gloria married Zachary, had a daughter, and moved to Port Elizabeth. We were in our mid-forties by then. It was great having her close. She, Rhonda, and I got together when we could, but Gloria was pretty busy helping Zachary with his practice, and being a wife and mother. Then we had the bright idea of getting the five of us back together." She fell silent.

After a long moment, Erin said, "Are you okay?"

"I'm fine." Shirley snuggled into her covers, gazing at the ceiling. "Okay, we decided to have a reunion the following year when we'd all turn forty-five. Gloria suggested a weekend touring Lake Michigan on her boat. She called Marilyn and Laura, and we all settled on a date. Gloria grew up boating, so we didn't need a driver. I forget they're called."

"Captains. I don't remember Gloria."

"When she moved back to Port Elizabeth, you were living in Denver fulltime and we didn't see much of you. Maybe one or two trips a year for Easter and Christmas."

"Yeah, well…"

"You don't have to explain it to me. Anyway, the first day out, Gloria drove us north for a few hours, then turned off the engine. We lay out in the sun, had a few gin and tonics, and all dove into the water to cool off, except Gloria. She said she didn't want to get wet and didn't want to drink while running the boat. We had dinner at a lakefront restaurant, then pulled into a cove for the night. The next day we headed for Harbor Springs and—"

Tony steered a wheelchair into the room next to Shirley's bed. "The doctor wants another MRI."

"Okay, but when can I go home?"

"If everything looks good, maybe later today. Do you think you can make it into the chair?"

"No problem." Shirley gasped as she swung her legs off the bed. "Shit, damn…"

"Erin," Tony said, "this might be a good time for you to go home. The test results are going to take a while. I'll call you if Shirley can leave today."

****

Erin and Eddie helped Shirley into her Paradise Beach bed later that day.

"Thanks for helping me, you guys." Shirley's eyes misted.

Eddie squeezed her hand. "Anytime, kiddo. Now, I'll leave you ladies to it." He left the bedroom, closing the door behind him.

"I want to finish telling you about Gloria."

"You can tell me tomorrow. You need rest now."

Erin helped Shirley into her nightgown, settled her into bed, then kissed her forehead before leaving the room. She found Eddie sitting at the kitchen table.

"Are you thinking what I'm thinking?" she asked.

"Yes, if you're thinking we need to keep our eyes on Shirley twenty-four seven from now on."

****

Erin rolled out of bed at five the next morning, her eyes grainy from lack of sleep. After making a pot of coffee, she pored over her notes. Was the name of Rhonda's, Laura's, and Marilyn's killer, and Shirley's attempted killer, among them?

"Erin!" Shirley yelled. "Come here. Now!"

Erin arrived in Shirley's room, out of breath. "What's wrong?"

"Nothing. What's wrong with you? You look like you just saw a ghost." Shirley sat against the headboard, with the morning news on TV.

Erin waited until her heart slowed down. "You scared me to death. I was afraid you were having an attack or something."

"Calm down and pull up a chair. And before you ask, everything still hurts, but I'm getting used to it."

Erin tugged a chair next to the bed and sat. "Do you want a pain pill?"

"No. They make me sleepy and I want to finish telling you about Gloria."

"Are you hungry? Thirsty?"

"Don't treat me like a helpless old lady, okay? If I need something, I'll tell you." Shirley grabbed the TV remote and turned off the sound. "Do you remember where I was?"

"You said it was the second day on the boat and heading for Harbor Springs."

"Right. Gloria drove while we soaked up the sun, talked about old times, and drank gin and tonics. There

259

wasn't too much traffic on the water, so every once in a while, she'd put the boat on autopilot and join us."

Erin could picture it. Five old friends laughing, sunning, drinking, and gossiping on a beautiful lake under a cloudless blue sky.

"It was late afternoon by the time we got near the cove where we'd spend the night. It was a pretty place with a beach hidden from the road by woods. Gloria dropped the anchor and four of us jumped in the lake while Gloria sat on the boat ladder, dangling her feet in the water. All of us, except Gloria, had been drinking pretty good and were starving, so she prepared dinner. Then we...I have to stop for a minute." Shirley unsteadily swung her legs out of bed. "I have to go to the bathroom."

"Let me help."

"No, I can make it by myself." Shirley limped into the hallway.

The toilet flushed, but when several minutes passed and Shirley wasn't back, she knocked on the bathroom door.

"Are you okay?"

"I'm fine," Shirley mumbled. "Be out in a minute." When she returned, her eyes were red.

Erin helped her under the covers. "Is something wrong?"

"I just want to get this over with." Shirley scooted backwards until she rested against the headboard. "Where was I?"

"Gloria made dinner."

"Right. We all wanted to help, but she said we'd be in the way." Shirley flexed her arms and winced. "The evening was warm and beautiful, but the wind was up and the waves were a little rough by the time we finished eating. It was late August, so the sun was low in the sky. Like I said, we'd had plenty to drink all day and then more at dinner. Gloria didn't drink anything except water. We were in a crazy enough mood to decide that forty-somethings going skinny dipping was a great idea. Gloria laughed, shook her head, and picked up a book. Me and the other girls stripped and dove in."

Shirley covered her face for a moment, then, with a deep sigh, dropped her hands. "I'm not sure who suggested we toss Gloria in, but we all thought it would be a hoot. We got back on the boat, picked her up, kicking and screaming, and laughed at her furious face as we tossed her in the water. I knew something bad happened the minute I heard a clunk. We scanned the water, but didn't see her. At first, we thought she swam to the other side of the boat to scare us. But it wasn't long before we realized she wasn't coming up. We jumped into the lake and dove underwater, but the water in the cove was murky. We swam around for what seemed like hours, but couldn't find her."

"Did you call the coast guard?"

"We weren't thinking straight from the shock and alcohol, and none of us knew how to work the damn radio. This was before everyone had cell phones. We didn't know how to work the boat either." Shirley raised a shaky hand to her forehead.

Erin grew uneasy. Shirley looked as though she was about to lose it.

"Relax and tell me the rest tomorrow."

"No. I gotta finish this. When we got back in the boat, we shined flashlights on the water and yelled Gloria's name until we were hoarse. As more hours went by, we knew she was gone for good. We couldn't figure out what happened. She should have been floating, at least. Thinking about it later, her head must have hit something on the boat that knocked her out, and a wave pushed her under it. Anyway, we continued watching the water until after two, then went down into the galley and talked about what we were going to do. Laura said we'd committed involuntary manslaughter and could go to jail. That hit us like a ton of bricks. But whether we lied or told the truth, Gloria would still be dead. So, we decided to lie." Shirley took a tissue from the nightstand and wiped her eyes. "We remembered what happened to that actress who was on a yacht with her husband, slipped off it in the middle of the night, and drowned. This was a long time ago."

"Oh, the dark-haired movie star in the sixties. Rhonda loved her."

"Even after all this time, no one really knows how she got into the water. That's what we used to come up with our story. We'd say we all went to bed about eleven and Gloria was missing when we got up the next morning. Her bed was slept in, but she was gone. We told ourselves she'd probably went up on deck to get something and fell overboard. We agreed that we'd never tell anyone what really happened."

"Oh, Shirley." Erin could barely breathe. "What a tragedy for Gloria's family and the four of you."

"I'm cold." Shirley wrapped her arms around herself and shivered.

Erin wrapped a blanket around her shoulders. "Are you sure you want to keep going?"

Shirley nodded. "While Rhonda and Marilyn stayed behind to clean the boat the next morning, me and Marilyn dinghied to the shore. Looking back, I don't know why we didn't think to use it to look for Gloria. Anyway, the two of us climbed through the woods to the road, where a woman stopped and drove us to a police station. Marilyn, being an actress, told our story so well, I almost believed her myself. The cops called Gloria's husband." Tears streamed down her face. "I've never forgiven myself."

"It was an accident."

"An accident caused by four drunk women who should have known better."

"Was her...body ever found?"

"Yes, a couple of months later, and the cops closed the case as an accidental drowning. One of the worst parts, though, was that Gloria had been pregnant. She didn't tell us." Shirley scooted under the covers. "Please bring me a couple of aspirins and a glass of water."

Chapter Thirty-Four

Erin prepared lunch as the horror of Shirley's story smoldered in her mind. It had to be the reason someone killed Rhonda, Laura and Marilyn, and tried to kill Shirley. She placed a bowl of tomato soup and a tuna sandwich on a lunch tray and set it on Shirley's bedside table.

Shirley pushed it away. "I'm not hungry."

Erin sat on the chair next to the bed. "Why didn't you tell me about Gloria before?"

"Because I didn't think it had anything to do with the murders. When Rhonda and Laura died, we believed Westside was the culprit, remember? But it wasn't until Marilyn died that I suspected the murders might have something to do with Gloria."

"Okay, but you should have told me then."

"Once I realized Gloria could be the link, I didn't have the courage to tell you we'd killed someone."

"It was an accident. No more secrets, okay?"

Shirley smiled weakly. "No more secrets. I promise."

Erin didn't speak for a moment, thinking about the four remaining suspects.

"What's up? You have that look on your face," Shirley said.

"Rhonda had an appointment with Zachary on the day she died. Maybe she told him about Gloria and he told Mrs. Masters. He'd lost his wife, and she'd lost a daughter. Revenge is one of the motives for murder."

"I can't think about this anymore." Shirley rolled over to face the wall. "Ouch, damn it." She rolled back. "By the way, if you think you can leave me out of the investigation just because I have a few bumps and bruises, you're out of your mind."

"We'll see. I'm going to tell the police about Gloria. They might want to question you."

"Fine with me. It's about time I came clean."

****

Erin called Justin as she left Shirley's room. "Can you come over? There's something I want to tell you."

Fifteen minutes later, Justin joined her on the back porch. "I'm sorry for what happened between us. I had no right to—"

"Forget about that." She handed him the cabin cruiser photo. "Four of these women are dead." She told him about the boat trip. "Gloria's accidental death has to be the motive for the murders, and why Shirley ended up in the hospital."

"Have you called the police?"

"No, I want to tell them in person. Maybe now they'll take another look at the so-called accidents and suicide."

He held out a hand. "Let's go."

****

Within the hour, Erin and Justin were in the Great Rapids Police Department, sitting across from Detective Mackey. Erin handed her the photo of the boat.

"Nice cruiser," Mackey said. "Looks like the ladies are having a good time. So what? Wait…" She brought the photo closer to her eyes. "Three of them died recently. What's going on?"

"Actually, four of them are dead," Erin said. She repeated Shirley's story while Justin held her icy hand.

"So, you think someone murdered Mrs. Brady, Ms. Nowak and Ms. Mitchell, then nearly killed Mrs. Cochran because they accidentally killed Gloria Smith? Interesting. Come with me." Mackey led them to an interview room. "Sit. I'm getting the chief."

The small room's scuffed gray walls, metal furniture, and opaque glass window reminded Erin of every low-budget interrogation room she'd ever seen on television. She leaned toward Justin.

"This place makes me feel like I'm guilty of something."

He squeezed her hand. "You're going to be okay."

A few minutes later, Mackey returned with the chief. He was younger than Erin imagined he'd be, probably in his early forties, and wore a this-a-waste-of-my-time frown. He held out a hand to Justin. "Good to see you, Rourke."

Justin nodded.

The chief turned to Erin. "Ms. Brady, I'm Chief Sloane. So, you're the one who's been proposing alternate theories for the cause of your mother's death."

"Right. I don't believe her death was accidental."

The chief and Mackey exchanged looks, then both sat facing Erin and Justin.

"How long have you been a forensic pathologist, Ms. Brady?" Sloane asked.

His patronizing tone infuriated her. This would not go well.

"You don't have to be an expert to know when

something doesn't make sense. I knew my mother, and your team doesn't."

Sloane folded his hands. "Detective Mackey said you have new information."

"I do." Erin handed him the photo and repeated Shirley's story. "I think my mother, Laura Nowak, and Marilyn Mitchell were murdered to avenge Gloria Smith's death. And as you know, someone recently made an attempt on Shirley Cochran's life."

The chief gave a skeptical smile. "If revenge was the motive, why were these women murdered fifteen years after the fact? That's what doesn't make sense."

Erin wasn't sure how much to tell him. "The women agreed not to tell anyone about what happened to Gloria on that boat, but I think someone recently did."

The chief raised an eyebrow and turned to Mackey. "Detective, I want to see Gloria Smith's file." After she left the room, he shifted his attention to Justin. "What's really going on here, Rourke? Why are you involved in this?"

"I'm a friend of Erin's and think she's onto something. Five women went to school together. Three of them died in Misery Cove within a three-month period. A fourth was injured in a hit and run recently. These four women were with a fifth when she died several years ago."

Friend of Erin's. Her heart sank. Telling herself and others that she and Justin were just friends was one thing. But hearing him say it stung.

"We've thoroughly investigated the three deaths, and there's no evidence of homicide. As for the Shirley Cochran incidents, we're actively working on it."

"Will the department at least consider the possibility that Rhonda Brady's death wasn't accidental?" Justin asked. "Erin talked to some people and gathered—"

"Stop right there. I don't want you or Ms. Brady interfering in police business and spreading rumors about women being murdered."

Erin was beyond frustrated. No arrogant jerk, unwilling to even consider the deaths were murders, would stop her.

Justin didn't respond, and an uncomfortable silence filled the room until Mackey reappeared. She handed the chief a folder.

He read through the file slowly, then said, "The medical examiner ruled Gloria Smith's death an accident. Now you're telling me it wasn't."

"It was an accident," Erin said, "but not exactly the way my mother and the others described it. They promised each other that they wouldn't tell anyone what really happened. But I think someone broke that promise. And now almost everyone on that trip is dead."

"Ms. Brady, I'm very sorry for your loss. We take every premature death seriously and have diligently investigated Rhonda Brady's, Laura Nowak's, and Marilyn Mitchell's deaths, and the medical examiner ruled no foul play was indicated."

"Chief Sloan, I think you should reconsider all the facts and—"

"Noted, Ms. Brady." He nodded to everyone, and left.

Mackey got to her feet and shrugged. "Well, that's that. I talked to Mrs. Cochran in the hospital and we have the color of the car, but not make or model, and a vague description of the driver. Someone with long blond hair. It's not much to go on. But if and when we find her attacker, we might get more info on the other deaths."

"Shirley needs police protection," Erin said.

"There's not much we can do. We don't know that the hit-and-run was intentional."

"I don't believe this," Erin said.

Mackey's features softened. "I told Mrs. Cochran she needs to be aware of her surroundings at all times." She gave Erin an intense look. "And you and your friends need to keep a close eye on her until we can determine if her run in with the car was a potential homicide."

****

Eddie sprang to his feet the moment Erin and Justin entered Shirley's room. "What did the cops say?"

What was going on with those two?

"They said the hit-and-run could have been an accident," Erin said. "They're looking into it."

"It wasn't a damn accident. That car was aimed at me." Shirley struggled to untangle herself from the covers.

"Don't even try it," Eddie said, pushing her gently back into the pillows. He turned to Erin. "What about the fire?"

"They're working on it."

Eddie frowned. "Idiots."

"How are you doing, Shirley?" Justin asked.

"Mostly just bored to death lying here. Wanted to take a little walk around the house, but this guy," she gestured toward Eddie, "said he'd tackle me if I tried to get up except to go to the bathroom."

"He's right. You should take it easy," Erin said.

"But how in the hell are we going to catch the killer if I'm stuck here? I need to get moving."

"I agree with Eddie. You just got out of the hospital yesterday," Erin said.

Justin moved toward the door. "Erin, I have to leave, but we can talk a minute?"

"Sure." She followed him to his car.

"You have a plan, don't you? Whatever it is, don't do it. You're chasing a murderer. They might already know you and the others have been asking questions."

"I'm not planning anything stupid."

"Maybe I should stick around, just in case."

Tempting, but the more they were together, the harder it would be to hide her feelings, and the more her heart would hurt because he was still engaged.

"Thanks for the offer, but Mick and Eddie are here."

"Okay, but stay out of trouble." He held her shoulders and softly kissed her lips.

Embarrassingly, her knees buckled. She grabbed his arm to steady herself. Why did he kiss her? On the lips? She backed away.

"Bye, Justin."

As he left the parking lot, Mick's car pulled in.

"How's Shirley doing?" he asked.

"Come in and see for yourself. But first, I need to tell you something." She'd worried about the best way to tell Mick about Gloria, but decided not to sugarcoat it. "Fifteen years ago, Mom, Shirley, Laura, and Marilyn tossed their friend Gloria off a boat. A cabin cruiser. She hit her head and drowned. It's the connection we've been looking for."

His eyes widened. "Holy shit." He paused for a long moment. "Are you sure?"

"Yes, Shirley told me."

"Mom had been so excited about that trip. You know, getting all her friends together in one place and going to Petoskey. For weeks, she talked about what to wear and what food and drinks to take. After the accident, she stayed in bed for a week. I asked her what was wrong, but she only said Gloria died. Did you ever meet her?"

"No."

"She was a nice lady. I can't believe Mom could..."

"I know. If you're okay, let's go in and see Shirley."

****

Mick bent to kiss Shirley's forehead. "You're looking pretty good."

She smiled. "Thanks for that."

Eddie grinned. "She always looks good."

Shirley giggled. "No, I don't" She blushed.

Oh my God. It was worse than Erin imagined.

"Erin told me about Gloria," Mick said. "Is it true?"

"Sorry to say it is."

"Are you tired, Shirley?" Erin asked. "Want us to leave?"

"Stop fussing. I'm not tired and not hurting much. Just frustrated. I want to catch the bastard who killed my friends."

Erin scanned the bedroom. Only the bed and one chair to sit on. "Do you feel well enough to eat dinner in the dining room and talk about how to catch the killer after?"

"Hell yes."

Chapter Thirty-Five

Erin loaded the dishwasher with the last of the dinner dishes and returned to her seat at the dining room table. "I believe Gloria's death is the motive for killing Rhonda and the other women who were on the boat that day." She glanced around the table and wondered for the millionth time if they were out of their depth.

"I think we're all with you on that, Erin," Eddie said. "Keep going."

She drew in a breath. "We haven't questioned the two suspects who were most affected by Gloria's death."

"Right," Eddie said. "Gloria's crazy mother and Gloria's shrink husband."

"What about Father Joseph, Erin?" Mick asked.

"He's off the list. I checked him out the morning before Shirley's accident and didn't get a chance to tell you. I visited the rectory when I knew he would be out and peeked at his appointment book when Mary Margaret left the room to make tea. He had had a Bible study class at the time Marilyn died and marriage counseling session the night Laura was killed."

"Now we're down to two," Mick said.

Shirley gave Mick a sideways glance, then turned back to Erin. "I hate to say this, but I think we should leave Melanie on the list."

"What the hell, Shirley?" Mick said. "Melanie didn't know Gloria."

Eddie cleared his throat. "But she has a personal interest in wanting the Westside project to go forward, right?"

The room went quiet for a moment, then Erin said, "Eddie and Shirley are right, Mick. If the Westside project goes through, she'll earn tens of thousands in commissions from the sale of the condos. And she'll be promoted to VP of Marketing."

"What do you all have against her?" Mick asked. "This is bullshit."

Poor naïve Mick. He had a blind spot where Melanie was concerned, but she had to say it—to warn, not hurt, him. "Doesn't it seem odd Melanie won't commit to a wedding date until the terms of the will have been satisfied?"

"What the fuck, Erin? We can get married anytime."

"Then why don't you?"

That came out too fast. She shouldn't have said anything.

"She—Just forget it." Mick stormed out of the room.

Eddie frowned. "He's got it bad."

"Shh, he's coming back," Erin said.

Mick stomped back into the room, holding a can of beer. "So, you're saying Melanie is only marrying me for money? Thanks a lot." He returned to his chair, tipped his head back, and poured beer into his mouth.

"Take it easy, son," Eddie said. "We're all on your side."

"So why would Melanie kill Marilyn? She wasn't

involved with the Westside project."

"We don't know that for certain." Shirley said. "Let's just keep going and see where it takes us, okay Mick?"

Mick gulped the rest of his beer. "Fine. But I'm still pissed off."

"Sorry," Erin said. "Next, we need to question Mrs. Masters, Zachary, and Melanie about where they were when the murders and Shirley's accident took place. Everyone except Shirley will—"

"Hey, wait a damn minute," Shirley said. "I told you that you're not leaving me out."

"You just got out of the hospital." Erin said.

"I agree with Erin." Eddie held Shirley's hand.

Shirley shook him off and gave an exasperated sigh. "I get why you're worried, but it's my life hanging in the balance here and I will not sit around on my butt waiting for someone to kill me."

"Okay, okay," Erin said. "Let me think a minute…How about you and I question Mrs. Masters together?" She glanced down at her tablet. "Eddie and Mick will question Zachary. I'll question Melanie. Our goal is to find out who has a verifiable alibi for one of the murders or Shirley's accident."

"You're thinking about questioning Melanie alone?" asked Shirley. "What if she's the killer?"

"I'll meet her for lunch or something."

"Okay," Shirley said. "By the way, the day before my tumble, Holly told me Mrs. Masters is on a wine tour in Traverse City with her church friends, but will be back tomorrow."

"Is there anything going on in Misery that woman doesn't know?" Eddie asked.

Shirley laughed. "I don't think so."

"So, let's get to work as soon as possible. If the person you're questioning doesn't have an alibi for the first murder you ask about, try another one if it doesn't look too suspicious."

"Me and Dad can catch up with Zachary during lunch tomorrow," Mick said. "I'll ask Holly where he goes."

"Good idea, Mick." As angry as he'd been, he hadn't walked out. She was proud of him. "Is three days from now enough time for everyone to contact their suspects?" Erin asked.

"It has to be," Shirley said.

****

The following day, Erin parked in front of Mrs. Masters' dingy gray bungalow. Her ancient minivan dozed on the sunny driveway.

"Are you ready for this?" Shirley asked.

"I think so, and I think I should go in alone." She'd brought Shirley along so she'd feel included but never intended that she to go into Mrs. Masters's house.

"No! I don't like the idea of you going in there by yourself."

"I'll be fine. And you'll probably scare her with your black eyes."

It'll be a miracle if Masters even lets her in. She lifted a bouquet of sunflowers, carnations, and lilies from the back seat and got out of the car.

"Good luck, Erin, and be careful. Even if she's not a murderer, she's a vicious old woman."

Erin gave a thumbs-up and walked to the porch.

The curtain on the window next to the front door fluttered. Erin waved. No response.

She knew this wasn't going to be easy and lightly tapped her knuckles on the door. "Mrs. Masters, I came to apologize for that day at the cemetery. Please open the door." She knocked again.

The door opened a few inches. "What do you want?"

Erin held out the bouquet. "To say I'm sorry and give you this."

She snorted. "I doubt it. Why are you really here?"

"I want to show you something."

"What?"

"Can I please come in?"

The door opened a little wider. "I'm very busy right now."

"Please take these." Erin held out the flowers again.

Mrs. Masters began closing the door. "I have enough flowers."

"Wait. I found something when I was cleaning my mother's room. I think you'll want to see it."

The door stopped moving. "Well…" Mrs. Masters gave her a brief once-over and strode inside, leaving the door open. Erin followed her into a living room filled with overstuffed floral furniture and smelling of lemon polish.

Mrs. Masters grabbed the flowers and tossed them on the coffee table. "Sit down, if you want."

Erin sat on the musty couch and eyed the flowers. They needed water, but she wasn't going to mention it. "How was the wine tour?"

"How'd you know? Never mind. That blabber mouth Holly told someone. And it's none of your business."

"Sorry." Erin took a photo from her purse and held it out.

"What's that?"

"A picture."

"I can see that." Mrs. Masters appeared to be wavering between obstinacy and curiosity. Curiosity won, and she held out a hand. "Oh my dear Lord, it's the girls. I took this picture at their high school graduation. Haven't seen it for years. Gloria packed up all her pictures when she moved away."

Erin removed two more photos from her purse and gave one to the older woman.

Mrs. Masters traced a finger over it. "I took this picture on Gloria's seventeenth birthday. See the station wagon behind her? Ten years old, but in perfect running order. It was her birthday present."

"I bet she loved that car."

"She did, but I only let her drive it back and forth to school. Getting an education was more important than gallivanting around town to the drive-in restaurants with her friends. She only took it out once without my permission and I locked away her keys for a month."

What a witch. Erin handed her the last photo.

Mrs. Masters looked at it for a long while, fat tears dripping down her cheeks. "I've never seen this picture. It must have been taken on the boat trip when Gloria drowned. Those girls let her drown."

"That's not what happened." Although Erin knew better, she said, "Your daughter fell overboard during the night."

"No. Rhonda, Shirley, Laura, and Marilyn were jealous of my Gloria. Had been for years, especially

278

when she married a doctor. They probably killed her to get even."

Unbelievable. "That's not true. My mother would never intentionally harm anyone."

Mrs. Masters blotted her cheeks with a tissue. "I was devastated when my darling girl died. She had a loving husband, a beautiful daughter, and an expensive house. Poor Zachary. He almost lost his mind. And then, when her doctor told him she'd been pregnant with the son they'd always wanted, he took it hard. He didn't even know she was pregnant."

"You both must have been heartbroken."

"We were. Zachary drank too much and started taking drugs. I reported him to child protective services because he wasn't capable of taking care of Sara. He lost custody. She should have stayed with me, but decided to live with her aunt in Arizona. I wasn't happy about it, but it turned out to be a good thing. I had a heart attack soon after."

"What about Zachary's practice?"

"Some psychology board suspended his license. He went to rehab and got clean. He's a good man now. Takes care of me and is a good father to Sara. Sees her in Arizona every chance he gets."

She had to rattle the old woman. "Mrs. Masters, did you kill my mother and her friends and try to kill Shirley?"

"What? No...no," she sputtered. "Why on Earth would you say a thing like that?"

Time to pull out the Cunningham technique. "I was driving on Marilyn's street the evening she died and saw you in front of her house. At the end of the block, I looked back. You were on her porch."

"That's not possible."

"I saw you. It was three weeks ago on Monday, at eight."

Mrs. Masters snatched a sheet of paper from the table next to her. "According to my list of TV shows, that was the day my favorite mystery series started. It came on at seven-thirty."

"Was anyone with you?"

"It's none of your business." Mrs. Masters got to her feet. "You're not the police. Get out of my house."

Erin didn't move. "I'm going to do whatever it takes to find out who murdered my mother and the other women. If you don't want to answer my questions, that's your prerogative. But I will tell the police I saw you on Marilyn's porch the evening she was murdered. They'll probably take you to the station and put you in one of those interrogation rooms and—"

Mrs. Masters gave Erin a murderous look. "Not that it's any of your business, but Mr. Wallace was with me."

"Mr. Wallace?"

"Roger Wallace. He's a widower and likes that series too. We'd both waited for the new season to start, so he came over for dinner at six and he stayed until about ten."

Erin picked up her phone. "What's his phone number?"

"No. I'll call him."

"Okay, but don't tell him what this is about. Just say I want to talk to him."

Mrs. Masters picked up her phone. "Roger, it's me. There's someone here who wants to talk to you." She handed the phone to Erin.

"Hello, Mr. Wallace, this is Erin Brady."

"How are you, Erin?" he said. "I'm sorry for your loss."

"Thank you. Do you remember where you were on Monday three weeks ago, between six and ten at night?"

"Hmm. Let me see now. Oh yes, I was with Mrs. Masters for dinner and we watched TV after."

"Thank you, Mr. Wallace." Erin ended the call.

"Well, are you satisfied?" Mrs. Masters flashed a smug smile.

Erin nodded toward the flowers. "Better put those in a vase."

"Well?" Shirley asked as Erin got into the car.

"She has an alibi for Marilyn's murder."

Chapter Thirty-Six

Erin dashed to Eddie's place through wind and heavy rain the next evening, wrestling with her inside-out umbrella.

Eddie opened the door, took the umbrella, and handed her a towel. She wiped herself off, then sat at the table across from Shirley.

Obviously, Shirley had been there for a while because she was totally dry. Erin raised an eyebrow. Just a few weeks ago, Shirley called him a sack of shit.

"What?" asked Shirley.

"Nothing. How are you feeling?"

"Fantastic, thanks to Eddie's cooking and this." She raised her nearly empty wineglass.

"Careful if you're still taking pain meds."

"Erin!" Shirley warned.

"Okay, okay, I'll stop."

Eddie handed Erin a glass of red wine and topped off Shirley's. "Mick had to talk to Melanie about something," he said, "but he'll be right along." He glanced out the window. "Here he comes."

When Mick opened the door, it flew out of his hand and crashed into the side of the RV. He caught it and stepped inside, dripping. "Holy crap."

Eddie tossed him a dish towel. "Sorry, the rest of the bath towels are in the wash."

Mick shrugged, wiped his face and blotted his

clothes. "Thanks." He grabbed a can of beer from the fridge, sat at the table, and took a long gulp.

"Melanie doesn't know what we're doing, right?" Erin asked.

"I told you I wouldn't say anything. Anyway, she's pissed at me because I've been MIA for the past few days."

"So sorry." Erin didn't mean for it to come out with so much sarcasm, but it was hard taking the adventures of Mick and Melanie seriously. "FYI, Mick, I'm having lunch with Melanie at Georgia's tomorrow."

"Don't be mean to her, okay?"

"I promise." Erin had to stifle a smile. Her brother in love was hilarious.

"What happened with Mrs. Masters, Erin?" Eddie asked.

"She has an alibi for Marilyn's death."

Mick scooted his chair back. "You believed her?" He grabbed another beer from the fridge.

"I think so. Her boyfriend said he was at her place that evening."

"Her boyfriend?" Shirley laughed.

"That's what she said."

"Why didn't I know she got herself a boyfriend?" Shirley said. "Anyway, I can see her revenge-killing if she thought someone killed her daughter."

"Right, but I believed Roger, her boyfriend. She's off the list for now, but we could bring her back in if we need to."

"Mick, tell the ladies about our lunch with Zachary."

"Sure," Mick said. "Holly said Zachary eats lunch at The Cove every day. Dad got him talking about the hockey finals and the game on the night Laura died. Zachary knew about the big fight on the ice. Dad knew the fight would have made the news and Zachary could have read it, so he said, 'What about that last goal?' One of the players made his 100th and tossed the puck into the stands where a kid caught it. Zachary knew all about it, even how the kid kissed the puck."

"Who was the player?" Erin asked.

"How the hell should I know?" Mick said. "Hockey isn't my thing."

"Do you guys think he watched the game live?" Erin asked.

Eddie nodded. "Think so. He knew everything."

"He still could have recorded it," Erin said. "We'll have to talk to him again."

****

"I'm so glad to see you." Georgia met Erin at the restaurant's door the next day. "How's it going with you and your family?"

Erin smiled. "It's been a little crazy, but we're okay. Is Melanie here yet?"

"Outside on the deck. I don't envy you getting that woman for a sister-in-law. Someone ought to take her down a few notches." She glanced toward the entry as a couple walked in. "Sorry, gotta go. You take care now. And let me know if you need any help with that Melanie." She chuckled, walking away.

"I will." Erin wound her way through the restaurant and out to the deck, where a young pony-tailed server placed a glass of white wine in front of Melanie.

"Would you like something to drink besides water?" the server asked as Erin approached the table.

"A glass of pinot grigio, please."

The server nodded, and Erin sat across from Melanie..

"I'm glad we finally got a chance to talk—just the two of us," Melanie said. "Listen, I know we got off to a bad start, and I'm hoping we can move past it. After all, in little more than a year, we'll be sisters."

Melanie's ingratiating smile and sugary tone made Erin's stomach clench. "I guess we will."

"As you know, I have a lot of friends, but decided that you should be my matron of honor and April, my junior bridesmaid." She spoke with the confidence of someone bestowing an extraordinary privilege.

Matron of honor? She must be joking. Bachelorette parties, bridal showers, and wedding dress shopping? Not going to happen. "Is it okay if we talk about it later? I told you I wanted to discuss the wedding, but that's not the real reason I'm here."

Melanie frowned. "Why then?"

"I think someone murdered Rhonda."

"The police said it was an accident."

"It wasn't."

Melanie picked up her wineglass. "You know, I'm sorry she's dead and all that, but what does it have to do with me?"

Erin forced herself to be pleasant. "More than you think. If I prove someone killed Rhonda, the authorities will look for suspects. And Mick had the most to gain from her death. He told me you two discussed the sale of Paradise Beach right before she died. What if the police find out and arrest him? He wouldn't be able to work on the motel and Dean will turn Paradise Beach over to the animal charity."

Of course, this was a stretch, but the possibility of

losing Paradise was having the desired effect. Melanie's face froze. Then her wineglass slipped from her fingers and broke apart on the deck.

"Are you fucking kidding me?"

Erin signaled a passing server and ordered Melanie another glass of wine.

"What can I do?" Melanie's hands shook as she picked up the new wineglass.

"I need to know if Mick was with you when Laura died."

"Laura, not Rhonda?"

"I think the same person who murdered Rhonda killed Laura. Was Mick with you when she died?"

"Of course he was."

Erin opened her phone to the notes app. "Mick told me he was supposed to go out with you that night, but you canceled because you had a few house showings."

"You wrote that down?"

"He guessed you might be cheating on him."

"No, I called him back and told him to meet me at Charlie's. We stayed until midnight."

Melanie obviously didn't know Mick babysat for April that night. Erin picked up her phone and pressed the phone icon.

"Who are you calling?"

"I want to know if Mick's memory is as good as yours."

"Wait. This was supposed to be about clearing Mick."

"It's about clearing you, too."

A full minute passed before Melanie said, "Promise you won't tell Mick what I say."

"I won't tell him unless I have to."

Melanie blew out a long breath. "I was with Lou Guthrie. We're business partners."

"When you were on the phone with him a few weeks ago. It sounded like you two were a lot more than business partners."

"You must have misunderstood."

Did Melanie think she was stupid enough to believe that? "Where did you and Lou go?"

"We stayed at his place."

"Can anyone corroborate that besides Lou?"

"Well, aren't you the nosy little detective? The answer is no. We were alone. Oh wait, we got a pizza delivery from Zinc."

"Did the delivery person see you?"

"He saw both of us."

"What time did the pizza arrive?"

"This is crazy. What difference does it make?"

"After Laura's funeral, you said you were glad she was dead. I wonder how Detective Mackey would react to that information."

Melanie's face twisted. "The pizza arrived around seven-thirty. You can take that judgmental look off your face. Mick and I aren't married yet." She held up her ringless left hand. "We aren't even officially engaged since you took my ring."

"What kind of pizza?"

"This is ridiculous. Why do you want to know the kind of pizza we ordered?"

"In case I check your alibi. What kind of pizza?"

"Pepperoni and pineapple. What about Mick? If he wasn't with me, where was he?"

"At home with April."

"So, this whole thing is a setup. You want to see if

I killed Laura and maybe Rhonda. Well, I didn't. Why would I?"

"For Mick's inheritance. I think you care more about the money than you care about him."

"You bitch. Mick loves me and I will marry him. Oh, and you can forget about being my matron of honor."

Erin laughed and got to her feet. "Thank you. I'll let Georgia know you're paying."

On the way home, Erin stopped at Zinc to verify Melanie's alibi. The bartender said the delivery person didn't work there anymore.

"Do you know where he is?"

"I think he's back in Ann Arbor."

"Do you have a phone number or address?"

"If we did, I couldn't give it to you. Privacy and all that."

Damn. "Can you check to see if there was a pizza delivery at Lou Guthrie's home about two months ago?"

He crossed his arms and sighed. "It's possible, but it's a pain. I'd need an exact date and time."

Erin slipped a twenty onto the bar. "May 20th in the evening."

"I'll see what I can do. It'll take me a while."

"I'll have a glass of pinot grigio while I wait."

He poured the drink, went to the office, and returned ten minutes later. "Wasn't too bad. Here it is. A pepperoni and pineapple pizza delivered to the Guthrie house at seven-thirty."

Melanie was at Guthrie's. She knew the type of pizza and the delivery time.

She's out.

****

April ran out of the house when Erin pulled into the motel parking lot. "Surprise, Mom."

Panicked, Erin clutched her daughter. "Why aren't you at Olivia's?"

"Mom, let go. You're holding me too tight. Is something wrong?"

"You need to go back. Right now. I'm calling Kelly."

April can't be anywhere around while they were looking for a murderer. She took her out her phone.

"Wait, don't call her. I *am* going back. Olivia's mom had to come to home for a few hours. Something about her work. I asked her to bring me here so I could pick up some clean clothes. She'll be here in a little while. You're acting weird. What's going on?"

It took a moment for Erin's heart to slow down. "Nothing. Let's go in." Erin gave April a squeeze. "Are you hungry?"

"Not really. I've been snacking since I got here, but I'd like a soda on the porch with you."

They sat on the rattan loveseat and watched the Hope Island Ferry's bow rise and fall with the undulating waves. "Mom, I have to tell you something."

"What?"

April squirmed. "Um...Can we go camping on Hope Island this summer?"

Why does April look so nervous? Erin had the feeling her daughter wanted to tell her something else. "Sure. We could pack a lunch, take an early ferry, and spend the day exploring. Once, an Aboriginal tribe lived on the island. We can search for their campsites and look for artifacts."

"When can we go?"

"When you get home from Olivia's cottage, we'll pick a day." If the murderer isn't in custody by then, she'll arrange for April to return to Denver. "Is that what you wanted to talk about?"

April looked down at her shoes. "Please don't be mad at me. Your tablet was in the dining room. I opened it and read the suspects list with Melanie, Doctor Zachary, and Mrs. Masters. Do you think one of them killed Granny?"

Why had she left her investigation notes out in the open? "My tablet is off-limits. It's private. Do not mention what you saw to anyone, understand?"

"Yes. I'm sorry and promise I won't tell anyone… There's something else. I looked Doctor Zachary, Mrs. Masters and Melanie up on social media, but only found Melanie and Doctor Zachary."

She'd considered checking the socials too, but something must have distracted her. "Anything interesting?"

"Nothing on Doctor Zachary except articles on mental health and pictures of him and his daughter. But I saw a video of Melanie at some party."

"Show me."

April opened the social media, then handed the phone to her mother. Erin watched the video for a while as it swept the party room. A woman, wearing a sleeveless white t-shirt, a small white veil, and a white skirt, waved. A bridal shower. Erin spotted Holly and Melanie in a group of women clinking martini glasses filled with something pinkish.

Her heart kicked when she saw the date on the post

was the date of Marilyn's murder. But the posted date wasn't necessarily the date of the shower. She had to find out when and what time the shower was held.

"Thanks, honey. You've been a big help. Share that with me, okay?"

"Sure, Mom." April's thumbs flew across her phone.

"Got it, thanks."

"I can help more if you want. We should look on other sites."

"No, that's okay. What time is Kelly coming?"

April looked at her watch. "Oh no, in about ten minutes and I haven't packed my clean clothes yet."

They hurried upstairs to April's room.

"Need help?" Erin asked.

"Mom, I'm not a baby. I can do it."

"I know you're not a baby."

But it didn't seem that long ago when she was.

April pulled some shorts and t-shirts from her dresser and set them on her bed. "I think this is all I need."

Erin packed the clothes into a duffel bag. "How about underwear?"

"Oh, yeah." April grabbed a handful and shoved them in the bag.

Erin hugged her daughter. "I missed you." She had a hard time letting go. If anything ever happened to her... "Be careful, okay?"

The doorbell rang.

"That's probably Olivia's mom," April said. She slung the duffel over her shoulder and bounced down the stairs.

Erin followed her to Kelly's car. "Thanks again for

having April at your place. I, uh…" Erin couldn't hold back tears as April jumped into the back seat.

"Is something wrong?"

"Nothing major, but would you mind if April stays with you for another week or two? She's still mourning Rhonda and, of course, being here reminds her of her grandmother." Stretching the truth, but not really a lie.

"Absolutely no problem. She can stay as long as you want."

"Thank you!" She leaned into the back seat and hugged April. "I love you, honey."

"I love you, Mom."

The car drove off. At least April was out of harm's way for a while.

When the car was out of sight, Erin drove to Stay and Shop and picked up a salad for dinner and a few other groceries. The store wasn't busy, and she was first in line at Holly's register.

"I hear April's having a blast at Olivia's cottage," Holly said. Her hands flew as she scanned and bagged the groceries.

Of course Holly knew. "She is. This is going to sound like a strange question, but do you know whose party this is?" Erin opened her phone to the video April sent her.

Holly roared. "Oh my God. That was insane. Sure. That was Jenny's bridal party."

Erin didn't know who Jenny was, but didn't need to. "Do you remember the date?"

"It was the day Marilyn died. Of course, we didn't know it then. She was the most famous person miserable Misery ever produced."

"What time was the shower?"

"About seven-thirty until ten." Holly narrowed her eyes. "I'm getting a vibe that says you're investigating something. I've had a few interesting questions from other people who hang out with you. What's up?"

Thank goodness no one was in line behind her. She weighed how much to tell Holly. "If I tell you something, do you promise not to tell anyone?"

"I know everyone thinks I'm a big gossip, and I guess I am. But I know how to keep my mouth shut."

"I don't think some of the recent rulings of suicide and accidental deaths are accurate."

"I knew something was fishy." Holly dropped a bag of hamburger patties on the conveyor belt with a damp clunk. "So you are investigating."

"Yes, but please don't tell anyone. It could make things dangerous for me and others."

"Cross my heart and hope to die. I'm here for you guys if you need anything."

Erin hoped she'd done the right thing.

Chapter Thirty-Seven

"I have a couple of things to say before we get started," Erin said. She, Mick, Shirley, and Eddie were finishing breakfast at the kitchen table. She loved the joking and laughter now, remembering her confusion and anger the day Eddie arrived. Her still unresolved feelings about Rhonda had collided with the shock of her father, apparently risen from the dead. But he'd worked some Eddie magic and was now firmly a part of the family.

"Are you daydreaming, Erin? What did you want to tell us?" Shirley refilled her coffee cup and passed around the carafe.

"Yesterday, I learned Melanie was at someone's house at the time Laura was murdered."

"What?" Mick jerked and spilled coffee on his jeans.

Shirley handed him a wad of paper towels.

"Thanks. Why didn't you tell me yesterday, Erin?"

"You didn't get home until after midnight."

"Okay, fine. Whose house was she at?"

This wasn't the time to educate Mick on his girlfriend's infidelity. "Doesn't matter right now. Another thing, I had to tell Holly we're investigating Rhonda's and the other deaths. She'd guessed what we're up to before I told her and she promised not to tell anyone. But in the future, we need to be careful what we ask her and make sure no one else can hear."

"Tell me where Melanie was. She said she was working."

"We'll talk later. Another thing, Melanie was at a bridal shower when Marilyn died."

No one spoke for a moment.

"If I'm thinking right," Eddie said, "Melanie is off the list because she has two verified alibis. And Mrs. Masters and Zachary only have one."

"At least you finally admit Melanie isn't a murderer," Mick said. "But because both Mrs. Masters and Zachary have alibis, do we have to start over?"

"Hell no," Shirley said. "Either Mrs. Masters or Zachary Smith are lying."

"But we checked out their stories," Mick said.

Eddie got up and stacked the dirty breakfast dishes. "Maybe we didn't do a good enough job."

"Do we need to add more suspects?" Mick asked.

Erin shook her head. "No more suspects yet. Those two are the most affected by Gloria's death. We just need more information on them."

"What are you thinking?" Eddie asked.

She reflected a moment. "We need at least one more alibi for each."

"Questioning them again might send up red flags." Eddie added silverware to the stack of dishes.

Shirley caught his arm, smiled and mouthed, "Thank you."

Eddie winked at her.

Oh my God, are they flirting? Eddie and Shirley being in a romantic relationship was unsettling. But cute.

"Someone might have seen Zachary or Mrs.

Masters at the time and date of one of the deaths," Erin said, "or know without a doubt where a suspect was. For example, Melanie was at a party when a murder took place."

"So, you're thinking we don't directly question the suspects, but check with other people, right?" Mick asked.

"Right."

"I have an idea," Eddie said. "Erin, didn't you say Mrs. Masters has a boyfriend?"

"Yes, Roger Wallace."

"I could start up a conversation with him and see if he was with her on the night of a different murder."

Shirley snorted. "He'd never talk to you. You don't even know him."

"Yeah, but I could knock on his door and pretend to…uh…be collecting for some charity. Then start talking about stuff. Maybe asked him out for a snort."

Mick laughed. "A what?"

"That's what us old guys used to call a drink."

"Seriously?"

Erin shot Mick a *stop-it* look. "Okay, Eddie will talk to Roger Wallace. Mick, how about taking on Zachary?"

"Hey, what about me?" Shirley said.

"You're staying here," Erin said. "We don't want you out in the open."

****

"This is it." Erin paced in front of the kitchen counter.

Between the motel work and questioning people, they hadn't been able to get together for two days. Mick, Shirley, and Eddie watched her from their seats at the table.

"After this meeting, we'll either have a good idea who the killer is...or not." She wasn't sure which was worse.

"So, at the end of the meeting, we probably won't know shit," Mick said.

Erin sat and eyed Mick wearily. "Thanks, Mr. Cheerful. Eddie, anything on Mrs. Masters?"

"Roger and I are good buddies now. I found out she has an alibi for all the murders, except Rhonda's."

Shirley patted his back. "Fantastic! How'd you do it?"

"Went to Roger's house asking for a donation for St. Jude's restoration, and before you know it, he asks me in, hands me a beer, and we start talking about Rhonda and Emma. That's old Mrs. Masters' first name. He said they spend just about every weekday together having dinner, either at her place or at The Cove, then watching TV. She asked him to move in and he's thinking about it. She must have something I don't see."

Shirley poked his arm. "But how about the murder dates?"

"I asked him point blank where he was on the day Laura died. He showed me his calendar. He and Mrs. Masters spent the night at the Running Deer Casino. Later, I called the hotel and told them a similar story Mick told the other hotel about Guthrie's room. They confirmed she was there that night. Roger also said Emma plays poker at the senior center at eight every Monday, Wednesday, and Friday morning. I went to the senior center and the manager, a nice lady, confirmed Emma was winning at poker when Shirley was run down."

"They play poker at eight in the morning?" Shirley asked.

He shrugged. "Guess so."

"Good job, Eddie." Shirley kissed his cheek.

Eddie's face grew pink, and Mick rolled his eyes. Erin smiled to herself, knowing exactly what he was thinking.

"Mick, what about Zachary?"

"Holly said he goes to either The Cove or Full of Beans for coffee every morning. I went to The Cove first. The new woman behind the counter said she doesn't know if he was in the day Shirley was hit, so I went to Full of Beans. Zachary had been there that morning. The counter person said she remembers because it was the same morning you were there asking about Shirley about an hour later."

"What time was he there?"

"She doesn't remember exactly, but between eight-thirty and eight-forty-five."

"That's the time you usually get there, right, Shirley?" Erin said.

"Yeah. When I walk, I leave here at eight-fifteen, get there a little after eight-thirty and by the time I order and gossip a little, I'm at the pharmacy by about ten to nine."

"Based on where you were found," Erin said, "you must have been hit around eight twenty-five. That gives Zachary about ten minutes to park and get to the coffee shop. Very doable."

"So, where are we?" Mick asked.

"Mrs. Masters has three solid alibis and Zachary has two squishy ones." Shirley said.

Erin drummed her fingers on the table. "Zachary could have recorded the hockey game. And timing-wise, he could have come into the coffee shop after running down Shirley."

"So, Zachary is our strongest and only suspect," Shirley said. "But why would he go on a killing spree instead of taking revenge on us by using something less…deadly?"

"He lost more than his wife the day Gloria drowned. The son he always wanted also died. Afterward, he lost custody of his daughter and had his license to practice psychology suspended. He must have snapped. All that pain and anger must have flooded back when Rhonda told him about that day on the boat."

"Yeah, that day on the boat. Somebody get me a drink, okay?" Shirley said

Erin poured her a glass of wine. Zachary was almost certainly the killer. Rhonda must have told him about Gloria, so he had a motive—revenge. But they had no evidence to take to the police. And what if they were wrong?

****

Erin needed sleep, but her mind wouldn't shut down. She'd scheduled a meeting with Mackey in the morning and wanted to appear confident and logical, not foggy with sleep deprivation.

She was almost certain Zachary was the murderer. Rhonda must have told him about Gloria during her appointment, and he murdered her that night. Afterward, he tracked down the other three women who'd been with Gloria on that trip. So far, Mackey wasn't convinced that the deaths were murders, but maybe the new circumstantial evidence was enough to convince her to take another look at Rhonda's death.

Right before she finally fell asleep, an idea occurred to her. If it worked, it might convince Mackey and Chief Sloane that she was right.

Chapter Thirty-Eight

After three cups of strong coffee, Erin's nerves zipped with caffeine and tension as she sat on the visitor side of Mackey's desk. "I believe Zachary Smith killed my mother and the other women."

"You gotta be kidding me."

"I'm not."

"I assume you have a good story."

"In fact, I do." Erin explained how she arrived at Zachary being the murderer by documenting alibis and eliminating suspects.

Mackey lifted a pen from her desk and twirled it between her fingers. Then let out an impatient breath. "Okay, I'll bite. What's the motive?"

"Revenge. Zachary was extremely possessive of his wife, and he fell apart when she died. When her obstetrician told him she'd been pregnant with a baby boy, it sent him over the edge. He began drinking and taking drugs. Lost custody of his daughter, and his psychology license was suspended. It took a few years, but he finally got it together, all the while believing Gloria's death was an accident. Then, Rhonda got terminal cancer." Her voice faded, and she leaned back in the chair. She was so tired of fighting for police support.

"Want water or something?" Mackey asked.

"No, I'm fine." She took a breath. "Rhonda visited

Zachary the day she died, supposedly for a counseling appointment. I believe she told him the truth about Gloria's death. I'm guessing she'd felt guilty for years and decided he deserved to know what really happened."

"So, she decided to ease her guilty conscience at the expense of Doctor Smith's feelings."

"She must have wanted to confess."

"Didn't she consider how Doctor Smith might react to Ms. Nowak, Ms. Mitchell, Mrs. Cochran, and herself, when he found out the truth?"

"I don't know." Time to try out last night's idea. "Did the police take photos when they examined Laura's and Marilyn's death scenes?"

"Normally, we don't photograph accidental death scenes. But initially, their cause of death was inconclusive, so photos were taken."

"Shortly before Laura and Marilyn died, I visited them at their homes. Could I take a look at the photos? Not the bodies, just the photos inside the homes."

"No, it's against the law."

"I might see something in the photos that's new or missing. I read that under exceptional circumstances, access could be granted."

Mackey paused. "Well, okay. I know how strongly you feel about this."

"Thanks, I really appreciate it."

"I'm removing the photo of the victims." Mackey clicked a few keys on her laptop, then turned it around so they both could see the screen. "This is Ms. Nowak's home." She slowly paged through the photos. "Anything pop out?"

"No, the living room and kitchen are the same as I

remember."

"If you move out of the way, I'll pull up Ms. Mitchell's file."

Once the photos were up and sorted, Mackey again moved the laptop so Erin could see the screen.

As Mackey paged through them, Erin stared at the photos so fiercely, her eyes burned. "Everything looks like I remember."

Another disappointment.

"I know you have other people working with you—no, don't try to deny it. If you're right about Doctor Smith, you and they are in danger as well as Mrs. Cochran."

"Will you help me?"

Mackey sighed deeply. "I just did. What you say is logical and believable. But as I've said many times, the accidental death cases are closed and the suicide case is open pending the toxicology report. There is no evidence crimes were committed. The exception is Ms. Cochran's hit-and-run, which is still under investigation." She got to her feet. The discussion was over.

"Thanks, Detective."

Mackey gave a half-smile. "I admire your persistence."

****

As Erin parked next to George's truck, still disappointed that nothing in the photos implicated Zachary, she scrutinized the motel's facade. It looked good. Actually, better than good and ahead of schedule. The crew had repaired the truck-damaged wall, installed a sky-blue roof on both the left and right rows of units, and replaced the windows. George said with the additional help, they'd still make the motel up-to-code date about two months away. Maybe a little ahead. Looks like Mick will get his inheritance after all. A feeling of territoriality and regret surprised her when she remembered Westside would control the property in less than a year.

Standing next to the RV, Eddie rested his hand on Mick's. They were laughing. Mick finally had a father, and it warmed her heart. Some good was coming out of this mess. For now, she pushed aside the disappointing meeting with Mackey and the ultimate destruction of the Paradise Beach Motel.

"Oh, you're back," Shirley said when Erin came into the kitchen. A cookbook lay open on the table. "Did the good detective let you look at the crime scene photos?"

"Some, and before you ask, she left out pictures of the bodies." Erin grabbed a bottle of water from the refrigerator and sunk into a chair. "Nothing's missing in the rooms."

"That's too bad. I know you were hoping Zachary was the souvenir-collecting type."

"Doesn't mean he's not. Maybe he took something from a drawer like a piece of jewelry. But he's probably too smart for that."

Her phone rang, and she listened to her doctor's automated appointment reminder. "Damn." She opened the calendar app on her phone.

"What?"

"I have an appointment for my annual physical tomorrow in Denver and forgot to cancel it." She called the doctor's office, canceled the next day's appointment and said she'd call back to reschedule.

"Tell me about the photos you saw."

"Not much to tell. Laura's place still looked like a page out of an interior design magazine. Nothing out of place. Nothing to suggest anyone else had been there."

"Are you sure nothing was missing?"

"Nothing I remember."

Shirley reached across the table and squeezed Erin's hand. "Must have been hard for you to look at the pictures."

"It was. They reminded me of the time I spent with her. I'd felt a connection and not just because she was Rhonda's friend. She didn't deserve what happened to her."

"If I let myself think about my three friends dying the way they did, I'd go crazy. We have to get that bastard."

"We won't stop until we do. I promise."

Shirley pulled a tissue out of her pocket and blew her nose. "What about Marilyn's house?"

Erin half-smiled. "In the same shape as when I was there. Open play scripts all over the coffee table, a sweater slung over the back of a chair, dishes piled in the sink. Papers stacked on her desk. Marilyn was comfortably messy. I really liked her."

Her phone rang again.

"Hi Mom, just wanted to tell you I love you and miss you."

"I miss you too, honey. Are you having fun?"

"I love it here. We definitely have to get a boat."

Not going to happen. "We can talk about it when you get home."

"Okay, I just wanted to say hi. Olivia is waiting for me on the beach."

"Have fun. I love you." Erin ended the call. Something nagged at her brain. Something about her doctor appointment. She opened her calendar app. Yes, she had an appointment for tomorrow. She'd booked it when she saw the doctor last year.

"Oh my God." Erin's chair fell over when she jumped up.

"What?"

"Marilyn and I talked about appointment books when I was at her cottage. She showed me the one her mother bought her for Christmas. It had a blue crocodile leather cover. She said cost about three hundred dollars. I don't remember seeing it in the photos I saw today…Wait, I'll look for it." She searched for a few minutes. "Here it is." She handed the phone to Shirley.

"My God. It costs four-hundred-sixty dollars. Are you sure that's it?"

"Positive. I'm calling Mackey."

"You have reached the phone of Detective Caroline Mackey. If this is an emergency, hang up and call 9-1-1. Otherwise, leave a brief message."

"Detective, this is Erin Brady. I would like to see Marilyn Mitchell's photos again. Please call me as soon as you can."

Two hours later, Erin's phone rang.

"It's Detective Mackey, Erin. What's this all about?"

"Can you send me the photos of Marilyn's house?"

"Impossible."

Erin made her voice as calm as she could while stifling the excitement. "May I come in and check them?"

"Why?"

She didn't want to mention the appointment book yet. "I remembered something Marilyn said and want to take another look at the photos if it's not too much trouble. Please."

Silence for a moment. "Erin, this is getting—"

"I know. Please."

"Fine, tomorrow." The detective hung up.

****

"You've got exactly ten minutes to go through the photos." Mackey's face was flushed with either annoyance or anger. Probably both. "I sympathize with what you're trying to do, but this has got to stop. I have other cases to work on."

"Thank you so much, Detective." Erin said. "I really appreciate everything you've done for me."

Mackey took a large manila envelope from her desk. "Let's go."

Erin followed her into an interrogation room. Her heart gave a thud. "Am I being questioned about something?"

"No. Sit."

Erin lowered herself onto a chair, and Mackey handed her the envelope. "I can't work while you're in my office, so I printed the relevant photos. You may not keep them and do not take pictures of them. If you do, I'll know." She nodded toward the camera in the upper left corner of the room.

"Thank you, I won't." She didn't need to take a picture of the photos. She just wanted to see if the appointment book was in one of them.

"Ten minutes." Mackey left the room, snapping the door shut.

Erin spilled the photos onto to the table, shuffled through them, and selected one showing the living room desk. The appointment book wasn't there. She examined the rest of the living room photos. Not there either. Then she looked through every photo of the cottage's interior. Nothing. A tiny trickle of hope. She replaced the envelope's contents and walked it back to Mackey's office.

Mackey looked up from her laptop. "Did you find what you were looking for?"

"No."

"What were you looking for?"

"Marilyn's appointment book. It was her desk when I visited her and it might contain the names of the people she'd seen the day she died. She could have moved it, though. Do you know if her family cleared out her belongings?"

"The cottage owners told them they can take as long as they want to pack up. The family said they'll be here in—" she typed on her keyboard. "They'll be here in two weeks."

"Can we get in and look around before then?"

"First of all, there's no *we*. Second, I'd need probable cause to get a search warrant and since there's no crime, there's no probable cause."

"But the owners could give us permission."

"No."

****

Erin left the building, slipped into her car and bounced her forehead on the steering wheel. *Why is everything so damn hard with Mackey?* She straightened when she remembered she'd stored Marilyn's cottage address in her phone. A search produced the private rental-by-owner listing and the owner's phone number. She called it and a woman answered with a wary "Hello?"

"Hi, I'm Erin Brady and I'd like to rent your Misery Cove cottage for the summer, beginning next week, if possible."

"Sorry, but we're not renting it out at this time."

"I know about the suicide, and it doesn't bother me."

"It hasn't been cleared out yet and won't be for a while."

"Can I at least get in to look around?"

"No, I'm sorry. We don't live in Michigan and I wouldn't want to take responsibility for the previous renter's uh…effects. Anyway, we're selling the cottage. You might want to look up the new owners in a few months."

****

Shirley and Eddie were on the back porch when Erin returned from seeing Mackey. Shirley closed her book. "What happened with the detective?"

Eddie pulled out his earbuds. "Was the appointment book on Marilyn's desk?"

"No." A tinny version of a country singer's voice leaked from the earbuds as she pulled a chair around to face them. "I called the owners of the cottage Marilyn rented, hoping they'd let me look around if I said I wanted to rent it. They said no. So, who wants to check it out with me?"

"Are you talking about breaking in?" Shirley's tone had a disapproving edge. "You could go to jail if you get caught."

"I don't care. Zachary has to get arrested so he

can't…get to you," Erin said.

"Thanks for what you're trying to do," Shirley said, "but I wish there was another way. Please don't break into that cottage."

"I'm good for a break-in." Eddie brightened.

"Don't do it. You'll both end up in prison."

"Not if we're smart," Eddie said. "Does the cottage have security cameras?"

Erin shot a sideway glance at Shirley, who was obviously not happy about where this conversation was going. "I didn't see any when I was there, either inside the cottage or outside. Eddie, do you have any ideas about how we can get in?"

"Well, I might have broken into a place or two over the years."

"You did?" Shirley looked impressed. "There's lots about you I don't know."

"Let's just say tough times require tough actions. When do you want to do it, Erin?"

She covered her eyes for a moment. "How about the day after tomorrow? Gives us time to come up with a good plan."

"Just a sec," Shirley said. "Since what you're going to do is illegal, how can you use whatever you find as evidence?"

"I'll think about that tomorrow," Erin said.

"Sure thing," Shirley said. "And just so you know, I'm driving the getaway car."

Chapter Thirty-Nine

After midnight, two days later, Shirley drove past Marilyn's cottage and parked off the road a quarter of a mile away. "You guys okay?"

"I'm good," Erin said. She really wasn't. She was scared out of her mind.

Eddie looked ready for battle. "No cars on the road. Let's go."

"I'll text you when we're finished, Shirley," Erin slid out of the car and into the cool air. What were they doing? This was beyond crazy. If they were caught, April would have a jailbird for a mom.

"Please, please be careful," Shirley said.

Erin looked over her shoulder at Eddie as they moved toward the cottage, hiding behind the bushes and trees lining the road. They'd dressed in black and wore black masks left over from Covid times. "Thanks for doing this with me," she whispered.

"You're my daughter and I'd do anything for you."

She nodded, still uncomfortable that he'd eased into being her father faster than she'd adapted to being his daughter. They rushed through the open space next to Marilyn's cottage. When they were close, she sprinted to the back door, with Eddie in her wake, and tried the doorknob. Of course, it was locked.

Eddie held a small flashlight in his mouth while he removed a little tool kit from his pocket, selected a tool, and picked the lock. The door swung open into the kitchen.

"Crappy lock," he murmured. "You okay, kiddo?"

She switched on her flashlight. "I'm fine. How about you search the living room, bathroom, and laundry room and I'll take the kitchen and two bedrooms?"

"Fine with me." He headed for the living room.

Erin dreaded going into the bedroom where Marilyn died. Even though she didn't believe in ghosts, she'd always believed some part of a person's essence survived in the place where they'd died. If she saw even a glimmer of Marilyn hovering over the bed, she'd blast out of the house screaming. But peace filled the room. Moonlight poured through the window's horizontal blinds, covering the bare mattress with bright strips of light. She began her search.

No appointment book on either bedside table or inside the drawers. The dresser and closet contained only Marilyn's clothing. The blue appointment book wasn't in the second bedroom, either.

After finishing an unproductive search of the kitchen, despair hit her. She kept running into dead ends, and it was wearing her out. Eddie joined her a few minutes later.

"You look happy," she said.

"I didn't find her book, but I found her cell phone. I looked through the desk to see if she'd written the password on anything. If she did, I didn't find it." He handed the phone to Erin.

"At least it's something. We better go." Erin texted Shirley to pick them up.

****

Twenty minutes later, Erin, Shirley, and Eddie sat around the kitchen table, staring at each other.

Erin shoved the phone aside. "It's not much good until we can unlock it,"

"I'll take it," Eddie said. "I'm pretty good at figuring out passwords."

"Good luck." It was almost three a.m. but Erin was wide awake. "Since we didn't find the blue book, maybe Zachary took it with him."

"Why would he do that?"

"Because his name might be in it," Erin said.

Shirley frowned. "You're not thinking about breaking into Zachary's house, are you?"

Eddie pounded a fist on the table. "Let's do it,"

"No!" Erin and Shirley shouted simultaneously.

"He might have thrown it away," Shirley said. "He probably has a cleaning service. If he does, Holly would know. I can ask her to ask the cleaning lady or man or whoever, if anything new and blue turned up about a month ago."

"Brilliant," Erin said.

Shirley stood. "I'm on it. Going to bed now, but in the morning, I'll do a little shopping."

"Not alone, you're not."

"It's just to the grocery store and back. Relax, okay?"

****

The next morning, Eddie grumbled over his third cup of coffee, "She's been gone more than an hour. How long does it take to buy a couple of groceries?"

Erin laughed. "It's not the groceries. It's getting away from Holly once she gets started."

They were still sitting at the table when Shirley

came into the kitchen fifteen minutes later and set a bag of groceries on the counter.

"You two haven't moved."

"Didn't think you'd take so long," Eddie said.

"You know Holly." Shirley pulled out a chair and sat. "She said she'd be glad to ask Terry, Zachary's housekeeper, if there's a blue appointment book in his house. She also said she knows for a fact that Terry goes through Zachary's trash because he regularly throws away good stuff. She keeps some and sells the rest on the online auction site. If the book isn't in Zachary's house, maybe she has it. Holly said we should get a picture of what we're looking for and she'll show it to Terry and tell her we'll give her fifty dollars for the book if she still has it."

"This is so great, Shirley. Thank you."

"I hope it works out. Do you still have the picture you showed me the other day?" Shirley asked. "Get it and I'll run it over to Holly."

When Shirley left, Eddie said, "Have you ever fired a pistol?"

"No, why?"

"We're getting into some pretty dangerous territory now, and I think you need one. I have a three-eighty in the RV. Come and take a look at it and if you feel comfortable, let's spend an hour at the range. I'll run you through handgun safety and show you how to take a few shots."

A gun. Erin never wanted one, but Zachary hadn't been reluctant about killing three women, so she shouldn't be reluctant about defending herself. "Let's go."

****

The next afternoon, Shirley rushed into the house. "Look what I have." She handed a Stay and Shop grocery bag to Erin. "Holly said Terry found the blue book in a paper bag at the bottom of the laundry room trash bin. She didn't sell it because she liked it."

"She liked it, but sold it to you?"

Shirley grinned. "I guess she liked the fifty dollars more than the book."

Erin looked inside the bag. "Thank God—oh, it's just the cover. Zachary must have removed the pages before tossing it away."

"Probably burned them. That's what I'd do," Shirley said.

"The cover still proves he had something of Marilyn's. I'm taking it to Mackey. Hopefully, it's enough evidence to look into Marilyn's case and eventually Rhonda's and Laura's."

Eddie came into the house, grinning. He handed Marilyn's cell phone to Erin. The home screen glowed.

"How'd you unlock it?" Erin asked.

"My little secret."

Erin checked Marilyn's email, texts, and phone calls. "Nothing helpful except an unknown person called her the day before she died." She found Rhonda's phone and turned it on. "It's the same number that called Rhonda on the day she died."

"So that's how he set up the meetings," Shirley said.

"Probably. We need to get the phone back into Marilyn's cottage before her family clears out her things."

"I'll take care of it," Eddie said.

"Don't tell me how you're going to do it." Erin

picked up the bag and started for the front door.

"Going to see Mackey now?" Shirley asked.

"I am." Finally, some physical evidence.

****

Erin knocked on Mackey's half-open door.

"Come in, but don't bother sitting. You won't be here long."

Erin held up the grocery bag. "Evidence."

Mackey sighed heavily. "Seriously, Erin—"

"Please, look." She handed Mackey the bag. "It's what I was searching for in the photos of Marilyn's house. It's the cover of her appointment book. Her initials are on it."

"Where did you get this?" Mackey's voice sharpened.

"From Zachary Smith's housekeeper. She found it in his trash the day after Marilyn died."

"So, you went looking for it because you hoped his name might be in it, with the time he was visiting her?"

"Well, yes. Unfortunately, all the pages are missing."

Mackey stared into the bag for a long while, then said, "This so-called evidence is useless. No chain of custody. Even if Doctor Smith's fingerprints are on it, there's no telling how or when they got there."

"But it's still pretty interesting, right? Marilyn's empty appointment book being in Zachary's trash?"

"I assume you convinced the housekeeper to give this to you. Maybe you even paid her for it."

Erin didn't respond.

Mackey opened a desk drawer and dropped the bag inside. "I'm keeping this. What if you're right about Smith and the housekeeper mentions the appointment book to him? You could get yourself killed. Stop this, Erin. I mean it."

"There's one more thing. Rhonda got a call from an unknown phone number the day she died. Marilyn had a call from the same number the day before she died. That could have been the killer setting up the meetings. Can you check it out?"

"Not unless the deaths are considered suspicious. And they're not. By the way, how did you know about Marilyn's caller? Wait, don't tell me. Let me just say that if anyone steals anything from a murder victim, for example, a cell phone, any evidence on that phone is inadmissible. And by the way, stealing a cell phone is a felony."

Brick wall. Brick wall. Brick wall. "Can't you do anything? You must see something strange is going on here."

"Erin, I appreciate your persistence and think I'd do the same if I were in your shoes. But even if I believed the deaths were murders, there's nothing I can do without evidence. As I've said before, I believe you and your helpers are in danger if you're right, so I'm telling you to stop what you're doing now before anyone else gets hurt."

"You mean *killed*, don't you?"

****

Shirley flung the front door open. "Well, what'd she say?"

"Not much." They walked through the house to the back porch and sat in chairs facing the lake. "According to Mackey, the book cover is useless as evidence."

"Chain of custody?"

"How did you—? Never mind. You're addicted to

cop shows."

"Comes in handy. Okay, what do we do now?"

"First, you need to call Steve and tell him you need two weeks off. Then I want you to pack. You're going somewhere Zachary can't find you. I have a lot of frequent flyer miles, so let's go online and pick out a nice resort in the Caribbean."

"No."

"Just no?"

"I'm not letting that asshole chase me out of town. Let's get the team back together and come up with a plan to catch the bastard."

"Shirley—"

"Don't Shirley me. I'm not budging. Eddie thinks we should bring George into the team and I agree. He and Mick already filled George in on where we are."

"They should have asked me first." She exhaled slowly. "Anyway, we can't protect you here."

"Then you better think of something, because I'm not going to some damn island and worry about what the rest of you are doing."

Erin was silent for a minute. "Okay. I'll work on it. Team meeting tonight."

Chapter Forty

"I have a plan to trap Zachary."

Erin sat at the head of the dining room table, trying to ignore the churning in her gut. The four faces around the table mirrored her apprehension. They were close to the endgame, and she had to remain strong.

"Zachary is smart and arrogant. A psychologist. A murderer. I wouldn't blame you if you want to back out."

In a way, she hoped they would back out. Hotheaded Mick might get reckless. Eddie would take risks to protect his family. George wasn't as emotionally invested as the rest of them and would stay calm and logical. But she worried that under severe stress, he might act impulsively. As for Shirley, she would be nowhere near Misery Cove when the action started.

"No way in hell I'm backing out," Eddie said. "He went for Shirley twice, and he's not gonna stop until he gets her."

"Twice?" Mick said. "Oh yeah, maybe the fire. You know I'm in."

George gave a thumbs up. "Me too."

"Shirley, how about you?" Erin knew she'd be against the whole thing.

Silence for a moment, then Shirley planted her elbows on the table and lowered her head. "I hate this. I wish there was another way."

"There isn't. We've interviewed people. Found evidence like the wine bottle and Marilyn's appointment book cover. We've concluded Zachary is the only person harmed by Gloria's death who doesn't have a solid alibi for the murders. But it's not solid enough for the police. The only thing left is to record Zachary doing or saying something incriminating."

"How?" Mick asked. "If he's so damn smart, he'll be on to us."

Erin grinned. "We're going fishing for him."

"What do you mean?" Shirley looked up. "Literally fishing with him?"

Erin left her chair and leaned against a wall to stretch her tense muscles. "Not with him, for him. We'll set out bait and reel him in when he goes for it."

"What's the bait?" Mick asked.

"Not what, who. It's me he wants." Shirley raised her hand. "I'll be the bait."

"You will not be the bait." Eddie glared. "You're no spring chicken, Shirl."

"No, I'm the bait," Erin said. "I'll tell him I know how he committed the murders. He'll deny everything, of course, but he'll want to shut me up."

Mick grabbed her hand and squeezed hard. "No, Erin."

She twisted away. "Yes, Mick."

"I agree with Mick," Eddie said. "You won't be bait, either."

"There's no one else. And Shirley, you're staying out of town until Zachary's arrested."

"Hell, no! You'll be in danger because of me. I need to help."

"The best thing you can do is stay out of the way so we don't have to worry about you. Please, Shirley."

Shirley scowled. "We'll see."

"Problem is, Erin, we won't know when he'll come for you," George said.

"If he knew Mick and Eddie wouldn't be home for a night or two, he wouldn't be able to resist coming for me."

"I'm not comfortable with this," Eddie said. "But let's talk it out a minute." He paused. "How about this? During our next poker game, I can say Mick and I are going fishing at Gun Lake."

George shook his head. "What if he doesn't come to poker?"

"He will. He hasn't missed a game all year." Shirley rocked back and forth. "This is way too dangerous."

"It's the only way," Erin said. "If anything goes wrong, we can call it off."

"I don't like it, either," Mick said. "What if he comes in shooting?"

"The police believe the deaths were accidents and a suicide," Erin said. "He won't want to mess it up with a murder."

"So now you're a mind reader." Shirley rocked faster. "What if he wants it to look like a burglary gone wrong or something?"

"I haven't told you the whole plan. I'll make an appointment with Zachary for psychological counseling. At the appointment, I'll say I can't sleep because I don't believe Rhonda's death was accidental, that someone killed her. In the next session, I'll tell him most of what I believe—that someone murdered

Rhonda, Laura, and Marilyn and tried to murder Shirley and that I have proof, but don't know who the murderer is. I'll say I'm taking the evidence to the police and hopefully, he'll freak."

Shirley frowned. "What's stopping him from killing you then and there?"

"At the second session, he won't be prepared for my knowing as much as I do. Anyway, what's he going to do? Shoot me and mess up his office? No. He'll know I'd have told you guys I have an appointment with him, so he'll try to get me alone somewhere else. And we'll help him with that—the fishing trip plan."

"I hope it works." Shirley sounded doubtful.

"I hope so too. At the poker game, Eddie will say he's going up north fishing with Mick for two days and a night. He'll believe you're alone with me, Shirley, so he'll think he's getting a twofer."

"I'll say you and me will be having a good old time while they're away," Shirley said.

"Good idea. He'll come to Paradise when he thinks we're asleep. Shirley, you'll be in a hotel."

"No way I'm leaving you alone."

Erin grasped Shirley's hand. "Don't take this the wrong way, but we'd get distracted worrying about you if you stay. Mick, Eddie, and George will be close by."

If anything went wrong, she could die. So could the others. But the alternative was to do nothing and have no clue when Zachary will kill Shirley. That can't happen.

"Where do you plan to be when he comes?" Mick asked.

"On the back porch. I'll have a light on and pretend to be reading or something, with Eddie's gun ready.

Mick, you can rig up video and audio recorders."

"What if, after all this, he doesn't admit to murdering Mom or anyone?" Mick asked.

"Trust me. He'll want to kill me when I'm done with him. But he's so conceited he'll brag about the murders first. When he attacks, two of you guys will jump in and restrain him and the other will call the police. Attempted murder is a felony. That should be enough probable cause for Mom's death to be re-investigated, followed by Marilyn's and Laura's."

Mick jumped out of his chair. "Are you out of your freaking mind?" he yelled. "No, no, and no!"

"No bloody way!" Shirley shouted.

"You've been watching the British murder mysteries again, haven't you, Shirl?" Eddie joked, then turned to Mick. "I'm as worried as you are, but Erin's idea is a sound one. Now we have to figure out how to make it safe as possible."

"I agree with Eddie," George said.

Plans were falling into place alarmingly fast. "Are you okay with this, Shirley and Mick?"

Shirley frowned. "No comment."

"I'm okay." Mick pivoted between Eddie and George. "We three need to stay as close to my sister as possible."

"Roger that," Eddie said.

"Okay, I'll call Zachary tomorrow to set up an appointment. I'll try to get a second appointment the day before the poker game, where you'll tell him about the fishing trip."

****

Three days later, Zachary led Erin into his office and gestured toward a plush loveseat. "Please sit."

"Thanks for seeing me so soon."

The room had a comforting, cozy charm. Would have been soothing if she wasn't alone with a multiple murderer.

Zachary took a leather portfolio from his desk, sat across from her in one of the matching chairs, and opened the portfolio to the legal pad inside. "I'm happy I could accommodate you. Let's start with you sharing what you hope to achieve here." His gaze was warm and kind. What was going through his mind as he faced the daughter of one of his victims?

"I'm a little nervous." She actually was a little, and it didn't hurt if he thought he had the upper hand.

"This is a safe place." Zachary eased back into the chair and crossed his legs. "The last time you were here, you asked me questions about your mother's emotional health. Is it something about her?"

"I think about her all the time and can't sleep. When I do, I have nightmares."

"About your mother?"

"It's the way she died." Answering him was easier than she'd imagined. Most of what she'd say would be true.

"What about that bothers you?"

"She was alone when she drowned. And she'd been drinking. I used to wonder if she killed herself."

He jotted a few notes. "This is the third time we've met, and you've seemed troubled each time. In the town square, you were upset because of Mother's Day. When you questioned me here, you were concerned about your mother's state of mind. And now you're experiencing sleeplessness, nightmares, and anxiety about Rhonda's death. Anything else going on? Are you frequently tired, feeling guilty, depressed?"

"Of course, I'm depressed. My mother died less than three months ago."

"I'd like to hear about your relationship with her."

She told Zachary about her life with Rhonda and hating Misery Cove. Did he think she'd been a terrible daughter? If so, he was right. She had been. Never considered Rhonda's feelings about being a single mom, raising two kids, and running a motel after her husband deserted her.

"What I find interesting is how your feelings about your mother parallel those of Misery Cove. You emotionally abandoned both while you lived at home, then physically when you remained in Colorado after college. How do you feel about that?"

His insight surprised her. "I don't know. I never put it together the way you did."

"Are there other areas of abandonment in your life we need to explore?"

"I don't think so."

"What about when your father left and Rhonda emotionally abandoned you and your brother? Often in situations like this, the children feel unloved. Is that how you felt?"

She swallowed hard and shrugged. That was painfully accurate. She'd always thought her mother didn't love her. That's why she started calling her Rhonda. To punish her.

"Rhonda abandoned you again when she died. Do you agree we have some work to do to unpack these layers of love and abandonment?"

"I suppose."

How could he have figured all that out? She didn't

like it. And she'd been as bad as her mother when she abandoned Mick for Denver, leaving him to cope with Rhonda, the house, and the motel. He was getting into her head. Time to change the subject.

"Back to Rhonda's death. I don't believe it was an accident."

"Quite a shift in topic, but let's go with it. You mentioned you suspected your mother killed herself. Do you still believe that?"

"Not anymore. I think someone murdered her."

His head jerked up. "Murdered?" He paused. "Let's explore that further."

She'd surprised him, but he wanted to talk about the murder. Wanted to find out what she knew or suspected. "It's because of a recurring nightmare I've been having."

"Are you comfortable sharing your nightmare with me?"

"I am." She'd spent hours coming up with it. "I was in a large, empty field, with Rhonda at the far end in the woods, calling me. I started running toward her, but couldn't get closer. Like I was on a treadmill. Finally, I broke free and stumbled on a bottle of her favorite wine. That's all I remember."

He wrote on his pad. "Why did this nightmare lead you to believe Rhonda was murdered?"

"It reminded me of something that actually happened."

"Tell me more about that."

"A few days after Rhonda died, I found an empty bottle of her favorite wine in the woods next to Paradise Beach. It was the same brand she'd taken from The Sand Bar a few hours before she died."

Zachary clicked the top of his pen a few times. "Was the same bottle in your dream?"

"Yes. I realized it might be important, so I snapped a picture with my phone and left it where it was. I'll show you." She scrolled to the photo on her phone and handed it to him.

His back stiffened as he expanded the image. "Looks like an old bottle in a junk pile."

"I read Rhonda's autopsy report. It said when she fell, her head hit a dock piling, causing the concave contusion on her head." She sniffed, grabbed a tissue from the box on the table, and dabbed the non-existent tears under her eyes.

"Please go on."

"May I have my phone back?"

He dangled it above her open palm for a long moment before dropping it in. "Have you shown the photo to anyone?"

"No, but I asked Detective Mackey if a wine bottle could have made the injury on Rhonda's head. She called the medical examiner, who said it was possible. I wanted the detective to reopen the case, but she said the M.E. reaffirmed the accidental death ruling."

"How did that make you feel?"

"Aggravated. They should at least examine the bottle. I convinced Detective Mackey to send officers to retrieve it. But by the time they came, the bottle was gone. I didn't think about the bottle again until a few weeks ago, when the nightmares started. I think they're trying to tell me something."

"That someone murdered your mother?"

"That the person who took the bottle killed Rhonda with it."

Zachary clicked his pen, paused, and wrote on his notepad. "From what I've been told, the detectives and medical examiner are certain Rhonda's death was accidental. Thinking it was anything else is causing your anxiety and stress. What steps can you take to move forward?"

She had to keep him on point. "There's something else. Rhonda had a visitor that night."

He set the portfolio down and got to his feet. "Would you like some water?"

"No, thanks."

He removed a bottle from the mini-fridge, twisted off the top, then sat and set the bottle on the table. "Are you certain Rhonda had a visitor?"

"Yes. One of her friends told me Rhonda called her around ten that night. While they were on the phone, the doorbell rang. The friend said she heard two voices—Rhonda's and a man's. I think that man killed her."

Zachary closed the portfolio abruptly. "That's a lot to explore, but our time is up for today. I'd like us to meet again to further explore your relationship with Rhonda. Soon to keep today's momentum going."

"Yes, I'd like that. How is two days from now?" The day before the poker game.

"Perfect. Is three in the afternoon good for you?"

"That works." He didn't consult his schedule. Either he's not that busy, which doesn't seem likely, given his popularity. Or he's clearing his schedule for her to learn what she knows.

"Excellent. Together we'll create a plan to guide you on a path toward healing."

"Thank you, Zachary." She'd gotten to him. She

knew it.

Erin started for the door.

"Erin, wait a sec. We talked about the possibility of your mother's death being a suicide. Have you had any thoughts about harming yourself?"

So that was how he was going to play it. "Not often, but sometimes."

"Please feel free to call me at any time of the day or night if you don't feel safe from others or yourself."

Right. Like he wanted Rhonda to feel safe that night.

"Thanks again."

****

"There he is," Erin whispered as she, Mick, Shirley, Eddie, and George followed a server to a table in Zinc later that day. Zachary was seated at the bar with a glass of wine. He looked up and saw her. She gave a friendly wave, and he raised his glass in acknowledgment.

"Can we sit over there?" she asked the server, gesturing toward an oblong table at the back of the room, far from the bar.

"Sure."

When they sat, the server set menus on the table and took their drink orders. She returned a few minutes later with two glasses of white wine and three beers.

"Shirley, good idea, spying on Zachary," Mick said.

"I wanted to see how he'd react to Erin after their session this afternoon. He's such a smug jerk. I bet he stops by our table."

Mick eyed Zachary's back. "How'd you play it at his office?"

"I started by saying I was having nightmares." When she finished, no one spoke for a moment.

"Whew, what a story," Eddie said. "You did good."

"You might have done too good." Shirley took a long sip of her wine. "What if he goes after you before we're ready?"

"I said I didn't know who the killer was. I'm pretty sure I rattled him, though, but not enough to kill me. He'll want to know what I know." Her phone vibrated. "It's Mackey. I'll take it outside."

Erin caught Zachary glancing her way as she left the restaurant. She ignored him. "Hi Detective."

"What the hell have you been saying to Doctor Smith?" The cold fury in Mackey's voice was unmistakable.

This wasn't good.

"Nothing, why?"

"He was at my office this afternoon asking if it was possible your mother's death wasn't accidental. You talked to him, didn't you?"

"Did he say why he wanted to know?"

"He said he was her psychologist and wanted to update his records."

A thin icy thread traveled up her spine. "What did you tell him?"

"The same thing I told you, that there's no evidence her death was anything but an accident. Now you tell me what prompted his visit."

"Well, I was having trouble sleeping and—"

"Bull. You went to him for a psych session, didn't you? You think he killed your mother and you're spending time alone with him? Probably questioning him about her. And here I thought you were smart. Stop poking the hornet's nest, Erin. I mean it. I think he's getting suspicious." Mackey hung up.

Of course, she was right, but Erin didn't know what else to do.

"What did Mackey say?" Shirley asked when Erin rejoined the table.

"That Zachary went to her office and asked if there's a chance Rhonda's death wasn't an accident."

"Why would he do that?" Mick asked. "He's the killer."

"He wants to know what the cops think," George said.

Eddie scraped the beer bottle label with a fingernail. "I agree."

The server appeared at the table. "Need anything?"

"Bring us two orders of french fries and lots of ketchup," Eddie said. "And another round of drinks."

After she left, Erin said, "We need to talk about a few things. First, my next appointment with him is in two days."

"And our poker game is the next day," Shirley said. "Mick and Eddie will talk about going fishing this weekend and I'll say you and I are going out to dinner, then home to watch movies."

The server returned with the drinks and fries.

Erin picked up a fry and bit into it. "Eddie, you need to say you and Mick are leaving early Saturday morning and coming back Sunday afternoon. That forces Zachary to try for me Saturday night."

Shirley pushed the plate of French fries toward Eddie. "Get this away from me. I get fatter just smelling those greasy, salty, delicious things."

"I don't want it near me either." Erin shoved the plate farther across the table. "What about you, Mick? Everything set?"

"Yep, while the poker game is on, I'll stick a tracker on Zachary's car. Don't mention that to Mackey. I'm not sure it's legal." Mick grabbed three fries and dunked them into the ketchup on his plate. On the way to his mouth, ketchup dripped on his shirt. "Shit."

"I'll get it out," Erin said. "To move on, I've been working out the logistics for Z-day, the day Zachary comes for me."

She caught a movement out of the corner of her eye. Zachary dug a wallet out of his pocket and handed the bartender a credit card.

"Zachary just signed his check and now he's walking over here," Shirley said. "Told you so."

"Nice to see you all." Zachary stood at the head of the table. His gaze shifted to George. "I'm afraid I don't know you. I'm Zachary Smith."

"I'm George Stevens. Managing the motel renovation."

"Pleasure." Zachary gave a nod that included everyone at the table. "You look lovely tonight, Erin. Maybe we'll see each other here another time. Have a wonderful evening, everyone," he said. Then turned and left.

What was he doing? Flirting? Trying to prove he has nothing to hide? He was probably taunting her, the arrogant jerk.

She couldn't wait to see him taken down.

Chapter Forty-One

Two days later, Zachary's fingers flipped through the pages of his legal pad. Those fingers clutched the wine bottle that bashed Rhonda's head. They pushed Laura down her basement stairs. They forced vodka and antidepressants into Marilyn. They steered a car into Shirley.

She wanted to smash them all, one by one.

"Ah, here we are." Zachary set his hand on the page and looked up. "Erin, you appear upset. Is something troubling you?"

Erin faked a smile. "I'm fine."

"Good. Any improvement sleeping?"

"No, and I'm tired of being tired. Tired of feeling helpless."

"As we work together, you'll find you have the power to change. Change the way you feel about your mother, the way you process her death, the way you live your life, the way you—"

She couldn't take any more of his smarmy condescension. "Did you know my mother's friends Laura Nowak and Marilyn Mitchell?"

"I knew them slightly. They lived in Misery Cove awhile back."

"Did you see them when they were here this year?"

He repositioned himself in the chair. "This is your session, Erin. And while I encourage you to ask any questions you wish, I'm more comfortable when we stay on topic."

"You know they died, right?"

"Are you having nightmares about them?"

"No, but something's been bothering me. Three friends, Rhonda, Laura, and Marilyn, died suddenly in the last three months. I got to know Laura and Marilyn this year. Some people said Rhonda seemed worried in the days before she died and I wanted to know if she'd said anything to them. If they knew of anyone who might have a grudge against her. I asked you too, remember?"

"Did you learn anything from talking to Ms. Nowak and Ms. Mitchell?"

"Not much. But then they died. I think someone killed them."

He clicked his pen twice and poised it above the notepad. "What I'm hearing is your concern that the police didn't properly investigate the deaths of your mother and her friends."

"What I'm actually saying is their killer is clever and made their deaths appear to be something other than murders."

He studied her face. "All right, for just a moment, let's work through that scenario. Who might have killed those women?"

"I don't know. I went to the police. Of course, they said there's no evidence of homicide in any of the three deaths. So, I began my own investigation."

"Let's look at the statistics. Two of the women fell. One in four older adults falls every year and some falls are fatal. And that age group commits eighteen percent of suicides in the United States, although they're just sixteen percent of the population."

"I believe the statistics, but they don't apply here. From what I discovered, the killer was either incompetent or didn't do their homework. They made mistakes."

"Losing your mother was a significant life event. You haven't had time to process it."

"The first mistake was throwing the wine bottle onto the trash pile in the woods. The killer didn't think it was important since Rhonda supposedly died falling off the dock. As you know, I found it and shot a photo. Unfortunately, the killer must have realized its significance and picked it up."

"Erin, I—"

"The second mistake was in Laura's death. To be fair, the killer probably didn't know she had mice in her basement and was too afraid to go down there. The exterminators weren't available for a week. A few days before the appointment, she died."

"Next, I assume you want to talk about mistakes in Ms. Mitchell's death?"

"Yes. It's the most interesting one. I visited Marilyn a few days before she was murdered and noticed a beautiful blue appointment book on her desk. She told me she used it for scheduling everything, including phone calls to her mother. The book disappeared. It wasn't in the crime scene photos. And according to my source, it wasn't in her cottage."

"Are you saying someone stole the book?"

"It's possible. Sometimes when people steal things, the items end up being sold online, so I started watching for it. Maybe Marilyn recorded her meeting with the killer in the appointment book. Or DNA or fingerprints would be on it. The book showed up on an online marketplace site a few days ago. I bought it and the owner said she'd send it the next day and I'd receive it in about a week."

"Are you certain the book cover was Ms. Mitchell's?"

"Her initials are embossed on it." Another mistake. He said "book cover." She hadn't said the pages were missing.

His lips formed a tight smile. "You say you found it online. How did it get there?"

"People going through other people's garbage occasionally sell their discoveries online."

She glanced at her watch. "Thank you for letting me get all this out. I didn't know who to trust so haven't told anyone else. I know you can't repeat anything because of client confidentiality, right...Oh, I just remembered something else."

"Yes?"

"My mother and her friends called themselves the Fab Five when they were in high school. Did you know that?"

"No. That was before my time."

"There were five friends, Rhonda, Shirley, Laura, Marilyn, and your wife Gloria."

He startled and dropped his pen, then bent down to pick it up. "I feel we've gotten off track—"

"I found a photo of them on your cabin cruiser when I cleaned out Rhonda's room. She died, didn't she, your wife? I looked up the newspaper report. It said she drowned when she and her friends were on Lake Michigan. You must have been devastated."

Zachary didn't move for a long moment. "We'll

have to leave it right there for now, but we must have another therapy session soon. Tomorrow, in fact."

Erin got to her feet. "I'd like to meet tomorrow, but can't. A township inspector is coming to check the motel and I can't miss it. I'll call or text you tomorrow to set up a date. Is that okay?"

"Let's make it as soon as possible. I'm very concerned about your state of mind."

"I'm fine. Just a little stressed."

"During our sessions, you've shown signs of depression, delusion, and an obsession with death. If you feel life is getting too difficult and are considering ending your… pain, contact me right away. I have some coping strategies you can try."

There it is. He's going to write "depression, delusional, obsessive, and suicide risk," in her file. "I don't think I'd ever kill myself. But if I get to that point, I'll call you."

****

Erin collapsed into her car, exhilarated. The way he acted when she mentioned Gloria said everything. But excitement faded as reality took hold. She'd played mind games with a multiple killer. To stay alive, she'd need help from people more formidable than Mick, Eddie, and George. She phoned Detective Mackey.

"Are you in your office?"

"What now?" The detective was clearly annoyed.

"I need to see you today. Please."

"I'm working on another case. One where a crime was actually committed. But if you want to talk for a minute, go ahead."

"Not on the phone."

"I need more information."

Erin hesitated. "I poked the hornet's nest you mentioned the other day. I think he'll try to kill me."

"Damn it, Erin. Can't you leave things alone?"

"Will you meet me or not?"

"Oh Christ. Okay. It's after one and I haven't eaten lunch yet. Meet me at the Courthouse Grille in Great Rapids at two."

"I'll be there."

****

The one-hundred-year-old Grille was nearly empty in the lull between lunch and Happy Hour. Erin found a booth next to one of the brick walls and ordered a glass of white wine. Mackey arrived ten minutes later and slipped into the booth across from her.

A server appeared almost immediately. "Your usual, Detective?"

"No, still working. Water is fine."

"Of course. Lunch?"

"Give us a few minutes." She turned to Erin. "Talk."

"Zachary Smith wants to kill me."

Mackey let out a frustrated sigh. "Erin—"

"Please, just listen. I met with him right before I called you and told him I know Rhonda, Laura, and Marilyn were murdered. And I told him about Laura's mouse-infested basement and Laura's blue appointment book. He said I was delusional and offered his help if I planned to kill myself."

Mackey leaned so far forward Erin could smell something minty on her breath. "If this guy is by any chance a killer, and not merely an innocent man pissed off because you're accusing him of murder, you've endangered yourself and others, including your daughter."

"April is with her friend's family up north. I'd never let her return to Paradise Beach with Zachary gunning for me and Shirley." If he wasn't in custody by the time Olivia's family came home, she'd take April to Denver before she had a chance to unpack.

"Okay, so that's one person out of the way. What about your brother, father, Shirley? Do I need to spell it out for you?"

"I'm desperate. I can't sit around and do nothing."

"Nothing you've said is enough to bring him in." Her eyes narrowed. "Exactly why am I here? By now, you must realize you have no substantive evidence against Smith, so I can't help you."

"Just wanted to give you a heads-up. Will you be around for the next few days?"

"Why?"

"Just in case he—"

"You're not telling me everything, are you? You have some ridiculous idea about capturing him. Listen to me. I will not allow you or any citizen attempt to bring down a multiple murderer."

Erin half-smiled. "So now you think he's a multiple murderer, too?"

"That was a slip. You are not equipped to handle this situation."

"I'm going to get him to confess to Rhonda's death, while Mick and Eddie record it."

It sounded incredibly naïve when she said it. Was it even possible?

"How are you planning to do that? By asking him nicely? And what if he comes in shooting?"

"Why does everyone think that? He won't. He'll

want it to look like I killed myself and is probably already updating my file to say I'm suicidal."

"He'd be right."

"Sometimes cops use victims as bait, right? I think he'll want me alive long enough to brag about how clever he is."

"You watch too much TV. Besides, I don't get the impression he bragged much to his other victims."

"How would you know? They're all dead."

"My point exactly. Just when is this so-called plan of yours going down?"

Erin didn't want to tell her yet. "I'm not sure. You have officers patrolling Misery Cove, right? If something unexpected happens, we'll call 9-1-1."

"Unexpected? You mean if someone gets killed, right? What in the hell are you thinking? I should arrest you right now."

"This isn't about me. He won't stop until he kills Shirley."

"You're putting me in a tough position. We don't have sufficient resources to cover every what-if situation that comes up. As far as calling 9-1-1, the team patrolling Misery Cove also patrols Port Elizabeth, so at any point in time, they could be ten to thirty minutes away. Not close enough to prevent something serious from happening. I want you to call this off. Otherwise, I can't guarantee I can have someone there in time."

"I get where you're coming from, but I wonder how you'll feel if something happens to me or Shirley."

Chapter Forty-Two

Erin watched Mick and Eddie load the RV with the last of the camping equipment, electronics, and guns. How she could feel so cold on this warm sunny morning? She tried not to think about the million things that could go wrong today and could only pray they didn't. "Everything ready?"

"The tracker I installed on Zachary's car last night during the poker game is still working," Mick said. "This morning, Dad and I checked the motion detectors in the woods, the audio and video recorders around the porch, and the parabolic microphone. It's all good to go."

Shirley handed Eddie a bulging grocery bag. "There's enough food in here to keep you guys from starving for a month."

"Good," Erin said. "Zachary probably won't show up until after ten tonight." Just saying his name sent shivers up her back.

"Thanks, ladies," Eddie said. "Ready to rock and roll, Mick?"

"Any time you are."

"Have fun up north," Shirley shouted, "And bring me lots of fish."

Mick checked the tracking app on his phone. "Zachary's at The Cove, probably having breakfast, so you didn't have to yell, Shirley."

"His *car* is at The Cove," Erin said. "He still might sneak past here to see if you guys are really leaving."

"Don't worry, honey." Eddie tossed the keys to Mick. "We'll drive through town, stop at The Cove, and pick up donuts and coffee. If he's there, we'll let him know we're on our way up north to catch us some bass."

Please, God or whoever's out there, keep them safe. "Are you sure you packed everything? Guns, binoculars, insect spray, and—"

"We double checked, Erin. We're good," Eddie said.

"Okay, let's go over the plan. After driving through town, you'll take the back roads to George's place and leave the RV in his garage. He'll hide you two and the supplies in his truck, then drive back here, parking as close to the woods as he can. I'll talk to him about the motel while you two grab your stuff and sneak into the woods. He'll putter around the motel for a while in case Zachary is watching. When George leaves, Shirley and I will go to Stay and Shop so she can buy lottery tickets. I'll—"

"Whoa." Eddie tapped a pencil against a small pad of paper. "Slow down, please. I'm taking notes." He wrote for a few minutes.

"Done?"

"Yes, thanks, honey."

"Then I'll pick up wine and snacks. When we're checking out, Shirley will tell Holly that you guys are going up north fishing, staying the night, then heading back home sometime tomorrow. I'll say Shirley and I are getting a carryout dinner from Zinc and spending the evening watching TV. Holly will tell everyone who comes into the store and word might get to Zachary."

"We're covered," Shirley said. "I told him that last night."

"Great. Questions anyone?"

Eddie shook his head.

"Mick, when you track me leaving Stay and Shop, text me Zachary's location. If he's not around, I'll take Shirley to the Portside Inn in Port Elizabeth."

"Got it. In the meantime, one of George's guys will drop him off here."

"Keep track of each other and stay safe. Mick, call Detective Mackey if anything goes wrong."

Eddie kissed Shirley's cheek and hugged Erin. "Okay, ladies, we're off."

Mick jumped into the driver's seat while Eddie slid into the passenger's.

"What is it with you and Eddie?" Erin asked, as the RV disappeared down the driveway.

Shirley grinned and shrugged. "Nothing." Her face grew serious. "I wish we could call off the whole thing. It's me who should be waiting for Zachary, not you. You had nothing to do with Gloria's death."

"Doesn't matter. There's no way I will ever let that maniac get near you again."

"But now he's after you, too."

Erin gave a weak smile. "Yeah, there's that."

****

An hour later at the Portside Inn, Shirley was still complaining. "I want to help. I swear I'll stay out of the way."

"You haven't totally recovered from your accident," Erin said, "and if anything happened to you—"

Shirley pulled her into a tight hug. "You better be careful, too." Then pushed her toward the door. "Okay, go on. Get out of here."

On the way back to Paradise Beach, Erin called Mick. "Where's Zachary?"

"His *car* is at his house."

Erin laughed. "You're never going to let that go, are you?"

Zachary's house was north of Misery's downtown, so he probably was home. Erin parked in front of the motel and crept into the woods, where Mick said they'd established a campsite.

"Everything okay, Mick?"

"Yep. We just got back from searching the woods around the motel, the woods on Shirley's property, and the house."

"We locked the front door and all the windows," Eddie said, "but not the back porch doors."

"And George set up a scouting relay," Mick said. "Me and Dad will check the woods while he stays at the campsite. Later, we'll switch off. I linked our phones to the security systems so they'll all vibrate if anyone sets one off."

"Sounds like you have everything under control," Erin said. "Please, please be careful."

George winked. "Don't worry, I'll keep my eyes on these two. You take care of yourself."

****

Erin went into the house, removed Eddie's pistol from the small gun safe in her bedroom, and headed for a chair on the back porch. Zachary will want her death to look like suicide or an accident, but how would he arrange it? Something like Marilyn's drug overdose,

344

Laura's slip down a flight of stairs, or Rhonda's crack on the head and drowning? Or would he try something completely different? She'll keep a close eye on him.

She'll be on the back porch when he comes. And if he pulls out a gun, she'll pull out hers. That was the worst-case scenario. Instinct told her he'll be more subtle.

Mick will monitor his parabolic listening device, so he'll know the right time to take action. That, along with a separate voice recorder hidden in the porch's eaves and her own cell phone, should catch every word. She had a sudden urge to hear her daughter's voice and called April's phone. After a few rings, the call went to voicemail. She almost cried with disappointment and left a message.

"Hi honey, it's Mom. I've been thinking about you today." Her voice trembled. She faked a cough and fought to make her tone cheerful. "I'm getting a cold. I hope you're having a good time with Olivia but I can't wait to see you again. Please don't call or text me when you get this voicemail. I'll explain tomorrow. I love you."

Fear and dread twisted Erin's insides. She could die tonight. She didn't want to die. She needed to be alive for April.

****

Shirley called at three-thirty. "Hey, I'm still here at the hotel going stir-crazy, in case you're interested. How's everyone there?"

Erin smiled to herself. "We're all fine."

"Bullshit. Tell me the truth."

She considered lying, but Shirley would see through it. "Okay, I'm on the porch, scared out of my mind, waiting for Zachary to show up."

"You're on the porch because you think he'll come during the day? I think he'll come when it's dark."

"I don't know when he'll show up. But I don't want to be trapped inside the house if he comes early."

"I can't believe we're discussing when a multiple murderer might show up." Shirley gave a loud sigh. "How are Mick, Eddie, and George?"

"They're doing a good job monitoring Zachary's location and scouting the woods."

"I can't stand sitting here just waiting. I'm calling a taxi and coming home."

"Don't you dare. It's hard enough worrying about the guys without worrying about you, too."

Shirley didn't speak for a moment. "Fine, but call me the minute anything happens. Never thought I'd get tired of watching police procedurals."

"Do not leave your room. I'll call you later."

Mick swaggered to the porch as the call ended. "The target's car hasn't moved from his house in half an hour. My gut tells me he's inside. Just wanted to let you know."

"The target?" She almost laughed.

"Yeah. Referring to the subject as a target helps to dehumanize him. I read that yesterday in a combat training book."

Mick had changed since she arrived three months ago. Her once irresponsible brother was making better choices, cared more about his family, and worked hard on the motel. And the ideas he came up with for catching Zachary were well thought-out. Intelligent. Maybe she hadn't noticed his good qualities before. Maybe she was the one who'd changed.

"That's all I had. See ya later and stay safe." Mick glanced at her over his shoulder as he disappeared into the woods.

She'd faced other moral dilemmas in the past, but never had to make a choice between two such dangerous paths. Do nothing and pray the police would eventually believe her and arrest Zachary, risking Shirley's life in the meantime. Or act now and hope her plan works without anyone getting hurt. Too late to do anything else. Too late to stop the speeding train.

****

The rest of the afternoon dragged. She tried reading, but couldn't focus. Walking to and from the beach helped, but she worried about getting caught out in the open. She hadn't practiced with the gun as much as she should have. After stepping off the porch, she removed the magazine and dry fired at trees. Her hands shook. Would she be able to steady them when the time came? Would she even be able to pull the trigger? Could she kill Zachary if he attacked her? She hoped so, but wasn't sure.

The evening sun's weakening rays didn't penetrate the forest, and shadows deepened in the places where Mick, Eddie, and George waited. Was Zachary really at home? When would he come? Was he coming? Her phone vibrated with an intrusion alarm. *Oh God.* She instinctively slapped the magazine into the pistol, dashed back to the porch, and texted Mick, then Eddie, then George. No one responded.

A figure dashed through the trees. She swung the gun toward it and tried to yell, but nothing came out. She steeled herself and tried again.

"Come out with your hands in the air or I'll shoot."

"It's me!" Mick burst out of the woods, hands raised. "Everything's okay."

"What the hell? You scared me to death. Why didn't you guys answer my text?" She lowered the gun and bent over, hands on knees, trying to catch her breath.

"Sorry. We were trying to find out what triggered the alarm. It was a deer."

"I hope that doesn't happen again. My heart can only take so much." She straightened. "Where's Zachary?"

"At Clique in Port Elizabeth, so you can relax for a while."

"Yeah, sure." She glanced at her phone. Eight o'clock.

An hour later, Mick texted,

—Z is still in Port Elizabeth but at Georgia's—

The night dragged on. Erin paced the porch, stopping to retrieve the empty storage bowl near the steps that once held what Rhonda claimed was Eddie's ashes. She grabbed the gun and tramped through the sand to the shoreline. No movement in the woods at all. A full moon hung above the lake. *Werewolves came out when the moon was full.* Why in the hell did that pop into her head?

At the shoreline, she turned toward the house. All the windows were dark. Zachary would think she and Shirley were asleep. A briny breeze wafted in from the lake, and with the darkness, the temperature dropped. Shivering, she returned to the porch, tucked the gun under a pillow and lit a candle.

Where was Zachary? Usually night sounds—chirping crickets, croaking tree frogs, and hooting owls, soothed her. Now, listening for Zachary, they put her on edge. When she couldn't stand the suspense any longer, she texted Mick.

—*Where's Z?*—

—*At Zinc*—

—*You didn't tell me he left Port Elizabeth*—

—*Didn't want to text you until I knew where he was going. You okay?*—

—*Yes. Not really*—

Her phone vibrated with a call. Mick.

"I couldn't keep typing. Are we doing the right thing, Erin?"

"It's the right thing, but I'm not sure we're the right people to do it. I'm calling Mackey."

Chapter Forty-Three

"Zachary's coming to Paradise Beach tonight, Detective. Mick, Eddie, and George are in the woods waiting for him, but—"

"For God's sake, Erin, I told you not to mess with him."

"Mick will call you when he arrives."

"Erin—"

She pressed END.

Mick strode out of the woods a few minutes later. "Zachary's still at Zinc."

"I keep telling you, you're tracking his car, not his body. What if he saw you just now? Think before you come out here again, okay?"

"He hasn't been there that long and couldn't get here that fast,"

"Zinc is the third place he's been tonight. He's probably had a drink in all of them."

Mick looked more worried than she'd ever seen him. "I don't like this."

"Neither do I, but it has to be done. Is everyone ready?"

"Yeah. The microphones are operational, and the guns are loaded. Dad and I are in the woods about a hundred feet from the porch. George is on Shirley's side of the woods."

They should have recruited more help.

"Stay hidden when he shows up. If he threatens me, make a racket. Yell and shoot into the air. When he turns toward the noise, I'll grab my gun. Tell George to approach Zachary from behind."

"How will I know when you want us to come out?"

"You want a safe word?" She half-grinned. "Or in this case, a 'danger' word?"

"Well, yeah. I guess."

"How about 'Help?'"

"That'll do it." He hugged her. "You are one brave woman, Erin. I love you. Please be really careful and don't do anything stupid."

"You too. No heroics, okay?"

"Right." He checked his phone. "Oh shit, his car is on Shirley's property."

Erin and Mick locked gazes.

An intrusion alert buzzed on Mick's phone.

"He's in Shirley's woods. Gotta go." Mick rushed into the woods.

****

Oh God. Her body pulsed with terror. She was just like those women in novels who made stupid decisions that got them killed. She never guessed she'd be like them. But she was. One of those stupid, stupid women.

Her gaze darted frantically, searching for any sign of Zachary, while her ears strained to catch even the faintest sound of footsteps.

Still, she didn't hear him coming.

"There's nothing more romantic than a beautiful woman on a perfect midsummer's night." Zachary's voice, warm, dark, and seductive, came from the shadows at the side of the porch.

She couldn't think. Couldn't move. Couldn't

speak. *Stop it!* She glanced at the darkened phone in her hand. He'd take it if he saw it. Turning toward his voice, she tucked it under the pillow behind her, next to the gun.

Zachary moved into the moonlight illuminating the porch stairs. Attractive in a white shirt tucked into fitted jeans. Attractive and terrifying. He held a paper sack.

What was inside? Gun? Rope? Knife? She gripped the arms of her chair. *It could be anything. Don't react.*

He lowered himself into the chair beside hers, opened the bag, and removed a wine bottle. She exhaled and closed her eyes for a moment. Not a weapon. The wine was the same brand as the one Rhonda took from The Sand Bar the night she died.

Three wine glasses appeared next. He set them on the side table. After twisting a wine key into the cork, he extracted it, poured two glasses, and placed one in her shaky hand.

"Thank for the—" *Damn.* What the hell was she thanking him for?

The rising anger strengthened her resolve.

He removed a handkerchief from his pocket and wiped the bottle, then lifted his glass. "Cheers."

She set her glass down. No way in hell was she going to drink with him.

"I hope you and Shirley had a nice evening. Is she asleep? Will she join us?"

Of course, he thought she was here. His plan was to kill her, too. "She's not home."

His eyebrows furrowed. "Oh?"

"Her aunt called last night and said she needed help with her broken hip. Shirley caught a flight to Fort Myers this afternoon."

"That's unfortunate." He frowned. "I'll catch up with her another time."

Oh God.

He touched his glass to hers, and sipped. "So, you're alone tonight. Expecting company?"

She shook her head.

Zachary rose from his chair. "Let's take our wine down to the lake. The moon is dazzling tonight. So are you." He held a hand out to her as if they were on a date and he was taking her on a romantic stroll along the beach.

Was he coming on to her and why the beach? Then her mind flew to Rhonda. He'd killed her on the beach. Her determination to bring him down grew stronger.

"No thanks. I'd rather stay here." She prayed Mick wasn't freaking out.

"Whatever you say." When Zachary returned to his chair, his jacket fell open, revealing a shoulder holstered gun. He shifted, covering it. Terror threatened again. *Stay strong. Stay pissed off. Did Mick call Mackey? Was she on the way?*

"So, you're all alone on a Saturday evening. I wonder if it's because Justin is with his ex-fiancée? Catherine, I think her name is. They were in Zinc when I was there earlier. Sorry to say, they were getting on rather well." He laughed. "Holly told me they'd broken up. Maybe she's taking him back."

She wanted to slap the patronizing look off his face. "I didn't invite you to my home, so why are you here, Zachary? No, wait, I know. You want to make sure I don't tell anyone you killed my mother, Laura, and Marilyn, right?"

"You remind me of Gloria. Beautiful, but often

single-minded." He took a deep sip of his wine. "I still miss her."

"Before she died, she planned to leave you, didn't she? Didn't even tell you she was pregnant with your son. I wonder why that was?"

"Not your concern." His tone held an edge.

Good. "How did you feel when Rhonda told you the truth about the way Gloria died? And how did you feel when you killed Rhonda? Satisfied? Vindicated? Didn't bring back your wife back, did it?"

"I think when all this is over, I'll move away from Misery Cove. Maybe out of the country. I've always wanted to live in Tuscany." He got to his feet. "Shall we take that walk?"

Maybe she should accompany him to the beach. The guys would have a clearer view of them. A clearer shot. When Mick saw where they were heading, he'll probably move everyone to the other side of Paradise Beach, the side bordering Shirley's property, where the trees grew close to the water. *Shit.* Her gun was under the pillow, but it couldn't be helped. She got to her feet.

"Okay." She'd play along.

"What changed your mind about walking out here?" Zachary sounded genuinely curious.

Erin stood next to him at the water's edge. The brilliant full moon, high in the sky, created shadows in the creases of his face. He looked older, calm. Scary calm. *Keep him talking.*

"I don't come out here much anymore. As you know, my mother drowned in the water near that dock." It sagged into the water about ten feet away. "I still can't believe she's dead. I bet you found it difficult when your wife died suddenly. Especially in such a tragic accident. How did you deal with it?"

No response.

Push him. "The wine you brought tonight was the same brand Rhonda took from The Sand Bar the night she died. It was her favorite. Did you know?"

"She might have mentioned it."

Strange, he didn't play the psychologist. Ask questions. Maybe he wanted to find out what she knew first.

"It has the same label as the empty bottle I found in the woods. Remember, I showed you a picture of it?" She turned toward him but kept a few feet away. "I learned something interesting on a true crime show a while back. The police identified a murderer's fingerprints from a photo of the water glass he'd handled. I checked online, and it's true. Forensic scientists can identify a person's fingerprints from a photo of the object the subject held. Isn't that amazing?"

His face tensed. "You believe your photo of the bottle has identifiable fingerprints?"

"The macro lens on my phone takes incredible close-ups, so yes." She didn't have a macro lens, but he didn't know that.

Zachary hesitated, then grinned malevolently. "Did you share the photo with anyone?"

She'd known the fingerprint information would get to him, but something in Zachary seemed to have flipped a switch. She saw it in his eyes. But he hadn't really threatened her yet or admitted killing her mother, so she had to keep at him. "Not yet."

"Do you have the phone with you?"

"No."

Zachary's steely gaze locked onto hers. "Where is it?"

How much more could she provoke him without pushing him over the edge? He'd wouldn't kill her until he had her phone. Would he?

"I'm not telling you."

In a single motion, he pulled out his gun and pointed at her face.

Her heart slammed. Was this it?

She was about to scream when he spoke.

"Is it on you?" He slid his free hand over her body. "Where is it? In the house?"

Oh, God. She wanted to gag but forced herself to think of ways to escape. Knee him and race to the woods? No, he hadn't done or said enough to get him arrested.

"Please put the gun away and let's talk."

"No, but go ahead and talk if you like. I have all night."

He laughed and chills crawled through her veins. She fought to stay focused. He wants the phone so he wouldn't shoot her yet. She hoped. How could she get him to admit what he'd done? Cunningham. Make a wrong statement to get a right one.

She glanced at the gun, then back at his face. "For the past fifteen years, you suspected Gloria's friends had something to do with her death, but you didn't know what. You'd grieved for Gloria and your unborn son, lost custody of your daughter Sara, and had your psychology license suspended. You believed you'd never find out what happened the day Gloria drowned, but had a plan ready in case you did. Rhonda told you about Gloria on the day she died and you put your plan into action."

"Wrong, I didn't—" He stopped, irritated and confused, lowering the gun for a moment, then raising it again.

Damn, he almost said it. "During our second session, you realized I knew you murdered my mother, Laura, and Marilyn."

"I knew what you were up to from the time you made your first appointment."

"What was I up to?"

"Some patients make up stories to impress me. I saw your improbable stories as a cry for help. A way to ease your conscience about the way you'd treated your mother."

"Then why go along with it?"

He smirked. "Because it amused me." The hand holding the gun wobbled a little. His arm was getting tired.

Keep pushing. "After your wife died, you lost it, didn't you? Drugs and alcohol. It's taken you a long time to convince people you're stable, but I don't believe you are. If you were, you wouldn't have murdered three women."

He bent his arm at the elbow and pressed it to his side. Resting it. Now the gun was leveled at her chest. *Don't look at it.*

"After only two sessions with you, and particularly today, I'm very concerned about your mental wellness." He slipped on his benevolent doctor face. "Your patient file doesn't paint a wholesome picture of your emotional state. I've been worried you might hurt yourself."

He's been planning this. She'd love to see what

he'd written about her.

"When my mother told you she and her friends tossed Gloria overboard the day she died, you were in shock. You canceled your clients for the rest of the day. All those years of grief and loss were because of what those four women did, and they had to be punished. Fortunately for you, everyone who'd been with your wife when she died was in town this summer and you spent that entire afternoon thinking about what you should do to avenge Gloria and your son."

"You have quite an imagination, Erin. Keep going." He laughed. "Sounds like a TV drama."

"Later that day, you called Rhonda and asked if you could visit her that night, and she agreed."

A lump grew in Erin's throat, thinking about Rhonda dressing up for him. Did she think it was a date?

"Don't stop." Zachary nudged her with his elbow.

She inhaled. "The two of you drank wine while walking the beach, then stepped onto the old dock. Rhonda must have said something that set you off and you impulsively hit her head with the wine bottle. She fell into the water and drowned."

Erin couldn't bring herself to say really happened. How he banged Rhonda's head against the piling until she was unconscious.

"It made you feel good. Powerful. And you decided to kill all of them, but needed a plan. You probably dated Laura a few times before she invited you into her home and you pushed her down the basement stairs. That was your first mistake. A big one. She told me she never went downstai—"

"ENOUGH!" He thrust the gun out toward her.

"Where's the fucking phone?"

She forced a laugh. "In a safe place. How does it feel being trapped, Zachary? Feeling like there's no way out? I hope you're terrified right now. Just as terrified as the women you killed."

"Shut up!"

A branch snapped in the woods.

Chapter Forty-Four

Zachary spun toward the tree line. "Who's there?" he shouted.

It had to be Mick. *Please don't move.*

Silence. Erin let out a relieved breath. Then froze as Zachary pressed the muzzle of his gun to her temple.

"I'm holding my gun against Erin's head and will pull the trigger unless you show yourself," he yelled.

"I'm not afraid of you." Erin hoped Mick caught that and understood not to react. That she was still okay.

No movement in the woods.

Zachary pushed the gun hard against her head. "Does anyone know we're out here?" Beads of sweat gathered on his brow.

She had to keep him talking, off balance. "Your arm is getting tired, isn't it?"

"Where is the fucking phone?" His voice was low and dangerous.

"The police know I've been researching Rhonda's, Laura's, and Marilyn's deaths. I told them about the wine bottle, Laura's basement, and Marilyn's blue appointment book. You won't shoot me. My death will convince them there's a murderer in town." Her voice held steady, thank God.

He didn't speak for several moments. "If they believed you, we wouldn't be here today." Another flip of his internal switch and his expression turned compassionate. "Erin, I'm so sorry I couldn't help you. You've struggled ever since your mother died and were so overwhelmed with grief, you sought my help. During our sessions, you said you didn't want to live."

Oh my God. He could say anything and the police would believe him, a respected psychologist.

"The medical examiner will say you committed suicide. They'll find a half-empty bottle of Rhonda's favorite wine next to you on the dock. Your hand wrapped around a gun. I'll be overcome with remorse when I tell the police I unsuccessfully treated your depression."

"Are you serious?" She forced a laugh. "You'll never get away with it. My family and friends know I'd never kill myself."

"Friends and family don't always know what's in our hearts. And that's what I'll tell them at your funeral if you won't cooperate." He pushed the gun against her head with such force she stumbled backwards. "WHERE IS THE FUCKING PHONE?"

The mask was off.

Erin's heart hammered violently. She stared at the moon's silvery path, shimmering against the deep, deep darkness of the lake and its calmness quieted her. She locked her gaze onto his. "You're right, no one really knows what's in our hearts. And I don't know what's in yours. But I sense you really don't want to kill me. You're having misgivings. I didn't hurt you like my mother and the others did."

Where was Mackey? Was Mick so rattled he forgot to call her? She didn't know if she could hold Zachary off much longer.

"Nice try." He studied her face, then lowered the gun. "If you give me the phone, we can pretend this never happened. You go your way and I'll go mine."

He must think she's an idiot.

"I don't trust you."

"I know it's been difficult for you to trust the people in your life, including me, practically a stranger. But I promise that after tonight, I'll never bother you again. Like I said before, I'm moving out of the country."

"That's a lie. You'll kill me, anyway. Make it look like I killed myself, then go back to Zinc or somewhere."

"Is it in the house?"

An idea flashed into her head. She prayed it would work. "It's hidden."

"Let's go get it."

Erin glanced sideways at Zachary as they walked to the house. Had he said enough to get arrested? He'd threatened to kill her, even laid out how he'd make it look like a suicide. But he was clever. He could make up a story about how this was some type of psychological treatment. He'd say she had paranoia and believed someone was trying to kill her. And he and she played out a scenario to lessen her fear of it. He'd say she was fine when he left.

The gun was still under the pillow. Her idea was flimsy, but had to work.

Zachary followed her up the porch stairs. She deliberately stumbled at the top, fell toward the chair, and grabbed the gun from under the pillow. Then whipped around, and aimed it at his chest. "Put your gun down."

"And just when we were becoming friends." He waited a beat, then swiveled towards the woods. "Heard you again," he yelled.

She spun in the same direction and scanned the trees. As her focus shifted, Zachary snatched her gun and hurled it toward the beach.

"Fooled you. Slight change of plans."

How could she have been so gullible?

"Your phone's in the house, isn't it? We're going in there and you're going to get it. Then we'll take another pleasant stroll to the dock."

"Help!" she screamed and lunged at Zachary.

He lost his balance and fell backward down the stairs. As she ran past him, he grabbed her ankle. She kicked his chest and sprinted toward the beach. He started after her, but turned when Mick bolted out of the woods with his gun and fired. The shot missed.

Zachary aimed his gun at Mick and pulled the trigger. Mick screamed. Erin watched in horror as he crumpled to the ground. Zachary lunged toward him and kicked the gun away.

A fierce protectiveness overcame her. She raced to her brother. Blood covered his right shirt sleeve and his eyes were closed. She knelt next to him.

Zachary came up behind her, grabbed a clump of hair, and pulled. "Get up."

"NO!"

Erin reached above her head and dug her fingernails into the back of his hand. He loosened the grip on her hair for a moment and she jerked it free. Then she half-rose and jammed both her elbows into his stomach and he staggered backward.

She must have shocked him because he didn't

make a move while she crouched down and raised Mick's shirt sleeve. A small hole oozed blood.

"Mick, are you okay?"

His eyes fluttered, then opened. She folded the sleeve over itself, placed it over the wound, and covered it with his left hand. "Press hard."

"Get up," Zachary screamed. "Now!"

Eddie blasted out of the woods. "God damn you, you fucking bastard! Leave my kids alone!"

Zachary fired. Eddie's leg buckled and he toppled to the ground. He rolled over and aimed his gun at Zachary.

"I'm gonna blow your fucking head off!" Blood seeped through his khaki trousers.

Zachary smirked.

"Did you hear what I said, asshole?"

"Shut up, old man, and put down your gun." Zachary waved his pistol toward Mick and Erin. "Or I'll shoot them both."

Rage and fear alternated on Eddie's face. He tossed his gun aside.

Erin started toward Eddie.

"Stay where you are," Zachary growled.

"How many more people do you intend to kill?"

She'd die before letting anything happen to her family. She raced to her father, crouched down, and worked his pant leg upward. Blood flowed from a hole in his thigh.

"You're going to be okay, Dad." Thank God the blood wasn't spurting. "Don't move." She removed his belt, wrapped it above the wound, then slipped the end through the buckle and tugged.

"Get up," Zachary said. "This isn't exactly what

I'd planned, but it'll have to work."

Erin rolled out of her crouch and sat on the ground, praying one of the devices was still recording.

Zachary glowered down at her. "Here's the new story. Your brother and father came home from the fishing trip early. You killed them accidentally, thinking they were intruders. When you realized what you'd done, you killed yourself."

"The bullets came from your gun. No one will believe I could take it away from you."

"It's unregistered. The police will say you probably picked it up somewhere. Maybe Denver."

"Goddamn idiot." Eddie raised his uninjured leg and hard-kicked Zachary's shin. "Take that, asshole."

As Zachary toppled to the ground, his gun flew into a deep thatch of beach grass. Erin bolted for her gun.

"Erin, look out," Mick yelled.

She turned. Zachary was back on his feet, racing toward her. Mick dove for Zachary's legs and both fell, twisting in the sand. Zachary slung an arm around Mick's neck and tightened it. Mick's eyes bulged, his hands scrambling along Zachary's arm.

Erin pointed her gun at Zachary's head. "Let him go or I swear to God I'll pull the trigger."

"I don't believe you have the guts."

Erin aimed above his head and fired. "Try me."

Zachary scowled, releasing Mick, and Mick rolled away, cradling his wounded arm. Then Zachary launched himself toward Erin. She fired again.

He howled and fell backward, clutching his leg.

"It's a good thing I'm a bad shot," she said.

Blue and red lights pulsated throughout the forest.

Then sirens blasted up the driveway and from the front of the house. Vehicle doors slammed and someone yelled commands. Then a loud sound of wood cracking. They must have bashed in the front door. Officers burst onto the back porch through the sliding glass doors, their gazes darting around.

Erin waved her arms. "Over here."

Mackey and three other officers rushed from the side of the house. "Everyone, face down on the ground," she yelled. "Hands where I can see them."

Erin dropped to the sand. "Zachary shot Mick and my father. He was going to kill us."

Mackey checked Mick's arm and Eddie's leg. "Someone get the paramedics back here." She held a hand out to Erin and pulled her to her feet. "You okay?"

"I'm a psychologist," Zachary roared, "and Erin Brady is my deeply disturbed patient. I stopped by to check on her and she—"

"Shut up." Mackey rolled him on his stomach, cuffed him, then turned him onto his back. She stared at the blood on his pants. "What happened to him?"

"He was choking Mick, so I shot him," Erin said.

Mackey raised an eyebrow, then turned to the nearest officer. "Check Doctor Smith's leg and stay with him. As soon as I sort out this mess, I'm arresting him."

"I need a doctor. And I want a lawyer," Zachary shouted.

"You'll get them," Mackey said.

Erin collapsed on a porch step, resting her head on her knees and sobbing. It was over. She was wrung out. Exhausted.

A voice from the woods called, "I'm coming out.

Don't shoot."

"Hands above your head and come this way," Mackey yelled.

Erin sat up and wiped her face with the sleeve of her shirt. *What the...?*

A sheepish-looking George stumbled out of the woods, hands held high.

Mackey laughed. "Oh, for God's sake, George. What are you doing here?"

"Supposed to be helping these folks," he said. He turned to Erin. "Sorry, there didn't seem to be a good time to join the party." He hung his head. "I was useless."

"Don't you ever think that," Erin said. "We all did our part."

"You would have been a foolish man to barge into a scene like this," Mackey said.

Minutes later, Erin and Mackey followed as paramedics carried Mick and Eddie to one ambulance, and placed Zachary in another. Both drove away, sirens shrieking.

Erin started toward her car.

"Where do you think you're going?" Mackey said.

"I want to be with Mick and my father."

"They're not in danger, and I need to talk to you now. I'll take you to the hospital later."

Erin glanced toward a pile of broken wood where the front door used to be. "Let's go around the back."

She led Mackey to the back porch. Moonlight shone on the empty yard and beach. Only a short time ago, guns fired, bodies tumbled and voices screamed. And chaos escalated when the police arrived.

"It's so quiet now."

"Won't be for long," Mackey said. "A swarm of detectives and other officers will come to collect evidence and question you."

"Can't you ask the questions?" Erin asked.

The air still reverberated, like in the aftermath of an explosion. Rhonda's killer was in custody, so why did it feel so anticlimactic?

"Let's get some coffee into you two." Mackey steered Erin and George into the house.

"I'll put a temporary patch on the front door first," George said. "It'll only take a few minutes." He headed for the renovation supplies.

By the time he returned, Mackey had made strong coffee and poured three cups.

"Now, you two are going to tell me the whole story."

Chapter Forty-Five

Four Months Later

If Erin ignored the headstones, St. Jude Cemetery could have been a park. Squirrels and chipmunks scampered through fallen leaves. Bird songs echoed through the forest's canopy. Benches dotted meandering gravel paths. Cool, pine-scented air carried a taste of winter.

She found Mick sitting on a stone bench facing their mother's grave. They'd purchased it the previous month and had a brass plaque inscribed with the title of her favorite song affixed to its back. Reading it, she always envisioned the long-ago night with her family gathered around a bonfire. When that song came on the radio, Rhonda spun under the starry sky, her waist-length hair and strands of beads twirled along with her. She'd looked like a goddess.

Erin's heart broke for the wasted years. The years she'd forgotten, or refused to acknowledge, the wondrous part of her mother.

"Hi, brother, slide over."

He looked up, smiled, and happiness coursed through her. They'd become close during the search for Rhonda's killer, closer than they'd been as kids.

When she settled next to him, he leaned over and hugged her. "Lunch with Mom is an awesome idea, Erin."

"Thanks." She'd started visiting her mother's grave most days after Zachary was arrested, sometimes bringing along her morning coffee or lunch. A few days ago, it occurred to her that her family might enjoy a meal with Rhonda, too.

"April, Shirley, and Eddie finished packing the picnic basket, but I asked them to wait a while before coming here so we could talk."

"Good, because I want to talk too."

She and Mick spoke often now, discussing motel business and family issues like how crowded the house was getting since Eddie moved into Shirley's room. "Okay, you go first."

He looked down for a moment, then back up at her. "The motel's been doing really well ever since we got the thumbs-up to open."

"I know. Thanks to the fall color tours, we're completely booked through mid-November."

"Right…And I…uh—"

Erin knew what he wanted to talk about. Westside's plans for the motel property when the will's conditions were met, and the sale finalized. Her feelings about Paradise Beach had dramatically changed since she arrived, and the idea of selling it filled her with bitterness and regret. But she'd agreed to sign her half of the inheritance over to Mick, so she would.

She steeled herself. "And…?"

"I know you were counting on giving half of the money we'd get for selling the motel property to April, but…I've been thinking. Maybe we don't sell. I liked working on restoring the motel with the guys, and now managing it with Dad. And I'm thinking about taking some management and hospitality classes at the community college." He took a breath. "What do you think?"

She pulled him into a bear hug. "I love you. I wanted to talk with you about the same thing. Don't worry about the money. I never believed it was ours, anyway. Shirley will be happy. She enjoys handling reservations and bossing around the cleaning crew. And Eddie likes the maintenance work." She still had a hard time calling him Dad, but she was working on it.

"Also, Dad and I can run the bar together. And when we have enough money, we could buy a boat and I can take guests on day trips to Hope Island and out fishing. We could also do winery and other tours."

"Wow, that's pretty ambitious. I'm so proud of you."

"I was hoping you and April will stay here. To live." He grinned. "And besides, Justin lives here."

"I planned to stay here, anyway. We're a family. I'd forgotten how great having family around felt...By the way, has Melanie contacted you?"

"I don't want anything to do with her, and I'm glad she's in jail. I'll never forgive her for burning down Shirley's house. Good thing we got the engagement ring back." He didn't speak for a moment. "So. we're not selling Paradise Beach and you're not going back to Denver, right?"

"Right. I've already talked to my editor in Denver. I'm going to work on travel pieces about Great Lakes destinations. So you're going to have to get used to having me around."

Mick pulled her into a hug. Relief. The massive weight on her shoulders was gone, and joyful tears crept down her cheeks.

The sound of voices came from the front of the cemetery.

April appeared weaving among the headstones, cheeks pink with excitement and the chilly air. "This is such a cool idea, Mom. I bet Granny will love it."

Erin dropped a kiss on her daughter's head. "Thanks, honey."

Eddie set up three camp chairs next to the bench while Shirley wheeled a cooler behind it, then pulled out a soda for April, cans of beer for Eddie and Mick, and poured two glasses of wine. She handed one to Erin and raised her own.

"To Rhonda, we wish you were here. I really, really miss you." Tears sparkled on her lower eyelids.

"I love you, Mom." Mick held his beer high.

"To Granny." April's voice quivered.

"To Rhonda, I wish…" Eddie hesitated. "I wish I'd been a better husband."

Erin's throat ached as she lifted her glass. "To justice for Mom. This morning, Detective Mackey told me Zachary's trial will take place next spring—three counts of attempted murder, one count of possession of an unregistered firearm. They're still researching the earlier incidents."

"Thank God." Shirley sat on the bench with Erin and April, while the men settled in the camp chairs.

"There's something else." Erin glanced at Mick. "April and I are staying in Misery Cove." No one reacted. "Isn't anyone going to say anything?"

"Honey," Eddie said. "Mick already told us he wasn't going to sell, so we knew you'd stay."

"I knew too, Mom. And I'm soooo happy!! Did Uncle Mick tell you about the boat?"

Erin shot a sideways look at Mick. "Thanks a lot for telling everyone except me."

Mick grinned. "You haven't been around much, lately."

"Oh, I have news too." Shirley said. "Holly told me the Westside building is empty. Apparently, everyone took off because the feds were onto them for something. She said the top brass are headed for some country that won't send them back to the States."

"Good riddance," Erin said. "Have you decided what to do with your property?"

Shirley glanced at Eddie. "We decided to rebuild my cottage and live in it. Together."

Erin wondered where the money would come from, but then decided she didn't care. Her father was one resourceful guy.

Shirley looked around the cemetery. "Where is he? Oh there. I see him now."

"Who?" Erin asked.

"I know this is a family event," Shirley said, "but Justin is family now, or will be soon, so I invited him to lunch." She winked at Erin. "Rhonda would have loved it."

He made his way to Erin. "Is my being here okay with you? I don't want to interfere."

She gathered him in her arms. "You're not interfering. Let's slip away before we eat."

They strolled hand-in-hand along the winding paths, kicking pine cones. It was one of those perfect Michigan fall days where the sky was brilliantly blue and the air fresh and crisp. Although maple leaves were fading, the greens, reds, yellows, and oranges turned fluorescent when touched by the sun.

She stopped in front of Gloria's grave. "None of them," her voice caught, "deserved to die. And I swear I'll keep after the police until Zachary is charged with three murders."

"I know you'll succeed." He pulled her into a long kiss, then released her. "Ready to go back?"

"Yes. For lunch with Rhonda and my family."

A word about the author...

Jan Rydzon began writing mysteries while working as an IT director, sneaking in chapters between meetings and deadlines. A lifelong bookworm and founder of the Michigan chapter of Sisters in Crime, she's especially drawn to small-town secrets, long-buried scandals, and the eerie charm of abandoned mansions and ghost towns.

She lives in Michigan with her husband and shares a lakeside cottage, and plenty of story ideas, with her two sisters.

Misery Cove is her debut novel.

****

If you enjoyed this story, leaving a review at your favorite book retailer or reader website would be much appreciated. Thank you!

Thank you for purchasing
this publication of The Wild Rose Press, Inc.

For questions or more information
contact us at
info@thewildrosepress.com.

The Wild Rose Press, Inc.
www.thewildrosepress.com